MANEUVERING FATE

By Megan Peterson

It was the end of an unusually warm day as the hazy red glow washed over the waves while the sun took its brilliance to the other side of the world. The light reflecting off the ocean momentarily blinded Anne with its random glittering making her shut her eyes, inhale a shaky breath and relish a solitary moment to watch the day come to a close. Her back felt slightly scratched from leaning against her favorite oak tree perched high on top of a hill that overlooked the reed ridden fields, sluggish marshlands and all the way down to the dunes railing the majestic Pacific Ocean. Her family's home had become a blessing and a curse, so much work for a young woman who never really wanted it...*but I love it, I just can't let it go.* Embracing the simple thought she closed her eyes and captured the peaceful moment. *All the daily work is done...now all I have left to do is go back inside the house and face the other millions of responsibilities waiting for me.*

The rough bark from the tree started digging into her back and was instantly comforting, adjusting her earphones Anne embraced the lyrics of David Guetta & Sia's 'Titanium' and thought about the past when she was young, all of the moments she'd unheedingly race to the trunk of the tree, searching for security, hiding from the world, and feeling the sense of being when her world became vulnerable. In her fantasies the huge oak was a magical guardian that protected her family, their house and the surrounding area, which for a child in a small town was their universe. Its dark gnarled limbs stretched up into the heavens spreading its massive arms to safeguard their home. She gazed up through the dark limbs staring at the blue sky which was beckoning night. Heaving a sigh Anne took comfort from the combined presence, especially on an unusually brilliant day that contrasted the dark, twisted branches barren of any leaves ominously stretching into the endless streaked blue sky.

A quiet wind rustled the remaining leaves forgotten by winter lying around her feet, making them dance in the air, still partially frozen with the winter chill creating the musky smell of dank thawing earth, decaying foliage and early spring in the air. Anne rapidly blinked at the darkening evening sky which was a residual from an unusually warm February day in Washington State, especially for the coast. But the temperature was quickly starting to cool with the night encroaching. She pushed herself off of the tree to grab the ignored rake as she kicked at the ground contemplating the practically nonexistent pile of leaves and the amount of remaining daylight. Hugging an arm around her waist for warmth, she paused and took one last wistful glance out towards the sea.

Suddenly Anne jumped and dropped the rake startled out of her reprieve by the loud crack from the back door being thrown open.

"Argh!!! Anne, come on. Are you ever coming in here tonight, or are you staying out here forever?" Beth, Anne's sixteen year-old sister's voice shattered her peaceful reprieve while her whining teen voice yelled unnecessarily from the house.

"Geeze Beth, hold onto your horses. I'm coming, I'm coming," Anne dismissed her with a random wave, calling over her shoulder as she kicked aside the unused rake and begrudgingly turned away from the beautiful scene.

"Good, because you've already missed the beginning of the awards, and you know that's the best part!" The slam of the back door resounded across the backyard as Beth went back into the house.

"Ah...lucky me." Anne tucked her hands into her jeans pockets, hunched her shoulders and walked across the lawn to the back of the house. Lingering for a painful second, Anne's breath caught in her throat while she stared up at the buiding, just like it always did when she saw her home. The house was a breathtaking Victorian standing on top of a slight hill with an exquisite view of the ocean. It had been crafted to preside above acres of land leisurely spreading over the area to create a boarding, training and working horse farm. For decades it had proudly stood three stories tall without the frivolous pompous lines on other houses of the same era. Its design was uniquely more angular and in a way, very simple. On the ground floor a large, wraparound porch added a warm welcoming feeling to the house, despite it being so imposing. The other two floors rose up in precise creatively arched lines. The white paint which was peeling and wood-bare in some areas shone in a rose color in the fading light. All of the shutter-clad windows facing the sea resembled brilliant jewels as they reflected the final glow from the dying sun.

The horse ranch had been a dream of their parents and had been maintained with pride while they were alive. Growing up, Anne remembered a similar proud feeling whether she was playing in the backyard or proclaiming that the beautiful house was her family's home. Until their Pollyanna future was shattered when a recent car accident tragically took both of her parents' lives. In the sudden upheaval of priorities the house had taken a backseat to all of the other tasks that needed to be resolved. Anne single handedly shouldered the daunting challenges of trying to raise her teenage sister, maintain their home and run a horse boarding/training business. The hectic combination constantly overwhelmed her.

The weight from her first step onto the porch produced a loud creaking, which immediately interrupted her thoughts. Anne despairingly looked down and noticed where some of the boards had rotted to almost nothing and would need replacing in the spring. Frustrated Anne aggressively rubbed her temples then kicked the side of the house while her thoughts began to seep back to the morning when she received the devastating call after moving to Seattle. She closed her eyes for a second and gave herself up to the forbidden luxury of recalling remnants of her gloriously short-lived freedom.

A forlorn smile slipped across her lips with the memories of how innocent she had been living in the big city and the unending promises when she had her entire life ahead of her. Anything seemed possible. After growing up in such a small coastal town, going off to college was the biggest adventure in her life. She never expected to appreciate dressing up to go bar hopping in Bell Town or shopping in thrift stores in Pioneer Square. Her favorite times were waking up late and sitting around with friends for most of the day at a local Starbucks, catching up on homework or whatever was happening in their current affairs. It was an amazingly distant world compared to what fate had in store for her; everything was simply memories now. A moment of unchecked frozen images flashed across her mind like a broken projector. Her heart filled with overwhelming sadness as unchecked tears welled up in her eyes. It was the outcome from an unassuming brief phone call that demolished her newfound life. She could barely recall the sound of Westport's local Sheriff's monotoned voice regretfully explaining the accident on the other end of the receiver. The last thing Anne remembered was his voice beginning to fade while she watched mesmerized as the receiver crashed, shattering across the floor. Her life quickly turned into a blur as she sped home to the coast.

Tentacles of another image crept through her thoughts. Dave, her high school flame who had stood waiting, like a sentinel firmly rooted to the porch. The warmth of his embrace and stoic presence seemed to make the tragedy real; he empathized while she became saturated in her grief and physically crumbled into nothing. It was his mellow brown eyes and persistently droning voice that begged her to reconsider college and move home to support her younger sister. Immediately after the funeral Anne dropped out of college to submerge her grief into the overwhelming tasks of running the ranch and becoming a single parent to a teenager.

Anne was startled to find that she'd unconsciously approached the end of the porch and found herself facing the closed back door. Taking in a steady deep breath she checked for tears with the backs of her knuckles, slowly opened the door and crept silently into the dimly lit kitchen. As she entered the haphazard mudroom, happy memories of the kitchen filled with sunlight and her mother perched at the bubble filled sink came flooding back. Anne's heart clenched at the memory of her mother's beautiful face as habitually she would turn around to give a welcoming smile and finished preparing another meal. The sound of Neil Diamond, Johnny Mathis or Elvis always lingered in the air as Anne scampered across the room to give her a huge hug, attempted to sample whatever was on the stove. A bubble of laughter was shared when she would receive a light slap on her wrist for her creative efforts.

Anne gave her head a quick shake to chase out the images, then despairingly glanced around the empty kitchen. As her illusion was broken, the obvious neglect revealed itself throughout interior of the house. She gently ran her hand across the delicate wallpaper decorated with sunshine yellow flowers, which her mother had treasured. Now it was old, faded to muted mustard and was peeling in random spots. Her gaze lingered on the once shiny countertops her mother loved that had become chipped, scratched or burned in a couple areas. The tired cupboard door handles were either mismatched, broken or fixed with rope or silver duct tape. Instantly she mentally decided not to notice the horribly marred floor, *it's better off forgotten*.

Pulling on the cuff of her coat, a slight sad smile crossed her face while she listened to the sound of Beth's rambunctious conversation with her BFF Suzie. Excitedly they competed against the blaring TV's volume rumbling from the living room. Anne tried to shrug off an engulfing sensation from the weight of responsibility as she struggled to shake off her coat.

"Ahhh… to be young again," she sighed as she tore off her baseball hat and quickly tossed it and her coat onto the pegs on the wall. Tiredly she sat on an ancient bench, carefully slipped off her dirty muck boots and tucked them behind the door. She carefully leaned forward trying to peek around the corner of the room then silently stood up and tried to determine where Beth was. Inspired by the constant noise from some heated disgruntled teen exclamations, she quickly darted across the kitchen making a stealth attempt to silently cross the room and tip toe up the back stairway to sneak into her room.

"Ohh...no way!!! Don't even tell me that you forgot what night it is."

Anne stopped short with one foot on the back stairway then guiltily turned in the direction of her sister's irritated voice. Immediately she had to bite her lip to keep a barking laugh from ungraciously slipping out the second her eyes focused on Beth's perpetually dramatic façade. In the stark kitchen light, Beth simply resembled an avenging Barbie doll. She stood elegantly poised and framed perfectly in the doorway with her blonde hair piled in chaotic curls, makeup skillfully but heavily applied and completed by their mother's 60's cotton candy pink chiffon prom gown. Her teenaged youth radiated as she irritatingly placed both hands on her hips and tapped her high heel, while an evident frown on her face registered her disappointment.

Anne covered her mouth with her arm to keep from hysterically laughing because the look that Beth had pinned on her face was exactly like one that only their aging Aunt Gertrude had mastered in her lifetime, *but at this moment Beth is giving Big Aunt G a run for her money.*

"Oh, no. She didn't." Suzie's voice echoed as her worried head popped unannounced into the doorway and became an exact duplicate illusion of Beth, except with her yellow chiffon dress cascading in waves.

"Oh, yeah...she did," the pair mournfully murmured simultaneously turning forlornly towards each other. They appeared to physically merge resembling Siamese twins with their arms intertwined, similar gaudy makeup and a confection of billowing dresses tangled around their feet.

Anne bit her lip again and rolled her eyes to the heavens as she thought to herself, *oh shit, I forgot what night it is. I could just kick myself!* For as long as Anne could remember this particular evening was a sacred tradition. Every year their family and friends would dress - up, mingle over appetizers and drinks to watch the Oscars. It was always one of the best nights of the year for all of them. After their parents' death, Anne vainly attempted to make sure that at the very least this one tradition could be a semi-normal evening for the two of them.

Anne's forced smile spread across her face while she maneuvered carefully around the outrageous girls. Without another word, she turned bounding up the steps and called back over her shoulder the moment she ran across the landing. "Oh, you two just stop. No, I haven't forgotten. But at least give me a couple of minutes to get cleaned up."

Smiling, Beth let out a whoop then a shrill squeal as she exaggeratedly spread her arms to twirl with Suzie around the middle of the kitchen. They both began to dance to the music coming from the TV and then ran back towards the living room after they called up the back stairs.

"OMG, you better hurry up because they're already walking down the Red Carpet. You just have to see all of the dresses this year. They are sooooo gorgeous!"

Sighing with relief Anne crossed the room to turn on the radio. As the Fugee's 'Killing Me Softly' moved through the air she slowed her pace while pulling her shirt over her head, unzipped her jeans to quickly shower and change. Her shoulders slumped while her mind dejectedly resigned that the evening chores were officially finished and she was committed to the couch watching the Oscars. She opened the closet door to grab a pair of sweats and a T-shirt then padded into the bathroom. With each step she got a little more excited about relaxing with a huge bowl of popcorn and watching some mindless TV.

Finishing the shower in record time, Anne wrapped herself in an old, threadbare towel to mechanically stand in front of the pedestal sink. Holding her breath she shivered and waited for the mist on the ancient, chipped mirror to dissipate. Impatiently she wiped off the last of the existing layer of condensation and habitually examined herself. She was always startled to find that the face staring back didn't have any of the youthful appearance that a 23-year-old girl should have. Her long brown hair hung in wet, limp strands tangled over her shoulders and trailing down her back. Frustrated, Anne combed the mass away from her face and gazed more intently at her reflection. The large dark bags stained the skin under her blue-grey eyes and making them look haunted and tired as they emptily stared back at her. A couple of years' hard work on the ranch had created a feather of lines around the corners of her eyes and mouth. During the winter her skin had become a pale white, compared to the summer months when working outdoors helped create a healthy glow. Rubbing her hands roughly against the sides of her face and gently pulling on her skin, Anne mentally compared her pallor to the underbelly of a frog. She slowly turned her head this way and that, trying to convince

7

herself that she was not only blessed with a good heart but also an semi-attractive face. *But lately, no one ever comes around to see me...especially men,* Anne begrudgingly thought to herself. *Not a single soul from town or Seattle. It's as if I've dropped off the edge of the earth.* Anne placed her hands on her hips and began to give herself a mental pep talk. She bravely recounted the days in high school and she had quite a few boys looking her way and begging to ask her out. At one time even the big-time jock, Dave, from the neighboring farm had pursued her and they'd briefly dated. But her parents had frowned on their relationship because he was a few years older, a little wild and the known bad boy of Westport. Anne abruptly rubbed her hands across her face as she turned away from the mirror and resumed her thoughts back to the present. She quickly grabbed her clothes, carelessly throwing them on and tied her hair up into a ponytail. Pushing the bathroom door open she headed down the front stairway of the house to watch the rest of the Oscars with Beth.

The moment Anne snuck into the living room, to un-graciously plop down onto the couch and threw her feet up on the wobbly coffee table, a commercial ended, "And welcome back to the night of the year" echoed throughout the room and enjoyed the glitz as the Oscars resumed. The introduction from the commercial break was intoned with welcoming everyone back with an overview of the show was very flashy and full of glamour. They streamed highlights of interviews with the stars that were available for comments, focusing all their attention on their outfits and whom the stars were with. The camera always seemed to be searching obsessively for the next big piece of gossip or scandal.

"Oh, I'm so glad you finally made it down! You missed most of the beginning, but this is usually the best part. They're going to announce the awards for the best actor and actress, my favorite!" Beth gushed.

Anne swiveled around on the couch the second she heard Beth's voice as the duo walked into the room carrying a huge green Tupperware bowl full of popcorn and a few glasses of soda. They happily displayed their outfits by sashaying around the living room, randomly pirouetting and then strategically positioned themselves on either side of the couch, sandwiching a suddenly claustrophobic Anne between them. The lightweight chiffon material from their skirts billowed out in sporadic layers almost completely covering the sofa, and Anne. Choking, she quickly pushed the piles of fabric off of her head and stared incredulously at her sister, who had become instantaneously engrossed in the show.

Rolling her eyes to the heavens again, Anne heaved an exasperated sigh. *We are so opposite.* After the aggravated thought, she got another catch in her throat remembering all of the years sitting in this same spot with their parents and friends. They would all try to make a concerted effort to dress up in some sort of exaggerated way. At the end of the night her mother would always announce that they had all dressed up out of respect to the talented people that they were watching, but Anne always knew it was simply a cherished night that her mother could leave their small town life and be somewhere or someone amazing, without ever leaving the living room.

Anne chuckled at Beth's unblinking eyes glued to the TV screen and automatically shoveled handfuls of popcorn into her mouth. When another dancing segment ended, the camera panned towards another area of the stage, Beth began to hop up and down while excitedly nudging her sister in the ribs.

"You are so lucky that you came down at the perfect time! They're going to announce the best actor award. Nick Taylor is up for it again. He's so dreamy," she finished her sentence with an elongated, high-pitched squeal.

Anne enjoyed her sister's excitement, grabbed the bowl of popcorn and resumed her attention back to the program. *Well…I've heard enough about this superstar, it's about time I'm finally seeing him.* A graceful image suddenly emerged on the screen, a beautiful buxom blonde dressed in an almost transparent dress that magically defied gravity as she floated across the stage towards the podium. It took a second for the applause to subside enough to allow her to present the names of the nominees. After the beautiful starlet read the description of each actor, the camera momentarily focused and then froze on each of their faces while a dramatic clip from their movie was displayed on a huge screen suspended over the stage. When the camera finally panned to Nick Taylor, a fervor of screams came from most of the females in the crowd. Anne's eyes widened in surprise as she thoughtfully chewed on her lip. *I have to admit he is one gorgeous man.*

The camera perfectly caught the wicked smile that crossed Nick's handsome face the moment his name was announced. He exaggeratedly tipped his head slightly, longingly gazed into the lens and cocked an eyebrow as he taunted the viewers, bringing their screams to a fevered pitch. The camera seemed to simply eat him up as he sat confidently, displaying his classically chiseled face, strong jaw line and full lips that were presently parted in a rueful grin. The exception to the rest of the other actors and his most recognizable asset was his startling silver blue eyes that topped off his trademark good looks. The camera remained riveted, recording his every move as he leaned towards his date. His highlighted collar-length hair moved sexily against his neck, as the stunning bombshell blonde woman covered her astonished mouth when he whispered something obviously outrageous in her ear.

Anne turned questioningly towards Beth and muttered, "Who's the sexpot with him?"

Beth gave her sister an irritated look before she answered with a disgruntled humph, "I can't believe you don't recognize her, she's the new 'it-girl' Ava…Duh." Anne made an unrecognizable acknowledging noise when she suddenly recalled Ava's picture spread across all of the covers of magazines promoting one of her new clothing lines, fragrance or upcoming movie. The camera stayed focused on the couple, especially when Ava looked alarmingly shocked by whatever Nick suggested. She animatedly slapped his thigh, then scooted a little closer while maintaining her cool, collected poise before the cameras moved on to the next nominee.

Anne annoyingly found herself drawn to Nick like a moth to a flame; *this is ridiculous I'm acting exactly like all the other thousands of sex deprived women across the country.* With the appearance of Nick Taylor, it seemed as if Hollywood had created the perfect male specimen for every lusting lonely female in the world.

Beth giddily bumped into Anne as she brought her knees closer to her chest and giggled as she beamed up at her sister. "I just know Nick Taylor is going to win the Oscar for best actor. He has to win this time, he is SO HOT!!"

Suzie seemed like she couldn't physically remove her gaze from the TV screen as she added with a distracted, "Yeah."

Anne rolled her eyes at the teens while she grabbed another handful of popcorn and started to eat it. "You guys, Nick Taylor is up for one of these awards almost every year and he has yet to win one. Just because he's attractive doesn't mean that his performance will guarantee that he'll win the award."

As the camera zoomed on the presenter seductively starting to open the sealed envelope and announce the winner, Beth hugged her knees closer to her chest and whispered, "Well, I don't care. He should win just because he's so HOT!!"

2

The post-party thrown for all of the Oscar nominees was traditionally located in the most exclusive hotels in Hollywood and always revered to be a spectacular presentation. This year it was conveniently located at the Sunset Tower Hotel, which graced prime skyline and overlooked the whole expanse of LA. The interior resonated nothing but old Hollywood. Draped in luxury, a multitude of windows and French doors opened out onto an enormous rooftop deck.

At that moment all of the doors stood completely open to allow the breeze to alleviate some of the heat radiating from the party. Proficient waiters assembled in crisp white uniforms skirted around a sea of circular tables draped in crisp red linens, adorned with china, crystal and champagne. The entire room was engulfed with the mixture of fresh flowers, food, an exquisite bar, dance floor, a DJ spinning music and a horde of people. But the most important detail that finished off the ensemble was the brilliant addition of all the beautiful stars that were calculatedly mingling while dressed in their finest attire. Each and every one of them were glowing like jewels as they socialized and relished in the spectacular privilege of attending one of the most sought after party invitations of the year.

Bored, Nick had pointedly chose a corner table for simply one reason; he didn't want to talk to anyone. At this vantage he felt minutely in control sitting alone in the desolate spot as he observed all of Hollywood's "new" beautiful people parading around like peacocks. He disgustingly shook his head, grabbed his drink and resigned that the evening was indeed an incredible sight merely because, *I can't believe that there are so many malnourished, eccentric egomaniacs packed into one room. I can't keep track of them, their ultimatums and what they're up to. This whole damn party's surreal, like a scene straight out of a dysfunctional segment of a Monty Python movie, except this entire charade is my reality and I've become a huge part of this sordid life.* Nick rolled his eyes and pinched the bridge of his nose anguishing over the thought of being associated with any of the immature drunken hordes, whose monotonous conversations were giving him an instant migraine. He inwardly moaned while another cluster of the press disengaged themselves from the newest laughing, smiling 'in' couple being interviewed and strategically made their way in his direction. With a single ominous look from Nick, the crew redirected their attention from him and onto another waif-like star. Nick suddenly realized, *I've attended the same party for so many consecutive years that I completely lack any appreciation for where I am or what I'm witnessing. Here I am again at the damn after party for all of the stars who were nominated, but didn't win. Don't they realize that I am better than this? All I want is to be at the Governor's Ball - the one where the winners are.*

What seemed like hours later, he stretched his stiff neck after countless interviews, photographers and well-wishers bombarded his peaceful sanctuary, expertly avoiding the onslaught he adverted his bored gaze, lightly tapped his fingers against the empty glass and wondering out loud, "Hmm, I wonder where Ava's disappeared to." Nick signaled a waiter to bring him another whiskey on the rocks, sighed and then ran his hand through his hair. Disregarding the interested looks thrown his way because he looked carelessly dashing while he leaned back in his chair to survey the room. In the limousine before they'd arrived at the party, he had removed his tuxedo jacket, bow tie, unbuttoned his shirt, exposing the base of his tanned throat and rolled back his sleeves. As Nick surveyed the arrival of another drunken bunch of stars, his brow creased as he half-heartedly looked for Ava. His mouth mischievously turned up in a cat-like grin, reflecting on their conversation during the drive to the party.

"I don't know why you're so upset. At least you were nominated for an award and got invited to go to this party. Just being here will give my career a boost and another excellent opportunity for us to get more exposure as a couple." Ava's honest but narrow-minded comments obnoxiously ping-ponged through his head. *Yet again...her single minded antics are uncaringly resumed at re- assuming her typical ignorant mantra that everything including our relationship is all about her.* Nick turned away from her searching gaze, so the back of his head and obvious brusque silence were his answer.

"Well." Ava exaggeratedly rolled her exquisitely made-up eyes as she gave him a petty little pout for being so openly ignored. With an unladylike "Humph!" she became instantly bored with the situation and began to dramatically rummage through her clutch. Pursing her lips tightly together, she pulled out a compact mirror and meticulously started to apply more ruby red lipstick, her signature color. "Well, for heaven's sake, at least act like you are having fun when we get out of the car. You know our fans will go crazy when they see us together," Ava said through the side of her mouth in a sulky childlike voice. "I hope you made sure that Kris and Kris have their invitation...you know how much I need them around." Nick closed his eyes and prayed for her to stop talking because the sound of her high pitched voice recently had become identical to fingernails on a chalkboard. From the beginning their sexually charged, heated relationship had instantly become the talk of Hollywood and everyone was always speculating which direction their affair was going.

Ava, was Hollywood's new sparkling glamour girl, who was currently, seemingly unhappily married to her high school sweetheart...*but has sworn that she supposedly filed for divorce*, CEO of her own modeling agency/product line, insecure enough to hire a pair of women to be at her beck and call, originally from a small farm in Ashland, Oregon. She'd found her success from climbing her way from acting in minute bit parts at the Oregon Shakespeare Festivals, modeling in malls, to making her way determinedly south to LA and stardom.

On the other hand Nick was the ever sought after, stunningly handsome bachelor who seemed to elude Hollywood by keeping his personal life undisclosed. Especially in a world where anyone would sell off their friends, let alone their deepest secrets, just to get the exposure and their fifteen minutes of fame.

When their limo leisurely pulled up to the building, a Red Carpet pristinely rolled out to the curb and lurking behind a gold cord, were frenzied paparazzi anxiously waiting for the car door to open. Nick took a steadying deep breath as he climbed out of the car while tons of camera's flashed, as photographers frantically trying to catch his every move. He turned to take Ava's hand and graciously helped her out of the limousine.

Here we go, Nick maliciously thought as he slid an arm around her waist, smiled and mindlessly waved to the crowd while he tucked her arm under his. On the Red Carpet Ava paused to pose, pulling Nick's momentum to a standstill while his intentions were to attempt to guide them nonstop through the sea of screaming fans, microphones and flashing cameras. He jumped, startled when he realized his arm was being viciously pinched and yanked, while Ava tried to make him accept an interview alongside her. Nick softly let go of her arm and reassuringly patted her shoulder, indicating that he was moving to stand politely behind her. The second he stepped out of her sight, Nick turned, making his way undetected around her back, never pausing until he reached the main door. Grabbing the handle before the doorman could react, he turned with a genuine smile, gave a jaunting wave to the fanatically screaming crowd and quickly ducked through the door. *Ha, I got through that without a scratch. I wonder when Ava will notice I'm not standing diligently behind her.* Pleased with his successful outcome from eluding Ava, Nick haughtily smiled as he straightened his lapel, clapped his hands, then strode arrogantly into the party and headed directly towards the bar. He made a mental note that it would be imperative to have a drink in hand before answering any questions about losing again. Lounging in his chair and taking another long drink from his half-empty glass, Nick chuckled and thought about how furious Ava was when she finally realized that he'd duped her.

Suddenly out of the corner of his eye Nick caught a slight disruption in the crowd and noticed Ava's minions separating a path through the dance floor. Nick blinked as he stared at the pair, trying to distinguish any difference between the two women. He became astounded when he realized that the Kris's were always two women who looked duplicate to Ava, always hovered anxiously for her every want, petty whim and unnecessary need. *Ava's unspoken rule is always simple…that there was always two and they always resembled their idol in every physical way.* Nick leaned back in his chair and enjoyed watching the two identical women dressed outrageously in gold, plow through the crowd, creating a human fence in an attempt to restrain the dancers from crossing their manmade path. A few seconds later a fuming Ava stampeded through the human barrier, irately in search of Nick. Launching herself away from the crowd she un- euphorically found him contentedly engaged at a corner table sipping on a drink, surrounded by a gaggle of stunning women, who were all too ready to sympathize with his loss and eagerly make him aware of their sexual availability for the evening.

"I can't believe you left me out there, alone!" Ava annoyingly chastised him as she stood towering over the table with one hand on her hip, as venom shot out of her eyes and visually dismissed the other hovering beautiful females with an overtly aggressive stare. The Kris's immediately rushed to her side, trying to sooth her nerves and began berating each of the lingering, hopeful women. Once the horde was successfully diffused, Ava regally took her place by noisily sliding a chair across the floor and creating a loud smack as it slammed into his chair.

"I don't know what has gotten into you. You should be delighted that you've made it this far and relish in your success! I could name quite a few actors who have never been invited to this party during their careers and would give their eyeteeth to be here." She eyed Nick's unresponsive profile. "Argh…you two know what I like to drink, go and get me another one." Ava haughtily commanded, as she waved her minions to do her bidding and retrieve a drink.

Turning his head to watch the pair scamper off he gave Ava a beguiling smile, Nick searched her beautiful face and then leaned forward, suggestively gesturing with his finger for her to move closer towards him. Ava knowingly lowered her lashes, bit her lip and smiled as she leaned seductively towards his mouth. Their eyes locked as he licked his lips, bent further over her protruding cleavage, lingeringly traced her exposed skin with his fingertip and suggestively whispered right above her luscious mouth. "You, should remember that you are only here because I brought you. So be a good girl and mind your P's and Q's...or I'll have to trade you in for a NEW and improved 'model'." Nick smothered his smile with his hand while he watched Ava's eyes widen in shock the second she registered his obvious innuendo.

 "You wouldn't dare." Furiously she shoved back her chair from the table, arrogantly stormed across the room and disappeared into the crowd. The moment Ava left, he deftly reached across the table, grabbed her abandoned drink, blew out his pent up breath and leaned back in the chair. Nick squeezed his eyes shut, taking a deep swallow of the sickeningly sweet pink drink, he tried not to recount how many times he'd attended the same party. Swirling the ice cubes around the glass as he listened to the DJ play 'Sweet Nothing' by Calvin Harris & Florence Welsh, Nick glanced around the room trying to determine what was going to happen by the end of the party. *How many different women have accompanied me here year after year? How many times by the end of the evening have I left drunk with someone, other than my date and not even cared?*

He noticed another slight disturbance at the edge of the dance floor caused by a small, dark-haired man cutting through the crowd and confidently maneuvering his way towards the table. Nick smiled at the sight of his agent and longtime friend, Mike. He silently watched while Mike painstakingly stopped to greet everyone as he slowly made his way to the table. Nick knew he was a good guy, especially for an agent. It seemed that Mike always had excellent direction, guidance, candor, and dedication to help him achieve every one of his career goals. All Nick ever wanted was to be the best, and Mike was always there to support him in every endeavor.

Mike heaved a huge sigh of relief as he slipped into the chair across from Nick and propped his head on both hands to watch his client. Nick squirmed inwardly while he felt the intensity emanating from Mike's gaze and took another drink to avoid his sympathetic eyes; instantaneously a young blonde actress bounced over to the table, bumbling started on a bland typical speech of the evening about how he was being overlooked, his amazing acting talent and how totally enthralled she was to be in his presence. After an overtly long stretch of daunting silence from either man, she lamely tried to confirm the possibility that they were probably staying at the same hotel, then gracefully stooped over to display a large portion of her cleavage and silently slipped him her room key across the table. "It's such a funny coincidence we'll be so close, so if you're in the mood and feel like to talking or anything else, please let me know." After another pregnant pause, she skillfully licked her lips, gave Nick a wink then gracefully sauntered away from the table. Mike appreciatively raised his eyebrow while watching her walk away with a very suggestive sway in her hips. He turned his attention back to Nick once she rejoined a small circle of giggling beautiful women and gave a low, slow whistle.

"Wow, now she was impressive. How many room keys does that make tonight?" Mike raised his hand to signal the waiter for another round of drinks for their table. As he turned back to Nick, Mike was startled at Nick's giant domino stack of room keys carefully laid from the center of the table to the edge; it resembled a multicolored river of sin. Quickly surmising the wearied look on Nick's face, Mike realized that he didn't care about any of the keys or the young actresses who were openly ogling the empty seats, oozing their invitations to sleep with him.

Mike uncomfortably cleared his throat as he turned to humor a disgruntled Nick across the table. "I remember the first time you came to this party years ago. You sat over there at the head of the room at the center table, reigning like a king and holding court with every woman fawning over you the entire evening." Valiantly trying to lighten the mood, Mike smiled at the memory and watched as Nick toyed mindlessly with the line of room keys on the table. "Ah, those were the days. Remember you'd have a list of questions about yourself that you asked each female contender. Whoever answered all of the questions correctly and looked good, received the, um, er…prize. I'll never forget that one year, which one was it? When you told me about the pair of twins from Paris, and what you guys did out on the balcony at your hotel. I think most of what you told me is illegal in quite a few states." Mike wiped his eyes as he laughed at the uncomfortable look that suddenly crossed Nick's face. Nick shoved all of the keys into a catawampus pile along the side of the table, seething and glanced around the room at all of the beautiful people. Right at that second, a roar of approval came from the crowd as Justin Timberlake's 'Sexy Back' started to play. All of them were mingling, dancing and enjoying themselves to the fullest, everyone except him. Nick leaned over the table and frustratingly raked a hand through his hair.

"I'm starting to become a living cliché. For the amount of times I've been nominated for any award, I haven't won. Even the gossip magazines have been sympathizing with my plight, I've almost accomplished winning the award so many times it's stupid. The only thing I have succeeded in is the knowledge that I have a table reserved indefinitely here at this party for the almost-achievers." Mike opened and shut his mouth like a broken puppet as he attempted to think of the appropriate response to he's revelation. Nick simply raised his hand to stop any of Mike's positive 'pick yourself up by your bootstraps' monolog. "Yes, I know that just being nominated is an accomplishment, but I want more." Nick's weary eyes rested on Mike trying to judge his reaction before he continued on. *I feel like I need him to understand and not because he's my agent but because he's become my best friend.* "I've been giving acting everything I have for so many years and continually ending up here stuck with the second string. I feel like I'll never get to the top, never become number one, and never really win. Right now I would sell my soul to be at the *other* party, the one for the winners. I just want a guaranteed chance to be one of the golden ones for the evening, instead of lucky to be second best."

Mike slowly leaned back in his chair and rested his chin on his steeple fingertips while he solemnly regarded his friend. "I expected you'd feel this way. I believe I have a proposition for you to consider." He signaled an approaching waiter over to the table, ordered another round of drinks and then turned back to Nick. "Let's go outside so we can have a serious discussion in private." Ending their conversation by abruptly standing up from the table as he spied another one of the giggling women disengage from the gaggle and confidently approach the table with her eyes steadfastly trained on Nick, like he was her human prey. Seconds before she pounced Mike stealthily moved to one side and stood directly in her path, blocking all of her seductive intentions. Not anticipating Mike's movements, she was instantly startled out of her intent, awkwardly pitched forward on her stilettos and nearly running over the little man in her determined, provocative walk towards the table. She kept her vision focused on Nick while she casually leaned over to listen to Mike. The second she moved forward, the top of her dress gaped open to expose a view practically down to her bared navel. Knowing he was looking she gave Nick a devious smile. Her eyes went frigid the second her sex fogged mind comprehended what Mike was saying, her smile abruptly vanished as she quickly stood up. Appalled at the intruding man, she hopefully glanced back towards Nick with a forlorn look and surprisingly with the agility of a circus performer she tried to side step around the insignificant man. Mike sternly planted himself in front of her, then dramatically shooed her off like a fly with his hands.

Nick chuckled heartily at the redhead's withering glare she gave Mike, then peevishly turned on her heel and stormed off. "That wasn't hard." Mike murmured while he brushed off his hands, shrugged nonchalantly and turned made his way towards the French doors leading outside onto a secluded deck. Nick obediently rose and followed.

Now I wonder what that little man has in store for me.

The view from the deck was breathtaking. The building they were in sat high on top of a hill that overlooked the city. Night was just descending and turning the brilliant azure sky into a rich midnight blue. Thinly streaked clouds in that floated across the sky shimmered silver as the lights from all of the buildings below glowed. The whole city sparkled like diamonds in the night. The Sunset Tower Hotel perfectly complimented the soiree; the audience attending combined with the view were worth millions of dollars.

There were a few straggling couples lingered around the expanse, enjoying a breath of fresh air and the view. Nick nonchalantly scanned the area, then sauntered over to a group of vacant chairs. Mike briskly maneuvered around and spoke discreetly to each of the guests. Disgruntled, Nick took a seat, swirling the ice cubes in his drink, noticed how each couple sympathetically glanced his way and after a second of Mike's probing they reluctantly moved inside. During the procession of retreating people a waiter brought out their drinks, set them on a table and subtly left the area. As Mike ominously closed the French doors on the last straggler, silence enveloped all of the party's gaiety, laughter and music. Nick physically shuddered at the sudden peace that transformed the serene outdoors, filling him with impending doom. Mike rapidly crossed the deck and took the seat next to Nick. The tension between them was deafening as the seconds ticked by. Nick regarded Mike out of the corner of his eye. *What is he up to? I haven't a clue what he has planned for me this time.* Nick uncomfortably sucked air in between his teeth before he opened his mouth and began to state the obvious, "So, here we are…sitting outside waiting for you to get on with whatever topic you wanted to discuss." The moment Nick finished his statement, a rowdy noise emerged as the doors opened and a waiter quietly stepped out with another round of drinks. Nick arrogantly turned his attention back toward the view ignoring the waiter, who was awkwardly glancing around searching for a spot to set down their drinks. Looking like he was a part of the circus sideshow, the waiter balanced the, tray laden with drinks while repositioning a table by sliding it loudly across the deck to their spot. Nick closed his eyes against the grating noise while the waiter strenuously pushed the table into place in front of their chairs.

"Is there anything else that you would like this evening?" he breathlessly asked as he stepped in front of them anxiously waiting for any other instructions.

Mike cleared his throat looked over at Nick and gave him a quick wink before he tucked a rolled wad of cash into the surprised waiter's palm. "Yeah kid, can you make sure that we're not disturbed, and keep the drinks coming if you see our glasses are low."

A glimmer lit his eyes while he reassured them, "Oh, yes sir. I'll make sure no one will be coming out to disturb you. My name is Kurt. I'll be around if you need me the rest of the evening." Kurt hastily left the couple, then clumsily bumped into the French doors as he backed away and frantically searching for the handle. A roar from the party exploded when the door finally opened, then the boisterous noise slowly diminished the moment he quickly shut them. Kurt snapped the lock with authority, then resembled a militant guard by crossing his arms in front of his chest, sternly braced his feet and defying anyone to pass.

"It always amazes me what a couple of 20's can buy nowadays," Mike heartily laughed as he picked up his glass and lazily took a swig. Absently nodding at his comment and looking back out at the beautiful view, Nick took a drink, anxiously waited for what Mike had to say. The silence stretched for just a couple of seconds. "Nick, I know that tonight was a big disappointment to you. I really thought you had the award with this part. Everyone thought so. But it just didn't fly." Mike turned to face Nick's ticking jaw. "Now we have to move on. I got an opportunity that I think is just what we need right now. I know that you typically have a vacation planned after one of these award things, but I am going to ask you to reconsider your plans and listen to what I have to say." Mike took a deep breath and launched into the rest of his speech. "I think you need to change your acting tactics and the direction in which your career is currently headed. I know you want to win this award. Hell, everyone in Hollywood wants you to win it. But I think it's time you start living your dream." Leaning closer to Nick and casting furtive glances around the deck to make sure that no one was listening, he conspiringly whispered, "I have a new contact and he has procured us the script of a lifetime. It's like nothing we've ever done so far, and I think it's the key to unlock your career right now."

Nick settled further into the chair cradling his drink with him. "OK shoot, what are the details and more importantly, what's the catch?" He knew from all their years together there was going to be some kind of catch. "Do I have to do another shaving cream commercial, sell cologne at the mall or make an appearance at another charity event?"

"No, no, no, it's nothing like that. I just need you to disappear for a little while." Knowing what Nick's reaction would possibly be with the delivery of the imperative information, Mike carefully leaned away from Nick, just out of arm's reach. "You have to leave Hollywood."

"What?" Nick lunged forward, slopping his drink onto his pant leg as the word escaped his mouth. He turned with an incredulous look at his friend, because he felt like he'd been slapped across the face with a brick.

Mike held up a protective hand and continued, "Now hold on. You haven't heard the entire sales pitch yet. And you can imagine that it must be something big, especially if I am sitting out here putting my career on the line by merely mentioning it."

Nick swallowed the rest of his drink and set the empty glass on the table. Aggravated he picked up Mike's extra drink, gave him a jaunty salute and took a long swallow from it. Leaning back Nick closed his eyes for a moment and allowed the warmth from the liquor to mellow his frayed nerves and took a deep meditative breath. *Remember, he has just as much riding on his career. Mike's vision of who I was going to become has made me the superstar I am. Maybe this is another one of his blind-faith situations that I just need to sit back and listen to. Hell, you never know, most of his crazy schemes have worked.* Reluctantly, Nick squinted over at his friend, only to find him serenely steeple his fingertips and looking at the view. Offering a truce, he repositioned himself by sitting back up in his chair, taking another gulp, and then gestured his hand in surrender towards Mike. "Ok, I've had my little fit, I'm ready to hear your newest sales pitch for my next successful role."

Mike held up a single finger as he stood up, emptied his drink and walked over to the French doors. As he tapped they opened slightly, Nick could hear him asking Kurt to order another round. He quickly walked back and placed his hands on the back of Nick's chair. "I thought we'd need another round before I explain the whole situation. Once I start with this, I don't want any interruptions." Recognizing the noise of Kurt fumbling with the door, Mike quickly intercepted, took the drinks back to the table and then settled into his chair. "As you know, this is all very confidential, so here it goes. A few weeks ago, I received a phone call from another agent in town. He started bragging about how he had been contacted by some unknown screenplay writer who was new in town, out of cash, but brilliant." Mike smiled over at Nick and shrugged. "You know the drill. I took the agent out to lunch, bought him a shit-load of drinks and by the end of the meal I had this 'amazing' writer's name. You know, Mike always gets what Mike wants."

Nick instinctively glanced down at the empty glass on the table and half empty drink in his hand. *Hmmm, I wonder how many times he's tried that trick on me.*

Mike excitedly turned towards Nick, lowered his voice and rushed on. "So, I go to see this guy, not really thinking anything about it because he's in this rundown, low income neighborhood. You should have seen the people's eyes when I drove up and parked my car. They were all freaking out, like crazy, man!" Nick laughed because he knew how much Mike's car meant to him. It was the first thing Mike had purchased for himself when he received his first large pay check from Nick's success. The car was a low slung, bright cherry red Ferrari and had instantly become an extension of Mike. The ongoing joke around town was if anyone spotted the car, Mike wasn't two feet away. He'd never allow anyone to touch it or even ride in it as far as Nick knew, not even Nick. "Anyway, I went in thinking nothing was going to come out of it, but holy shit, the writer is amazing! I introduced myself after he answered the door. He lamely wandered off like he didn't know who I was! When I walked inside the apartment, I noticed he was packing all of his belongings. I asked him what was going on and he replied that things hadn't been going his way and he was going back home to Washington State." Mike squirmed in his seat exactly like an excited child at Christmas and continued on. "I told him that I had just heard about him and asked to look over one of his manuscripts. He hardly noticed I was there as he continued to pack and just waved me over to a corner where a pile of material had been discarded on the floor. I grabbed the nearest stack of papers and started to read." Mike took his drink off of the table and took a long pull. He closed his eyes as if he was savoring the moment in his mind. Nick's frustration began to surface as he fought the urge to shake him until his teeth rattled. "The manuscript was amazing. When I finally looked up, he was sitting on the couch watching me. I was so engrossed with his writing that the afternoon had moved into evening and I never even realized it." Mike sat forward and looked at Nick. "I didn't know what to do. Here was this gold mine, and he was leaving. So I grabbed all of his work, threw it in a box and told him to grab his coat. I threw him into my car with all of his work and drove to an out-of-the-way restaurant so I could talk some sense into him."

Nick leaned forward to the edge of his chair waiting to hear the rest. "First off, I can't believe you had another human being, besides the boxes, in your car, and then what did you do?"

Mike quickly turned back towards Nick and said, "I have him tucked away in a hotel outside of LA. He's agreed to work in private on your next script, but we're going to have to do things fast. We have to get you out of here to work on it quietly and there is only one way to do it. I'm going to get an outline from him and set up everything that has to be done to get you into character. I need you to lay low while this is all developing and work on rediscovering yourself for this part. It's the one, I know it in my gut. But you're going to have to trust me and follow my directions explicitly. We can't let anyone know what I've done with this guy and his work, or he could walk. The plans are a bit shaky but they have to start rolling fast or we'll never keep this guy, especially if anyone realizes what he's working on, and for whom."

At the precise moment the door slammed open the second Mike's sentence ended. An irate Ava had accomplished the impossible, pushing past Kurt and stormed across the deck. Kurt was diligently trailing behind, desperately trying to redirect her back inside while he cast a nervous glance at the seated men and they curiously at the Kris's flanking Ava's side. Without a word, she skidded to a halt in front of Nick, as the identical duo scrambled to support Ava, while she started to indignantly tap her toe.

"What the hell is going on out here? I have been looking everywhere for you. I thought you might have been up to one of your famous disappearing acts with another woman this evening, but I see you were just having a pity party with Mike. You should be in there escorting me to ensure that everyone has seen us! I really don't want to miss out on such a huge opportunity." Ava ended her waspish tirade with a flip of her hair and an irritated huff. The Kris's added their two bits with a unified "Yeah."

Nick wearily rubbed his hands over his eyes while Ava stood ominously waiting for his answer, he decided to though his hands up in mock surrender. "Okay, okay, you win. I'll have you hanging on my arm for the rest of the evening. Just don't start with your ranting for the rest of the night. Like you said, I could still 'conger up' one of my famous disappearing acts." Nick raised a suggestive eyebrow at Ava, making her huff and pivot away. He stood up from his chair and looked back down at Mike. "And I'll talk to you soon, right?"

"Cheers." Mike raised his glass, saluting the backside of Ava as she indignantly ignored him and turned to make her way back towards the party. Mike refocused his attention onto his friend. "You know Nick, I think this opportunity couldn't have come at the perfect time for you. I can imagine that after tonight you'll need a break from whatever moral "obligations" you feel towards that married tramp."

"Yeah, I think you've hit the nail on the head." Nick smiled at his friend's assumption of his relationship and unsteadily followed the waiter trailing in Ava's wake. As he approached the opened door, Nick staggered back from all the noise and heat radiating from the party.

He quickly realized that Ava had quickly moved ahead, flanked again by the hovering Kris's, instantly engulfed by another group and matronly motioned him to follow her. He lifted his hand and motioned for her to wait then started for the bar. *I might as well make this an evening that I would rather not remember in the morning...especially since I'll be Ava's little puppet for the rest of the night.*

Taking a quick detour, Nick sauntered across the room and bellied up to the bar in one stiff motion. He held up his hand to get the bartender's attention so he could order another drink. Suddenly he felt the hairs stand up on the back of his neck the second he felt Ava's malicious stare burn a hole into the back of his head. A sad, sly smile crossed his features as his imagination ran rampant about what their conversation would be during the ride home. Nick hummed along with Maroon 5's 'Moves like Jagger' absentmindedly, simply because he drunkenly couldn't quite place who was singing while he lounged against the bar for support. After the set was done, he realized he'd become completely engrossed with a toothpick as he had sat down at the bar and patiently waited for his drink. Suddenly he felt a determined tug on his sleeve that brought him out of his current toothpick dilemma. He casually turned to find another beautiful woman smiling coyly at him.

"Ummm, excuse me. Could you pass me a napkin?"

Nick licked his lips as his gaze lingered on her face, and then roamed across her openly displayed assets, promptly ending at the edge of the bar. He noticed that there happened to be a stack of napkins next to his arm, and one neatly tucked under her elbow.

"Ahem, don't mind me." Nick deftly reached over, intentionally grazing her breasts with his palm as he lifted her elbow to pick up the napkin tucked under it. "Don't mind helping a lovely lady in distress."

The music and memory of Ava faded into the background as their gazes heatedly locked as he slid up next to her body, his eyes never leaving hers. A seductive smile crossed his face as he inched a little forward making the fabric of his shirt press against the woman's chest and brushed his hand up her indecently exposed thigh. *I wonder if Ava will notice if I bag out of here early, and without her...*

3

Nick carelessly smiled then paused to enjoy the warmth of the early morning sunlight while simultaneously locking the door to his mod 60's styled house. It was situated on a prime piece of property that spread across from the pristine Malibu beachfront. He gave his keys a blasé toss into the air, began to whistled, turned his face in the direction of the sun, and contemplated about the great turn of events. Nick tapped his toe as he whistled an off-key version of Rod Stewart's 'Maggie May'. While he uninterestedly observed the small army of help maintaining the yard, and continued to leisurely walk down the paved path in front of the beautiful home that lead to a large triple-car garage. His grin widened as he approached the sleek black Porsche Panamera GTS sitting picturesquely in the driveway. *Can't beat receiving this for a gift after finishing that shitty movie last year. I love my job!* He continued whistling while thoughtlessly waved off numerous offers to assist him from the staff and offhandedly nodded to the head gardener tending a large palm tree. He opened the car door reverently and sensually slid down into the snug driver's seat. Nick emitted an impatient sigh while he waited for another hired hand to finish polishing the car. "I love this car," Nick murmured as he ran his hand over the leather seat, which hugged his body perfectly, closed the car door and gazed up at the rearview mirror. His sparkling baby blue eyes flashed as he let his sunglasses slide down his nose for a second. Admiring his million-dollar smile, Nick gave his reflection a quick, audacious wink then redirected the mirror towards the rear window. He momentarily paused while he turned the key and instantly the engine leapt to life. Nick gave a respective salute as the quiet purr of the engine complimented 'Life's Been Good' by Joe Walsh as it suddenly blared over the stereo. Glancing over at the passenger side of the car, he reached over to pat the black leather duffle bag that occupied the seat and glanced at the sealed manila envelope. He took a sobering breath and gave one last look to memorize his house sprawling house that overlooked a huge expanse of the ocean. The yard was manicured to perfection by an army of gardeners and to the right you could catch a glimpse of the pool with an extended cabana. It was fashioned in the likeness of a low-key mid-century modern. Excluding the expense; it was the perfect home for a superstar.

"Lord, I love my house." Nick allowed the engine to warm up as he thought about being rudely awakened at daybreak when Mike had unexpectedly called. Blurrily, Nick had tried to listen while Mike immediately dove excitedly into reciting some of the pages from the script, which he exuberantly promised would be the miracle that would change his career. The concept of the script sounded good while Mike fumbled through his proposition, except he never gave Nick any concrete information about a plan or anything. He rubbed his aching head listening to Mike's rambling, rumpling his hair as he attempted to mentally catch up with the scheme. It had only been a day since the Oscars and he had almost forgotten about their whole drunken endeavor.

"Hey Mike, I'm not complaining, but I think you're asking a lot from me right now. There isn't even any substantial light outside yet and you want me to commit to a life-changing decision." Nick whispered into the receiver as he stood in front of the enormous bedroom window just as the beginning of the sun's shimmering rays sprawled its fingers over the murky ocean. He felt pretty calm despite being rudely awakened by the piercing sound of the phone at the surreal time of morning.

"I know, I know. But this is going to be HOT. Either we jump on it, start everything rolling and have this guy signed, like yesterday, or we might as well hand everything over to your competition, sit back and watch while they walk away with next year's Oscar."

"Let me digest this whole idea of yours for a moment and see if I comprehend it correctly. I have a choice; either agree with your insane proposition by getting into my car this afternoon, in which you've left me a packet in a bag with instructions to some hotel in San Francisco with provisions, vacate my life and begin training for a script that I haven't even agreed to read yet...or stay where I am and fail." Nick heard a slight moan that emitted from the direction of his bedroom. He quickly turned away from where Ava laid, unladylike spread eagle in bed, softly snoring. Stealthily, he maneuvered around their discarded pile of clothes, opened the door and silently made his way into the kitchen. "And if I accept this crazy idea, then I'll have to lay low for possibly nine months. During this time I'm supposed to be developing my character from a script I know nothing about, but during my exile, you'll supply me in bits and pieces. All the while you'll be here in LA, finalizing all of the minor details for a movie that has yet to be slated, produced or backed. On top of all of this you are guaranteeing that my months of patience and sacrifice will ensure that I will win the Oscar, hands down." Nick ran his hand over his face. "I have to admit this situation is slightly different from all the other scripts you've ever procured for me."

"Look Mike…" When Nick attempted to complain again about not having any essential information, Mike nonchalantly interrupted him.

"Nick baby, you've got to trust me on this one. All you have to do is simply follow all of the directions that I'm going to leave in your car to a 'T' and you'll be the next golden star. Who's believed in you since the evening I stumbled across you bartending in that sleazy hole years ago, huh? It'll be a piece of cake. Trust me."

"Whatever, Mike. Just make sure it's all set up in the morning, I mean in a few hours."

"Nick baby, have I ever let you down?" were the fateful last words from Mike.

Nick disbelievingly shook his head, after recalling what had transpired, he reached over and grabbed the manila envelope. He quickly ripped it open and took inventory of the contents. It consisted of a Google map, simple driving instructions to head north on Highway 101 to a hotel in San Francisco and to take the duffle bag in with him. Inside the bag was another packet with more information about his venture into the unknown and expectations with accepting the proposal. "Whatever, Mike. Fucking control freak." Nick arrogantly shrugged his tense shoulders as he threw the car in drive and slowly headed down the curved, palm tree-lined driveway, picking up speed with the Eagle's 'Life in the Fast Lane' blaring through the opened window.

"Yeah--" Suddenly Nick felt a touch of fate tingle down the base of his spine. He lightly touched the brake pedal and slowed the car down to a crawl, as he suddenly had a strange feeling that this might be the last time he'd be enjoying the sight of his home. Nick nervously laughed at himself and unheedingly gunned the car down the rest of the driveway, laughing harder while making a few of the workers frantically leapt out of his way before they got hit. Surging towards the end of the drive, he tapped slightly on the brake then sped out onto the busy street, causing oncoming cars' brakes to squeal while others swerved out of his way. Uninterested and slightly annoyed at all the havoc he'd caused in the street, Nick cranked the stereo and headed into the unspecified future, without a single thought of abandoning Ava while she peacefully slept.

4

"Ok Kate, that sounds great. Then we'll expect him by, I guess in a few days...right. I really want to thank...yes, I realize...thanks again for thinking about us, and it's no problem." After glancing out the rain-sprayed window, Anne closed her eyes and pinched the bridge of her nose in earnest. Her jumbled thoughts went directly outside to the two bright yellow slickers emerging from the barn and racing awkwardly through the mud towards the house.

"Thanks. Yes, I have the contact number in case, yes...and hey Kate-- Thanks again for considering, yes...bye." Anne hastily snapped off the phone and closed her eyes while she stood petrified in the middle of the kitchen. She couldn't bear to open them as she carefully set the received back in its cradle. Searing pain began to creep up the back of her skull while Anne felt another monster headache coming on. She tentatively opened one eye into a tiny slit to stare accusingly at the phone for a second, pondering her rash decision. "Ah shit, what did I just do?" Anne ran both her hands roughly down her face as if she was trying to erase the last few minutes from her memory. At once she began to rub more vigorously up and down, when the back door crashed open and she soberly listened to the two girls stumble into the house.

"Hey Anne, we've got another runner!" Beth hollered as both she and Suzie stormed in through the mud room, squeaking their dirty muck boots across the kitchen while their dripping slickers quickly made pools of water on the floor.

"Shit! It isn't Demon again, is it?" Anne grabbed the nearest dishtowel and threw it on the floor directly across the girl's feet.

"You're not going to believe it, but its Ginger this time," Beth soberly informed her as she began to drag the towel around with the toe of her muddy boot.

"What? There's no way she possibly could have..." Anne murmured while she stormed over to the back door and grabbed her dry yellow slicker off the wall.

"Well, she did. It looked like she leaned onto that broken corral door. And OMG, looked like she was headed straight over to Dave's place, again."

"Shit, shit!" Anne shrugged into her coat and started to pull on her boots just as the phone began to ring. Anne paused to silently lock a knowing gaze with Beth's as she let out an exasperated breath and her shoulders slumped in defeat. Her feet felt like she was wading in mud while she made her way across the kitchen to answer the phone. *Shit, shit, shit.*

"Hello—Oh, hey Dave." Anne dramatically rolled her eyes at her sister while she gnashed her teeth and prayed for patience as she waited to continue her conversation. The muffled sound of an irritated male voice could be heard through the receiver across the dead calm of the kitchen. "No...everything is just fine here. Oh really, Ginger this time? Huh, I didn't realize..." Anne tightly shut her eyes as she desperately tried to keep her headache at bay. The pain seemed to come in waves as she listened to the masculine voice begin to condescendingly lecture her about responsibilities and their runaway horse.

"I realize we need to secure the animals appropriately, we're trying to get everything maintained and squared away around here. But you know, there are only so many hours in a day." Anne tried to placate their neighbor with a falsetto-singsong voice as she eluded his aggressive questions. Beth and Suzie sympathetically watched Anne struggle with her frustration over the situation and having to deal with Dave. They nervously glanced at each other, because neither knew what to do to help in their youth and ignorance. Instantly they stepped closer together in a silent, but naïve show of support as they quietly anticipated Anne's decision about their situation.

"No, I don't need your help around the ranch...not at this moment. But thanks anyway for your offer." Anne pinched the bridge of her nose and squeezed her eyes tighter while she tried to find a way out of the conversation. "Yes, yes...I realize. No. You don't have to bring Ginger back over here. I was just going to send Beth and Suzie over to get her." Anne waved her hand at the girls, forcing them to obey her silent command.

Beth nudged Suzie with her elbow as they hesitantly sidestepped towards the back door. Each girl listening for Anne to finish with the insulting conversation and let them know what they needed to do. The girls jumped in unison when Anne abruptly stood ramrod straight, clutched the receiver tighter and narrowed her eyes into tiny, seething slits while anger surged through her. "Dave...like I've said, your help is always appreciated around here. But, I think you're overstepping yourself with your assumptions. I think we are doing just fine here...alone. I really would appreciate it if the direction of this conversation stopped right now. Thank you." Anne gave her sister a heartfelt fleeting glance, then continued on. She pivoted her body so she was facing the window over the sink and watched the rain fall in torrents. "Look...I didn't want to say anything too soon, but I've been working on something that is going to help out with the ranch. So, you don't have to overly concern yourself with us. Once this opportunity starts, we'll be able to keep up with everything."

Beth instantly froze with her hand on the doorknob, intrigued by the outcome of the conversation and watched her sister skeptically. *Hmmm...I think I'm going to wait for an explanation about that comment and whatever is the solution to our situation.* Frustrated, Anne kicked the cabinet and tried to finish the conversation. "What...well, whatever Dave. Just bring the horse back over here then. I'll see that you get in the barn when you get here." She slammed the receiver back into the cradle while she mentally berated herself for being baited. Anne closed her eyes and inhaled another soothing breath before she turned her full attention back on Beth. *Shit, shit, shit. I wish I had more time to figure this all out.*

Beth calmly slipped out of her slicker and hung it on the peg on the wall. Suzie quickly imitated her friend's actions seconds before they both walked together across the kitchen and leaned against the butcher block. Beth leisurely folded her hands, rested her chin on her knuckles and innocently batted her lashes as she watched her sister. Anne blew out her breath in an exasperated huff as she quickly avoided her sister's overtly perceptive gaze and walked over to the sink. Distracted, Anne made an unnecessary clamor while she searched through one of the cupboards for a coffee cup. She mentally kept busy as she made a pot of coffee, waited a few minutes to pour herself a cup, attempting to compile her chaotic thoughts.

"So, what's this amazing solution that you've found to end all of our problems?" With wisdom beyond her years, Beth stoically braced herself while she pointedly delivered her question, for the plain reason that she knew her sister all too well. If anything was too difficult, Anne would find a way to not discuss it or just plain ignore a bad situation. It was never a question of whether she could handle the hard labor around the ranch, but she couldn't quite cope with the more important issues of dealing with their ever-existing struggle, trying to figure out a way to keep from simply losing their ranch. Anne tried to focus her thoughts from the oncoming migraine, struggled with the appropriate words while she mechanically turned around to face her sister. She glanced at Beth and her heart was engulfed with misery at the overwhelmingly difficult situation they had been thrown into dealing with. *She's sooo young.*

"OMG, stop with the silent pity party over there! I realize that it must be pretty bad if you can't figure out how to get it out yet. You're killing me. Please, tell me what's going on!"

"Right--well, here it goes. Since you've overheard me explaining some of the situation to Dave, I'll try not to overlap everything. I don't know if you've noticed that everything around here has been a little overwhelming for me to keep up with lately." Anne noticed Beth's eyebrows progressively rise into her hairline and with a dumbfounded look she openly mocked her sister' honest admission as if silently saying "Duh--"

At that second, it took every fiber of Anne's existence to take a deep, soothing breath and to not allow her instantaneous, sibling fueled gut reaction to simply bitch slap Beth silly.

"I can't imagine how on earth our parents kept this place running so smoothly. There is so much to do every day, and the house maintenance on top of that puts everything over the edge. I just can't keep up." Beth held her breath while she silently waited for the ominous, invisible shoe to drop. Suzie invariably sensed her friend's emotional distress and scooted closer to offer her support while they waited for Anne to finish. "So, the other day I received a phone call from my old college roommate Kate, asking for a favor. She was looking for kind of training and work for a down-and-out friend who needs a break. She promised that he was more than willing to help, work with the horses and learn the ropes, just to get a chance to learn some kind of trade." Anne took a comforting sip of her hot coffee while she paused before she continued. "We were actually the only ones that she considered since we could provide a trade, work and housing for him."

"HIM?" Beth squeaked. The rush of her adolescent interest instantly perked her up as she locked astonished eyes with Suzie while Anne's final word still hung in the air. Anne raised her eyes towards the ceiling as she prayed to her parents for any kind of strength to deal with her sister.

"Look, I'm sorry. I would've told you earlier, but everything moved so quickly and I had to make an instant decision. I was actually getting off of the phone with her when you two came crashing through the door. I think that this could be a great opportunity for this tourist season. Besides, we desperately need the help around here." Anne mentally crossed her fingers as she asked, "So. What do you think?" Beth and Suzie leaned into each other as they whispered behind their shielded hands. Anne clutched her coffee cup in a death-like grip as she held her breath from across the kitchen as seconds ticked by on the faded, old clock. When their chatter ceased; Beth looked solemnly over at her sister.

"So-- You're saying that you made the decision to hire a stranger to not only help around the ranch but also live here with us, sight unseen. And...you can live with the fact that we only have your old roommate's guarantee that he's a decent person and won't murder us in our sleep. Even though you haven't seen her since you've moved back home and she could be a whack job herself."

"Yeeeaahh--" Anne hesitantly responded at the brutally honest description Beth painted that her rash decision put them in. The weight of her spontaneous decision settled heavily on her shoulders, while unnerving tension hung in the air as all of them digested the unusual situation at their own pace.

"Well Anne, I think it sounds great. Does this guy have a name, when does he start, do you know where he's coming from, what he looks like?" Beth leaned over, firing the questions in one breath and gave her sister a heartfelt slug on her shoulder.

"The only definite thing I know is that he'll arrive in a few days." Anne rubbed her arm and stuttered the only direct answer she could come up with before they realized someone was yelling outside. "Ahhh, SHIT...its Dave."

"Ok. No problem. We'll go, stall him and take care of Ginger." Beth and Suzie eagerly spun around to grab their slickers off the wall. The girls buzzed and bumped into each other with excitement as each of them animatedly chattered while they made their way outside.

"OMG, What do you think he looks like?" Suzie half sighed and half whispered as she tugged on her coat.

"I hope he's hot!" Beth helped while she tugged on the door handle.

"I hope he's tall and blonde...I like blondes."

"I can't wait!!" Their babbling rose to a fevered high pitch as they stepped outside into the rain. Anne smiled at their innocent exuberance, continued to pour another cup of coffee and ponder her rash decision. The door suddenly burst open emitting Beth's face engulfed in the yellow slicker as she popped unexpectedly back into the house. "Hey Anne… have you told Dave yet?"

Anne met her sister's searching gaze to merely give a silent, negative shake of her head. Beth's eyes widened while her mouth formed a perfect circle in pseudo shock, pointed an alarmed finger at her sister and theatrically backed out of the door.

"OOMMGG, you're in SOOO much trouble--" Beth squeaked as she tried to dodge the soggy dishrag that Anne threw at her head and slammed the door in her haste to leave.

"Shit," Anne mumbled as she ducked like a fugitive in an attempt to avoid the windows so she could keep out of Dave's view.

***

It took half a day of driving before Nick started to question his sanity at making such a hasty decision, especially while being extremely hung over. *I should've demanded Mike give me more information about this script. What are the exact details of his brilliant plans? Shit. I shouldn't have drunk so much the other night! I sure as hell wouldn't be in this predicament right now.*

The selection of music between the radio and his play list the last few hours hadn't been any consolation to all of the exhausting questions that bombarded his thoughts. Beside the simple fact that he'd given everything up and left without notice to anyone. By the end of the day he reached a decision that he wouldn't be a victim to his life; it was a perfect opportunity for a change in his career and a new look at his purpose.

The beautifully illuminated city stood proud in the filtered blue dusk light. Evening was about to darken the sparkling sky when he finally reached the main juncture just outside of San Francisco. Nick took the appropriate exit and followed the directions Mike had specified on the note. After driving around for what seemed like forever on gazillion one-way streets, he realized where the hotel was located, carefully drove his car through congested San Francisco traffic and strategically pulled up in front of a nondescript hotel building. A shiver snaked down his spine as Nick physically cringed at the name of the moderate chain hotel as he pulled into the underground parking lot. He became frustrated at having to drive around forever in the dark parking garage trying to find decent parking, until he finally decided to double-park in a handicap spot at the front of the lot. "Either this place is the ugly part of Mike's big scheme, or it better be a very bad joke," Nick mumbled as he shut the Porsche off. Once out of the car, he irritably strode around, yanked open the door and grabbed the unwanted duffle bag. He immediately slammed the door shut and rubbed his tired, numb butt trying to erase the long drive. Exhausted, Nick walked across the creepy garage entirely engrossed in disbelief that this moment was the fruit from all of his hard working years of success. He picked up his pace to gain some momentum while he strode up a sidewalk towards the glass doors leading into the dingy hotel. Nick visibly stumbled when the soles of his shoes practically squealed, coming to a screeching halt an instant before his face hit the dirty, marred glass.

"You've got to be shitting me." Nick dropped the duffle bag exasperated at the audacity that the doors hadn't automatically opened and annoyingly glared down at the two protruding handles. *SHIT. What kind of hotel doesn't have automatic doors now days?* He thought as his overtired hands lividly grabbed a door handle, pulled back forcibly and flung it open with every ounce of strength. The sound of the door cracking against the wall resounded throughout the lobby. Every person who'd previously been engaged in the room now openly paused midsentence, their complete attention was captivated by Nick's entrance. A low, nervous murmur began to buzz as dozens of eyes watched to see what the angry intruder was going to do next. Nick irately huffed as he stormed through the doorway, intending to create an ugly scene at the reception desk about his inconvenience. Muttering profanities under his breath, he was disgusted about the situation while his irritation began to surface, simmering to the point that he was almost ready to turn on his heel and depart. *I could always check into one of the other hotels on Nob Hill and call this whole experience a vacation. Mike would just have to figure something else out, this is ridiculous.*

All of the buzzing commotion from the onlookers came to a complete halt, silence fell across the entire lobby. Nick lifted curious a brow and cockily smiled to himself when he realized what exactly was starting to happen. A startled hush engulfed the lobby the instant guests and staff began to recognize who he was. *That's right bitches, I'm a superstar.* Nick slowed his stride to a snail's pace while he continued aimlessly in the general direction of the reception desk. He assertively looked everyone in the eye and egotistically smiled as the confirmation of his identity registered on their shocked faces. By the time Nick arrogantly sauntered over to the counter, most of his anger had dissipated, replaced by vanity. He leaned a casual hip against the reception desk and swiveled to serenely smile at the awestruck woman standing behind it. In an instant, he pumped up his demeanor a couple of notches, displaying his dazzling million-dollar smirk, making her mouth hang open in astonishment. Nick sexily slid his sunglasses off, shook his hair so it grazed his shirt, leisurely traced the marring on the counter top and gifted her with a smoldering quizzical look with his signature blue eyes. Suddenly the woman's eyes grew enormous and with a startled look quickly realized that her mouth was unattractively hanging ajar. Nick sympathetically narrowed an eye, then openly winced as he watched her physical discomfort the moment she promptly snapped shut her gaping mouth with a resounding gnash of her teeth. *Gee, I hope she didn't break anything.*

Uninterested in her careful monolog, Nick watched her face distractedly while she went through the typical check-in routine even though he was obviously uninterested in the hotel's protocol. He scrunched his eyes, intently checking her out and imagined that she had probably been attractive in her youth, *but age is catching up with her quickly.* She appeared to be in her early 50's, but it was evident that once she washed off her meticulously applied makeup, she was really headed for her late 60's. Her hair was dyed a youthful, highlighted blonde and cut in a flattering style for her features. She had tied a jaunting, bright scarf around the tell-tale sign of her ageing neck. Nick's gaze traveled down her blouse, which was unbuttoned a little too far south into cleavage country to retain any sense of the proper stuffiness that was desired by her snug, hotel business attire. She finally recovered from her awkward moment by clearing her throat a few times and tugged her uniform top lower.

"Good evening and welcome. My name is Sue. How can I help you?" Sue purred as she gazed dreamily into Nick's eyes once she regained her composure.

Nick saucily used his usual alias and then patiently waited for his room key while she took her sweet time checking him in. "Hello, why I'm Clark Kent."

"Well, um-- Mr. Kent, will there be anyone else joining you while you enjoy your stay here? Perhaps a Mrs. Kent…" Sue looked up at Nick from under her lashes indiscreetly as she finished her inquisition. She was determined not to finish with the final paperwork until Nick gave her a negative answer. She forgot half her work ethics, began chewing on her lower lip, under the assumption that he was captivated by her sly innuendo as he stood watching her.

"No. Not that I know of…or at least not at this minute." He gave her a dashing smile at her feeble attempt at being nosy.

"Well…if you need anything, again my name's Sue and I'll be here at the desk until 11:00 this evening. Just ring the front desk and I can take care of ANYTHING for you." Sue leisurely explained where his room was located in a suggestive tone, while she handed over his key. Nick was startled to realize that somehow, she ended up holding his hand in the process and giving it a suggestive little squeeze. As the pressure registered, he quickly glanced at her over the counter. Sue had leaned over a little too far so her shirt gaped open even more, allowing him a full view of her cleavage. He quickly looked back up at her leering smile, like a predator she intensely watched his every move looking for any indication of him accepting her offer. It took him a second to summon an appropriate response as he decided to silently nod and humorously smile back. *WOW, but unlike her, hopefully I don't have bright pink lipstick smeared all over across the front of my teeth*. Nick turned to grab his bag and moved in the general direction she'd pointed out to find his way to the room. Suspicious at her reaction to his departure he watched her from the corner of his eye, while slightly shaking his head. Sue was enchantingly draped across the reception desk, her eyes openly devoured his firm, retreating ass as she traced the top of her blouse. Without any disgrace at her actions she began to heatedly fan herself in front of the busy lobby, complaining in a particularly loud voice. "My, oh my, it sure is HOT in here! I better call maintenance because it seems that I need to have the air conditioner checkout out up here, behind the desk in reception. Whew--My OH My."

Once Nick thankfully turned his shoulder against the awkward situation, while it only took him a few minutes to wind around a couple corners and find himself standing in front of the door to his room. He inhaled deeply while mentally prepared for whatever lay ahead in his idiotic journey and slid the key through the lock, opening the door. Dingy yellow light floated through the air from a single window, illuminating the narrow room. It had been decorated in the late mid-80's motif containing a chair, side table and a queen bed covered with a non-descript scratchy, multicolored comforter that had seen better years. Nick quickly walked into the room, pulled the lock across the door, tossed the duffle bag onto the bed and sat next to it as he disbelievingly glanced around the small room, while the bed happily squeaked in protest.

"You've got to be shitting me." Nick whispered and tiredly rubbed his face.

5

"Dear lord." The disbelieving words snuck out after a slight groan escaped Anne's lips while straining to push the heavy, overflowing shopping cart filled with all of the necessities they'd need to get them through the next couple of weeks. The old, rickety wheels of the cart habitually veered towards the right every couple of feet, as if its intention was to willingly smash itself into one of the aisles in the Westport Local Feed Store. Anne braced her feet while she firmly heaved it towards the front of the store. With some effort she belatedly pulled back on the cart and paused in front of a small area that displayed an assortment of equestrian products ranging from brushes, bits, treats, shampoo besides grooming supplies. Anne placed a hand on a hip, bit her lip and casually searched the wall trying to find the last few items on her list. She blew out an exasperated breath when her thoughts started drifting back to her rash decision of hiring their unknown hand and her brief unnerving discussion with Beth that morning. *I don't see why my decisions have anything to do with Dave. Shit...I don't even know why I ever decided to hire that guy. Oh yeah, that's right...I need all the help I can get. Even if it's from some down-on-their-luck transient, possible felon that needs a handout to get back on his feet. Shit...can't wait till this news gets around town.*

Anne quickly realized that she was daydreaming again, angrily snatched the last salt lick on the shelf and turned to heave against the resisting cart to continue up towards the front of the store. Just when she was about to give the cart a last huge shove, Anne's feet magically skidded to a halt, making her body involuntarily pause, spotting a lone someone lounging at the only register, but instead the cart had a mind of its own. "Uhhh...no you don't." Shoving with all her might creating another simultaneous loud groan, emitting not only from the cart but also her lips, Anne felt her stomach plummet to her feet, as she wheeled her purchases up to the one person that she had prayed that she wouldn't run into...*Lois.*

Unbeknownst to anyone breezing through Westport on holiday, then happened to stop into the feed store, they'd think that Lois was the nicest and most helpful person they'd ever encountered. But ask any of the locals where to get any slanderous gossip...they'd point you straight towards Lois. The town cowered at the power she wielded, amazing just about everyone around Westport. On a turn of a dime she always knew everything and was willing to reveal anyone's darkest secrets at any given moment. The idea of what she knew made the most decent people become as skittish mice in her ominous presence. The perfect example seemed to be when a church abiding local business owner was selling something illegal out of the back of his store, overcharging for his products and sequentially 'visiting' quite a few of the town's available ladies on random nights. To the dismay of the ladies, his instant exodus transpired after a chance encounter with Lois in the fruits and vegetables at the Red Apple Grocery store. Once the news began to leak out from the feed store, the last thing anyone saw of him was red taillights leaving town in the middle of the night.

 Anne realized her palms began to sweat profusely by merely approaching the counter. Her basic instinct screamed to run and leave the heaping cart, but common sense made her continue towards the checkout. Instead she gave Lois a quick friendly smile, secretly giving the other woman a thorough assessment through her lowered lashes. No one in the entire town dared to attempt estimating Lois's exact age, because from the moment she stepped foot in it her annoying mantra demanded that she was continuously a mere 35 years old, even a passing skeptical glimpse betrayed that she was obviously older. She wore her stark, brown hair cut in a short, 60ish mod bob with a clip alongside of the part, a large section of bangs covering her forehead, with an ever-present pencil tucked behind her ear. She seemed to ware minimal makeup, except the frosted pink lipstick meticulously applied, false eyelashes, piles of foundation and hip, retro-shaped reading glasses. Her tight, fuchsia polo shirt was tucked into her high-waist 'mom jeans' as she twitched her round ass in time with Beyonce's 'Single Ladies'. No one would suspect anything awry on any particular day in the store when everything seemed typical, except it was what lay menacing behind those meek glasses that made people stray away from confronting her, and the intensity of her hawk-like stare silently exerting any interesting tidbit of news floating around that could be applicable to her next victim.

Anne took a calming breath for courage, forcefully pushed the catawampus cart towards the checkout of doom. Lois' calculating eyes lit up with exceeding interest, observing the mass of items piled up on Anne's cart as it suddenly catapulted forward and smacked directly into the base of the ancient counter.

"Morning--" Anne mumbled out of the side of her mouth, as she began to nervously shift the items onto the conveyer belt, while Lois held the gun-like price scanner limply in her clutch, as if she controlled Anne's future. Lois delicately cleared her throat then unhurriedly scanned each of the purchases, relinquishing in a mode that possibly they were made of porcelain, suddenly brored she leisurely allowed the rest jammed up on the back of the belt.

"Well, Miss Anne, from what I can tell you certainly can't be stocking up for winter, especially since Christmas passed. I'm wondering what is going on in your world that would warrant so much stuff." Lois gave her chewing gum a loud, measured snap at the end of the statement as if punctuating with it. Her shrewd eyes never left Anne's features, while she desperately attempted to deviate from being appraised and continued to load everything on the ancient conveyer belt.

"Yyyeeeaaahhh--I just figured I'd stock up for a while and save an unwanted trip into town."

 Lois speculatively all of the items with her narrowed beady eyes as her glasses slid forward, carefully searching Anne's features for an uncomfortable reaction. Anne inadvertently registered that the entire time Lois was mindlessly scanning each item... her single intent was to catch Anne in something devious. Silence loomed between the battling sounds from the thump of Anne tossing her items out of the cart, wheeling of the belt and the annoying beep of the scanner. Suddenly Lois' obvious scrutiny was rudely interrupted by the beeping of a void from an unmarked salt lick. She leaned her overly endowed body across the register, authoritatively grabbed an ancient microphone, irritated heaved it over her chest, jammed a hand on her hip and gave a forceful snap of her gum before she announced, "Chuck...I need a price check on aisle one." Aggravated by the gridlocked situation, Anne rolled her eyes, shoved her hands into her jeans' pockets and rocked back on her heels. *Are you shitting me? It's not like she doesn't know the price of the only salt lick in the whole freaking store! Besides, there is absolutely no one else in here and the shelf is five yards away. Can't she get off her nosey ass and go look for herself?*

Trying to maintain a calm disposition, Anne distractedly glanced around her vision roamed the entrance, vacant aisles and parking lot to reconfirm that she was held prisoner in their awkward situation. Anne's unsettled gaze riveted on Lois' irritated profile and the continuous ticking of Lois' jaw muscle mesmerized her as she watched her chomp her gum. An extra loud snap from Lois' gum brought her attention back to the checker as Lois exaggeratedly shifted her weight and attempted to get Anne's full attention. Anne's eyes quickly darted over to Lois' impatient face, realized she got caught staring and didn't catch the question. "Sorry Lois, I was just daydreaming. What did you say?" Anne politely asked in a sing-song voice, trying to cover up her embarrassment.

"No problem, Hun. So – Anne, anything new and exciting going on with you lately? I haven't seen that handsome devil, Dave around here for some time now. Maybe, you've seen more of him up at your place than we have lately." Lois made her eyebrows slowly migrate past the point of normality and disappear behind her blunt bangs to punctuate her openly suggestive remark.

"WOW--," Anne racked her head trying to diffuse the awkward situation. "Hey Lois, do you want me to run over and get that price for you? Looks like Chuck is going to be awhile. You know what, now that I'm thinking about it, I think I might have left something cooking on the stove and need to get back to the ranch." She turned in a feeble attempt to go check on the price, turning to make her way over to the shelf. Lois quickly reached across the counter and laid a hand over hers as if she was insisting to keep her available. Sensing that something had changed, Anne lifted her questioning eyes to Lois' narrowed ones. Instantly Anne knew exactly how a trapped fox felt when they released the hounds before the hunters rode out with their death warrant. Lois enjoyed the feeling that she smelt blood and wasn't going to relent until her curiosity was satisfied.

"No, no, Honey, he'll be along in a minute. So...how's that hunky neighbor of yours? Like I said, I haven't seen much of him around here. Damn shame if you ask me." Lois gave her gum a quick, solid snap. "You two been keeping each other BUSY up at your places?" The blatant insinuation resounding in the tone of Lois' question rolled off her tongue, as she relished in making such an obvious inappropriate suggestion.

"No." Anne simplistically batted her lashes and gave Lois an idiotically innocent stare while she solemnly replied, "No, no. Come to think about it, I haven't seen Dave for quite a while either." Lois gave her another quizzical look while she scratched her chin, contemplating Anne's answer and tapped her pursed lips with a long, manicured nail.

"Hmmm...that's funny. Because he was just in here a few days ago picking up feed out back, mentioning to Chuck about how one of your horses got out and landed in his yard again." A sneaky smile crossed Lois' mouth as the invisible words flashed across her face: Checkmate. For an insane instant Anne wanted to jump over the counter and throttle the opposing woman for manipulatively cornering her so easily. Her conscience began irately screaming "NO!", while her face betrayed it as a heated blush engulfed her face, vision blurred from frustration while she racked her brain for any kind of flimsy excuse.

"Well, I guess I forgot that had happened. I've been really busy trying to get ready for the summer tours and…oh great! Look, here's Chuck." At the sound of clomping footsteps approaching, Lois' shoulders slumped, momentarily deflated by the newcomer's intrusion. With an irritated sigh, she turned to address the tall, gangly older man meandering slowly from the back recess of the store.

"Hey Chuck. Stop right there and tell me the price of that salt lick." Lois regally waved her hand in the general direction of the display rack where he came to a complete stop.

"What? Lois are you insane, you called me away from the loading dock for a price check?" He gave Lois a heated, insolent stare and openly refused to even glance at the rack. "Lois, you damn well know the price of that because it's been the only one we've had in stock for…I can't count how many years. It's $19.95." Before Lois could open her mouth to interfere, Chuck disgustedly shook his head, loudly mumbled a few choice profanities under his breath and turned to leave. As his figure faded into the darkness Chuck continued his diatribe loud enough for Lois to hear about some people being some nosey, good-for-nothing worker until he disappeared into the shadows.

"Humph, old codger." Lois indifferently snapped her gum and continued to mechanically scan the last few items on the conveyer belt. "Alright-y then… you want me to put everything on your charge, right?" Before Anne could say a single word, Lois was deftly leafing through the little black book that had been preciously tucked under the register. Lois offhandedly licked her fingers in between flipping each of the pages and began to hum off-key with Martina McBride's 'Suds in the Bucket'.

"Yeah, that'd be great," Anne mumbled as she tentatively wandered over to the packed cart, allowing a second to muster the courage she'd require to finish what she intended to accomplish. Lois thrust the book down to the end of the counter so Anne could sign next to the total for the day. Quickly Anne ineligibly scribbled her name, then hustled back and gave the cart a huge shove. Summoning up all of her courage she hastily called over her shoulder as the cart painfully began to inch away from the counter. "Lois--While you have the charge book out, I need to add someone onto my account for future purchases." Anne tried to avert her guilty gaze away from the other woman, but relentlessly found herself looking back at Lois as if she had some kind of magnetic pull. Anne had to stifle a nervous laugh when she giddily registered the gossip-queen's frozen, stunned expression. The older woman's mouth was stuck mid-chomp, eyes astonishingly wide, and eyebrows completely lost beneath her bangs.

"Really--" Was the single comment that slipped through Lois' pursed lips as she distractedly tapped the cover of the black book with her pen. Anne watched while a feline-like smile spread across the opposing woman's visage, causing a frigid chill sweep down her spine, recognizing that at that precise moment Lois was mentally calculating the exact order she'd start calling Westport's cronies to spread Anne's little piece of gossip. Anne gnashed her teeth in frustration, wanting to haul her body over the counter, grab her ill-fitting, snug polo shirt and shake her until Lois spit out or chocked on her day-old gum. *I'm overtly positive that perfect Dave's name will be at the top of that freakin' list.*

"Yes, I'd appreciate it." Anne attempted to use an authoritative tone, concluding the conversation as she struggled in vain with the overloaded cart. Anne stepped back to give in to her frustration, surged forward and single-mindedly gave the cart a gigantic shove. As it unexpectedly shot toward the door, Anne stumbled in its wake and casually called out, "His, his name is Rick Short and he'll be here in a couple of days."

"But...what...how--?" Lois stuttered unbelievingly watching as Anne forcibly propelled the cart through the door and stumbled out of the store.

"Hey Lois, thanks for all of your help. I'll talk to you later." With that Anne continued through the door, banging the cart into the front of the building as she awkwardly headed for the truck. Lois watched Anne quickly throwing everything into the bed of the truck and then raced the wobbling cart back up to the side of the store. Without allowing a guilty glance back into the store, she rapidly ran back, jumped into the cab and gunned the truck out of the parking lot.

"Hummm, interesting..." Lois off handedly murmured while she picked up the telephone receiver and began to rapidly speed dial.

For the last hour, Nick sat on the edge of the bed staring at the nondescript leather black duffle bag, contemplating what surprises was awaiting his undivided attention. He briskly rubbed his hands over his face, deeply inhaled and nervously chuckled while he slowly unzipped the bag. He hesitantly glanced inside noticing a bunch of items stacked neatly in the bottom and a short, handwritten note on top. *Well, Mike, what do you and fate have in store for me now?*

Nick Baby,

If you are totally serious about advancing your career and becoming the biggest star in Hollywood, you need to follow every instruction that I'm giving you. I know it's a little sketchy right now, but it'll all make sense later.

1. All of your personal belongings must be put into this bag and placed outside the hotel room by the end of the night. You cannot keep ANYTHING that has any significance to who you are.
2. There are new clothes, cell phone, car keys, contact lenses and hair dye in the bag; you need to change everything about your identity and actually become this character. Plus, you will have to stop shaving. Always have some sort of facial hair until you come back to LA.
3. Remember you have to leave ALL of your belongings...including your car keys in the bag (Don't worry. I'll personally take care of your car and possessions).

In the morning, you'll need to leave promptly at 6:00 a.m. through the back exit. A car will be waiting for you, parked in the same spot where you left your car is tonight. There is a short description of your character profile, new name and an outline of more character changes at the next stop in Portland, Oregon. If you accept the agreement you will check into the next hotel by tomorrow night. If not, bring the car and everything else back to your house and we will start on a different idea for your career. But if you DO agree and continue driving to Portland, there is no going back. This may take six to nine months. You'll get a call when we're ready for you. It's all your decision...but I'd do it if I was you.

Good Luck, Mike

After he quickly rescanned the note, Nick leaned over, grabbed the bag and dumped the entire contents out onto the bed: a plain white polo shirt, khakis, underwear, socks and tennis shoes, a box of hair dye, a cheap prepaid cell phone, a box containing brown contact lenses with a care kit, generic key to a car and a cheap wallet only with a fake ID. Nick curiously grabbed the box of hair dye, weighing it in his hand and silently pondered the mystery of what he was agreeing to. His options were simple: *commit to the unknown for a about a year, or go back to a career that's failing. It's not too hard to figure that one out...I'm going to go ahead with the plan.* Nick deftly stood and stretched for a second, tossing the box of color into the air and caught it midstride, arrogantly strolling into the bathroom to commit to his endeavor.

He switched on the lights after walking into the bland taupe bathroom with his spirits high, placed the box of dye next to the sink and stared into the mirror at the familiar image of a movie star. His reflection mirrored a glamorous lifestyle: longish styled, highlighted, blonde hair, sea-blue eyes, straight white teeth, a chiseled, clean-shaven jaw line, a full mouth, a small dimple in the corner of a cheek and all wrapped up in an expensive suit. Nick's smile devilishly deepened. *The face that is staring back, is currently featured on every magazine cover across the world, man I'm good.*

His gaze traveled down taking a quick inventory of his lavish attire that he'd decided to wear out after the last article he was featured in GQ. It consisted of a stark white shirt, unbuttoned at the base of his neck, black slacks and an Italian leather belt, a simple outfit worth thousands of dollars. *Man, I feel like a snake that's going to be shedding his skin.* Nick gave a quick mental shake and turned away from the mirror. He lingeringly started to strip each layer of clothing off, slowly discarding them one at a time into a heap on the floor. He shivered after everything was taken off, feeling unreasonably cold standing stark naked and mentally preparing to become a new individual. Nick quickly tied a towel around his hips, grabbed all of the neglected clothes and quickly stuffed them haphazardly into the empty duffle bag. He determinedly strode across the room, ready to set the bag outside the door and then paused for a moment as something shiny caught his eye; his expensive Italian wallet and key ring innocently laying on the end table.

"While I am at it, I better throw these in too. If I'm going to go through with this half-assed plan...I'm going all the way." Nick tossed them both in a moment before soundly zipping up the bag, opening the door to place it outside the room. He confidently dusted off his hands, turned after the door closed and headed back towards the bathroom. "Ok, now the next step."

Nick carefully read the directions on the back of the box of color, mixing the two tubes together and started applying the dye all over his hair. He studied his reflection in the mirror once he squeezed the last few drops of the hair dye onto his head. His beautiful, shoulder-length, highlighted hair immediately looked like it was encased in a cocoon of honey. He turned away from the mirror and strolled back into the bedroom. *Hmmm...I didn't do too badly, if I do say so myself.* Nick switched on the ancient clock radio, picked up the packet of papers as he sat on the bed and began to read the outline of the character's personal description. Unconsciously, he began to hum along with Wings' 'Maybe I'm Amazed' as it began to play along with irritating static.

Name – Rick Short

- From the southern California area (parents moved around a lot, possibly military)
- Has had a shady past, possibly some jail time (not willing to discuss any background)
- Wants to start a new beginning and is willing to work at anything, ultimately training horses.(training horses is imperative for your role, learn and become confident)

Employment

- With the help of an acquaintance, Rick has been hired as a laborer through a friend (Kate) at a mutual friend's horse farm in Washington State.
- Rick's responsibilities will be to become a "Jack of all trades" and most importantly learn how to handle any horse, at any time.

Nick glanced up from the page and rubbed his hands across his forehead in frustration. *That's it! Rick Short...couldn't Mike come up with an alias better than that? What the hell? I've never even been around a horse; on a horse or let alone work with one...he knows that.* Exasperated, he pinched the bridge of his nose and inhaled a long breath before he continued to read the rest of the page:

*The commitment will be for nine months to a year. If there are any discrepancies about this commitment or the duration of time, you can leave and the endeavor will be canceled. If you accept, you will be contacted when the preparations for the movie are ready to involve your character the call will be from my phone to the cell phone found in the bag…no message will be left. You will have to leave immediately, no questions asked and come back to California.

I will be mailing parts of the main sections from the script in a manila envelope as they pertain to your character. Please keep these strictly to yourself and destroy them once you've memorized them.

Remember two things –

First - This is an opportunity of a lifetime to turn your career around, so please work on changing your identity and seriously prepare for this role.

Second - Knowledge about who you are, what you are accomplishing and the project must be kept secret. There will be more than just your life affected by this endeavor. Respect the family who you will be working with. No contacting ANYONE in Hollywood, the press or informing a soul about who you really are, ever. Not even after your commitment is over.

In consideration of the success for you career and with all hope, you'll actually follow through…I'll see you on the other side of the podium, Mike.

Nick's mind reeled as he chuckled at the audacious notion that no one in society would recognize him, let alone miss his presence being away from Hollywood for nine months. *Ha, how could anyone NOT know who I am? Let along the simple fact that someone as famous as myself, will be missing for months. Hollywood will be in an outrage. This whole idea is going to tank. My picture is everywhere, everyone in the world knows who I am!*

Minutes ticked by as he silently became engrossed in his narcissistic thoughts, merely attempting to wrap his mind around the meager concept of the proposed letter. Nick distractedly glanced up from Mike's delusional pages, trying to digest the impact of his impulsive decision. Suddenly the situation became too much and the constant tingling searing across his scalp not only made him scratch aggressively, but also itch different areas of his face and neck until he finally registered that the color was definitely irritating his skin. *I wonder how long this stuff is supposed to be on, when did I put this shit on?*

Spreading his arms up above his shoulders to lethargically stretch, Nick slowly stood, gave his cheek a final scratch and walked across the room to retrieve the discarded box out of the trash. He scanned the instructions, simultaneously eyeing the the clock, trying to calculate how much time had been allowed for the color to develop.

A curious, slight shuffling noise occurred outside the door, as if someone slowly paused and then receded. Nick took a second to halt mid-scratch to watch a darkened shadow from the crack under the door, slowly pacing outside in the hallway. His boggled gaze slid from the clocks red illuminated numbers that had just turned past 11:30, towards the door as a soft muffled knock sounded from its general direction. Realizing what the time indicated, Nick smiled wickedly as the immediate image of the nervous, lipstick smudged smile female perched at the front desk and her blatant underlying propositions. Nick eagerly swiveled, tugged his towel indecently low on his hips and sauntered across the room to answer the door. As he timidly turned the door handle, his smile widened mischievously mentally preparing to enjoy her shocked reaction when he allowed her to intimately spy his sculpted body. *What's her name again...oh who cares, I'll give her something that she'll remember for the rest of her life.* He quickly linked a thumb into the top of the towel, threw open the door, casually slid his body along the jamb to sensually settled a hip against the frame.

"Hey there, you've got something for me, Sugar?" Nick hoarsely whispered in his sexiest movie star voice, coyly toying with the loose knot that semi-secured the top of his towel and cocked an eyebrow with an open invitation. Just as he suspected, it was Sue, the overanxious blonde from the front desk, who currently stood guiltily transfixed on his lower region, fidgeting in the hall carrying an armful of useless towels. Nick readied himself for the gushing flood of shocked awe then adoration, bumbling sexual offers and outline of her physical accessibility to flow out from her over glossed pink lips.

Instead, Sue suddenly became absolutely frozen, her face void of any emotion relating to the undying devotion he'd expected, instead she mutely stared up at his face with unbelievably huge eyes. Her pink mouth gaped obnoxiously open, a hot flush raced up her neck and face, as it became an unattractive mask of horror.

"I, umm. I…I thought, maybe you could use some more towels," Sue stuttered while continuing to stare obnoxiously at his face. The second reality sank in she instantly, and blindly thrust the towels somewhere in the general direction of Nick's chest, a lame attempt to redirect his attention. "Ummm, hope you enjoy your stay." Without another thought she forcefully shoved the towels into his barely occupied hands, abruptly turned away and bolted down the hall before another word could transpire. Mystified, Nick bumbled with the unwanted towels and the edge of the one dangling from his waist to stare at her retreating back. She threw a strange glance back at him before picking up her pace, hurriedly turned the last corner at the end of the hall.

"Wow, now that was weird," Nick muttered and then inquisitively leaned forward farther out into the hallway to make sure that Sue had actually scampered away, checking to make sure there wasn't anyone else around and shrugged, "Damn, I've never had that kind of effect on a woman before." His vanity struggled with her abnormal female reaction to his assets, rejection loomed over his shoulder while closing the door. Nick mentally chalked her reaction up to insanity, walked over to the bed, threw down the extra towels, started to check the time and re-determine the directions on the box. He roughly scratched his head while he thought out loud, "Well, I think this shit's been on long enough." Nick hastily grabbed a couple of Sue's extra towels, walked back into the bathroom and negligently tossed them onto the counter while glancing into the mirror.

"Oh my…AH, SHIT!" The sight of his reflection made him instantly become rooted to the floor, because staring back wasn't the image of a superstar, but the mirrored mask of horror pasted on an abnormal looking man with greasy, black, oozing, slicked back hair. Not only was his hair encased in black goo, but also the top upper half of his forehead, black stained streaks etched down random areas of his face, the unmistakable residual from having scratched. In addition large black spots had splattered everywhere across his shoulders, chest and torso, a stained map of where it had dripped during the application.

"AH, Shit…no wonder the old broad ran away in terror. I fucking look like a freak!" Nick muttered a string of profanities under his breath, reached into the shower and angrily turned on the water. That's when he noticed that the palms of his hands were completely stained black also. "Damn it!! This shit better come off!" He mumbled while his irritation rose tugging off the towel around his waist to jump into the shower and began to attempt to scour off the residual. Nick scrubbed his skin until it felt like he was going to bleed, when the marks refused to diminish he surrendered his head against the stark shower wall as the water began to run cold, wondering what kind of demise he'd gotten himself into. He took a deep, cleansing breath, finally turned off the semi-tepid water and jumped out of. Closing his eyes of a couple of seconds, his lungs felt like they were going to burst from the lack of air while he held his breath and slowly cleaned off a large circle on the fogged up mirror standing perfectly still, awaiting to view the damage. His teeth felt like they were going to pop out of his head, as they slowly grated, being tightly clenched while he mentally prepared himself for the reflection.

The result of his transformation was completely shocking, his hair wasn't the slightly darker honey tone that he'd seen when he first applied the color; now it was almost black, including his scalp, ears and an inch-wide area all along his hairline. "How did I get the shit down there?" Appallingly he inspected his marred image from the blackened hairline roaming all the way to the rest of his body where a multitude of splatter marks stained his face, neck, shoulders and some lower extremities. "Well, it can't get much worse than this." Sighing, Nick despondently swiveled, turned out the lights walked back into the bedroom, picked up the unwanted wardrobe off the bed and set the bulk on a chair. He rolled his eyes and pulled back the obvious itchy medium grade covers to climb into bed, set the alarm and switched off all the lights. In the dark he carefully laid back, bleakly closed his eyes, trying to forget what just transpired, accepting his decision to commit to the endeavor and willing sleep to take him into oblivion.

6

"What in the Sam Hell, what is that racket?!" Anne half asleep found herself alert sitting straight up in bed, barely able to crack open a dreary eye, to contemplate a very persistent pounding surging through the house. She gave her scarred, closed bedroom door a maliciously evil look, throwing off the covers and flinging her legs determinedly over the side of the bed. "There freaking better be a fire with this racket, or I know somebody going to be dead!" she mumbled. Anne rolled off her comfy bed with an elongated groan and began to stomp her way to the window. "Oh my...lord." Immediately she stopped midstride, the second her brain registered that the freezing, cold dampness seeping through the wood floor that found its way straight into her bones. Quickly she re-swiveled, ran across the room and launched herself into the sanctuary of her closet.

"Geeze...cold, cold, cold," Anne chanted, diligently hopping from one foot to the other while she desperately tried to ignore the prickly, stinging feeling that tortured her brain as it registered that her toes were probably turning blue. Besides her head began to beat in time with the constant, irritating pounding in the background. "F-ing..." She gave an aggravated grunt while steadily rummaging through the depths of her closet, until happily spying her father's old worn out, slippers. She euphorically snuggled her toes deep into the soft sheepskin lining with a grateful sigh of contentment. Distractedly, she simultaneously threw on a pair of worn-out Levi's and an oversized sweatshirt while marching to the window.

"You've got to be shitting me," Anne murmured, as her breath became a visual cold, frosty mist against the cold window pane. Disbelief ran through her thoughts the second she caught a glimpse of the sleek black sedan parked in front of the house. Anne closed her eyes tightly, wearily pinched the bridge of her nose and leaned her forehead against the frigid window. *Shit...its Dave.* The house immediately seemed unnervingly silent compared to the constant pounding that had thankfully subsided for a blissful second. Anne took that quick minute to take a deep, calming breath, subduing her nerves before leaving her room. Yet again, the noise immediately resumed except this time it became quite louder. The idea that Dave was concededly creating the noise made her eyes narrowed and lip curl with disgust as she angrily pivoted, storming out of the room, in her haste tripped on the landing and clumsily stumbled down the front stairs.

A large, man-shaped shadow clouded the threadbare shade drawn over the front door's window. It began shaking as the pounding continued to resonate up the stairs, reverberating through her body as if it was greeting her scrambled approach. Skidding to a halt at the bottom of the stairs, Anne paused to mentally retrieve a moment of sanity. As she tucked her body into the shallow corner, hiding next to the door, a crooked, malicious grin lit across her face. She closed her eyes taking a blissful second before confronting Dave. Her thoughts slid to the luxurious image of her carelessly grabbing the knob, defiantly throwing the door open, becoming her own Joan of Arc and striding out onto the porch. In rare form, she'd not only verbally rip him a new asshole about his abusive pounding, but also giving him a secure piece of her mind about his constant manipulation, insinuated sexual advances and whatever other 'issues' he'd had with her and her family...forever. With the tip of her pinkie, she attempted to slightly lift the corner of the material to peek around the blind. Seeing the dark body, she suddenly lost her nerve while cocked a timid brow towards the safety of the stairway, considered high tailing it back upstairs, throwing the blankets over her head and indignantly waiting until he decided to leave. *Stop...you're being a chicken; just open the stupid door and get this over with, cuz he's not going anywhere.* Anne closed her eyes, took a slight second to compose herself by shaking her head to chase away all of her negative convictions, the second she grabbed the deadbolt, yanked it back, turned the knob and yelled. "Hold on to your horses! I'm getting the door."

She forcefully yanked open the door wide enough to barely stand in the doorjamb, but not enough to allow any insinuation of a friendly invitation inside. Anne casually leaned on the marred door and opened her eyes exaggeratedly wide, as if innocently surprised by Dave's persistent presence. "Why, Dave. What a pleasant surprise." She shifted, leaning out of the doorway poking her head out a little bit farther, glanced around the yard and the obvious early morning sky. "Wow...It's so early, and on a weekend. I can't imagine what would warrant such an unnecessary visit."

Dave's silent mask of an unresolved look froze on his face, undeterminably dismissed her asinine comments, as he attempt to assimilate a civil thought about a reply while he nervously shifted from foot to foot.

Anne tried to retain some kind of pity for him as she watched him clumsily try to articulate his thoughts. His handsome face became suddenly scrunched up as if he had eaten something tart, while his eyes darted to anywhere else on the porch, anywhere but on her.

"Look, Anne. You know, I'm not good at this sort of thing." His large frame cast a shadow over the sky as he loomed before her, taking a hesitant step in her general direction. Anne's heart plummeted into the pit of her stomach, mouth started to water and she wanted to gag as her nervous gaze darted up to search his soft brown eyes. *Holy Shit. I hope he isn't going to bring the whole dating exclusively thing up or hint at marriage today. It's too early, and I don't have time for this crap.*

Dave rubbed the back of his neck, took a second to clear his throat and shoved his hands deep into his front pockets. Anne hopefully wished she seemed genuinely interested, even though she was desperately searching the horizon for any indication that hopefully fate would bring anyone up the drive and save her from the unwanted situation. But to her distain, there wasn't a car in sight for miles.

"Well, all I'm going to say is..."

Anne waited with baited breath for him to continue, while a bubble of anticipation fed her dread, boiling to the surface waiting for the moment that he would stumble through their uncomfortable situation, making her lose the contents of her stomach on his boots.

"What in the HELL, do you think you're doing?!" Dave leaned across the thresh hold, taking an aggressive step forward with every intention to intimidate her by positioning himself securely inside her personal bubble.

"What?" Startled by his unexpected attack, Anne took a cautious step back from being verbally assaulted, realizing that she'd read the situation completely wrong.

"Do you even know what you're getting into, or have any responsibility for your actions?" Dave exasperatedly asked as he lifted his hands in question, swung around and began to angrily pace the porch.

"You know Dave...I really don't know what you're talking about," Anne replied in a patient tone while she tried to redirect his obvious tension by using a calm, almost mother-like voice. Frustrated by his inconsiderate outburst besides the silent treatment, she mildly shrugged her shoulders watching him methodically stride up and down the side of the porch. Listening to the intense moan that began creaking from the decaying wood, Anne nervously jumped off of the doorjamb when an apprehensive thought popped into her mind. Giggling, she bit her lip as an imaginable thought crossed her mind, *Shit…I hope he doesn't step on one of the rotting, soft spots of the planks and crash through the porch.* She struggled to repress a chuckle at the image of Dave arms helplessly flaying about and then suddenly disappearing through the porch, but caught in their current dilemma, she decided against it. *Watch out…don't forget Karma.*

"Ummm… Hey Dave." Anne started to raise her hand, instinctively attempting to redirect his pacing and warn him of the dilapidated condition of the boards. At the same time, he turned aggressively around, disgustedly curled his lip and rudely examined her with his overtly tormented eyes.

"How could you consciously make the decision to bring another man around? And, and…into your home?" Dave flung his hands around signifying the enormity of her responsibilities and silently insinuating that the decision made her a brazed hussy.

Anne disbelievingly opened her mouth to give him a set down, closed her eyes and prayed for patience, just his intonations while delivering the statement made it obvious what their conversation was about. She took a quick second to compose her rebuttal, before dealing with a wounded Dave. He stood at the top of the porch stairs that lead out down the path to his parked car. His mournful demeanor, slumped shoulders and exasperated disposition, told her everything she needed to know. *Are you shitting me…fucking Lois.* Anne turned around, grabbed the door, slammed it shut so hard that it made the windows shake and deliberately maneuvered her way around the seeming devastated Dave. Irritation at her pathetic situation fueled her steps, spurring her into a fast march down the path, through the broken gate, until she paused next to his car.

"Are you shitting me? This entire morning drama is because I hired someone to work around the ranch? You've got to be joking!" Anne disbelievingly turned to watch Dave's silent approach as he followed her lead from the porch.

"It's not like you, to hire just anyone to help you out, let alone some strange guy!" Dave looked at her as if his explanation made some sort of defining point.

"Well Dave, who else am I going to hire? Tell me…who? Some down-and-out local who doesn't want to work? I'd have to deal with their family issues or someone who I have to check in with constantly because of their chemical dependency? I don't think so." Anne felt a flush of anger burning her cheeks, while she pivoted around and launched blindly in the direction of the barn; forcing herself not to stop and resume her rant at Dave. That was until his emotional voice muttered a few profanities, then rose an octave and stopped her in her tracks.

"Well, Anne, you could have at least tried. I've been offering you my help for years and you've never once accepted. Why are you all of a sudden into hiring some nobody? You don't even know if he could be someone like the Green River Killer, Ted Bundy or some other mass murderer!" Feeling a pang of guilt, Anne returned her angry pace then began to pick up speed, with each step echoed his honest comments, irking her composure as she blindly made her way towards the barn door. She grabbed the broken door handle with one hand and began to repeatedly yank on it, without it budging. Frustrated, Anne dropped her hands in defeat and helplessly turned around to face Dave. Standing in the morning light, she offered him a silent moment of truce, gazing up into his ruggedly handsome face and gave a grateful smile.

"Dave --you know, I've always appreciated you and your kind offers to help me with all of the work around here. But you have your own place to think of and I really need to try to make this whole think work the way I think is best." Invisible tension hung thick between them as silent seconds ticked by. Anne's anger had completely deflated by the end of her statement as Dave appeared to concede with her decision and turned on his heel to leave.

 "Great." With a deep sigh of relief at being blown off, Anne returned her attention back to the stuck barn door.

"Don't you ever care about what people are going to be saying around town? What they'll be thinking with you two girls along up here…alone, with some strange man? Didn't you ever stop to think this whole thing through or care about anything, or anyone else…but yourself?" Dave's frustration at the situation grew as he said each carefully articulated word and moved to tower over her. Exasperated, Anne took a hesitant step back, looked up at him, wondering how he had the nerve to even pose such inane questions. *Because Anne…they're exactly all the questions you've been tossing around yourself.*

"You know, Dave, I hope they all see the situation for what it is; that I am trying to make this ranch into a flourishing business; that I'm intelligent enough to hire someone who is willing to work, not because that I'm into something sordid, but because I need the help." She took another step back, pointedly glared at him as she hurried on to continue. "Besides, if anyone has a problem with my decision to hire somebody or has anything malicious to say about it. I don't care…because it's really none of their DAMN business what I do."

With that, she ended the conversation by swiveling on her heel, storming back to the barn door and began to determinedly wrestle with the latch. The second it euphorically popped loose, she recognized the heavy crunch from Dave's footsteps fading away towards his car. Anne pushed open the door, solemnly walked into the barn, relieved that he'd decided to take a hint and simply leave. She turned around once she safely stepped into the darkness of the opening, watched him get into his car and squirreled down of the driveway. "Aw, shit." Feeling something oddly squishy, Anne glanced down at her soggy feet and realized that she had never changed out of her father's slippers. Then she noticed a blatant white tag protruding out of the collar of her sweatshirt, evidently not only was it on backwards but also inside out, happily indicated by the tag hanging out. Suddenly deflated by the confrontation she blew out the residual of frustration, closed her eyes while quietly mumbling into the darkness and to absolutely no one. "Shit…did I do the right thing?"

***

Nick's body felt oddly surreal as he stood up to walk across the stage, the applause became deafening and felt his hands tingling in anticipation from finally winning the award. *I did it! I am Hollywood's Golden Boy.*

He embraced the thundering applause as he squaring his shoulders, lifting his chin to defiantly make his way towards the podium and receive the award. A beautiful young woman gracefully sauntered across the stage carrying the illuminating, golden statue. Nick held his breath reverently accepted the statue, turned to smile at the crowd, emotionally cleared his throat and opened his mouth intending to begin his acceptance speech…then instantly froze.

A uncomfortable lump of fear lodged in Nick's throat, because instead of seeing all of the familiar faces of Hollywood's jet set, adoring women, screaming fans and camera crew; out in the audience there was only a sea of Sue's yearning face with her smeared, hot pink lipstick-toothed smile floating duplicated across the theater. Untapped fear surged through Nick's veins the second he turned his confused attention back to the beautiful woman, making a desperate snatch for the perfect golden statue. She started laughing at each grab, with the reflexes resembling a ninja, she continuously moved it out of reach and tormented him as she teasingly darted across the stage.

 Nick stumbled behind her every step bringing him barely out of reach, but just far enough that he knew that he'd never be able to succeed. Disorientated, he took a second to catch his breath, shook his head and beseechingly searched her face; only to discover the beauty had been replaced by the overwhelming image of Sue's lipstick-stained teeth and glossed mouth puckering as it made loud, smacking, kissing noises. Then she audaciously winked and teased him by rubbing the statue along the side of her face. Provoked beyond comprehension, Nick tried to seize the award out of her hand; except with each swipe, just when his hand skimmed its surface a loud alarm sounded. Sue mockingly jockey his attempts by outrageously grabbing any available part of his body after each of his swipes. Startled by her first pinch, he desperately tried to repeatedly grab it, except every time he managed to graze the golden prize Sue's mouth would open and emit a piercing loud alarm.

Nick miserably groaned, fitfully turned over in his bed and tried to return to sleep, until the shrilling noise from her pink gaping mouth, persistently pulled him out of his dream. He opened a blurry eye, glanced at the bleating clock's face and then moaning, slammed a hand down onto any button making the radio instantly play Muse's 'Madness'. *Really…5:30 in the morning? You've got to be shitting me. Thank you, Mike!* Closing his weary eyes and heaving a sigh while sleep deprived rolled out of bed, grabbed the heap of foreign clothes from the chair and stumbled into the bathroom. Groggily, he switched on the bright bathroom light and midstride turned to catch a glimpse of his image in the mirror.

"AHHH SHIT…I forgot." Nick carefully shut his eyes against his blackened, spotty reflection, despondently reached over, switched off the light and mutely attempted to get ready in the dark. A few minutes later he methodically walked across the room dressed in a white polo and khakis to sit dejected on the side of the bed, resting his head in his hands, then flopped backwards across the bed, threw an arm over his face and grumbled. "Shit. What have I gotten myself into?"

A slight shuffling noise strangely sounded from directly outside of the door. Nick lifted his arm to spy a plain, white envelope that had secretly slid under the door. Rubbing his face to wake up he rolled to the edge of the bed, stretched over and grabbed the envelope. He tore it opened while quickly laying back onto the bed; a single car key fell out, along with his new ID as Rick Short and a message from Mike all landed on his chest. Nick picked up the key, tucked the ID into his pocket and rolled onto his side to read the message out loud in an overtly condescending tone:

Nick,

Good morning! I hope you're still up for this amazing chance to change your career. I can only wonder what you're thinking about me at the moment…maybe not. Just remember, I believe that if you follow through with this commitment you're going to succeed like you have never dreamed imaginable.

I have picked up the duffle bag. There is a car parked where yours was last night, on the passenger seat are specific directions, another bag with more information about your character, necessities and parts of the script in it.

Your next stop will be Portland, Oregon sometime this evening. That's going to be a push to get there in a day, so you better hurry. Check into the hotel that is indicated on the directions with your new alias and follow the instructions provided in the bag.

Everything is falling perfectly into place here, but it's going to take some time. The dice has been cast, and sorry buddy you're not able to come back. I really believe all of this will end up producing your best success yet!

Take care and remember I'll be in touch when we're ready, Mike

---

"Ah shit...freakin' mother...argh." Was the only thing that came out of Nick's mouth while he crumpled up the letter and threw it at the door. He sat unmoving on the bed, pondering everything that he'd just sacrificed and unknowing his fate with agreeing to the insane situation. Finally he resolutely sighed as he tucked the crumpled letter, Rick Short's ID and car key into his pocket. He walked into the bathroom and decided to keep the light off while he tried not to notice his black splattered reflection. With the help of the soft light illuminating from the other room, he quickly put in the brown contact lenses as suddenly an overwhelming feeling engulfed him. *I feel like I'm going to leave something behind.* He carefully made his way around the room to make sure everything was cleaned and any traces of his stay were placed safely in the new duffle bag. Nick hesitantly stepped through the open door, glanced back into the room and instantly paused when he started to close the door. *Damn. I still have a feeling that I'm forgetting something.* Nick's hand abruptly shot out and stopped the door from locking. He hastily examined the room hoping to find something but closed his eyes in defeat when he realized that what he was leaving behind...*it's ME.* With that he accepted his decision, lightly lifted his hand to let the door softly close, quietly walked to the end of the hallway and exited the hotel with the feeling of a condemned man.

* * *

Anne nervously wrung her hands while appraising the small, dingy room located in the back of the barn. She attempted to squint her eyes in a vain to make all of the cast off furnishings look nicer than they could ever be, even when they first purchased. Anne found herself torn between regretting ever accepting the offer to hire a stranger, the idea of sticking him in the apartment in the back of the barn and undertaking the unthinkable of trying to make the makeshift room look decent. Throughout the afternoon of finalizing cleaning, she found her thoughts drifting repeatedly recounting the argument she'd had with Beth the prior day like a scratched vinyl record.

"OMG, Anne. You can't expect anyone to actually live out in that crappy room...oh wait...I mean closet in the back of the barn! We've never even used it, except for storing crap, even when mom and dad were around. I don't think it's right to make someone live out there in that friggn' mess!"

 A headache began to build making Anne pause from washing the dishes while her sister finished cleaning up dinner, which had become another family ritual to have dinner every evening, even if they didn't have time to cook and it ended up being cereal. It was the only time they had to really sit down and spend any quality time together. After taking a deep soothing breath Anne closed her eyes, desperately tried to channel some patience and guidance with her sister's naivety.

"Look, we don't know this guy...like at all, and I don't care who asked me for a favor. I contacted all of his references and he seems safe, but we just don't know who this Rick Short is or anything about him. I want US to feel and be safe if we're going to be stuck in this living/working situation with a stranger." Aggravated with the entire mess Anne finished with the last dish, wiped off her hands and turned around to face her sister and hopefully drum some sense into her adolescent ideas.

"Beth, I need the help right now. I can't have all of these never ending projects hanging over my head that either I don't have the strength to finish...or the time to even begin. I want to get the trail riding available and make some extra income this summer when all of the tourists come into town. We really could use any extra income, but I just can't worry about what this guy is doing all the time."

 The kitchen became engulfed in uncomfortable silence as an unspoken sadness overwhelmed the atmosphere; each of them struggling to hold off the grief of their parents' death, besides the dilemma that they were fighting to hold onto their family's home and their parents dream...alone. Beth quietly moved over to Anne and slipped her arm around her waist, giving her a reassuring embrace.

"I know. I just, well I wouldn't want to stay out there by myself. I didn't mean to cause any problems Anne. I know you need more help with the ranch."

 For a heartfelt, uninterrupted second they comforted each other while they tried to deal with their situation. Beth gave Anne another squeeze before she stepped back, winked at her and saucily turned to make her way up the back stairs.

 "Well...just to let you know sis...I'm just happy you won't be hassling me about helping mucking out stalls anymore...that's a bunch of shit. Besides, I hope he's HOT. Damn...after all of this we could use a little eye candy around here!"

 Beth squealed the second another sloppily wet kitchen towel that Anne had thrown with the precision of an Olympian wrapped her head like an octopus as she attempted to race up the back stairs.

* * *

It was still cryptically outside when he strode dreary eyed out of the hotel in downtown San Francisco. The second the secured door clicked closed with the finality of a coffin, Nick offhandedly realized that he was definitely locked out of the building, but on the opposite side of the garage from his car. Feeling the brisk chill snaking through his thin clothes, Nick started rubbing his arms briskly against the cold morning and quickly made his way across the garage. He kept his head and eyes shamefully cast down while the image of what his appearance popped to mind. Dark smudges from the colors dark stain evidently still covered most of his exposed skin around his face and neck. He picked up the pace and scooted in between a couple of parked cars thinking; *Shit…looking like this I sure as Hell don't want to run into anyone at the moment.* Confused and attempting to find his baring for a brief second, Nick slowed his pace, glanced around the garage and approached the stall where he'd double-parked his car the night before. Nick shook his head in denial as he froze directly in front of the parking space where his pristine Porsche should have been parked. Instead of his sleek vehicle residing in the general area, a practical, nondescript, white, Honda Accord was parked in the stall. Nick pinched the bridge of his nose and tried to stem off the migraine that was forming at the back of his head. Suddenly his eyes lit up amidst his despair as an idea rushed through mind, joyfully embracing a thread of hope, he started to slowly circle the car and gleefully gazed around the garage.

"I get it…Ah ha! This is Hidden Camera…isn't it? Ha, ha, ha, you guys got me. You have me acting stupid on camera and this is all just a practical joke, right?" Nick puffed up his chest with a lot of bravado and arrogantly walked up to the car door. *This whole thing is a hoax; I am probably being filmed because something stupid is going to happen and being PUNKED! I'm going to kill Mike when I get a hold of him.*

He paused making an exaggerated scene of whipping around to display the unwanted key, slipping it into the Honda's lock, turning it and patiently waited for someone to spring out from the dark garage to surprise him. Except the precise moment the key popped opened the lock, no one walked over with a microphone or jumped out of the shadows. "All right, I've seen these shows where people get set up. You've had your fun, now can we get serious and get on with my life?" Standing in the opening of the car door, his diminishing hope perked up as he watched someone silently cross the garage. As they maneuvered around a parked truck they spied him standing, creepily waiting in the garage, quickly unlocked their car and drove away. "Hey, is anyone out there…please?" Nick practically yelled the first words, then the rest deflated into a squeak, only to have silence answer the question. He instantly felt miserable, laying his head on the top of the cold car and heaved a breathe trying to calm himself. *This isn't some kind of joke or a new sitcom… is it?* The feeling of defeat wrapped its spines around his heart, slowly slid into the driver's seat, closed the door and dejectedly lay his fore head on top of the steering wheel. He closed his eyes for a moment, trying to collect his frazzled, sleep deprived nerves. Minutes ticked by as they seemed endless, making him turn his head, opened his eyes to slowly focus on a note innocently propped on the passenger's seat. It took a second to recognize what he was looking at before it registered, he reached over and grabbed the enemy that was brazenly addressed to his new alias in Mike's bold handwriting...Rick Short.

Nick –

All right, you are officially committed to this project. Just one more stop and you'll be on your way!

Go to Portland and check into this hotel. The room is paid for and under your new name, Rick Short. All of your information and provisions are in the duffle bag in the trunk. Don't forget that I'll be in touch with you later.

Good luck!

Mike

"Bastard," Nick mumbled as he angrily crumpled up the note, threw it across the passengers' seat and turned the key to start the Honda's engine. Without another thought he pulled the car out of the stall, drove out of the garage and towards the directed highway. He switched on the radio, found a decent station and turned up the volume as R.E.M.'s 'It's the End of the World' came over the speakers. He pulled the car out into traffic, then drove through the Sunset district, onto Highway 101 deciding to take the scenic route at the last moment while he headed out of San Francisco and towards his next destination, Oregon.

Nearly nine consecutive hours later, Nick noticed the green highway signs began indicating Portland, Oregon was approaching. The scenic drive had become a droning task to no avail, not even the numerous spectacular vantage points could encourage any fluctuation in his dismal mood. He'd given into stopping a handful of times, but to simply use the facilities, stretch, eat and purchase a baseball hat to cover the dark stains. The only thing that flashed through his mind while speeding down the highway was a simple looping thought that became his mantra: *All I want is to get this whole thing over with, the sooner I get there...the better. I'll show everyone what kind of determination I have and win that shitting award!*

Suddenly Nick snapped out of his negative, mental fog and noticed the large green sign finally signifying that the next exit was his. Uncomfortable from the countless, excruciating hours sitting in the strange driver's seat, Nick adjusted his position and neared the off ramp. He awkwardly slowed the car down, fumbled with the strange console to put on the blinker to exit the freeway and blindly follow Mike's jumbled directions. After missing a couple of lights he turned down a darkened side road and slowed to a crawl while he followed the instructions that Mike had written in the note. He tried to squint his tired eyes, occasionally rubbing them because they burned from the new contacts, lack of sleep and strain from the drive while apprehensively waiting for the address indicated on the note. At a four-way stop he slightly paused and then turned the car down a quiet tree-lined lane. The headlights from his car picked up the details of his surroundings while searching each of the numbers haphazardly nailed on the run down houses. The area had once been a nice neighborhood from the look of the architecture, yet with time and transition of families over the years, the neighborhood had fallen into decline. In front of some of the yards, chaotic fences were either falling down or had missing pickets, old items were strewn across the lawn and broken down cars were parked anywhere. Most of the streetlights still worked illuminating the street, but an average person with any sense wouldn't walk around this area at any time of night. Nick noticed the faint glow from a reddish neon sign at the end of the street. He immediately stepped on the gas trying to reach his destination quicker and thankfully end this juncture of the journey. As he approached the establishment, he physically let out a conscious moan, closed his strained eyes in a fit of agony. *Ah shit, I should've guessed.*

Nick timidly pulled the Honda directly underneath the blinking neon sign that eerily illuminated the front of a one story building and turned off the engine. He unbelievingly shook his head in defeat while, leaning carelessly over the passenger seat and stared incredulously out the window at the ancient hotel's shabby exterior. The building's bluish-green paint was constantly flickering in time with the broken neon sign, which happily displayed that it was peeling in large zebra-like stripes. The words on the sign haphazardly blinked on and off, not because it was supposed to but because a couple of the letters were trying to burn out. Instead of the unwanted luxury of the moderate chain hotel from the prior evening, this time Nick found himself in front of the Travel Inn Motel. He threw open the car door and stood motionless in the rain slickened road as the pavement glowing red and green from the wet reflection of the neon light. Anger radiated from his body as he walked around the car to the trunk, threw it open and grabbed the despised bag. Immediately slammed it shut, he threw the bag over his shoulder and started down the sidewalk towards the entrance of the motel. Nick strode through a small, weather beaten opening that led into a miniature courtyard. The cracked, paved pathway meandered around a darkened corner, leading to a small window where an ineligible hand written sign simply said "CHECK IN HERE" with a red arrow pointing at a small opening carved out of the glass. He marched directly up to the window while stealthy scanning the grounds.

The interior of the yard was developed with a straightforward plan; monitor all of the guests while they stayed at the motel. Each of the rooms' weather beaten doors and windows faced the large, rectangular, dimly lit grass courtyard. The entire interior itself had been decently maintained, shrubs had been cut back to display all of the numbered doorways and/or personal activity conveniently from the small windows, viewed from the check- in window. Only a couple of the rooms had a sickly, yellowed light falling through ancient venetian blinds, the rest of them were a vacant pitch black. The entire setup became an instant reminder of the old detention rooms tucked away in grade school, where all of the misguided children would find themselves sitting quietly before a matronly teacher; who was in her own angry way trying to prove her mettle by relentlessly working year after year to reform each one of them. *Hmmm…I always imagined that the matron's deepest, dark secret was to let her grey hair out of its tight-assed bun, throw on a pair of stilettos and thigh highs, secretly yearning to join the OTHER side of the room.*

A humorous tick tugged at the corner of Nick's mouth as he rotated his tired shoulders and returned to approaching the service window. He put his bag on the ground with a thump and peered through a smoke stained window into a dimly lit, wood paneled room. Directly behind the glass sat a sleeping, large older man slouching in a worn out computer chair; his head thrown back, glasses hanging precariously off his nose, mouth open and snoring. Nick smiled devilishly as he gave into an impulse and rang the service buzzer next to the window, then sheepishly laughed while he watched as the man startled awake. Jumping as fast as his bulky frame would allow him, awkwardly causing the chair to topple over in his haste and then begrudgingly righted himself. Fuzzy gray hair stood on end, while clueless he scratched his head, slipped his bifocals on and unseeingly glared towards the window.

Nick's brow raised a notch while he watched the muttering man; *this is going to be my HOT reform school teacher this evening…MEOW!?!*

"What…do you want?" Disgruntled the man adjusted his cock-eyed glasses then squinted into the darkness trying to determine whom he was addressing.

Nick sighed tiredly and replied, "I have a room reserved and I believe it's been paid for. My name is…is… Rick Short." He almost choked as the strange name rolled off his tongue in more of an unwanted garble, than the effortless smooth of his usual alias. The old man suspiciously examined Nick from head to toe, then grumpily began to shuffle through the mountain of papers until he found a card and a key.

"Room 3; Keep it clean, keep it down…and keep to yourself. Absolutely no funny business, and get out by 11 am." At the end of his rehearsed speech the old man pushed an ancient key through a small pass-through cut in the window; his unwavering gaze never leaving Nick's face while they shot daggers of distrust. *Crazy old man…who does he think he's talking to, some lunatic?*

As Nick reached arrogantly for the key, he caught a passing glimpse of his reflection in the blurry glass. He had a day's growth of stubble darkening his jaw, couldn't restrain from rubbing his hands against his arms to keep warm from the dampness hanging in the air and his baseball hat was pulled extremely low over his eyes to hide the multitude of stains across his face. He smirked as he humorlessly thought; *Guess I can't blame the old guy for giving me a bad time. I do look a little rough around the edges.* Nick snatched the key off the ledge, retrieved his bag and started to wind his way across the courtyard, ancient light fixture casting a hazed glow illuminated each doorway he passed. Glancing suspiciously around, he stepped up to the door marked with a shiny black #3 sticker, jammed the key into the rusty lock and mumbled to himself, "Bet he couldn't even see this far." Since the second he left the check in window he could feel the old man's distrustful eyes boring a hole in his back. He barely restrained his intuition to turn around and wave at the audacious man, then give him an obvious one fingered bird. Instead he kicked open the scarred door, walked into the room and quickly shut out the yellow light by rapidly closing it.

The smell of must and mildew permeated his senses a nanosecond after he click of the latch. Nick blindly ran his hand up and down the grooved wall, while he blindly searched for a light switch. He heaved a giant sigh of relief when finally felt a lump on the wall with the help from the glow that was barely illuminating through the blinds from the light outside. Nick held his breath, not knowing what to expect as he switched on the lights and then miserably glanced around the room, which didn't improve his mood. There was a lumpy twin bed abandoned in the middle of the room with an orange bedspread that looked like it had seen better days...*like from the 70's.* The TV was chained to the wall, stationed on top of a fabricated end table; there was no phone on the small night stand and a single uncovered light bulb dangling from the ceiling by a cord. As he tilted his head to one side, he noticed that there was another dented door that sadly led into a bathroom with a shower, a couple folded warn towels and stained toilet.

Nick dropped the duffle bag down on the floor and sat heavily on the bed, creating a plume of dust that wafted into the air. Sneezing profusely, his disgust manifested while critically examining the ancient, dingy room from the brown, shag carpet, unidentifiable spotty ceiling, to the forgotten but thoroughly used fly strip and finally bent, tobacco stained Venetian blinds covering the window. While his revulsion surged to the surface, he menacingly glared at the black, shiny leather of the bag and suddenly resented the fact that neither of them were compatible with the environment of the room.

"Well...you're the one that got us here... and don't look at me like that."Nick absentmindedly shook his head abruptly realizing; *I've become so detached with the entire outcome of this situation that delusion has finally set in, almost making me feel like I'm sharing this disgusting room with the bag, and it's developed an identity.* He lifted an arrogant brow while assessing his black, shiny nemesis and thought to himself. *I wonder what you'd say about all of this if you could talk...Mr. Black Bag. Would you console me, or laugh in my face at my decision? I'd want to know...so I can figure out what the hell was going on.* Nick aggressively rubbed his face with his hands, trying to dissolve the situation, make the room disappear, except he only had the strength to wearily mumble in defeat, "I'm too tired, too confused...and too shitting far to go back." He yanked off the baseball hat to run his hands through his hair while he leaned over, grabbed the bag and dumped all its contents onto the orange bedspread.

In the pile of items he found a pair of clippers with a single guard attached, stained, crooked teeth implants with directions, faded jeans, a vintage, rock T-shirt, thick socks, flannel shirt, work boots, a cheap brown, faux leather jacket, a flannel jacket, backpack and another vehicle key. After he rummaged through all of the articles he found a note from Mike that was hidden in between the clothes and the bed.

Nick –

This is the last stop before you get to your destination. There is some more information and just a few changes you have to make before you get there.

To complete your disguise –

Same routine, after you change, put everything in the bag and set it outside the door. There is a set of prosthetic teeth to enhance your appearance (I thought they'd be a nice touch). They may be uncomfortable, but please wear both the contact lenses and teeth at ALL times.

There's a pair of clippers with a large guard, you will have to shave your hair shorter. Once you have cut your hair you don't have to maintain the length, the more unkempt the better and again, try to keep some sort of facial hair. (Remember, we absolutely need to make sure that no one recognizes you while you're in character)

Also in the bag are some clothes, set of keys, a wallet with some cash, another bag and your new ID. While you are working as "Rick Short" you will have to live only on the amount of your paycheck from the job, so budget wisely!

Update on your character –

You are a guy who has been wrongly accused of a crime (but never convicted) and now you are trying to start a new life in a work release program set up by the mutual friend (KATE) who has gotten the job for you. You will be living at a horse ranch, as an extra hand doing odd jobs, but the real reason you are there is to learn how to handle horses for your next part. The more you learn and it comes naturally, the more believable you'll be.

Last, but remember, not least –

Don't forget, you will be contacted once the movie is underway, that's the cell phone. I will call you when we're ready for you to come back and start your part. Keep the phone by you. When you receive the call you will have to leave immediately. DO NOT TELL ANYONE!

Again the timeline of your commitment at this point is six to nine months.

Be safe, work hard and see you then.

Mike

"Shit." Nick dejectedly laid his head in his hands, turning from side to side as he processed everything that had finally compiled his commitment. He slowly splayed his fingers apart to speculate the haphazard mass that lay strewn across the bed. An enormous wave of anxiety coursed through his body, causing him to only hear sound of blood pounding in his ears. Even though the feeling of defeat caused his limbs to feel heavy, he stretched across the bed, rummaged through the pile, lifted the clippers and balanced them in his hand to measure their weight. Nick tiredly braced his feet on the floor while he unsteadily stood up from the sagging bed and crossed the small room to the bath. He switched on the flickering overhead light as he studied his changed reflection in the mirror and scratched his head. *Well shit, what's a little bit of hair anyway?*

After several frustrating minutes of searching the tiny bathroom, he found an outlet under the sink and plugged in the clippers. Nick took a deep breath, bending over, and braced himself with one hand on the wall while warily flipping the switch to turn them on. The sound of the constant whirling hum emitted from the blades instantly seemed more soothing in the cramped bathroom than compared to the churning he was experiencing inside. Nick inadvertently decided, *I think it's better if I bent over while I keep my head tilted forward... below the rim of the sink...I really don't want to see anything.* Bending over until his nose almost touched his knees he started to mindlessly hum the Jeopardy theme song, Nick casually inspected the patterns on the tiled floor while thoughtlessly grabbing a handful of hair with his unused hand, lifted up his other arm and ran the clippers across the back of his head.

His eyes instantly stung when he felt the first painful tug from the long hair at the nape of his neck, he immediately snapped his eyes shut tighter. The wavering low sound of the clipper motor reverberated indicating that it was having a difficult time hacking through his hair. Suddenly he felt a slight lightness as the whirling sped up and his hand began to lift, with a large mass of hair clutched in it, reaffirming that he wouldn't want to notice all of it falling onto the stained floor. Turning his head from side to side he rapidly grabbed more handfuls and randomly guided the clippers across his scalp.

As the weight from the pile of hair dumped on his feet, he turned off the clippers after finishing the lower sections and ran a shaking hand over it to make sure that it was completely shaved. Sucking in an indecisive breath, Nick gradually lifted his head to face the mirror and wearily opened his eyes to examine his reflection, the person watching him was the image of a complete stranger. The transformation seemed incredible within 24 hours, a combination of shadow, sunken rings around exhausted brown eyes, dark five o'clock stubble, black hair and a half-shaved head with the remaining hair sticking out in every direction making him resemble a character from a Yu-gi-oh or Japanese animation. Turning his profile, he desperately searched the transformed face in front of him but couldn't recognize any part of himself; *from the man who hob-knobbed with the stars, that had driven away in the warm California sun just a day ago, to this hollowed out stranger staring back, what the hell have I done.* Slowly, without blinking he masochistically watched while he flipped the clippers switch on, raised them to the top of his head and unblinkingly shaved off the rest of his hair. He unemotionally took every second in; each calculated moment was nailing him even more firmly to his commitment. Nick calmly turned off the clippers once the last of his long, dark hair lay on the bathroom floor, silently cleaned up the evidence, tied up the garbage bag and tossed it next to the door. Then he numbly removed the brown contacts, stripped down and got into the shower. It wasn't until the impact of his actions began to sink in and he felt the surreal prickling sensations of being frozen standing in the Luke-warm shower, that was until the water started to run cold. Nick quickly dried off from the shower with a dingy, threadbare towel, wrapped it around his waist and raced out of the bathroom, never pausing to glance at the mirror. He grabbed all of his discarded clothes off of the floor, marched into the other room, and automatically stuffed everything into the friendless duffle bag "Sorry buddy…you've gotta go". With a quirky smile he wandered over to where he'd tossed the garbage bag, grabbed the bagful of hair, whistled gaily and placed it on top of all the unwanted clothes. *Might as well…Mike hope you'll love that.*

 As Nick heaved the bag off of the bed, he took a quick survey around the room, zipped it shut and opened the door to abandon the bag on the step. The night had stopped raining for a second making him pause outside to take a deep breath, before he let go of the bag in the golden glow. Even with all of the turmoil swirling throughout his head, life had continued on as the night turned surreal standing in the damp evening air. An incredulous chuckle escaped his lips as he noticed the old man behind the window had fallen back asleep. Disbelievingly that nothing, not even a natural disaster had transpired outside the door, Nick shook his head and shut the door. *Funny how life goes on….*

Nick grabbed everything that remained on the bed, shoved it into the backpack and tossed it on top of the night table. He crossed the room to turn off the bathroom light and lethargically made his way back over to the bed. The strange glow that crept through the blinds cast patterns on the wall as he set the alarm on the beaten clock. He couldn't bring himself to realize what he'd done while he silently slid into bed. Under the worn, scratchy blankets Nick tightly shut his eyes and tried to put a halt to the incomprehensible images from the last couple of days flashing across his mind; steeling himself for the morning, the unpredictability of the rest of his journey and the next nine months.

***

"Hey Buddy...you need to get out of there!!" A loud thumping rumbled from the door accompanied with a gruff voice.

"What...what the hell?" Nick called out at the door as he rapidly rolled over. He suddenly realized that he was lying in a disgusting bed, someone was pounding on the door, making him instantly jump up and disoriented stumble across to the window. In an eerie, bluish light, Nick leaned against the door in nothing but his boxers trying to get a glimpse through the dirty blinds. He glanced around searching for something to use as a weapon while he inched the door open a fraction and jammed his foot behind it to deter anyone from forcing their way in. Holding his breath and ready for an attack, Nick glanced out the crack of the door...directly into a pair of old rheumy eyes that glared back at him.

"Hey, buddy, you better get out of that room or you'll owe me for another day's payment and you sure don't look like you can afford it. Especially 'cuz they repo'd your car last night...HA...knew you were trouble."

"Umm..yeah." He stood in shock, motionless against the door and listened while the old man lumbered away, muttering down the walkway. Nick tiredly closed his eyes, leaned his head against the doorjamb and took a deep breath. Without another thought he moved backwards into the room and grabbed the clothes he'd left out. As he pulled on his pants, he glanced at the clock on the wall and realized that he only had a few minutes to get out of there. *Shit, it's nearly 11 am and it's still dark outside...ass backwards place, no wonder the old guy's fucking grumpy...probably never even seen the sun.*

Nick quickly finished shimmying into the rest of his clothes, then grabbed the discarded backpack and stepped into the bathroom. He started to toss everything remaining strewn across the sink into it, until he switched on the light and instantly halted midstride. "Whoa, what the FUCK have I done?" As he unbelievingly stared at the reflection, he leaned closer to the mirror while his hand slowly inched towards his shaved head. Nick had a moment of sheer panic when his fingers glided across his scalp, only registering the prickliness of the soft, flat stubble as his hand lingered on his shaved head. "It's OK...I just have to remember there is a goal to all of this insanity. There has to be some sacrifice, just remember...become your character." Nick listened to the blood pounding in his ears deciding to determinedly face the mirror, placed the brown contacts into both eyes, grabbed the teeth implants and shoved them into his mouth. Watching the instantaneous transformation happening within the dingy mirror, Nick awestruck found a different man metamorphosing and staring back at him.

I've finally found Rick Short. The man that stood before him was raw, a chiseled chest in a tight AC/DC t-shirt, jaw darkened with stubble, pitch black hair, shaggy from being uniformly shaved enhance his edge. When he smiled his teeth looked slightly crooked and his brown eyes looked dull, with the help from the implants and contacts. Nick stepped away from the mirror and stood there while he processed his entire modification into a different person. *Hmmm...funny, I feel different, but better... in a weird way.*

He re-scanned the bathroom, snatched up the remaining cases for his lenses and teeth to shove them into the backpack. Without another thought he walked into the room, sat on the bed, quickly threw on his thermal socks and tugged his work boots on. Nick leaned over to the night table to grab the key ring and wallet, shrugging on the flannel shirt and took in a quick survey of the room. A stream of mid-morning sun finally filtered through the blinds as he opened the door and left without a second glance back. As he confidently strode across the empty courtyard and noticed the old man perched behind the window comfortably stationed back in his little room. Nick gave the old geezer a brief nod and noticed an odd smile that lifted the corner of the man's mouth. He pondered for a second about the sudden change of the man's attitude as he walked by the entrance towards where he had parked the Honda.

"Damn...it's cold here," Nick mumbled to himself and quickly buttoned up his flannel coat against the Northwest winter/spring chill. He immediately came to a screeching halt after rounded the corner of the ancient building, jaw gaped open and couldn't believe his eyes. Proudly parked in the spot where the Honda should have been was a deep, turtle-green, 1975 Ford pickup truck...dents, rust and all. "No way, how am I going to drive that thing?" A thousand thoughts about how he was going to tell off Mike swam through his head while he cautiously approached the truck's door. Without another word he inserted the key, opened the door and thoughtlessly hopped up into the cab. Slamming the cab door shut he listened to the foreign sound of the ancient seat springs squeak in protest against his weight, as he scooted back and tried to reposition his butt away from a large sag. His hands awkwardly clenched the steering wheel while he focused his inner strength and tried to willingly force himself to start the truck. Finally he sighed in forfeit, jammed the key into the ignition and attempted to start the engine. The truck gave a tired little shutter and a loud barking, cough as it attempted to start but with no success. Nick took another deep breath, pumped the gas pedal a few times and tried again. This time the engine coughed and sputtered to life, making the entire cab start to shake as it idled. The jumbling, shaking movement became reminiscent of the plastic teeth toy that chattered inconsolably when you wound them up. He urgently glanced around the dash as the fingers of cold started to seep through his flannel while he tried to find a heater switch. He finally spied it then quickly slid the leaver over to high, causing a blast of ice-cold air to shoot out of the vents. Shivering he snapped it off; *I better wait for the truck to heat up before I try that again.*

 Nick decided to take advantage of the annoying situation and tried to orient himself with the unfamiliarity of the cab. He curiously stopped his mission when something odd outside caught his attention while adjusting the review mirror, a single dark figure stood motionless near the entrance of the motel. He narrowed his eyes as he tried to focus his vision in the foggy mirror, without avail he turned around to get a better view. The old man from behind the window stood out in the empty street blatantly watching all of Nick's frustration and could almost feel the geezer's belated mockery seep into the truck through the cold windows. Ignoring him, Nick glanced around the dashboard trying to find some kind of CD player, but realizing that there was only the original AM/FM radio. "OHHH, are you shitting me?" An astonished groan escaped his lips while he leaned over to switch it on and determinedly cranked the ancient knob in any direction, intent on finding decent station. Nick sighed heavily, his resolve relenting its control to the reality that the only channels were either Country or Classic Rock; *I'll chose the latter.*

The dark shadow in the mirror boldly stepped farther out into the wet street, intently watching the rumbling truck. Nick made the decision to try the beast out a mere twenty minutes waiting for the heater to warm up; *Screw it, I'm never going to thaw out from the shitting cold waiting for this freaking thing to warm up.* He stomped on the gas, loudly revved the coughing engine a couple of times and magically caused the heater to start kicking out some heat. Nick rolled down the window to lean his head out and survey his ability to move the beast around. Checking his mirror he spied the shadow, slapped the truck into gear, stuck out his free hand and then gave a jaunting one-fingered salute to the grumpy old man standing in the cold. As the truck coughed, struggling to life, stamped on the pedal and lunged forward making him ease off of the gas. Nick leaned over to turn up the radio just as Bruce Springsteen started to sing 'Glory Days', but he could barely hear the song over the immense noise of the engine. Between the continual coughing engine, blaring music, and rumbling of the truck Nick headed down the deserted street on the way to his final stop and absolutely disrupted the peace of the neighborhood.

7

While the old, turtle-green pickup struggled to lumber over the crest of a semi-steep hill, the city of Aberdeen came into view. A massive, black cloud hung over the tiny town, waiting to pelt its rain on anyone who dared to venture outside. The view from the summit showed an ancient lumber town perched on a murky waterway, struggling to stay productive. A huge mill sat to the south, with timber lying in front of a building just adjacent to the bay. It looked as if an errant child had been playing with giant Lincoln Logs and neglected to clean them up. The entire town sprawled out across from the river and consisted of a bunch of small clusters of structures. Assembled side by side, they were a combination of brand new construction or ancient buildings that were sadly deteriorating. It was as if each century of construction was challenging the other to stand up against the test of time, lack of interest and the unforgivable weather of the bitter coastal region.

Nick's hands ached from the continuous shuddering caused by the extreme jerking of the steering wheel as he tried to maneuver the truck through traffic. He could feel the painful reward from hours of constant reverberating throughout his forearms while trying to control the truck from lurching to either direction was beginning to take its toll. *Damn... I feel like my innards have turned to Jell-O from shaking the entire drive since I left Oregon...I'll never be the same again.*

In an attempt to keep his sanity, he mentally kept a tally of the outlandish ongoing puzzle that the weather provided while driving across Oregon and Washington towards the coast: *The many ways how a person can appreciate the different types of rain in the Northwest.* So far he had driven through a range starting from a light mist, pattering sprinkles, sideways hail/rain, pounding large droplets, a torrential downpour and even a flurry of snow. It was during the last occurrence of a mammoth rainstorm that the truck broke down and he had to replace a broken water hose. *At least the fucking truck had only overheated three times on the road,* he annoyingly thought while having an unusual upbeat moment and tried to be optimistic about each time the hood began to billow smoke he pulled over on the side of the road, wasting hours waiting for the hot steam to stop flowing and attempted to continue his drive. With each mechanical time-out, Nick found himself developing an extreme black sense of humor, besides a bad habit of talking to himself. The only other source of company was then inconsistent radio with only two stations, overridden by static interruption when the forest became too dense or the drumming rain was too intense. The third time the truck began to overheat he was lucky enough to be pulling into a gas station. Nick recalled how excited he'd become about talking about the weather with the mechanic while he replaced the water hose, more than getting the actual help. Leaving the station his spirits tanked when he realized that the purchase had depleted most of his meager funds and his clothes were still horribly damp from standing chatting in the rain.

I think I can actually feel my suntan fading while I'm becoming a mindless drone in this endless gray. I can't believe that anyone would prefer to live in such a dismal state instead of anywhere else in the world. I haven't noticed anything of interest for a couple hours...let alone two days. Shit, this movie better be worth all of this crap or Mike is going to be looking for a new job. Nick was deep in thought as he brought the truck to a shuddering stop as he approached the traffic light at the bottom of the hill. As he scanned the area, he realized; *Shit the only point of interest are the buildings create one long strip mall, with Wal-Mart towering over the other local stores like a dominant queen.* Surveying the traffic, it seemed that everyone's sole intent was to drive around the department store's parking lot with the main intent to locate a prime parking spot. *Wonder if anyone ever actually makes it into the store before it closes, after wasting all their time searching for a front parking spot.*

The crackling on the radio paused long enough for Bob Seger's 'Hollywood Nights' to begin to bellow out through the ancient speakers. The singers heartfelt, gravelly voice broke through Nick's melancholy mood making him smile like a teenager and crank up the volume. His outlook lifted as the song's familiar lyrics gave him an optimistic reassurance that he'd be going back to California sooner than he thought. *This must be some kind of an omen letting me know everything's going to be all right.*

Horns began to blare through the open window and seemed to keep time with the song as he unheedingly sang along with the song. He looked out the windshield watching the sky for the slightest sign of rain and glanced in the rearview mirror. Listening to the honking Nick abruptly realized that all of the noise was aimed at him because the stoplight had turned green. Startled he stomped on the gas pedal, making the truck irately sputter and then billow out black smoke as it crawled through the intersection. Nick kept indifferent humming in time with the song while the rest of the traffic sped around his ancient truck as he crossed over a bridge and continued to follow the signs towards Westport. Nick noticed that the only indication the town had ended was that a tiny, local mall flew by, the speed limit went up from 30mph to 55mph on the two- lane highway, while large black thunderhead clouds began to encroach upon the horizon of a lack of homes, bogs, reeds and cattails. On either side of the road the landscape drastically changed distracting him from the boring drive when he realized he'd definitely left city limits. On the right were glimpses of pooled water that funneled into roadside bogs from the ocean and through the wind-shaped pine trees. On the other side were foxtails, skunkweed, and lily pads growing in the ditches overflowing with murky water. The light from the sky started to darken with the threat of an incoming downpour drenching the area at any second. Switching on the truck's headlights Nick sped up, trying to locate all of the backwoods markers he'd memorized that would indicate the turn off for the house. After he crossed the first bridge out of town and made the wide turn at a large sign indicating woodcarvings and totem poles for sale, he slowed down. Astounded, Nick gazed out the passenger window as he saw a mermaid, bear and crab all carved out of driftwood in front of a house that was creatively fenced with old fishing nets, buoys and glass floaters strung on ropes tethered in between the driftwood posts.

"Wow…looks like somebody's found a creative hobby." Nick raised an eyebrow at the interesting sight but refrained from muttering another word and picked up more speed. Without thinking, his tongue traced the outline of the teeth implants where they had worn the inside of his mouth raw. Involuntarily flinching, he tried to keep his oral movements to a minimum. He started to slow the truck down when the road began a slight incline down a small hill. He spotted the deserted dirt road on the left and a street sign that indicated he had finally made it to his destination. Suddenly it seemed as if the heavens decided to open up and started to dump buckets of water everywhere. Nick carefully turned the truck onto the dirt road, which turned to be another hill causing him to carefully drive at a snail's pace.

The main house perched at the top and was completely breathtaking with the rolling clouds lurking behind it. Nick let out a low whistle while he parked the truck directly in front of a picket fence. He unconsciously turned the engine off and sat back to survey the premises. *Somebody must have been the big show around here back in the day. At least I'll have a decent place to stay, not like that roach motel from last night, Shit… I can't think about it or I'll start itching.*

The house was a tall Victorian that was poised on top of a hill as if it recognized its importance and reined over the existing land besides the views. The white paint seemed to eerily glow in the rain darkened sky. Most of the windows were dark except for one upstairs and a couple on the main floor. There was a huge, covered, wraparound porch and an inviting cluster of wicker chairs that flanked the sides where the view of the ocean was the best. The rest of the walkway was overrun with a multitude of discarded items, desolately laying around as if frozen in a forgotten moment. It gave the appearance that someone had good intentions to start a hundred different projects; except never ended up beginning, finishing or even caring about them in the first place.

Eyeing the chaos, Nick reminisced some of the homes that had different objects artistically decorating their front yards as he sped towards the coast. He had encountered tons of yard art, old tools, broken old wheelbarrows, rusted tin cans, ancient out buildings, claw footed tubs and even a toilet or two. They all had one thing in common…flowers planted in or around them to decorate them. But nothing could compare to the onslaught of leftover items that created such neglect, nondescriptly littering the yard of this grand old house. *Someone should be ashamed of the way their living.* Nick thoughtfully reached across the seat, grabbed his damp flannel coat and threw it on as he tried to brace himself to venture out into the weather. He lowered the bill of his hat before opening the truck's door, trying not to allow rain to billow into the cab and immediately drench the interior. He squinted against the torrential rain, jumped out and smack dab into the largest puddle he'd ever seen. Nick cursed under his breath as he slammed the truck door and waded across the puddle towards the house. Shaking out water from inside his soggy boots, he found himself quickening his pace after stepping through the broken gate, and nearly tripped down the cracked, uneven slate walkway. Nick cautiously ventured up the steps in front of the house and paused to shake the water off his coat. As he looked around the neglected porch and noticed a few of the planks were broken or missing, besides the house was in dire need of a fresh coat of paint. *If Mike signed me up to help some elderly couple renovating their house...turning me into some Good Samaritan or whatever while I'm here, he's stupid. I only want to get this job done, get home and get out of this dreary, wet place.*

With a sigh of frustration, he assertively turned back towards the front door and intentionally knocked loudly. As Nick waited he tried to peer through the ancient shade covering the window of the door into the darkened house. There seemed to be a decent sized entryway that was completely bare, except for a small table with a basket full of mail perched precariously across it. Through the gloom he could make out the first few steps of a staircase that seemed to be covered in an old, threadbare runner.

A huge gust of wind whipped out of nowhere and pelted the entire right side of his body with the cold rain. Nick's teeth clenched while uncontrollably shuddered as the chilling wetness sank through his clothes, settling against his skin. He instantly huffed a frustrated sound, resounding through the back of his throat and diligently pounded on the door with a little more conviction. Nick stood back startled by an indistinct noise resounding through the house, it appeared a human alarm had gone off at the reaction to his obvious frustration. Lights began to switch on from room to room upstairs as someone made their way downstairs to the door. The light proceeded into the dimly illuminated stairwell, while the shadow of a single figure began to tentatively make its way towards the door through the darkness. The sudden brightness when the entryway lights unnaturally blazed on through the window, momentarily blinded him. Nick quickly turned his head, trying to forcibly blink his eyes back into focus just as the door cracked open a smidgen. He could hear the suspect noise of a trivial security chain that prevented it from opening any further.

"Ummm...Can I help you?" a slight feminine voice came from behind the door and through the crack.

"My name is Rick, ummm, Rick Short. I'm here about the job." As he estimated her to be a teen from the sound of her voice in the dark, he uncomfortably noticed that the teeth implants made him articulate his words with a lisp. He ran his hand down his face trying to wipe off some of the wetness seeping down his face and dripping off his chin. Closing his eyes searching for patience, he momentarily willed some of the ridiculousness of the current situation away. The door cracked open a little more, just enough that he was able to see the flimsy chain across the doorjamb and feel some of the heat radiating from inside the house. Rick shivered at the sensation as the heat permeated his wet clothes; *Come on…throw me a bone, haven't I been through enough? I wish whoever is behind the door would invite me in…I'd pay.*

Huge, doe-like eyes and the freshly washed face of a teenager popped into view of the door's crack. "Anne should be coming up at any moment, just hang out on the porch…umm, if you'd like." With that quickly said the door was immediately slammed in his face.

"But…I…uh…SHIT." Nick anxiously stretched out his hand towards the closed door, only to unbelievably hesitate as he watched the lights quickly turned out and the girl's footsteps hastily receded into the depths of the house. Annoyed, Nick turned away, swore and determinedly kicked a planter full of dead plants that perched next to the door. *Don't you know who I am? I am a superstar, damn it! If I said a single word, I could buy this place and the godforsaken town you live in! Shit, my signature alone is worth more than your dilapidated house and ranch put together.*

He slumped down into one of the wet, white, wicker chair forgotten on the porch. Nick dejectedly placed his elbows on his knees and plopped his head into his hands. He let his guard down for a moment as he closed his aching eyes from the long drive and gave into the honest thought. *Of course you don't know who I really am and you never will. I'm just some transient who is down on his luck and looking for a hand out. Shit, how did I agree to this?*

Just then Nick heard an odd, offhand noise coming from the opposite side of the house. He raised his head in surprise, squinted and attempted to scan through the rain across the yard towards the barn. Through the haze of the downpour a silhouette started to leave the old barn at the back of the property. A bright yellow slicker moved quickly as the person determinedly strode through all of the mud and muck too rapidly make their way towards the house. As whoever it was approached the house, the person completely enshrouded in the slicker mechanically turned to enter the gate and walked towards the front door. The mysterious person intentionally moved familiarly around the porch and as a single hand, silently motioned for him to follow around the back of the house. Without thought Nick jumped up at the chance of warmth and hurried over to follow the stranger towards the back door. The rotted planks moaned in protest while he diligently made his way around the porch and tried to keep up. He slowed down his momentum for a moment when he noticed the yellow slicker standing in front of a darkened back door. A small hand emerged out from the coat to produce a key, open the door and silently beckoned him to step into the warmth of a room. As the door stood open and shivering from the feeling of the gush of heat, he readily followed the sinister form. After enter the house, Nick started to shrug off his wet coat, only to have the shrouded figure immediately hold their hand up indicating him to stop, causing him to stand frozen in the closed doorway. Nick found himself deposited in a small mudroom at the back of the house and tried to quickly take everything in. The house was tidy, but very dated. He bumped into a wall of coats haphazardly hung facing opposite the door with a myriad of shoes lined up under each hanging item.

The room appeared that it had once been wallpapered in a cheerful floral print. But now it was faded and peeled in some spots all the way down to the wallboard. The kitchen was more than generous with vaulted ceilings, an oversized ancient butcher block that swallowed up the center of the room and an old chipped countertop encompassed the edges, dividing the upper and lower cabinets.

Still wondering who or what was under the slicker, Nick respectfully stood next to the door, instinctively ready to bolt if anything wen sideways. He started to feel uncomfortable as he listened to the water drip off of his coat and began to create a small puddle on the floor next to his drenched feet. From under the hood of the slicker a soft, velvety voice began to answer a nonexistent question; suddenly Nick's interest went from innocently confused to quite piqued as he realized three things. *First- whoever is in the slicker's on a cell phone, second - whoever is a woman and third - she's got great voice.*

"You know Dave, this isn't necessary. We are always very appreciative of what you do...yes...yes...well you let me know if you decide one way or the other. Yes, I think you've already made yourself clear about your feelings towards this situation the other day. I...well...whatever." Nick watched the woman end the call, angrily walk over to the butcher block, put the phone down and as she started to shrug out of her yellow slicker Nick's eyes widened in surprise.

Whoever she was, she stood taller than average, curvy in an athletic way and shoulders tense from being guarded. Dressed for the weather, she was wearing a black, long sleeve turtle neck sweater and a pair of old blue jeans that fit her like she had borrowed them from her boyfriend the old jean material was worn and buckled enough in the right places to give some kind of interest to the mystery that was hidden underneath them. Her hair was pulled back in a ponytail under a baseball cap so he could only tell that is was dark brown and trailed down the middle of her back. Nick's mind started reeling, wondering what she was going to look like as she slowly turned towards him.

"Sooo, you're Rick Short. We didn't quite know when you would arrive today, sorry for the unprepared... ummm, welcome." In a single motion she pivoted around while she spoke, then walked across the room, hung up her coat on one of the unoccupied pegs next to him and turned to extend her hand. "I'm Anne, Anne Jones."

She had an average but attractive face, slightly angular features and a full mouth. Her most striking asset was her light blue eyes that shone with intelligence and inquisitiveness. Nick's acute knowledge of reading people from years of being in show business, assessed that all the hard work and strain had started to set in on her physical attributes. Her complexion was gaunt, shadows stretched under her eyes, besides their weariness, and her tired mouth had crease around the corners mirroring the edges of her eyes that were premature for her age.

Rick nonchalantly took her hand and shook it. "Glad to meet you, Anne. As you know, I'm Rick."

Anne quickly dropped his hand as if he'd attempted to bite and walked over to the sink. "Care for a cup of coffee? I need to warm up before we head back outside." She took down a couple of cups and started to pour coffee before he had time to answer. As the comforting aroma of the coffee filled the room she replaced the coffee pot and walked across to where he stood. Anne handed him a large, oversized mug then walked to the butcher block, nonchalantly pivoted and neglectfully leaned against it.

She quietly surveyed their newcomer from over the rim of her mug of steaming coffee while indifferently took her first sip. Nervousness bubbled from her stomach making Anne choke on the hot coffee when she realized that her mysterious new comer looked more than a little rough, assessing the stubble on his face, short ruffled hair and disgruntled demeanor.

When Beth had called down to the barn to let her know that Rick had finally arrived, Anne unconsciously registered the large knot of apprehension amassed in the pit of her stomach that had been forming all day as they waited for him to show up. *Ahhh, just the fact that he's in a work release program from prison is enough for me to start hiding all of the sharp knives, tools and pawn-able items in the house...let alone Beth.* Anne wanted to give herself a huge kick in the ass for being so impulsive and not weighing all of the possibilities of what her rash decision was getting them into. She admitted historically, that she had the knack of jumping into something before really thinking it through. *You'd think that one of these days I'd realize not to go with my first instinct and actually think about the outcome, but noo...not me.* Everyone in town had been telling her for the last week that she was crazy. Besides the obvious fact that the combination of two girls alone in an isolated house with a strange hired hand was insane, they were all counting the days until they'd find them murdered in their beds, so their story could make a great television mini-series. The main gossip was that no one could believe anyone from their family had lowered themselves to hiring riffraff; *and to be honest neither can I, but we need the extra pair of hands and I still have my pride. We just need to float through another season, until I can cinch up the details of an outrageous opportunity that'll turn everything around.*

"So Rick, have you ever worked with animals or on a ranch of any kind?" Anne graciously cleared her voice when she realized their obvious lack of conversation, because silently they had been sizing each other up.

Coffee awkwardly sloshed over the rim when Rick jumped, startled out of his currently awkward dilemma by her abrupt question; he'd been silently contemplating how to ask if she had any creamer. *I can't fathom drinking anything other than Italian coffee. I want to fill this freaking mug halfway with creamer and tons of sugar just to get past the harsh smell of cheap coffee.*

"No, I haven't had a pet of any kind since I was a kid." He chuckled then had a good laugh at the end of his response imagining toting any kind of dependent animal around back in California, but when he glimpsed her reaction, instantly he realized his reply wasn't the appropriate one.

"So, no pets...hu?" Anne's instant curiosity was piqued while she snidely asked, "Why do you want to work here, a ranch of all places then?"

"Look, just because I haven't had a pet, doesn't mean that I've never wanted one. While I was growing up and even up to now, my life has simply never had enough room or time for one." Rick compiled his thoughts quickly trying to pull a story together with pieces from his own childhood. "Besides, I have always been drawn towards horses. I think they are amazing and always wanted to work with them. Just couldn't put them into a studio apartment, I think the landlords would have complained."

"You're probably right about that." Anne gave him an apologetic smile as she took another sip. Rick's stomach did a huge summersault as he involuntarily caught himself avidly watching her mouth the second she smiled. He clenched the mug as he noticed the natural beauty that came out in that one innocent gesture. *Hold on buddy, this is your boss for the next few months. You need to think straight and keep whatever you're thinking about in your pants. You've come this far, don't screw with everything now.*

Anne definitively placed her cup down on top of the butcher block, started ringing her hands and took a deep breath. Rick tried to take another quick sip, started to choke from the harsh taste of the bitter coffee and gave himself an imaginary pat on the back while resiliently keeping the burning liquid down.

"Well, here's the history behind our family's ranch." Anne took a second to clear her throat as she began with her story. "We've lived in this town most of my life. My parents had regular day jobs, but always wanted more when they started to have a family to provide for. The horse ranch idea had been their dream. When this property came up for sale years ago, they jumped at the idea to refurbish the house and grounds to create a thriving business; boarding, training and leasing horses." She gently rubbed the back of her neck as she contemplated how to unemotionally finish. *I wish I didn't have to retell this story again.*

"They both passed away a few years ago, with them gone, it's been a constant struggle to maintain everything and plus it isn't quite a lucrative business year round around a small town like Westport. We try to rely on the seasonal tourist income; with the unpredictable weather around here it's mainly active in the summer, but the rest of the time we simply board local horses. Which sadly are few and far in between." Anne took a deep breath, attempting to push down the solid lump in her throat while she grabbed her cup and walked across the kitchen to pour some more coffee. She was attempting to take a calm minute to regain her composure she'd felt slip momentarily from the honesty of her situation.

Rick tried not to openly check out her backside while she walked by, but it didn't work. *Not bad, nicely round and physically firm, just enough to grab*, he pleasantly thought with a Cheshire cat grin spreading across his face just as she turned around to offer him some more coffee. Silence engulfed the room as Anne held the coffee pot out to top off his mug and caught the direction of his gaze. She arrogantly lifted an eyebrow, brazenly indicating that she'd caught him staring. Without another word, she gently placed the pot back on its burner, unplugged the machine and turned to abruptly finish their conversation in a firm, militant tone.

"Your job is going to be helping with anything in and around the barn, pastures, corrals, horses, and sometimes on the main house. There is a daily schedule that is going to be your gospel and if I decide that anything out of the ordinary needs to be done, I'll let you know. When I feel like you're ready, I'll introduce you to the care and training of the horses, but only when I think you're ready for the task. It's going to be hard physical work and I hope you are up for it, because I'm not going to be available to walk behind you to make sure everything is done properly."

Rick was tempted to stand at attention to salute her when she finished her abrasive monolog and inform her that he wasn't going to be around long enough to care. Instead he decided to take the high road and absentmindedly nod in agreement.

"Sure--"

"Your living area is located in the barn, there is a small apartment in the back. It is more convenient to have you out there, available at a moment's notice. There is a washer and dryer here back in the mudroom for you to use. Your days to do laundry are on Sunday and Wednesday. There is no reason for you to be in the house other than that. If there is a need for anything there is a phone is the barn with the house's number. Please call or come to the back door if you have a question. If there is an emergency, you can reach me at any time on my cell phone, but only for emergencies." She walked over to a stack of papers and picked them up. "This is the basic schedule for each day. It will become routine, but for the time being it'll be easier if you make sure you have it down for each day. If you have a question about a job, ask me, that'll make it easier on the both of us." She walked over to Rick and handed him the papers. "Do you have any questions?"

As he took the stack of papers Rick looked directly into her eyes, smiled and cockily replied, "No, ma'am."

Anne rolled them to demonstrate her appreciation of his arrogance, irritated turned and grabbed her coat as she headed towards the back door. "Okay, let's go see to your job and living arrangements."

Rick thankfully set his cold offensive mug down and hurried to follow Anne back out into the rain drenched world. He shivered as the cold enveloped his newly warmed body, and then abruptly had to lightly jog as he tried to follow Anne down the porch, around puddles and areas of mud while they made their way across the flooding yard. As they approached the barn, Anne bent over and struggled to pull the door open. After a few attempts it loudly protested as it slid along its rusted tracks while the noise rumbled over the sound of the ever-constant rain and together they wordlessly walked into the old barn. The musty smell of hay, dirt, horse and dung hit him like a ton of bricks. Sucking in a protective breath, he desperately wanted to pull his flannel collar firmly across his nose to block the stench. Except eyeing his employer Anne didn't appear to notice the stench, so Rick decided to follow her lead, kept his breathing at a minimum and followed her though the barn. Anne walked over to a random stall door just as a golden horse poked its head over to see who was disrupting the evening.

Rick tried to check his gaping jaw at his circumstances and looked unbelievingly around the decrepit barn. On the right side where they were stood was a row of about seven horse stalls with planks laid unevenly over the ground in front of them. The rest of the area was a large indoor arena that was brightly lit by flickering overhead lights. A large double door hung crookedly from age that led out to the outdoor corral. The place looked even worse than the house, with holes, broken boards, even boarded up windows here and there. Anne's sharp voice brought him abruptly back from his open inspection of the barn.

"Ah-hum-- We start early here, 5 am. I provide breakfast and sometimes lunch, you're on your own for dinner. We try to make it into town about once every other week. So if you need anything you can either ride in or make a detailed list and leave cash." Anne pushed away from the stall and indignantly turned towards the back of the barn, and silently gestured for him to obediently follow her down the haphazard trail of uneven planks that lead to a poorly lit corner. AAs he started to move he incredulously realized that they were headed towards the end of the plank walkway where tucked in the darkness was an old unused door. *You've got to be shitting me...I not living in this disgusting place.*

Anne took an uncertain breath for courage, then slowly opened it to give way to a small, dark room and switched on the light. Rick quirked an inquisitive brow as he carefully inched forward, trying not to brush up against any overtly protruding part of her body while passing on his way inside. Glancing around the room, instantly his shoulder slowly drooped as he vainly tried to keep his back to the door, primarily so Anne wouldn't notice the physical display of his thoughts that ran across his face, from dismay to disgust.

In the flickering light the room couldn't compare in size to his closet back in Malibu, it was barely half. It seemed like the room had been furnished in desperation, simply with a twin mattress covered in an overtly used heavy blue comforter with a single pillow on top; across the room from the bed was a small wooden stand with a tiny TV that still had rabbit ears accompanied with tin foil, and an old dresser against a wall. He walked in squeaking pass the bed to look around the corner to find on his right, an ancient refrigerator with a microwave on top and the tiniest stove he had ever seen with two cupboards overhead for storage. He leaned forward to switch on another light to discover a bathroom was barely squished together with a toilet, corner shower, and sink precariously attached to the wall. Rick closed his eyes and rubbed his face while he thought to himself, *I thought that the last hotel was small! Shit, I'll never complain about any traveling conditions after this. Well, at least this place is clean.* He opened his eyes to the muffled sound of Anne uncomfortably clearing her voice. Rick moved to poke his head out of the bathroom to see what she had to say.

"Hope this is a step up from your last residence." Anne smiled weakly across the room as she stood in the doorway feeling a little odd being in such a cramped space alone with him. With a heroic attempt to diffuse their uncomfortable situation, she stumbled on. "I know the room is small, but it's all we have at the moment and hopefully it will suit you. Do you need any help collecting your things out of your truck?"

Rick glanced down at his wet clothes while he gestured at his body, "Other than a back pack with a change of clothes, this is it...everything I have in the entire world right at the moment."

"Oh, my...well." Anne's smile quickly faded as her thoughts strayed to his mysterious past. "We'll have to go into town sooner than I planned to get you some supplies. Until then I'll make sure you have dinner every night after work."

A small pit formed in the bottom of her stomach at the thought of Rick's situation, *Wow, I can't believe he has nothing and no one.* She tried to shrug off the overwhelming idea of being so misplaced in the world and wondering what he was thinking. *He's probably grateful at the chance to pick himself up and make something of himself. Don't even doubt what the room looks like, this could be the best place he's been in for a while. Maybe he was homeless.*

Ricks eyes were disbelievingly vacant while they sadly stared to reassess the room. *I can't believe I have to live in this shit hole. I'm going to fucking kill Mike. I wouldn't consider having anyone live in this hovel...even if I hated them! This freaking movie better pay off big or Mike's living here for the rest of his life!*

She quickly spun around as the sound of tires crunching down the driveway and the squeak of breaks caught her attention. "Ah shit." Anne eyes swiveled directly back to Rick to mournfully reassess his appearance. Taking in his rugged, good looks and edgy appearance Anne sucked in her breath laced with apprehension as he openly surveyed her back. She closed her eyes knowing that Rick didn't realize who was parking and what was possibly going to transpire, she ignored his rude appraisal and muttered under her breath, "I really don't need this right now. Damn it!" She grimaced back at Rick, mentally dismissing him as she limply raised a hand, sporadically waved it around in a vacant way and dismissed him like an unwanted guest. "Make yourself at home..."Anne bit the inside of her cheek while the odd movements of her hand became suspended, as if she was contemplating what to do with him at that precise second, either shove him under the bed or pray that he'd disappear. "Excuse me, give me a quick second. Umm, I need to see about a situation."

Rick opened and shut his mouth in astonishment at her treatment, but before he could say anything Anne abruptly turned around and stormed down the planks towards the front of the barn. Curious at what had incited the developing situation, he watched while her body language became exceedingly more and more rigid with mounting tension as she marched towards the opened door. He openly chuckled to himself at her dilemma. *This is going to be something. Whatever has gotten the Dragon Lady's panties in a bunch has to be good. After a day like today I deserve to enjoy a little drama.* Rick casually walked over to lean in the doorway so he could openly watch what was happening, but safely enjoy whatever was going to transpire from a distance.

A slight, sly smile quirked the side of his mouth as he noticed Anne's female form had picked up quite a momentum and practically launching herself across to the barn door. At that exact moment a disembodied hand appeared solidly on the door, as someone began sliding it open wider. She came to a sliding halt, angrily shoved her hands on her hips and waited for whoever was standing in the darkness to appear. The shadow of a tall man stood motionless outside while the headlights from a car illuminated his form through the rain.

"Ah shit, let me guess... the welcome wagon is here to greet me," Rick mumbled while he aggregately ran his hand across his forehead then down his face. Blowing out a frustrated breath he shook his head. *Shit...know what, I really couldn't give a fuck. I'm just going to kick back, relax and simply watch the show. It's nothing to me anyway. I'll be leaving this shit hole in a handful of months, back to my amazing life, while this guy will grow old trying to be the big fish in a little pond. I almost feel sorry for the asshole.*

"Dave, I thought I mentioned that you didn't need to come by this evening, I have everything under control." Anne said quietly through clenched teeth as she narrowed her eyes at the man and rudely remained planted in the door way. He looked intimidating dressed in his work clothes, boots and hunting jacket while the lights from his car shot through the night. Dave stepped forward, making Anne take a hesitant step back into the lit barn and glanced around the room as if he was trying to detect what exactly was amiss.

"Well Anne, I took it into my own hands to swing by here and make sure that everything and everyone…namely you, were OK. Plus, I'd like to meet our new resident for myself." Dave looked down at the fiery young woman who now stood ramrod straight and impatiently tapping her foot.

 Rick assessed the obvious opposition, Dave stood a few inches above Anne's head and looked to be a few years older. He had a kind face that was a little weathered and age had crept in quicker because of living in a coastal area. Lines that creased the sides of his mouth and eyes softened his arrogant appearance. He probably once had a full head of dark brown hair in his youth, but with age it had receded to the point where he should have shaved it short; instead he was still trying to style it reminiscing his glorious high school days, a sudo comb-over created a noticeable difference in thickness between the sides and the top of his hair. *Hu…he probably was the captain of the football team, surprisingly a decent looking guy for such a small town.*

Anne's anger dissipated a little at the thought of his genuine concern and registered that oddly his presence always had a calming effect. She blew out a defeated breath then looked up, Dave's most striking appearance was his brown/hazel eyes that could turn your knees to liquid; and had accomplished exactly that with quite a few girls in town over the years. *Remember Anne, he's a charmer; better keep your guard up.* Since her parents passing Dave had instantly remained helpful around the ranch, at least as much as he possibly could while maintaining his own property. Since her arrival from Seattle, he had approached her with several attempts to take her out for an evening, but she always found herself declining his offers with the flimsy excuses that the grief from her parents' deaths and lack of time prevented her from having any kind of social life.

Anne stepped directly in front of Dave, trying to block his path when he stealthily tried to maneuver around her. Irritated at his inconsideration of ignoring her request she infuriatedly jammed her hands on her hip and resumed tapping her toe, creating the perfect picture of an irate female. "I appreciate your concern about OUR welfare, but I believe I have THIS situation under control." She un-ladylike let out an exasperated pent up breath to punctuate the end of her sentence.

Dave leaned forward and gently lifted her chin with the tip of his finger so he could look deeply into her eyes. "You've always had spunk and determination with your decisions in life. That's what I like about you." He evaded her stance simply by placing his arm around her shoulders and physically guiding her towards the back of the barn. "You can't save every stray puppy Anne, it's about time you start allowing someone in your life to help you out and lean on once in a while."

Oh yeah, I bet you'd like it a lot if I leaned on you more! I've seen this trap coming on for a few years. Anne thought to herself as she unhappily surrendered her control of the situation, trying to stall the inevitable while Dave manhandled her across the barn towards the back. A lump of nervousness welled up inside her when she spotted the dark silhouette of her new ranch hand lazily leaning in the doorway, leisurely watching the entire scene unfold. *GREAT, I'm sure he didn't miss a thing. Damn.*

"Look Anne, you need me to see if this stray of yours is going to bite or it might even have rabies, you never know what you're getting into with these types. I WANT to give you my support and opinion of his character BEFORE things go too far gone and you start having trouble with him."

Anne immediately wanted to sink both feet into the floor like a cartoon character and attempt to drag their approach to a grinding halt. *I am SO mortified that Rick had to witness and listen to our entire conversation. I can't imagine how this is making him feel.* Instead she squared her shoulders, walked swiftly along with Dave across the creaking planks, passing each stall making the horses question their intent and whinny at the disruption. Any threads of pride Anne had, ruptured and then dissipated the second she raised her gaze to see how Rick had thrived their conversation with their approach. To her surprise, Rick seemed unaffected by their negative banter while he leaned negligently in the doorway with a cocky grin spread across his face. A shot of heat went through her the second she reassessed his rugged looks with his long lean muscular frame lounging against the wall dressed in jeans, black shirt, worn plaid flannel, with his dark hair short and disheveled. The dread that began to engulf her about the oncoming confrontation rose a notch, because he looked exactly the way Dave was expecting him to. *He definitely looks a little dangerous.* Anne suddenly realized that she didn't know anything about this man and became slightly embarrassed to mentally admit that she was grateful that Dave had shown up to investigate. She guiltily looked down at the ground, desperately wanting it to open up and swallow her whole to give her salvation as they slowed to a snail's pace in front of Rick. Dave stopped a few feet away and physically puffed out his chest in an effort to intimidate the stranger. He gently disengaged his arm from around Anne's shoulder and turned to softly pat her on the back as if to comfort her.

"Honey...you can just wait right over there for me, this will only take a second." Her startled gaze rocketed to his face, while he arrogantly winked in return and gave her shoulders a quick, supportive squeeze.

Dave pivoted around to size up the opposition, trying to determine how to approach this newcomer. "So -- where did you come from?" The comment seemed like a vague question, that anyone would hospitably ask to someone when they first met. But it was the condescending intonation in his voice that made it obvious that Dave expected Rick's reply, which he was from the slimiest pit of the earth. Dave impatiently cocked an eyebrow and nodded his head as he readily waited for Rick to answer his simple question.

Heat rushed through his body the second Rick's frustration skyrocketed; *Shit, I don't think I've ever felt so low in my entire life...until this moment.* He immediately racked his brain trying to conger up what the whole interrogation was about and why this guy was acting like a spoiled bully in a schoolyard. He slowly raised his hands and rubbed his face trying to wipe out either his frustration or fatigue, as he thought about how to answer the simple question that was suspended in the air. *Well DICK…I'm from one of the most beautiful and prosperous places in the world, the city where you could barely afford to dream, let alone vacation. You idiot! I can't believe someone is actually speaking to me like this. When I am through here, I'm going to come back to this half assed place and show this overstuffed peacock who he's really dealing with, just so he can try to apologize about being such a horses ass.* Rick slowly pushed himself off of the doorway, stood haughtily proud and quietly regarding the other man with obvious aversion. The silence stretched out between them and bore down as if they were two gunslingers waiting for the draw at dawn in the Wild West. "Well…let me think. I've lived here and there. Nowhere that you've ever been to, or ever will…now that I think about it." Rick waited for Dave's response trying to anticipate his next answer.

"Well, now that's peculiar. Folks around here have lived in this area their whole life, proud to have for generations before that. This is a small town, where everyone knows everyone…and everything." Dave turned his head to glance back at Anne for a second and volunteered another friendly wink. Anne's response was to roll her eyes and overwhelming urge to kick the crap out of whatever was lying next to her feet. The second Dave returned his attention back to Rick any sign of friendliness had instantly dissipated from his face while lowered his voice to a death-like whisper. "We don't take too well to strangers around here and I am going to let you in on a couple of things. Keep your nose clean and stick to your own business. I'll be watching you; trust me I'll know what you are doing…before you even think of doing it and I'll be here for Anne, always." Dave raised his voice an octave as he concluded, "So, if you need anything, Anne knows my number. Just have her give me a call and I'll do everything in my power to help you out in any way." At the end of his semi-gallant speech, Dave turned back to Anne and draped his arm protectively around her shoulder while he announced, "At least now I can be confident we all understand where we stand. It's been real nice meeting you…Rich, right?" Before Rick could correct Dave or say anything, he'd turned and started to escort Anne firmly towards the front of the barn.

Rick wanted to punch something, but instead he decided to take the easy way out and aggressively kicked at the ground. *Condescending prick, don't worry about anything there, mister mother-fucker. You're just like a small, yapping dog protecting your territory. Don't worry she's not my type, probably couldn't hold her own with me. I'll be out of here before all of you can blink an eye.* Rick gave the couple's retreating backs a quick single finger salute. *You are sure going to feel stupid once you figure out who I am.*

Anne tried to give a furtive glance over her shoulder while Dave's steel clad hand guided her out the barn door. "Hey Rick, remember we start early around here. There's an alarm clock in the room, its set for 5 am." She attempted at giving him an encouraging smile. "See you in the morning." Rick noncommittally shrugged his shoulders in response and then walked resentfully back into his room. Surveying the tiny room with disgust, he started to undress, and quickly switched off the light on his new jail cell.

Grappling in the dark for the edge of the bed, his thoughts leisurely turned to a typical scene of the sunny beach outside of his California home. Rick closed his eyes while his touch found the edge of the bed and imagined sliding into a lounge chair next to Ava lying seductively with one arm raised above her head like a 60's pin-up girl, waiting for him in a new, crocheted white bikini, holding an icy cold martini, beckoning him with a single finger to come and enjoy the pool. Rick held his breath as he walked over to the edge of the pool and mindlessly dove into the cool, clean water. But instead of being in the pool he ended up on top of the rangiest mattress he had ever slept on in his life. *Well... except for the one I slept on last night.* Closing his eyes tighter, he started to murmur a continuous sentence into the unforgiving darkness, the sound became soothingly rhythmic. *Six to nine months is all I have,* then fell into a fitful asleep.

8

"Good Morning South Puget Sound! It's going to be another typical Washington day...surprise, surprise the forecast calls for intermittent showers and some partial sun breaks. Look...it's going to rain again so just get your hinny movin' this morning! I'm going to send this one out to all of the early birds because the time is hitting 5 am and you're late!! So here comes a little Garth just to get your tail in gear." Rick slowly opened a bleary eye to pinpoint where the persistently annoying voice that was booming from somewhere in the pitch-black room. He rolled onto his side as the first strains to Garth Brooks 'Papa Loved Mama' started to play, moaned loudly and pulled the blanket resentfully over his head. As he blocked out the muffled singing, heaved a sigh of relief and contentedly started to drift back to sleep, a sudden pounding came from outside the room startling him awake.

"What the hell!" Rick swore as he ripped the blanket from off of his head and glared at the blurred light illuminated from around the doorframe that shone like a beacon through the darkness. He strained to hear what was causing all of the commotion while someone quietly murmured undistinguishable words from outside the door. Without another thought, Rick angrily jumped out of bed and stormed across the room to see what was going on. Just as he reached for the doorknob another knock, louder than the last, instantly startled him out of his intended berating. The underlying urgent sound of the rap caused him to pause for a second as he took a deep calming breath before throwing the door open and handing someone their ass.

Standing in the dimly lit entryway was Anne. She looked like crap, as if she'd just rolled out of bed wearing an oversized man's sweatshirt and a pair of baggy sweatpants that had one of the legs tucked into a large pair of black muck boots. Her hair was tied up in a messy knot of top of her head and a large smudge of dirt across her cheek; her overtly expressive eyes became round as saucers when her brain registered what physical condition Rick had answered the door in.

He seemed not to have a stitch of clothing on standing intimately close, until upon wavering expectation she noticed a pair of unbuttoned jeans that were precariously hanging off his hips. His body was just as she suspected it to be; long, lean and bronzed to a deep golden brown. His skin was perfect from his chin all the way down to his hips and a small patch of hair on his chest that lightly traveled in a small trail all the way down to the zipper of his pants. Just inside the edge of his pants there was a long scar that marred his perfect body. *Hmm, wonder where he got that?*

"Well…what do you think? Do you want to stand there to take a picture or just come inside and taste a sample?" Rick leaned slightly forward causing his pants to gape wider, easily exposing more, mockingly stared directly into her eyes and daring her to look.

"Ummmm–, ahhhhh--" Anne coughed uncomfortably as she vainly tried to collect her rambling thoughts while she desperately recited, *damn…now why did I even knock on his door?*

"I know…it's a little early for a little something, but I don't mind if you don't mind, Baby." Rick spiced up his approach while he trailed his fingers down the length of his chest ending below the button of his jeans, then mentally laughed while her naive face turned beet red and she attempted to register everything with her overtly awkward glance. Especially, since she seemed to be having a hard time keeping her curious eyes locked on his, the issue mainly being because they constantly migrated slowly south down following his fingers.

 Anne anxiously bit her lip while an obvious tell-tale blush continued to stain her cheeks, a curse from teenage years that was still extremely embarrassing and causing her to slightly stutter then rambling on like an idiot, fumbling with any decent intention to explain the disturbance. "Oh, I… I…I'm sorry to disturb you. But…but I think I need your help."

When Rick's over-zealous, over-sexed brain finally registered the honest urgency that emitted in the tone of her voice. Immediately his face became a blank canvas, adrenalin instantly surging through his veins as he pushed himself off of the doorway. "What's going on?"

"We have a mare, who's pregnant and having a hard time. It's going to be necessary for you to keep her moving while I make a call for the vet to come in and lend us a hand. I need to have you walk her around the arena while I wait for him." Anne stopped for a second and took a deep breath. Her frightened eyes searched his for a moment, looking for something she didn't expect to find. When his features registered apprehension and he didn't immediately answer, her pride took a back seat to the urgency of the situation as she practically begged. "Look, I really need your help. Are you okay?"

"Okay, okay…sorry. Just…just give me a second to get my clothes on." Rick gave her an unsure, lopsided grin punctuating his hesitant reply and grabbed his jeans up tighter around his waist. Without another thought he quickly started buttoning his jeans, turned into his room to grab his shoes, throw on a shirt and grab the semi-damp flannel coat. Hurrying back into the barn he spotted Anne leading a beautiful, but obviously very pregnancy Palomino around the arena. *Okay remember…this is why you're here. You need to get your head full of this crazy, backwards horse lifestyle.*

He fearfully paused before he entered he arena, doubtfully watching Anne naturally interact with the animal. She quietly coaxed the reluctant, tired horse to follow her with soft murmured words, then when the horse stopped or pulled back on its reins she delicately redirected her and started to walk again.

"Here...let me help you." Rick confidently entered the arena, strode up to the horse and quickly made a grab for the reins. *Shit, this will be a piece of cake. I don't know why she's so touchy about walking some damn pony.* The Palomino instantly reared up its head in protest at the stranger's assertive approach, then it began to violently toss its head back and forth while simultaneously backing away from him. The strength of the horse's instinctive actions pulled Anne's entire body and with its retreat seemed to stretch her arms to the point of making them pop out of their sockets as she desperately tried not to lose control of the reins.

"Watch out!" Anne semi-shouted as the horse whinnied and was still trying to figure out how to allude the stranger. She determinedly held her ground, redirected the horse and gently tried to re-focus its attention back onto her. "Shit. You really don't know what you're doing, do you?" Slowly Anne regained control of the shying horse and began making soothing noises, attempting to calm her down. After a couple of apprehensive minutes the horse seemed less agitated, and Anne angled her aggravated attention back towards Rick. "OK--Lesson 1 – Slow movements around any large animal. The last thing you ever want to do is spook a horse in a small, contained arena, or for that matter in any area. Especially when you don't know what you are doing, this is for both for your safety and the horse's. The last thing I need around here is either a crushed worker or an injured horse."

Anne cautiously walked the horse over to Rick and guided its head gently down to his chest. Rick eyes widened in fear at their approach as he realized how massive its head really was. "Now raise your hand up under her nose and let her smell you so she knows that you're friendly. Remember, no sudden movements, she's typically gentle... but right now, since she's a little on edge from being in pain, I can't guarantee what she's going to do." Nervous heat began to radiate through his neck when Rick raised his shaking hand, unwillingly reached out and placed it directly under the animal's nose. He held his breath while he imagined the horse opening its large mouth, bear its gigantic teeth and take off a couple of his fingers. Sweat started to bead on his upper lip while he apprehensively started to murmur reassuring words to the beast in a soothing tone.

"Ummm-- Nice horsey, pretty horse...I'm going to be your friend." The horse seemed to silently question Nick's sincerity while it regarded him with its large, shimmery eyes then hesitantly bent her head down and brushed her nose across his hand, taking in his scent. Lifting her head slightly and tipping it to the side, she immediately responded by exhaling, forcefully blowing large droplets of liquid, goo and dirt out of her nose that practically covered Rick's hand. *Yuck, disgusting. Shit, I wonder if I'd hurt its feelings if I wiped off all of this snot.*

"Wow…well Rick, seems Bella likes you. Now pet her slowly down her nose, she really enjoys that."
The way that Anne intimately spoke about the horse made Rick turn his head and look at her for a
second. While she stood next to the horse shadowed in the dim light fading down from the rafters, a
serene look passed over her face as she gently stroked the horse. He was immediately struck at how
at ease she was with herself and the unwavering concern she had for the animal. *It seems like the
damn horse actually knows what Anne's saying and with each touch she understands how it feels.*

Any illicit thought flew from his mind when Rick felt the color swiftly drain from his face while
becoming petrified as the horse raised its head and immediately towered over him. For a second he
couldn't think of anything coherently to say or what to do next. The sheer strength of the animal
intimidated him while he tried to figure out what to do in the present situation. Rick glanced around
furtively, trying to figure a way out of touching it, let alone help. *I thought these things were little. Are
you shitting me! And if she thinks that she's going to leave me alone with this thing for one second, her
brain needs to be checked out!*

"Are you okay? Rick is there going to be a 'problem', because I really can't have this kind of 'issue'
right now. This horse needs immediate medical attention and if you can't help I'll try and find
someone who can."

Rick desperately tried to register something witty to say, except his brain was still frozen from his
complete surge of fear. He tried to respond, but found his dry mouth mechanically opened and close,
but nothing came out except some incoherent mutterings.

"Damn it, I'm going to have to call Dave. I hate this shit!" Anne said to herself as she rolled her eyes
and stifled herself from screaming at the rafters. She hesitated embracing a moment of hope and for
a brief second waited for Rick to change his attitude, to attempt to dislodge his head out of his ass.
When he physically refused to budge, Anne solemnly exhaled as the weight of the dire situation
settled completely on her shoulders. Defeated, she turned in disgust, gently tugging on Bella's reins
while she started to coax the horse to lumber towards the outer arena wall.

"Hey, I'm fine," Rick abruptly shook his head and tried to rally, with the simple thought that of all his
hard work for the movie was leaving, harmoniously in time with the sway of the horse's ass, except
his words came out in a juvenile squeak. "Look, I needed a second to wake up. You can't expect
someone just to jump into this situation, without any information and just roll with it. Look, show me
what to do and I'll make sure everything is taken care of while you get the vet." Anne lifted a skeptical
eyebrow and silently regarded Rick for a split second, then gave him a beguiling smile that lit the
room.

"You can't imagine how imperative this is. All you have to do is keep her calm, walk around the arena and…simply keep talking to her. I'll be back before you know it." Anne didn't want to give him a chance of freezing up again so she chanced fate, jammed the reins into his hands and ran. She rushed out of the arena, skidding across the planks and bolted out the barn door. A second after she visually disappeared, Anne poked her head back through the gaping barn door and called out. "Hey, Rick --"

"Yeah?" Rick blew out in an exasperated breath while he eyed the giant horse and attentively touched its nose.

"Ummm…I just wanted to let you know that if Bella freaks out and well, attempts to run…you need to get your ass out of the arena ASAP, just jump the fence and get out of her way. I can't afford to have you all banged up on your first day." Anne gave him a jaunty salute, then magically disappearing and leaving Rick mentally frozen, besides semi-hysterical.

Terrified, he raised his head up to gape at the horse looming above him. Rick searched for some kind of minute thread of confidence, while his brain painfully registered that his face was only mere inches away from the horse's massive mouth. Her huge, misty, brown eyes watched his movements with curiosity and caution as he tried to determine what to do. Rick tentatively reached up and moved his hand down along the length of her soft nose. He watched as her eye turned to liquid, instantly responding to his gentle touch. "So Bella, you…um, come here often?" Rick gazed up into her gentle eyes, his confidence spiraling and making the determination that he was safe from her viciously baring her teeth and doing any damage. "Ha, well I have to admit, that little pick-up line generally works in LA," he chuckled nervously while he gently pulled on her reins and began leading her around the arena at a leisurely stride. "Well, since I have your complete attention and we're in private, what would you say if I told you a huge secret?" Rick glanced covertly around, then proudly tapped his chest and waved his hands trying to silently demonstrate his importance. "I'm a huge celebrity!" Rick paused as he gave Bella another long sweep down her nose causing her head nudged closer to his body. He smiled up at her open acceptance of his presence and reassuringly stroked her again. "I know! Can you believe it? A famous movie star…stuck in a shitty place like this. Trust me, I can't even believe I'm here either, shaved head and all because of some asinine idea my manager has so I can make it big! Like BIG- BIG, not just big." Her huge body knocked slightly into him causing him to stumble, losing his footing for a second. "Hey, you're pretty sick aren't you? Well, let's start walking around and get you moving like the Dragon Lady commanded." Rick turned and started to guide the horse back around the arena, the entire time he explained the curious situation of how he ended up in such an ass backwards place. Every so often Bella would snort, whinny or make some kind of "horsey" sound as if agreeing with Rick's ongoing monolog and Bruce Springsteen's 'I'm on Fire' floated softly in the back ground. He began to genuine relax while describing his beautiful home, the beaches of California, his amazing cars and all of the extreme excess of his glamorous life that he'd

93

left behind. A few times during their walk Bella would pause and act like she couldn't take another step, which triggered Rick into another story about his success, coaxing her to start moving by shaking the reigns gently or softly petting her nose.

"Wow, you must be tired, I wonder how long we've been at this? You sure don't feel well do you, girl?" Rick glanced up and hope coursed in his chest when suddenly headlights shone through the darkness in front of the barn door. The foreign sounds of a car door slamming, anxious voices whispering while shadows approached the barn door instantly became music to Rick's ears. "Here comes the Cavalry, hope that I've helped you out there Baby Doll. Maybe we can get together more after this is all over, but under better conditions. But remember, no talking to anyone...what I told you is our little secret." Rick gave Bella a heartfelt smile and one last lazy rub down her soft nose as the barn doors swung open wider to allow Anne and the vet inside. The two were deep into their conversation about the patient, while quickly maneuvering across the arena to where Rick silently stood.

The Doctor was an older man, who also looked as if he'd also just rolled out of bed. His gray hair was standing on end, shirt half tucked into his checkered pajama pants and he wore identical dirty muck boots.

"Doc Jones, this is Rick Short, our new help here on the ranch." Anne made the quick, but lacking introduction before she strayed over to soothingly pet Bella.

"Nice to meet you, glad we have an extra pair of hands today." The vet gave him a quick, firm handshake.

Rick silently nodded and kept his hand possessively on the horse's flank. "Well we're going to have to check her out. Anne could you assist me as a nurse since you know what I'm looking for...and Rick, I need you to just hold her steady while I'm working." Rick silently nodded in agreement while he protectively took the reins in one hand and began stroking her head with the other. Anne and Dr. Jones started to meander around the horse discussing what was wrong in a clipped, quiet manner. Every once in a while Dr. Jones would place his hands on the horse to feel an area, grunt and then push in to probe. Bella's eyes would get fearful and dart around nervously as Rick held tightly onto the reins. *What is the hell are they doing to this poor animal? It's not like she isn't already uncomfortable and in pain. Shit, I wish they would tell me what is going on.*

Right then he realized Dr. Jones was addressing them as a team and call out, "Okay, I think we'll put her down, get her quiet and see what is going on. Rick...you keep her still while we get her down."

"What?" Rick unintentionally hollered as he quickly glanced around the head of the horse. Anne and Dr. Jones didn't seem to hear him while they talked over the horse's back and slowly made their way towards the back-side of the animal. Rick nervously tightened his hold on the reigns and stroked her head even more. "I don't think I like the sound of all of this. I really don't like that whole 'putting you down' comment he just made," he muttered out of the side of his mouth to Bella as he watched the unsuspecting pair. "I don't trust what those two are up to."

"OK Rick, we're ready. Just start to gently pull on the reins and bring her head down to the ground. That should be able to get her to lower her back for us," Anne called out as she placed her hands on the horse's back and Dr. Jones walked indiscreetly over to a black case that was lying nondescriptly out of the way on the dirt floor. As the latch snapped open to display the plethora of shining utensils placed securely in the case, noticing them made Rick even more agitated. Dr. Jones leaned over and began to meticulously rummage through the depths, as if trying to determine what he needed and retrieve something imperative. Rick skeptically narrowed his eyes but didn't have time to doubt on what the devious doctor was doing because

Anne began insistently instructing him about the task he was supposed to do. Rick absently nodded at Anne while he gently coaxed Bella to lower her head with a few halfhearted pets, as simultaneously Anne guided her with a single hand from behind. Bella began to slowly lower her overtly swollen body thankfully down onto the ground, except the entire time her large soulful eyes locked onto Rick's with unfathomable trust as he murmured soothing praise following Anne's explicit instructions. Amazed, Rick squatted in front of the horse's head while she gracefully lowered her massive body onto the dirt floor. He continued to pet Bella's nose, quietly talking to her while Anne stayed next to her hind quarters and settled to kneeling down on the ground. Rick glanced up the second Dr. Jones approached Bella's rear, with the largest syringe he'd ever seen in his life.

"Hey, what are you going to do with that?" The second Rick deserted Bella's head, the doctor swiftly pierced Bella's flank with the shot punctuating his last word. Bella whinnied startled by the pain, then bolted upright and lunged forward. Her over-powering body fiercely knocked Rick to the side and made him stumble directly into the mud.

Anne rushed over to Rick floundering in the mud, grabbing the collar of his shirt, tugged hard and guided him towards a small door that exited the arena. Standing safely outside the arena's fence, the small group solemnly watched as Bella kicked and raced around the arena.

"What in the hell is this all about? Was that SHOT really necessary and what is going to happen to her? What...what -- are you going to put her down...like dead down?" Rick looked accusingly between Anne and the doctor, defensively crossed his arms across his chest while he fired off the myriad of questions, squared his shoulders preparing for battle and standing like a tall sentinel, feeling as if he was the only advocate for Bella.

Anne rolled her eyes, cast an apologetic glance over at Dr. Jones who merely shrugged his shoulders and then they mutually regarded Rick's indignant stance with a common understanding. Irritated by his opposition, she huffed out a disinterested breath then turned back to evaluate Bella, allowing some time for Rick to cool down and make sure the horse wasn't going to injure herself. As Bella slowed down into a light trot around the arena, Anne exasperated returned her attention to Rick, she felt sleep deprived but ready to answer his inane questions. With a cocky look Anne barely acknowledged his heated stare while he tried to burn a hole through the side of her head and simply returned his attitude with a droll, withering glance.

"Bella's at the end of her pregnancy and is having complications. We think the baby's breech. We gave her a sedative so she'll be calm while we continue with our evaluation, which will make everything extremely easier for all of us. Hopefully we've caught this complication early on and can help her…and no, we aren't putting her 'dead down'…that would be stupid." With an arrogant cock of her head, Anne aggressively pushed opened the arena's gate and walked back into the arena with a noticeable lack of humor at their immediate situation. With each of her deliberate steps, Rick realized that Bella was slowing down, groggy and coming to a staggering halt in front of Anne while she instinctively placed a comforting hand on the animal.

"Ahem, you might want to go out there and give her a hand, Son. She'll need it to lay Bella… down without any injury." Dr. Jones nodded towards where Anne stood with the wavering horse.

Shit…I feel like a complete ass. Rick quickly made his way through the arena's door and over to Anne's side. She was delicately holding Bella's head, stroking her nose and whispering words of gentle reassurance. As she stole a sideways glance at Rick's deliberate approach she gave him a nod of gratitude and whispered, "Just try to make her comfortable while we secure her safely on the floor." Rick found his resolution and followed each instruction implicitly while Anne explained how to handle the large tranquilized animal. Slowly they were able to get the giant body down comfortably to the ground without any complications.

"So you're having a bit of a time with your babe. You'll be okay, I promise." Rick quietly whispered once she was safely lying on the ground, stroking Bella's soft nose as her eyes turned more liquid and fluttered closed as Dr. Jones approached with his ominous bag. For the next few hours Rick sat quietly as Anne and the doctor underwent the enormous, ordeal of examining her.

***

After the doctor left in unison with the ebbing, dismal gray afternoon, the remainder of the day became a huge reality check while Rick tried to accomplish everything on his daily list of chores. The stress from being abruptly woken up and dealing with Bella's dilemma had squelched most of his energy for the entire day, let alone the week.

As evening descended, Anne found Rick standing, exhaustedly staring into an imaginary void in front of a stall with a neglected shovel in his hand and gazing blankly at the disgusting interior. For a handful of undeterminable minutes, he'd unbelievingly been stretching his mental capacity, attempting to get some sort of resolve and physical tenacity...to actually shovel real shit.

"Hey...how is it going?" Anne said while she leaned over the fence causing Rick to jump, completely startled out of his dilemma by her interruption.

"Ummm...I --" His tongue became awkwardly tied while he watched her open the arena gate, unseeingly switch on the radio and casually inspect the first of many stalls. With each of her approaching steps he worriedly glanced down the barn assessing every ignored stall. *Shit, I haven't gotten anything done.*

"These should have been cleaned out hours ago...that is, if you're going to accomplish everything else by the end of the day," Anne glanced down at her watch and noticed the time. "Well, I don't think you're going to get all of this done by yourself. I going to go, grab the extra shovel and help you out."

Anne disappeared around the corner the second Bruno Mars's 'Locked out of Heaven' started playing and came back with a wheelbarrow with another shovel lying inside. She aggressively maneuvered across the raised planks, then parked it between the two of them with a loud thud. Without another word she grabbed the shovel, walked over to the stall next to his, started whistling in time with the song and began to shovel out the mixture of old hay with horse manure.

Rick stood completely still while his mouth began to fill with saliva at the disgusting thought of having to replicate her actions. With a semi-deep breath, he channeled all of his courage, clenched the shovel and walked into the empty stall. Bending over he found himself faltering while the sound of the metal scraping the mixture began to seep into his brain. As he scooped up the first oozing load that seemed to uncontrollably wobble and move away from the edge, his eyes began to water, mouth went dry and stomach did a reverse flip from the stench.

"This wouldn't be so bad if I'd had a little help from Beth, but it seems like she's either absent most of the day or lounging in front of the TV," Anne's disembodied voice mumbled from somewhere behind the wooden slats of the stall.

"Um, who's Beth?" Rick tried to redirect his mind with the simple question, simply because he was trying not to vomit and make a bigger mess than the one he was working with.

"Oh yeah, you haven't met my sister. Beth is the quintessential teenager who is totally absorbed in herself and is noticeably unavailable, or unreliable when it comes time to do work of any kind." Anne ended the sentence with a thoughtful chuckle. "Ooohhh--, I'm sure you'll meet her, and her BFF Suzie soon enough."

"BFF?"

"That means best friends forever, you'll have to get used to the abbreviations and lingo that comes out of her mouth sometimes."

"Hmm --" Rick gingerly scooped up the remaining goopy hay and quickly placed it in the wheelbarrow.

Anne leaned across the opening of his stall and surveyed his job while casually leaning on her shovel. "Hey, not too bad, now we only have 5 more to do." Rick let out a loud groan, hilariously emulating the noise that sounded exactly like a spoiled teen. "What the--. Aw…man, you've got to be joking!"

"Shit, you sound exactly like Beth." Anne shook her head, smiling at his discomfort and understandably waved him off. "You've probably had enough for your first day. I'll get the rest of the stalls and close up, just make sure you're on time for tomorrow. I can't be picking everything up after you all of the time; I've got my own responsibilities that I've got to tend to, so you can't be slacking tomorrow."

Uncertainty racked his back as Rick narrowed his eyes and instantly wanted to hit her in the side of the head with the flat side of his shovel. But instantly squished the inane idea, resolving to take the higher ground by gently setting the weapon on the stall wall, concurrently weaved his way away from the unwanted work and steadily towards his room. *Better leave before the Dragon Lady changes her freaking mind.* He tried not to consider the unappealing idea of his cramped dwelling as he slammed the door, inadvertently without chancing to glance back and find her speculating upon his hasty retreat.

"Ahhh --" Rick contentedly sighed with relief while immediately shrugging out of his grotesquely dirty shirt and hurriedly crossed the miniscule room to turn on the shower. He paused a moment after he walked into the bathroom, had unbuttoned his pants and leaned in to turn on the tap because he'd heard an odd sound.

"What the hell?" He hesitated for a second and listened. Suddenly he recognized the acute sound of muffled feminine voices that were snickering, attempting to contain their giggling, soft whispering.

Ignoring the wanted invitation of the running water, he nonchalantly whipped around, retraced his path into the tiny room and grabbed an unused towel. *Hmmm, let's see what will happen...especially if my suspicions are correct.* Turning towards the interior of his 'bedroom' he sensuously raised the towel high above his head, allowing his jeans to drop an inch lower and stretched into a sexy yoga pose. The giggling intensified while a distinct female voice cautiously hushed causing the noise immediately diminished.

At that exact moment Rick's stealth-like searching gaze spotted a small hole, bored in the wall next to the refrigerator. He knowingly glared at the hole, stormed across the room, throwing the door open and causing an unnatural resounding slam.

"What the..." Across the barn, Anne physically jumped at the unexpected loud commotion that interrupted P!nk's 'Just Give Me a Reason' and turned around to see what was going on.

"Hey, hey Anne -- I think I know where your errant sister has been hiding, and more than likely co-hearts with her friend...or should I say BFF."

Instantly confused at his aggressive attitude, Anne momentarily lifted her head and a questioning brow at his errant comment until he empathetically pointed in the direction of his vacated room.

The sounds of clamoring, bumping and outrageous giggling seeped from somewhere outside the walls of the barn. She unbelievingly followed his condemning finger towards the back end of his room, when mysteriously two silhouettes caught her peripheral view, humorously running through the corral trying to escape from being apprehended in the barn and bunglingly made their way to the house, seemingly unnoticed by a very aware Rick.

"I'm sooo sorry...um...I'll...I...I can handle this -- don't you worry this won't happen again!" Anne's voice became horse while she found herself instinctively appreciating his half naked appearance, her eyes ran down his lean body mesmerized by each inch and ended only by the opening of his jeans that completely exposed a slight trail of shadow ending where her mind furtively wanted to go.

"Yeah, well... you better do something about those girls...or next time they might see a lot MORE than just this." Rick made a sweeping gesture towards his gaping pants, tight abs, bare naked chest and sexily disheveled state, making his jeans drop lower.

"I...I...um --"Anne's voice embarrassingly cracked before she swallowed the large lump in her throat, while instantly her mouth went dry from the simple sight of his toned, tanned body that was invitingly exposed underneath his jeans. "You know...Rick. I'll get right on that." She blushed furiously at the unintended innuendo stumbled out of her mouth, but obvious double meaning of her comment instantaneously registered in his mind.

"Right –"Rick condescendingly mocked back while exaggeratedly lifting a brow. "Yeah...you know what...I'm not so sure you can handle of this right now. Huh!" At the end of his diatribe Rick punctuated with a huff, then primly yanked up his jeans, turned on a heel to angrily stride back into his room, continuously tugging on his errant pants that hung precariously off his hips and slammed the door.

Anne bit her lip to contain a bark of a laugh at his outrageous assumption. Glaring out the open night at her invisible sister, she ran a tired forearm across her forehead before throwing down the shovel to scamper across the uneven planks, switched off the radio and lights then paused with the broken barn door. Frustrated because the latch had yet again decided to take a couple times to dislodge allowing it to heave closed, the entire time her mind kept reverting back to daydream on how good Rick's body looked. The second the latch decided to click, she quickly swiveled around and started to hurry her way towards the house listening to the rapid crunch of her shoes. *Damn, Beth and Susie!! What the hell did I get myself into!! And why does he have to look like Adonis with a hot 5 o'clock shadow? Why couldn't he look more like someone, I don't know like...like Pee-wee Herman??!*

9

Days later Rick found himself clutching the errant wheel of his truck tightly, slowly steering through the ancient town through the continuous vibration, focusing to mentally intent on remembering where Anne had off handedly described the location of the Local Feed Store. *It hasn't helped that the weather's turned worse and now isn't just a mass of rain, but now freakin' blustery wind storm.*

Earlier he found that the attempt to simply leave the house, the weather had turned so angry that he was barely able to pull his coat tightly against his chest, sprinting across the yard to hurdle into his truck. Unbelievably sitting in the cab he shook off the water dripping down his face, reminiscing about being trapped in the elements while he managed to close the barn door, feeling like he'd taken a shower...*with all my clothes on.* He shivered at the memory while the wetness seeped further through to penetrate against his skin. *I should've paid more attention when Anne drove me through town the other day.* He pulled the truck to a shuttering stop at a red light and pondered about the previous day.

With the trucks wipers slapping in time with Mona's 'Lean into the Fall', Anne had valiantly tried to maintain a jovial disposition and gave him the grand tour of the single street that made Westport a town. He couldn't recall what exactly set her off, either the stress of Bella's complications, Beth's teen absentness, or his continued mumbled, degrading comments on anything and everything.

When they finally pulled back up in front of the house she grumpily slammed the door and stormed down the houses path, ominously mute. Right then Rick resolved to take the higher road by keeping out of her way, effectively accomplishing every job, reevaluating his cramped room and moved the refrigerator to cover the peep hole, anticipating another voyeur-ish attempt. Embracing his decisions by the morning, while rearranging the tack closet, a very militant Dragon Lady swooped into the barn and delivered a stilted, verbal inventory of all the projects he needed to accomplish for the day.

"Look, between mucking the stalls and feeding the horses, the most important thing that you need to do is run into Westport and pick up some supplies at the Local." He'd barely had the chance to nod his head in agreement, before she turned on her heel, openly ignoring his comment and made her way haughtily barn. *That's fine with me... this errand is going to get me out of her hair, that barn and shoveling shit for the rest of the afternoon.*

Rick's thoughts quickly flooded back to the task at hand when he noticed the beat up sign indicating that the Local Feed Store on the corner and pointed the truck in the general direction of the parking lot. He indifferently parked the shuttering truck haphazardly at the front of the lot, turning off the engine, bundled up his coat and ran for the front door.

Sprinting through the downpour, he blindly ran for the front of the building, the second he approached the building the ancient door crashed open, making him accidentally burst into the store and become engulfed by the welcoming warmth from the interior.

The store seemed oddly darker than outside with its dated wood paneled walls, ancient lighting and beamed ceiling. The interior reminded Rick of an enormous trade store from some scene out of a classic Wild West movie. He automatically paused to euphorically utilize the benefit from the sudden heat, while nonchalantly shaking the rain off his coat and meandering over to grab a cart. Rick paused a second to pull Anne's sacred, crumpled list from his back jeans pocket, instantly feeling an out of body sensation, and realizing that someone was openly staring at him from behind the checkout counter.

Trying to attempt an evasive demeanor he began to push the cart while it uncontrollably veered right, he man handled it up adjacent to the check- out counter, nodded casually in the general direction of the woman and undeterminably headed deeper into the depths of the ancient store.

Rick chanced a sneaky look over his shoulder, realized that she was keeping a creepy but interested stare on him actions while he maneuvered out of sight. Rick felt a slight shiver of apprehension race down his spine while he pondered the extreme oddities of the locals in town. *I wonder if everyone's lost their minds, probably been on the Discovery Channel as some suspicious town that's been nuclear contaminated, zombies or hiding aliens. I should've watched more mindless TV.*

Exasperated after an hour of meandering, Rick glanced around to reassess his bearings trying to determine where the last item on his list was located. *It's taking a lot longer than I expected to figure out the layout of the store... Anne's going to be pissed. Well, hell. I can't see shit in here; maybe I should let that lady know that they've invented electricity.* Rick swung the cart only to realize that he'd been turned around and unknowingly been standing with the last item tucked behind him. Irritated he snatched the item, threw the packaged vitamin drops into the cart and resumed to trek back towards the counter. As the interiors darkness receded, he found himself approaching the front of the store and suddenly realizing that he felt nervous about meeting someone else from town.

He took a deep breath and mentally registered an average looking, middle-aged woman perched behind the counter...*Weird, I kind of feel like she's been watching me like a hawk.*

Rick tentatively approached the counter with the agonizingly, veering cart and noticed that music seemed to be coming from a tiny radio perched behind her and became uncannily louder with each step. By the time he saddled the cart up bumping against the counter, he recognized the song finishing was Justin Timberlake's 'Sexy Back', recalling his audacious evening at the Oscars and chuckled. *Ha, what a great night, but such a fitting song for such a typical woman in a small town. I bet this tune gets her going in the heat of the moment...if that ever happens.* Smiling he shook his head and enjoyed the thought about the thousands of women, exactly like her demographics that he'd met throughout his career. Typically they were a certain genre of woman that seemed to brazenly embracing their power by defying time and relishing in their open sexual awareness, inappropriate clothes and amazing ability to camouflage their age with an exquisite makeup application. *In California's terms a woman like her would be more like a Saber Tooth, and not a Cougar...even though she'd like to think she is. Damn, when I get back, I need to appreciate how the ladies down south maintain themselves, they would so chew her up and spit her out...and I bet she's probably not even 50 yet.*

 Rick's thoughts became lost for a brief humoring moments while he unloaded the purchases onto the counter and then realized he was humming a few bars along with the next song, Pearl Jam's "Elderly Woman behind the Counter". *Ha, it must be purely coincidental that the song started while I'm paying a silent homage to each and every one of these aging gals.*

Rick continued to toss all of the items onto the counter until he had to lean farther into the cart, grabbing the last item that had been awkwardly lodged in the back. Realizing that his shirt had slid up along his back, he suddenly felt the hairs on the back of his neck stand up and realized the woman had resumed her open, sexual appraisal of his body. As he instantly straightened from bending over the cart, uncomfortably tugging down his shirt and noticed that she sat smiling like a cat, saucily throwing out a hip, attempting to place a hand suggestively lower on it. The scene was perfectly paired with the invitation in her eyes and the odd, rhythmic snapping of her gum in time with Lenny Kravitz's 'Are You Gonna Go My Way.'

"Hi. What an amazing day, hmm --" Her eyes instantly danced, enjoying eating up the entire length of his body while she completely ignored the large pile of items on the conveyer belt. She sensually balanced the scanner with a single finger, while giving him her best coy smile. "So--." Her voice lowered an octave as she leaned slightly towards Rick attempting to display some cleavage and asked in a husky voice, "How are YOU doing?"

"Um, WOW, just fine...thanks." Rick's voice cracked like a 14-year-old's as he shifted uncomfortably under her unflinching observation. The look that continually crossed her face was the combination of blatant ecstasy with her acute imagination of peeling off every stitch of his clothing with her teeth and calculating how much room was available on the cluttered break room table.

"Well, well…just passing through?" She practically purred, as she casually began to uninterestedly and completely unhurriedly scan each of his items.

"No, ma'am -- Actually, I'm the new guy in town." Rick initiated an introduction by extending his hand across the counter. Lois' eyes gleamed with unrepressed interest as she fumbled to try to tug the scanner back from the belt, catching her arm in the cord and tried to semi-graciously accept his hand. She momentarily paused, embarrassed by having to struggle with the ancient cord as it caught uncomfortably against her hip and squished between the register. Rick watched her curiosity as her frustration continuously peaked while she attempted to save her pride and giddily ogle the hot stranger standing in front of her.

"Nice to meet you…I, I'm, um, Rick Short. I'll be helping up at the ranch and um, giving Anne a hand for a while." Rick instinctively thrust his hand out, attempting to bridge the awkward gap.

Instantly at the revelation of his introduction, Lois' languid, almost yearning hand abruptly froze in mid-air by the end of his fumbling lame explanation. An inquisitive arced penciled in eyebrow shot up with his answer, until it magically disappeared under her bangs, all the while seeing repulsed by pulling her hand back and rudely refusing to touch him. Lois keenly narrowed her eyes while reassessing his demeanor, abruptly turned her back on him to lower the volume on the radio and swiveled to completely ignore his piled up purchases.

"Really--." Lois dejectedly murmured through tense white lips and then with a flip of an invisible switch, indifferently continued to wield her scanner and began to silently ring up his items.

Confused by her complete change of attitude, Rick sucked in a hesitant breath as he realized that her demeanor had switched from frothing hot lava to frigid ice queen in a matter of seconds, merely by the mention of his name and employment at Anne's. Their battle of silence stretched out uncomfortably while she continued to ignore him, while the only sound disrupting the environment was the continuous beeping from the scanner and he allowed his extended hand fall back to his side, unaccepted.

"Sooo…how do you like it up at the big house?" The loud snap of her gum punctuated her question as she rummaged through a booklet, as she intently searched for a missing price.

"Fine…um, thanks." Rick felt like he was strategically circling a rattlesnake, but in bare feet as he tried to anticipate her next round of questions. *Damn it, I know she isn't finished with me just yet.* "Oh, I almost forgot. Anne mentioned that she'd called in an order of feed and hay."

"OH, that's right – Rod, right? If you'll excuse me for a second." Lois rudely turned her back on Rick as she picked up the ancient microphone and practically yelled into it. "Hey there Chuck, I need to see if that call in order is ready yet." Silence waivered as they uncomfortably waited for the invisible Chuck's reply, Lois continued to blatantly display her disapproving back and moved to crank up the radio as Lady Gaga's "You & I" began to play. She took the opportunity to critically eyeballed Rick for a few seconds, before she grabbed the bull by the horns and continued on. "So…where do you come from?"

"Here and there, you know…nowhere in particular." Rick tried to alleviate the uncomfortable situation by giving her a nonchalant shrug of his shoulders, exaggerated wink and humorous chuckle.

"Hmmm. Well, just to let you know, folks around here live a bit quietly, definitely keep to themselves, don't trust just anyone who we don't know and take care of our own. I can't seem to figure out any reason why someone from 'nowhere in particular' needed to come all this way to find work." Lois punctuated her antagonizing tirade with an overtly droll look.

Rick raised a brow silently questioning her open hostility, making Lois happily pop her gum in a perfectly, tactless way to acknowledge that an invisible gauntlet had been down with a vengeance. She crossed her arms defensively, turned to seemingly gaze bored out the window and superiorly waited for his ill equipped answer.

"I've come to notice, that would be the majority of peoples attitude about new comers…actually from experience a few times recently. Look, I'm just here to work for the summer. I don't mean anyone any harm… so don't sweat it, I'll be gone soon enough." Rick desperately tried to defend himself, placate the uppity woman, stem his anger and not intentionally, verbally rip her head off.

"Well, I hope you just take this as some kind of friendly advice, but those girls up there have been through enough for one lifetime. Don't you come waltzing into town and think you're going to mess with them or anybody else, for that matter. People talk, and let me tell you -- I wouldn't be too surprised if the entire town's going to be keep an extremely interested eye on you while you're working …and that's a guarantee."

"Thanks for the warning." Rick tried not to be offended at her barbed warning, all the while remaining ramrod stiff, still too afraid to do or say that would cause retribution. *She still has that aloof disposition like she might, at any second call the police and have me hauled away for nothing, just to prove a point.*

"Hmm, yeah we'll see." Lois narrowed her hawk-like gaze, focusing intently across his face as if she was deconstructing him piece by piece. "Hey, haven't I seen you somewhere before?"

"Nooo--, I really don't think I've ever stepped foot in this town before." Under her scrutiny, Rick uncomfortably tried to turn slightly away without giving her any indication about his sudden apprehension at her appraisal.

"Yeah...I feel like there's something that I recognize about you. I never forget a face." Lois leaned back for a second and rubbed her chin as her mind visibly whipped through its vast index.

Rick held his breath in trepidation while the Eagles began to play Tequila Sunrise' over the radio.

Lois took a second and tapped her lips, "Have you ever been on TV?"

Rick's mouth went dry as his stomach plummeted to his feet, while his hands began feel clammy. He nervously shifted his stance and began to perspire under her intense scrutiny while she unnervingly reassessed him with her hawk like eyes. *Shit! If this bitch figures out who I am, I'm dead! She's going to blow everything. Damn it all to Hell!*

"Nooo--. Ha-ha...me? I don't believe I've ever been on TV; at least not in the past few days." Rick gave her a quirky, lighthearted smile that gently creased his face while he tried to keep his movements casual as he began to walk over to claim the cart. He maintained his composure as he casually walked around and offhandedly tried make sure all of his purchases were securely positioned inside.

Suddenly the stressed moment was broken by the scratchy, static infused sound from the microphone connection and a low male voice emitted over the speaker, "Yeah Lois, I've got Anne's load waiting for to pick up back here."

"Humph...OK, Chuck...thanks." Without another thought Lois arrogantly finished ringing up the purchases, grabbed the black charge book and stoically slid it across the counter towards him. Rick noticed the tension in her unwaveringly tight grip as he tried to pry it away from her claw-like fingers to sign it. He wanted to glare back at her and blow out a frustrated breath once he manhandled the book away from Lois, while images of leaning across the counter to give her a Judo chop to the side of her neck floated through his thoughts. Emotionless at the woman's control freakish attitude, he efficiently scribbled his name, closed it with a snap and reassuringly slid it back to her. *Give me a break; the old bat is acting like I'm going to run out the front door with a stupid charge book, idiot.* He impatiently waited for her to give him the carbon copy of the receipt for the pick-up, which Lois held hostage between two fingers as she attempted to give him physical damage, eyeing him one last time with a malicious demeanor. She shifted slightly forward to ungraciously extend the slip, practically waving it in front of his face, until he reached for it and at the last second irritatingly pulled it back.

That's when her face became a frightening mask of distrust and she leaned forward to whisper in a shrewd voice, "Don't forget Rick Short, I never forget a face. I promise... I'll figure out where I know you from, I'm hoping more sooner than later."

Aggravated by her hostility, Rick snatched the slip from her grasp, rushed over to push the cart out of the store and the second the ancient door slowly opened he heard Lois murmur in a loud, distinctive voice, like throwing stones towards his retreating back. "Well, well...Looks like I'll be catching up on Crime Stoppers, Local News and Cops every night on TV from here on out."

 Rick took a deep, cleansing breath as he quickly darted through the rain, trying to calm down before he stormed back and gave Lois a piece of his mind. He threw the purchases onto the passenger seat, ran the cart back vacating it outside the front of the store and cranked on the truck. As it sputtered to life he distractedly followed a faded sign indicating to the back of the store where the loading dock was located. *Fucking hag, probably can't even wipe her own ass. Who does she think she is anyway?* He carefully rounded the corner until he saw the loading dock, backed the truck up to the edge of the platform and jumped out. Rick ran up through the rain to hurdle up onto the solid concrete platform. He searched around the darkened area for a second and finally noticed the shadowy form of a tall, gangly, older man standing at the end of the platform talking on an old phone connected to the wall. *Let me guess, my money's on the obvious who's on the opposite end of the receiver, it couldn't be anyone but the annoyingly nosey Lois.* Rick defensively crossed his arms against the freezing rain while it blew its way under the overhang and coated his body while he waited patiently for the man to hang up. He let out a dismissive sigh when he realized the other man kept continually pausing on the phone to agree about the invisible person's extensive negative appraisals of the newcomer. Rick was about to lose his temper when Chuck just grunted something into the receiver, hung up the phone and ambled over towards Rick, seemingly at the pace of a wounded banana slug.

"You here for Anne's call in?" Chuck mumbled over the sound of the rain pelting against the side of the building and tin roof.

"Yeah," Rick said through gritted teeth as his body distinctively shivered from the cold.

"Over there." Chuck gave his head a slight nod in a very general direction, turned and began to able back towards the interior of the building where it was warm and dry.

Rick figured out what exactly he was supposed to pick up after a couple of quipped questions about where everything was and what he had to do. Chuck response had been only a few short grunts for direction, dismissive hand waving and exasperated sighs; giving every indication that he was absolutely, a man of minimal words.

In mild desperation to leave the vicinity, Rick shot around the platform searching for each item, responding to each movement with lightning finesse. Soon the supplies were completely loaded in the bed of the truck, which left a sopping wet Rick panting from overexertion, racking his brain wondering if he'd forgot anything.

Opening the door to his truck he turned to give Chuck a quick indifferent wave, but found him standing eerily silent, arms crossed, and leaning against the wall of the store tucked out of the rain. Rick's hand hung in midair as he paused, registering the strangest feeling, that he was being critically observed and evaluated. *Creepy...he kind of reminds me of a prison guard watching over his inmate.* Without another thought Rick decided to throw Chuck a very formal, militant salute, jumped into the truck and cautiously made his way out of the potholed parking lot. Just as he was about to turn onto the main drag, AC-DC's 'Back in Black' began to play. Without a backwards glance at the Local Feed Store he cranked the volume, gunned the truck and skidded out on the slick pavement. Rick felt a lighthearted surge in his chest, while the he bumbling sang along with the song, flipped the bird to the crazy people in the store and gunned his truck through the rain back towards the ranch.

10

Incensed Anne paced desperately in front of the half closed barn door, continuously throwing an anxious glance back over her shoulder into the lit up building. Her nerves had erupted into shreds hours before when she frantically scoured the house trying to find Beth and realized that once again, *she's infamously come up missing during another critical situation.*

"Argh --" Anne wanted to scream and hit something because she felt completely bookended, *between a situation that I never wanted and my moral responsibilities.* Chills raked her spin momentarily as a strange moaning noise resounded from the darkened arena and shattered the silence that had enveloped the barn. Anne closed her eyes, attempted to clear her angry thoughts and mentally prayed for strength from anywhere in the universe that was possibly listening.

Instantly her eyes popped open as she recognized the distant rumbling of Rick's truck, as it laboriously made its way sputtering up the hill in front of the house. Anne wanted to burst into tears as she spun around, grabbed the barn door and struggled to push it open enough to allow her to stand in the frame. Her frame disrupted the light flowing from the interior of the barn, creating a shadowy triangle of darkness across the slickened mud lake formed by the constant rain. Anxiously Anne watched as the headlights rose over the hill, then as he slowed the truck down enough to carefully maneuver around the drive and continue on towards the barn. Abruptly the truck made a hesitant U-turn while he slowly backed up the bed towards the opened barn door.

Counting the desperate seconds ticking by, once she was certain that Rick was finished with his elite parking job, she ducked her head into the hood of her slicker and made her way carefully towards the cab. As she felt the slimy mud encase her boots, she made her way directly to the cab and rapidly tapped her hand against the foggy window right before he opened the door.

"Where have you been?" Anne desperately tried to contain her tone from screaming at him, by asking the innocent question through her clenched teeth.

"Um, I don't know. Maybe I went into town to purchase everything you instructed me to get." Rick's mind angrily reeled as any reign on his defenses gave way, making him want to unleash all of his pent up frustration from the feed store and verbally punish Anne.

Anne's anger dissipated abruptly as she took a second to search his angry face while the rain flowed over hers. "I tried your number, you didn't answer. Why do you even have a phone if you're not going to answer it?"

Rick guiltily hedged his answer around her question, "I don't usually have my phone on me. It's mainly for, um, other emergencies. Besides that, it's none of your business. What's got your panties in a bunch?"

"Well, we've… I mean I've got an emergency." Anne hurriedly tried to explain as she motioned for Rick to follow her inside the barn. With each step Anne's agitation resurfaced to a boil as she tried to remain calm and inform Rick the gravity of her predicament. "Beth disappeared again, I couldn't get a hold of you, the line at the store was busy and Bella went into advanced stages of labor. I've called the vet and he's indisposed for the evening." While they entered the barn a strange un-human noise met the couple, causing them to pause in unison. Anne's breathing started to sound like she was on the brink of hyperventilating, while she began to pace besides the stalls and threw up her hands in defeat. "I've never done this before by myself and need help! I can't believe this shit, I don't think I can do this!"

Rick quickly placed his body in front of her path imitating a human road block, frantically waved his hands in front of her face as he tried to redirect her desperate rambling. "Hold on, you need to calm down." He laid a gentle hand on her shoulder and gave it a supportive squeeze. "Just breathe for a second. I'm here, it can't be that bad. Let's go and take a look. You never know, you might just trust that I might be able to help."

Anne gave him an indecisive look, released her breath and then abruptly rolled her eyes to the heavens. "I can't believe I'm saying this…but I should go and call Dave."

Completely ignoring Rick's offer, she abruptly pulled away from his grasp and began to make her way to the back of the barn where the phone was located. With each step Anne tried to instantly wipe everything out of her mind, including her pride and mentally prepared herself to accept or initiate anything from Dave. *I can't believe that I'm doing this, but I'd do ANYTHING right now just for some kind of cohesive help, even freakin' go out with him again or…whatever.*

"Yikes!" A startled squeak slipped out of her mouth the moment she felt Rick grab her arm and forcefully turn her around. Her startled eyes leapt up to his as she tried to steady her balance and unconsciously braced her hands against his chest. Shocked by his actions, she was overwhelmed by the warmth of his body, especially when a jolt of electricity emitted through her hands.

"Look, I realize you're in a sticky predicament. But you need to lighten up for once. Shit, with the way you wield your independence, waltzing around here like no one else can do anything, it's no wonder you're finding yourself continually abandoned and trying to make this whole thing work by yourself. Anne...I'm here, trust me...I can help."

Anne assertively opened her mouth to give him a verbal set down about his assumption of her, but found herself biting back a million retorts while the ebbing truth behind his insinuations demolished any of her objections. "Look, I don't have time to sit here and argue. You want to help...fine, let's go."

 A loud painful sound overwhelmed the barn, without a second thought she turned and rushed headlong back into the dark arena. Rick took a second to squeeze his eyes shut knowing; *I've never been in a situation like this. Shit, I don't even know if I want to be here!*

Bella was agonizingly lying on a hastily thrown pile of hay with her distended belly pointed directly up towards the heavens. Anne slowly approached her while watching the beautiful horse go through another hard contraction. She knelt down on one knee so she could manually examine her with her hands and try to figure out how to help.

"Shit." Anne realized that Bella had become more advanced than she had thought. Looking over her shoulder, she glared in the general direction where she'd left Rick standing. "Rick! Damn it...get your ass over here."

Anne un-humorously watched while a wide eyed Rick hesitantly wandered into the arena, fingering his way along the fence while his frightened eyes locked on Bella large body consumed in her plight. The second his feet hit the uneven dirt of the arena, it caused him to slightly stumble forward as the action prompted him to instantly determine to either fall flat on his face or pick up speed to maintain his momentum forward towards Bella. His eyes became larger than saucers, making him look slightly crazy as he scrambled across the dirt and abruptly approached to two of them.

"What...what do I need to do?" He knelt beside Anne, obediently waiting for specific instructions while his horrified gaze never left Bella's swollen body.

"Hey, Rick." Anne found herself laying a comforting hand on his knee to give him a quick, supportive pat. Rick's eyes abruptly disengaged from Bella and locked onto Anne's face with an astounding amount of compassion. He gratefully took her hand in his, caressed it with his thumb and gave it a reassuring squeeze. Anne felt her voice whoosh out in a whisper at his touch. "Just, just make her comfortable and be ready to help me with anything I ask you to do, even if it doesn't make any sense."

"Alright," was all he could say as he squeezed one last time, then left her with a lopsided, boyish grin and obediently made his way up to Bella's head.

Anne felt her stomach do a tiny flip at his smile while she watched him lay a gentle hand compassionately on Bella's nose and begin to speak to her softly. "Good girl, now it's all up to you, Bella." Anne took a deep breath and prepared herself for the grueling amount of time they'd be there delivering the foal.

Countless hours later, Anne tiredly bent over the proud mother as they watched the beautiful foal trying to stand on its own. The only sounds permeating the air were the heavy breathing coming from Bella, the frustrated movements from the baby and soft music coming from the radio. She felt something on her face and realized it was tears of relief. Anne quickly wiped them off in an attempt to regain control and become stoic during the end of an extremely emotional moment.

"Uh-uh...I saw that." Anne startled when she realized that Rick had crept so close to her that he was able to whisper in her ear.

"Oh, well Rick, you can't tell me that this entire experience didn't move you in the least." Anne hurriedly wiped her fingers under each eye to confirm the tears had completely vanished.

"No...well, to be honest it's just nice to see that you have a little tenderness hidden somewhere, Dragon Lady." Rick smirked at her startled look when he reached up and gently wiped away the smudges of dirt she'd unintentionally smeared under her eyes. In the silence she absently recognized the first few notes of Katy Perry's 'The One That Got Away' as it began to play. Anne held her breath while the comforting feeling of his fingers gently traced down her cheeks and began cleaning up the rest of the smudges. She hastily turned away from his touch, embarrassed because of the hot blush that had crept its way up her entire body.

"Um, Rick. Thanks...thanks for everything."

"Hey...no problem." Rick flippantly answered as he silently chastised himself for touching her while he turned back to watch the beautiful pair began interacting together. After a few tranquil moments he felt an odd, cold heaviness on his pants and looked down to assess the damage of his ruined clothes. For a second he tried to identify what all the undeterminable pieces of goo splattered all over him were, but when his mouth began to profusely water and visions of vomiting all over Anne's muck boots rooted in his brain he quickly decided to advert his gaze.

Anne noticed his absolutely dirty clothes, watering eyes, gaunt look and chuckled. "Well, it looks like we'll be going into town sooner than I anticipated."

"Yeah…I think this was my last pair of jeans." Rick held his arms rod-ram stiff out away from his body, attempting not to contaminate anything else by dripping the goo anywhere else. Without another word he began to shuffle away imitating a penguin towards the back of the barn, carefully waddling with each step, warily keeping his appendages apart so he wouldn't feel any goo in the process.

Anne couldn't suppress her laughter and began to wholeheartedly laugh, while she watched his masculine, but obviously uncomfortable form amble awkwardly towards the back of the barn.

Disbelievingly his shrewd attempt at staying 'clean', Anne shook her head at his retreating back and then returned to watching the pair uniting themselves in the arena. A serenely beautiful smile touched her lips, wistfully sighing as she dreamily whispered, "Aren't they a beautiful sight. I can't put my finger on what it is, but…it's just so amazingly beautiful and natural."

Rick abruptly paused in his laborious trek and turned to cast a dumbfound look back at her lounging form. For a split second he felt speechless by her innocent beauty as she inquisitively looked back at him. His ire went up a notch when he realized she was curiously regarding him without inhibitions and shook his head in disgust as he gave her the daftest look imaginable.

"Are you serious? I don't know what on earth you're thinking about, but all of that…" He waved his fingers disgustedly towards the pile of destroyed hay completely covered with the obvious residual of goo from Bella's birth, "and all of this…" Attempting to not think about what was splayed, causing him to momentarily gaping at a loss for words, but instead of pausing he waved more dramatically at the goo covering himself. "First off, watching that whole process was not beautiful, it was downright messy. That would be, in my own particular words, a major source of birth control and every teen should experience watching that. Besides, what that horse just accomplished…sure as hell isn't anything near 'natural'."

Uncontrollably Anne barked out an unfeminine laugh as she watched him succeed in nimbly turning the door knob with his pinky and thumb, barely getting into his room without contaminating anything else with his slime splattered clothes in the process.

Turning to give her one more glare and nudge the door closed on Anne's hysterical laughter. Struggling while it refused to close, Rick held his breath as he tapped the door closed with the tip of his toe to firmly block Anne's laughter and tried not to vomit when he looked down at his clothes. Rick began to desperately search his room for any idea about how to disrobe and mumbled to himself. "Shit…How the hell am I going to get this shit off without throwing up if I touch anything slimy or step in anything on the floor?"

11

The stressful events of the previous evening took its toll, resulting in ravaged nerves, eyes bloodshot and stained, besides a pounding headache the second she tried to wake up the next morning. After stumbling blindly through her daily routine she found herself rushing off in her truck to make the unexpected trip into town, with a disgruntled passenger.

Anne rubbed her aching eyes and blinked rapidly while diligently attempting to focus on the highway, which was becoming more and more difficult as the trucks windshield wipers failed to keep up with the impeding darkness and sheets of rain. The entire world seemed like a dank, watery blur as they sped their way from Westport towards Aberdeen. With the onslaught of miserable weather, a drive that typically should have taken them 45 minutes on a decent day, would now take them well over an hour.

She tried to catch a glimpse of her passenger's face, but in the dim light she could only make out his angry profile, as he seemed completely engrossed with the passing scenery. *This is the exact moment that I wish that I had a new truck with a kick ass radio, so I could crank up my music and not even care who I was offending.* She closed her eyes for a second and summoned a little patience with her passenger, but only for a second, with all of the water on the road it made driving way too treacherous to close her eyes. Lately it seemed like the rain hadn't stopped for days around the area and the landscape was beginning to show signs of its impact. The bogs next to the road had started to overflow all the way to the middle lines of the highway and ocean waves seemed to heave more water over the dunes. It was like driving on top of a Popsicle, with any sudden movement you could feel the wheels start to hydroplane and continue in whatever direction they desired. Anne tried to focus while she thought; *it's probably exactly what kind of evening mom and dad were driving the night of their accident.* Her knuckles grew white from the strain of tightly gripping the wheel as her mind automatically wondered to the day she received the fateful call. *It was a usual day at college hanging out with Kate in the dorm room, discussing what party we were going to attend that evening.*

"Hey Anne, what do you think about slumming over at Greek Row? I heard that the guys are hot and the drinks are strong. It would absolutely be a sure way that the evening will be a success with the men, even if we don't remember it in the morning." Mysteriously Kate had popped her head out of the bathroom seeming completely naked, saved barely covered with a towel. She was an aspiring theater major from Tacoma and with her natural talent, Kate would morph into different characters and at any token place or time that she could share her love of drama, she did. She gracefully stumbled over to the couch where Anne sat reading the last few pages of physics homework, determined to finish by the end of the day, her butt laboriously anchored in the exact same spot. Kate walked seductively over to the other end of the couch, dramatically draped her legs and flawlessly improvising a risqué burlesque performer.

Anne knowingly raised her eyes over her book to gaze at her newfound best friend of all but a handful of months, humorously smiled at Kate and beguilingly batted her lashes, "As I recall -- I really don't think that's the safest combination. I know, let's flip it to the safe and sane side. I was thinking about a nice coffee house where the drinks are hot, the topics strong and the men are weak."

Kate gave Anne her signature disappointed pout, one that she'd perfected and most women would sell their soul to be able to give and then audaciously winked. "Well, how about this...at the party we make your drinks weak to help you get caught up in a hot situation, then when you wake up with a strong guy, you can thank your safe and sane side that you brought some protection!"

At the end of her amusingly insane diatribe Kate leaned forward and wiggled her eyebrows at Anne as she waited for another answer. Surpassed in their battle of wit, Anne simply shook her head while she watched her audacious friend. Kate had tried to get her to go out almost every weekend since they'd started school, each time Anne refused. Unbeknownst to Kate, with every invitation Anne refused, she secretly actually wanted to go but quickly declined without a conducive explanation.

"Ok, ok you jackass...you win, I'll go." Anne had given her irrational fear a lot of thought and decided that the only reason she wasn't going was mainly because she was insecure about herself and how she felt about living in a large city.

"Yeah!!" Kate let out an unpredictable holler that Anne was sure their neighbors would complain about in the morning. "Don't you worry; I'll make sure everything will be alright. But first I'm going to do your makeup and hair, and then we'll worry about what you're going to wear." The telephone started to ring just as Kate finished her excited monolog and began to disappear into her bedroom. "I've got it! I don't want you to have any kind of distractions and use it as an excuse. You keep reading... I don't want anything else on your mind tonight but hot sex, drinks and rock and roll."

It was at that precise moment her memory seemed to slow down as if was trying to process what had happened, simulating a freeze frame film, stilting everything while suspending each moment in midair.

"Hello--," Wiggling her brows at Anne, Kate kicked up her slender leg and saucily answered the phone still wrapped in her towel. "You've reached a couple of lonely luscious babes waiting for a good time."

Instantly the apartment went dead silent for a few token moments, until the slight creak from the couch while she swiveled to look at Anne, captivated by the unknown voice at the other end.

The first odd reaction that caught Anne's attention was the complete anguished look that seemed to wipe out Kate's radiant face and re-sculpted it like a mask shaved out of ice. Suddenly a chill of fear snaked down Anne's spine and she began to hear a soft buzzing sound resounded in her ears, while an enormous sinking pit plummeted into her stomach. Instinctively she dropped her book onto the floor, to bring her knees cathartically up to her chest. She anxiously waited in a fetal position for Kate to nonchalantly dismiss whatever telemarketer was on the phone and return to her mindless primping for the evening. Kate kept regarding her silently while an endless sadness enveloped her eyes.

"It's for you–," Kate seemed to silently float towards Anne with nonexistent steps, her arm raised and the receiver extended out in front of her, as if whatever was on the other end was contagious.

Anne delicately took the receiver, but kept a wary eye on Kate's obsessively wringing hands while she remained hovering nervously over her. "This is Anne, wh-who is it?" Anne timidly asked as the sinking feeling slowly turned into a swirling numbness as her friend pivoted and began earnestly pacing. "Hello?"

"Umm...Anne, this is the Sherriff from Westport Police Department. I hate to be the one to inform you, but a terrible accident happened this evening. There's no easy way to let you know...but your parents were in it and they're both in critical condition at the moment. We need to get you back home."

Anne's eyes swam blurrily as she simply watched the phone fall to the floor in slow motion, while a foreign numbness overcame her fingers and she wasn't able to grip it any longer. It seemed like the receiver simply shattered into a thousand pieces, simultaneously she recognized the distant sound of someone hysterically ranting. That was the moment when her brain registered Kate's firm hands on her shoulders, making all of the numbness melt away and cruel reality came flooding into her consciousness. Through a haze Anne suddenly realized, it was her own voice babbling in an incoherent screech while Kate calmly formulated her departure.

That's the last time I remember seeing Kate, funny she called me after all this time. Anne shook her head trying to clear her mind from venturing back down that dark broken path. She took a deep, cleansing breath, uncomfortably cleared the tightness from her throat, and un- clenched her teeth, racking her brain for some interesting topic of conversation. "Sooo...Nick, I don't really know a lot about you. Um, have you seen any movies lately or enjoyed anything in particular on TV?" Anne tried to seem nonchalant with her delivery, except her voice seemed way too loud and anxious in the tight confines of the cab.

"No, I haven't seen anything currently...kind of been a little busy lately." Nick's sulky answer seemed to ricochet his negativity off the window from across the darkness.

"Oh, yeah -- sorry." Anne suddenly felt guilty for broaching the subject. *Nice one Anne. The guy probably hasn't been able to do anything for years because he's been too broke...or whatever.* Anne guiltily squirmed in her seat as she tried to dig herself out of making him feel like an uncomfortable ass. "Oh, well, I know what you mean about being busy. I usually miss all of the big movies for the year, still end up watching the Oscars and not knowing what all the fuss is about. I've found enjoying music is easier to keep up with, simply because you can have it around you all the time." She motioned to the radio in the truck as if giving a lame example.

"Yeah, so who's your favorite artist at the moment?" Rick decided to throw her a bone, compromise his dour mood by engaging in the discussion.

"Um, P!nk, U2, Chris Isaak, Katy Perry, some country, rock or right now, Brandi Carlisle is the artist that I'm really into, but I'm always switching artists and genres around." Anne turned for a second and asked, "Ever heard of her?"

"Nope."

"Oh, well I happen to have one of her CD's right here. Wanna hear it?" Anne didn't wait for his answer and automatically pushed the CD into the player. "Sorry one of the speakers is out, but the CD still works."

The music was soft and beautiful, but what startled Rick the most was the woman's powerful voice when she began to sing. "Hmm -- nice."

"Yeah, I've really enjoyed her music. She's inspired me, like so many other talented artists. They all start out so young, put themselves out there with their unique ideas, talent and make something out of it all. I think it's amazing and it gives me something to aspire to...that is while I'm figuring out how to run the ranch." Anne bit her lip and felt foolish rambling on while she gave him a sidelong glance. "I bet you didn't know that she's from Washington?" She merely smiled when she saw the negative shake of his head and began to hum in time with 'The Story' while it began to play.

"So, you don't find any movies or anyone out of Hollywood interesting or inspiring?" Rick fished around in his seat and watched her carefully drive the truck.

"No, Beth's the one all wrapped up in the glitz and glamour. If you ask me, I don't think any of them are really that talented. Doesn't take too much talent to frolic around for an afternoon, get paid tons of money to get your hair done, make out, smile and cry on cue. Besides, it seems like they are all so arrogant and stuck on themselves, completely narcissistic...why would anyone want to aspire to be someone who thinks the world revolves around them?"

"Huh...really?" Rick arrogantly drawled as if he took personal offense and didn't enjoy the words sliding off her tongue. For some reason the tone of his voice made Anne unnervingly uncomfortable at her comments and tried to peer through the darkness to determine why Rick sounded so curt.

She abruptly caught herself staring at the back of his head, realizing that he'd reverted back to silently staring out the window and tried to redirect their conversation. "So, did you figure out everything that you'll need in town?"

The only answer that emerged from the direction of her traveling buddy was a not so enthusiastic, "Hmph, yeah I think so."

"Well...I know it's not the big city, but you should find everything that you need. I try to only come out here once or twice a month. So, keep that in mind and stock up on anything you'll need for the time being. Of course if there is an emergency, I'll make an extra trip. But I'll let you know way in advance when I'm going, so you have time to put in your request and let me know if there's anything in particular you need." Absolute silence greeted her attempt at breaking the awkwardness between them. Between Rick and the road, Anne became irritated and mentally exhausted simply shrugged then rolled her eyes. *Shit. You'd think that with his insipid, teenager attitude he was going to be hog tied, flayed alive or getting his teeth pulled. Damn, even Beth is better at doing this than this guy. I really don't see what the big deal is about a quick run to Wal-Mart.*

Anne eased up on the gas as they pulled into the parking lot in front of the store. She slowly drove around the large area and luckily found a decent parking spot that wasn't too far back, credited for the lack of customers on such a miserable day. She shut off the engine, turned to her silent passenger and waited for Rick to say something, except he was still sulkily looking out the window moping.

"Well, I usually don't leave the doors unlocked, but since we won't be shopping in the same departments, I will this time. It'll make it easier to get back. I guess I'll meet you back here in an hour?" Anne tried to prompt him into a better mood.

"OK, whatever." The window became misted by his answer.

118

"Fine--." Anne incredulously found herself snapping back, irritated beyond her normal limits she shoved open the door against a giant gust of wind and rain. Anne pulled her baseball cap securely down over her eyes, slammed the door and ran diligently in between the puddles to the front of the store.

Rick twisted in his seat, silently watching her rain blurred silhouette darting towards the building. He closed his eyes, a feeble attempt to purge his bad mood and started to rub his hands annoyingly across his face. *Well-- Mike, wherever you are… you bastard. I think I could guess exactly what you'd be doing if you were here… either hysterically laughing about this whole thing or choking while I strangle you, enjoying every second.* "Shit, I don't think I've ever stepped foot in a Target let alone Wal-Mart." Rick shrugged deep into his borrowed, bright yellow rain slicker, grabbed the top to cinch it around his face, shoved the door open and made a mad dash out of the truck towards the front of the store.

Feeling the trickling wetness run down his face, he immediately got blinded when he entered by the bright fluorescent lights. For a quick second he stood perfectly still, allowing his eyes to adjust to the interior. Blinking Rick inwardly groaned as an invisible person's muffled voice crackled through an intercom calling for a price check on tampons while eyes began to focus more clearly.

"Welcome to Wal-Mart. Can I help you sir?" The question came from the direction of a woman who was standing next to the door, monitoring the soggy entrance.

"Um, no…no. But thanks anyway." Rick began to scan the interior of the store and hastily spied the men's clothing department. He achingly listened to his shoes squeaking, soaking from the rain as he crossed the entryway and began to maneuver around miscellaneous racks, trying not to attract any attention. He mechanically surveyed the vast mismarked clothing aisles, trying to determine where the women's clothing left off and where men's began. Pacing back and forth in between the racks he started to get a little agitated, suddenly realizing that he was in the middle of the men's section and the obvious lack of selection.

"Hmm," Rick made a peevish voice as he mockingly complained to himself. "Wow…Wranglers or Levis, flannel or thermal, Hanes or Jockey. Shit, with the enormous selections to choose from, I just don't know where to begin." He snatched a few pairs of jeans out of their cubbies, dumped them along with a few shirts in his cart and anxiously scanned the area trying to determine the location of a dressing room. After a few frustrated seconds he noticed a low slung sign with an arrow, surging forward he abruptly parked his cart in an aisle, darted into the first available dressing room and threw the jeans down on the ground.

Shit, this must be the smallest dressing room I've ever been in. He turned around to get his barring while his elbows rubbed against the sides of the white laminate walls. Groaning he grabbed the scruffy blue curtain hanging in the doorway and tried to tug it across the opening. *Of course, the damn curtain is too small to fit the stupid opening.* Rick struggled in the small vicinity while he stubbornly stretched the curtain a hundred different ways, until he fitfully gave up. With a sigh of resignation he left the curtain standing half-mast in the doorway, shrugged his shoulders and started to undress. Distracted by his close confines he carefully tugged off his shirt and fumbled with the buttons on his pants, but the cold air that inadvertently billowed in chilled some part of his constantly exposed body that had found its way outside the curtain, making him extremely aware of his vulnerable position. *My luck...some busy body notice my bare ass sticking out of the curtain.* Deploring the situation Rick sighed and began mumbling to himself, "To think...just last month I was at one of the most exclusive boutiques on Rodeo Drive with my stylist. I think I was there for hours trying to decide what was perfectly hip for my interview with all of the morning talk shows. They served mimosas, hors d'oeuvres and the occasional back rub until we were finished with my purchases. Now I'm in a small, po-dunk town trying on Levis with my frigging ass hanging out of the dressing room."

Rick's ears perked up when he noticed a small feminine cough, accompanied by uncomfortable clearing of another woman's throat, instantly alerted him that he wasn't alone.

"Ah-hum, excuse me...Sir."

Rick instantly paused, frozen in his monolog, the Levis slid partially over his butt, attempting to visualize which part of his body was hanging out of the curtain and apprehensively acknowledged the woman's voice.

"Yes?" Unsure of his exact position, he turned accidentally catching the curtain with his elbow exposing his complete state of undress and embarrassingly realized that the entire store could see inside the dressing room.

Transfixed by his sudden movement the young female worker stood completely dumbfounded while her roaming eyes appreciated every inch of his partial nakedness.

A sudden fear sank to his stomach while he fearfully clutched his gaping jeans, waiting for the moment when the sales woman would unbelievingly point her finger, start hysterically screaming and gushingly ask for his autograph. Since his quick rise to fame, he had found himself stuck in semi-similar situations hundreds of times, but usually dressed.

Rick diligently held his breath and watched the employees frozen demeanor melt, when she felt the female customer physically anxiously grab her shoulder and indulgently hovering at her elbow. With a loud gulp Rick planned his escape route, the entire time preparing to bolt. *Oh shit, I blew it. What am I going to do? Better yet what are they going to do?*

"Um, Sir, this is...uh, the dressing rooms for women." The timid employee tried to assess the situation and uncomfortably diffuse it. "The men's area is on the other side, right around the corner." As the employee politely finished she managed to not crack a grin and pointed a humiliating finger, redirecting the idiot in the correct direction of the men's dressing room.

"Oh, wow...ok" Startled Rick fumbled with keeping his unzipped pants in place while he anxiously grabbed everything, dropping a few items in his haste and started to leave the room. "Ladies, I am so sorry. I didn't realize, that I was in the wrong area." Securely clutching his pants, attempting to make sure they didn't fall off, bumbling with his merchandise he crashed against the wall to ensure a clean departure around the gawking duo and turned to make his way quickly out of the dressing room. Rick had a sick, sinking feeling that any second he'd hear the intercom come on, scratchily asking for help in the dressing area and the threat of security showing up. Distracted with his rambling thoughts Rick ran smack dab into Anne. Shocked by being completely oblivious to his surroundings, he instantly dropped all the armful of items and almost his pants on the floor.

"Hey, do you need any help there...Hot Shot?" Anne mockingly said at his stunned expression, and bent down to retrieve his heap discarded items scattered on the floor. The few seconds it took to have everything tucked away in her arms gave her enough time to realize the awkward predicament she was in, squatting down a hair away from his knees. Anne sucked in her breath when abruptly racking her brain and intently studying his bare feet and nicely manicured toes, trying to find a respectable way to get out of standing up. Gritting her teeth trying to choke back a devilish smile, she slowly raised her head with an unblinking stare, leisurely admired his taunt mid-section and nice tanned skin an inch away from her nose. What seemed like eternity, she finally finished her interesting journey from squatting, caught her tongue achingly between her teeth and then paused pasting an uninterested look on her face to meet his piqued gaze.

"Yeah...seeing that I'm more than partially naked, could you possibly point me in the correct direction of the men's dressing room? I'd really appreciate it," he arrogantly whispered through tightly compressed lips.

"Sure...allow me," Anne jauntily said while she spun around with his heap of clothes tucked in her arms as hostage. Devious thoughts flew through her mind causing Anne to indifferently shrug her shoulders to his blatant haughty attitude, spontaneously deciding to take the long way around and snaked through the racks of women's clothes with unknowing Rick in tow. *Serves you right to be paraded around half naked, since you've been nothing but rude since we left the house.*

Embarrassed Rick clutched his pants, hurried in her wake and ducked his head trying to avoid the curious stares coming from the cluster of females shopping in the surrounding area. He blew out a huge sigh of relief when they made a final turn around a wall and found himself planted in front of the men's dressing rooms.

"Ok, here we are." Anne went into the first stall and set his items on a small stool. Eyeballing the distance between them she shimmied her way awkwardly around trying not to touch his half naked body and gave him a swift, innocent smile, "Hey, I'm all done with my shopping, so I'll wait out here for you until you're finished."

"Oh, you don't have to wait." Rick tried to physically wave her away but instantly realized that if he did his pants would drop dangerously south.

"It's a big store and I don't want to lose you before you're done shopping. It'll be no problem." Anne casually leaned back against the wall and began to examine her nonexistent fingernails.

Rick exasperatedly rolled his eyes as he went in and tried to make the curtain fit across the door, again without success. After a few uncomfortable moments he decided to simply stick with the Levis he was wearing, threw on his old shirt, disgustedly left the dressing room and found Anne lounging against a rack of multicolored T-shirts. He meandered over to her and threw his miniscule purchases into an empty shopping cart that was vacant next to her.

"Is that it? Is that all you're getting?" She vaguely inquired.

"Yeah, something wrong with that?" He bit the inside of his cheek, striving to keep his temper in check and was immediately ready to leave.

"Well, you'll need some more shirts, socks and other personal items. Besides that, you'll need to get your household items and food."

Frustrated at the thought of running into any of the gawkers, Rick sighed and rubbed the back of his neck. "Show me what to get and let's be done with it." Anne quickly directed him to a selection of appropriate clothing for work, barely containing her attention while he chose boxers over briefs, afterwards without another word swept him over to the household and food department. Anne stopped the cart in front of a large expanse of canned food. Rick gave her a preposterous look as she grandly gestured towards the wall of premade food with a sweep of her hand like Vanna White.

"What...is there an issue Rick?" Anne annoyingly replied at his insolent look.

"You're kidding right – Are you expecting me to eat this…ummm… stuff?" Rick disbelievingly scanned the entire length of multicolored cans and boxes stacked neatly on the shelves, he tried to visualize eating what was inside.

"Well, if you could imagine what your work day is going to consist of…every day, you'd be able to figure out, there's not going to be a lot of time to prepare a 'decent' meal. So, canned and frozen items are going to be your best friend when you're in a pinch, which could be…um, every day." Rick refrained from making a rude comment about what she could do with her premade, preservative glutton selections and more importantly uneatable choices. He painfully resolved himself to silently walk up and down the aisle trying to make a selection. "Remember that we try to only come into town once a month so get enough to last you until March," she said with a huge grin knowing that his choice of chili, ravioli, and a bunch of frozen dinners would be less than desirable by the end of the month.

"I can barely think about, let alone be creative with my meals right now. I…ok, let's just get out of here." After he chose a variety of items, hey ambled up to the front of the store so Rick could finish and pay for the merchandise. At the sight of Rick, the extremely attentive cashier suddenly became slower than a snail while scanning his purchases. Rick lost complete interest of the situation and started to casually glance around the store.

Instantly he froze, realizing that they were directly in front of the men's department and realized how he'd gone into the wrong dressing room, inwardly groaning reminiscing about the humiliating moment.

Rick pulled out his wallet as the cashier suggestively mumbled his total, as he turned around he spied the men's dressing room that Anne had embarrassingly redirected him to. Suddenly a realization occurred making him pause in mid swipe of his card, that the men's dressing room was conveniently located directly behind the women's; which obviously wasn't the way she had lead him. She *paraded my indecent ass throughout the entire store*. He swiveled to accusingly glare at Anne. *She'd actually marched me through the entire women's department instead of circling around the corner to the men's dressing room.* Confused Anne followed the direction of his hostile gaze and instantly knew he'd figured out what she had done.

Smiling sheepishly, she casually shrugged her shoulders and pointed a finger at the cash register. "She's ready to cash you out."

Rick opened his mouth to make a crass comment, but decided not to give her the satisfaction. He immediately paid for his items, silently following her back through the rain to the waiting truck and made sure that all his bags were juvenilely stacked into a bulletproof wall in between them on the seat.

At the sound of Anne cranking on the engine Rick heatedly shut the passenger door with a disgusted grunt. She tried to give his profile an amused look as she turned the truck bumpily out onto the road, giddily chuckled at their semi-calculated miss-haps and realized that it was going to be a long, quiet drive through the rain back to the ranch.

12

After the Wal-Mart incident Anne and Rick's relationship continued being strain fully business like, but with a growing mass of tension reverberating between them.

It took several days after their shopping expedition for a silent mutual truce to be acknowledged. Mainly because of the rigorous daily routine they had to accomplish on the ranch was decisively hinged on working together. Except by the end of the fourth week, their dreary nonverbal days seemed to become nonexistent, seamlessly blending into one another.

Rick had become willing to learn the ropes, work with the horses and take over some of the odd jobs left uncompleted, by day's end the amount of work that was finished became a pleasant surprise to Anne. The only insistent problem was the nagging guilt she felt leaving the barn each day. A typical evening Anne found herself trying to keep a balance on the time away from her wayward teenage sister and work. The image of Rick alone fending for himself with canned or frozen food in the dinky room gnawed on her conscious every time the barn door closed.

Alone for a precious moment, Anne paused at a corner of the outdoor arena, leaned against the post to enjoy some stolen time and the weather that surprisingly staying steadily mild for a Northwest spring. The sky was dusted with a few billowing clouds as the sun decided to make its slight presence a slightly longer each day. The trees in the yard were beginning to bud and some of the flower bulbs were making their presence known through the earth. The air had a touch of crispness to it and after a long day cleaning the barn, it was welcomed.

Turning her head towards the back of the barn, Anne noticed a hazy blue light from the TV screen emerging from the doorway at the back of the barn. A slight smile touched her lips as she recalled one of the busiest days post Wal-Mart, when Rick's presence had unexpectedly become accepted and created a comfortable routine.

It was on an unusually early morning when he bumbled into the mudroom on his appointed laundry day. Anne kept herself scarce upstairs while suspiciously listening to him rustle around, awkwardly start the washer, close the lid and immediately leave.

Unable to contain her curiosity Anne crept down the back stairway to see what was going on. The only thing she noticed was a semi-empty hamper on the floor and laundry soap sitting on top of the dryer. Glancing around the room she heaved a huge sigh of relief, dismissing her distrust and mentally reprimanded herself for being too curious. Mentally listing off her errands for the afternoon she hastily grabbed a cup of coffee and got ready to leave before Rick came back to finish his laundry. Sweeping through the kitchen she threw on a coat, slammed the door, jumped into the truck to drive into Westport to order some feed and escape the house for the rest of the day.

Stepping into the house later she was greeted by Beth and Suzie giddily cooking dinner and discussing boys; which lately seemed like the center of their conversations besides beauty, movies and fashion. They finished an enjoyably great meal and immersed themselves in the cleaning up when Anne suddenly realized she hadn't noticed Rick around the yard.

"Hey…have you guys seen Rick around today?" Anne absently asked.

Beth rolled her eyes and placed a sudsy, wet hand on her hip as she retorted, "Well…if you weren't such a slave driver, maybe you'd see more of him. He's probably been passed out in his room all day from being exhausted with what you expect him to do around here. You know, it is his only day off."

"Look, I have him doing the things I need or just can't get to, besides he's never complained." Anne crossed her arms in defense.

"Right, like he'd complain to you. You're an insanely driven workaholic. No one could keep up with your work ethics and expect to live a long, healthy life."

Anne picked up a washrag out of the sink and threw it at her sister's head. Beth let out a loud squeal, grabbed the rag to dart across the room attempting to fling it back in Anne's general direction while Suzie ducked up the back stairs and into the safety of her bedroom.

Anne picked up the wet cloth and tossed it back into the sink, finding herself staring out at the darkened barn. "Maybe you're right, I need to give him a break."

"OMG! I wish I had a recorder, Anne admitting a fault." Beth screeched as the sopping rag landed smack dab on her face.

The next morning Anne enjoyed feeling the sun breaking through the clouds warming her shoulders, breaking into a vivacious hum of Elvis's 'Suspicious Minds' as she made her way towards the barn. Silently squeezing through the slight crack of the door, she aimless wondered around the stalls, thoughtlessly puckered her lips to continue with in a whistling the tune and carefully walked across the planks. Rounding the corner she faltered with the tune as she unexpectedly caught herself appreciating Rick's backside. Anne realized that her pace halted to a silent standstill, enthusiastically continued to enjoy the view, knowing that he was completely unaware of her presence and that half his body was conveniently sticking out from one of the stalls as he diligently mucked it out.

126

"Ah-hum…Hey Rick, I was just thinking," Anne graciously cleared her throat to give him a moment to collect himself and redirect her thoughts to what she'd come in to discuss. She quirked her brow with curiosity, when Rick seemed hesitant at the sound of her voice slowly standing up, obviously negligent to leave the dark enclosure. "Ok, well…"She suddenly froze mid-sentence watching his peculiar actions while he stalled in the darkness and then slowly crept out of the shadows to stand defiantly in front of her the dim morning light.

"What…the…hell." Anne's eyes went uncharacteristically wide besides gasping in astonishment. Realizing she was being rude, she instantly tried to cover her mouth diffusing an amused snicker, until an unladylike cackle escaped through the cracks of her fingers. Anne tried to regain some composure by coughing over her mirth, dropping her hands and attempting to seem nonchalantly wipe away the tears from her eyes.

"Look, Anne…" Rick began by holding up his hands to visually persuade her to stop, until he noticed the sleeves of his shirt. "Damn…I know I look stupid, so don't say anything."

"Wow--." Her thoughts buzzed disbelief and astonishment as she attempted to formulate a decent response to his predicament, *SHIT, he looks completely normal…EXCEPT every piece of clothing's he's wearing matches…in color. Not only are his jeans blue, but everything…his shirt, sweatshirt and even undershirt are all dyed the same brilliant shade of blue.*

Anne again coughed loudly into her clinched fist stifling another giggle, until she realized he was menacingly crossing the uneven planks to approach her. Rick slowly raised a hand appealing for silence, her face became beet red from using an extreme effort to restrain her humor at his circumstances. Tears welled making her cover her mouth harder, this time with both hands while struggling against the rising laughter.

 Rick resentfully crossed his arms across his stained blue shirt stretching across his heaving chest, silently regarding her with an aggravated stance and waited for some sort of flippant comment.

"Let me guess…um, you didn't separate your clothes before you washed them." She innocently batted her eyes, attempting to mildly verify the reason for his obvious blue dilemma.

"Yeah --. Funny thing is, nobody ever told me that I needed to separate my damn clothes. Wow…what a novel idea. Next time when I go out and spend a shit load of cash on new clothes, I'll definitely remember to do just that," He peevishly announced through clenched teeth, tensing when her actions became motionless, eyes raking his clothes, hands covering her mouth and tears streaming down her face.

He held his breath. *Oh yeah, I'm just waiting for the next barb to fly out of her mouth or possibly she'll fall on the ground and give into her enjoyment, then I'm really going to give her a piece of my mind. Fuck, I know I look stupid...like a freakn' Smurf.* Fuming, Rick still had the residual from feeling dumbfounded, standing in the mudroom astonishingly pulling his clothes out of the washer, realizing everything been stained the same shade of blue. *I'm so pissed.*

Anne nobly cleared her throat while her eyes continued to brim with tears, merrily dancing at Rick's unusual predicament. She relished for another second, struggling with her pent-up laughter, but enjoying every single moment.

"OK --. Ah-hum, I'll help you. Um, could you go and grab the rest of your 'blue' clothes and bring them up to the house...especially the white top you have on. I'll see what I can do to...um, 'un-blue' them."

Rick jaw dropped shocked by her gracious, seemingly sympathetic suggestion, but didn't hesitate to contemplate for a second. Immediately he turned to obediently comply, quickly raced back into his room, gathered up all of the blue items and resentfully shoved them back into the laundry hamper. Quickly glancing around the room, he spied a black shirt hanging on the back of the bathroom door and pulled off his blue-ish shirt. Tearing off the repugnant shirt and disgustedly tossing it in with the rest. Shirtless he turned haphazardly between tugging on the black shirt and bending over to heft the basket up to leave. Instantly he caught a movement out of the corner of his eye, realized Anne had innocently followed him to his room and was unnaturally mute, shocked standing in the doorway.

Anne's eyes had become interestedly wider when she realized that she had innocently stumbled across watching him change out of his shirt, and became wider assessing the utter chaos littered throughout the room. There were open tin food cans spilling out of the garbage, unwashed dishes heaped in the sink, clothes scattered around, mail perched everywhere and unknown items discarded all over the floor.

"Sorry about the mess. I'm not used to picking up after myself, don't like to wash dishes and I've never really cooked either," Rick commented trying to defend his living conditions while watching her appallingly inspect his room. The evident look of repulsion that settled across her face ignited his wounded ego. He tentatively slid a dirty shoe to the side with the toe of his boot to create a feeble path through the debris so he could walk unhindered towards the door. Rick directly maneuvered his body in front of her, blocking her critical stare of his living conditions.

"Umm...yeah, I can see that." Anne incredulously muttered through the side of her mouth, trying not to aggravate the situation any further. She kept her eyes adverted, backed away from the doorway while Rick regally carried his hamper past her and slammed the door shut with his foot. Shaking her head at his rigid back she watched him promenade down the planks, and obligingly followed him out of the barn.

"Hey Anne," He kept an irritated but steady pace while Anne thoroughly enjoyed the view from behind, having a great time, at his expense, recounting the moment she saw his audacious blue clothes. "You know…Um, I really appreciate your help." Rick almost choked as the humble words stumbled out, walking through the fence and up onto the porch.

"Hey -- no problem. I can't predict that I'll be able to get it all out, but at least I can try." As they approached the back door Anne turned, timidly smiled and gently lifted the laundry basket out of his hands. "Besides, I don't think I could handle seeing you, dressed in a different shade of blue…every day. I wouldn't be able to get any work done."

They shared a quick, humorous smile while Rick reached around Anne and opened the door for her. After he pushed it open, he barely brushed her arm drawing away and instantly startled they both uncomfortably searched each other's reaction, simultaneously feeling a slight jolt of electricity.

"I should have all of this done by tomorrow morning." Anne uncomfortably muttered.

"Great. Thanks again," Rick awkwardly replied, rapidly stepping back giving the peculiar situation wide berth and shoved his hands deep into his pockets.

Anne's smile seemed to turn faintly quizzical, turning into the mudroom, placed the laundry basket on top of the washer and began to rummage through the cupboards searching for detergent.

Watching her back, Rick quietly pulled the door closed behind her and pondered the unusual change of her attitude towards him. *Maybe some of my charm is beginning to soften the Dragon Lady up a little bit.* At his quirky thought Rick immediately and spontaneously embraced his enlightened mood, primarily by the idea at the possibility of a new development between them.

That was until he heard Anne's voice erupt into hysterical laughter, the sound caused his foot to falter on the last step. His disbelieving eyes turned towards the back door, while she loudly shouted for the girls to come downstairs.

"Hey you guys, you have to come down here and take a look at this. Rick turned all his clothes blue!" The rumbling sound of footsteps, hastily running downstairs echoed outside of the house making Rick stop dead in his tracks. "Beth, you aren't going to believe what he did this time…blue clothes. Damn, even the inside of the washer is blue! You've got to come and take a look!"

The pounding of Beth and Suzie's feet could be heard from outside, including the continuous "OMG!" in unison with their uproarious laughter at his 'blue' situation.

"Well, that just killed any idea I had about her new found graciousness." Rick mumbled through his teeth, as he attempted to duck underneath the windows and hurried undetected back to the barn, the entire way the only thing reverberating through his head was the girl's hysterical laughter.

Rick dispassionately kicked a rock, making his lonesome trek safely back into the barn with the single intent of mucking the stalls and forgetting everything about the morning. Once inside the building, away from the echoed cackling, he wondered over to the radio and turned it up as Red Rider's 'Lunatic Fringe' came on. He dispassionately bent over to pick up the abandoned shovel and thoughtfully paused as something slightly askew caught his attention.

"Are you shitting me?" Rick muttered after taking a couple of seconds to determine what was amiss and notice his socks. *Shit...they're freaking blue too.* "SHIT! I'll never live this one down." Rick angrily readjusted the shovel, continuing mindlessly with his work, until a satisfied smile crossed his face as a semi-malicious thought entered his mind, *I'm going to save these blue socks, so when this whole thing is done, I can go back home and burn them with the rest of this crap... maybe I'll frame them and hang them next to my Oscar. hummm....*

13

Washington's indecisive weather created a long, grueling few months since the end of February. But with the continuous help from the unusually warm weather, May brought the return of spring and everything propelled itself into a new direction. Flowers were in bloom, trees were budding, the locals were out from their seasonal hibernation (everyone seemed nearly stripped down to traditional northwest warm weather gear; consisting primarily of khaki shorts, t-shirts under fleece vests and socks tucked under Birkenstocks) as weather consistently was becoming sincerely pleasant. The combination actually made life in Washington tolerable.

Rick had begun to feel like a drone with his daily tasks. He'd volunteered to finish any of the endless projects that had been aborted throughout the yard and house. The continual frustration of biding his time and trying to build some trust with Anne, simply so he could learn how to handle horses was beginning to wear on his nerves. Lately his only reprieve was either on the weekends when he was able to set up a rickety chair to sit undetected in the open arena all day without his teeth or contacts in, reading the weekly snippets of the script sent from Mike, or on the warmer evenings finding himself trekking out alone to walk the beach. The roar of the water combined with the luminosity of the moonlit sand and the star filled sky made life seem endless, as if he was the only person on earth. Trying to distract his thoughts he typically concentrated on working intensely on any project outside of the barn, mainly because if he found himself in a slight proximity of being near Anne, his attraction to her was becoming an issue. There were too many moments where they were alone in the barn and watching her had become a fascinating pastime. *It's only because of our close working confines and lack of any other available females that this is happening, especially since the weather has continued on a warm streak and her wardrobe had diminished to t-shirts and shorts.* The flimsy thought had become his reiterated excuse for his growing interest and as the heat continued to increase, she tended to work with the horses with less and less on. The distraction of her body was driving him a little crazy. So when the opportunity came to fix the outlining pasture fence, he instantly jumped at it.

Rick took a deep breath, lifting up the last of the fencing supplies and shut the back of his truck. Wiping the sweat off his brow, he took a quick second to inventory that everything was loaded and resolved to attack the extensive repairs on the broken fencing that surrounded the lower half of the property, an idea that had struck when Anne off handedly mentioned that because of the hazard of broken bays, the horses were restricted from being let out into any of the existing lower pastures. The blatant neglect on the property had crept past the house, revealing in the crumbling wooden fence line, broken gates, overgrown grass and weeds that had become a nagging reminder of Anne's perpetual lack of help.

He mentally checked off the towering stack of lumber, appropriate equipment and tools in the bed of the truck that he'd need to finish the impending jobs. With an agreeable nod, Rick was eager to be off of the property for the rest of the day, walking around the truck whistling off key with Neil Diamond's 'Sweet Caroline' while he opened the door, ready to hop in and get on with his work.

"Hey Rick...hold on a minute!" A sing-song voice hollered from the direction of the house.

Rick looked over and saw Beth racing across the porch holding a brown paper bag. He chuckled at her youthful exuberance as she approached the truck with her hair flying, bearing down on him at a galloping skip and carelessly swinging a brown paper bag in the air.

"I brought you some lunch for the afternoon. It's going to be hot, so I stuck in a couple of extra bottles of water."

"Thanks, I appreciate the thought. I've got to admit that eating out of a can has exceeded its limitations." Rick smiled his appreciation and turned to sit in the cab.

Beth's girlish laugh sounded forced while she smiled so hard that Rick was sure that light rebounded off of her pristinely white teeth. Her impish attitude suddenly changed as her head guiltily snapped down and her interest instantly became consumed with making circles in the dirt with the toe of her shoe.

"Um -- I... I just wanted you to know that I'm going to be heading over to Suzie's house this afternoon."

"Sooo, why are you telling me?" Rick asked suspiciously. "You should be telling your sister."

"Well, Anne isn't around. She went to check out that potential boarder down the coast, remember? She'll be stuck doing that all day and well, I just wanted someone around here to know where I'm going to be."

A huge red flag of warning popped up in Rick's brain while he half-heartedly listened to the one-sided conversation. Beth's naivety at the lack of ingenuity for a story was reaffirmed because she hadn't raised her head, her sentence trailed into a mumble out of the side of her mouth and refused to look directly in his eyes. Rick gently took Beth's chin in his hand and physically made her look up at him.

"First things first...Beth are you lying to me about going over to Suzie's house today?"

Beth dramatically opened her eyes wider than necessary, seemed rather piqued at his interrogation and answered with an unconvincingly blunt, "No."

"Look, I'm going to trust you." Rick watched the deflating change in her reaction to his honest statement. He recognized his gut instinct was right on the money, noting the instant elation that crossed her face at the prospect of getting off scot free, only re-confirmed her adolescent deviousness. "But, before you go. Just to cover my ass...I want you to write down three numbers where I can get a hold of you and a note to Anne explaining your intentions in exemplary detail."

"OMG –!" She looked crestfallen as a sullen look exposed her uneasiness at having to comply with all of his demands. "All right, I promise it'll all be on the kitchen counter."

"Good, because right now I don't need to get into any more trouble with your sister." Rick gave her hair a spontaneous light toss, shaking his head at her youthful innocence before he ambled into the truck.

"Hey, knock it off." Beth swatted his hand away, combed her hair back into place and started back towards the house. "Rick...thanks."

"Don't sweat it; just make sure you're going to follow through. I don't want to be made a fool of and I don't like liars." As the end of his sentence left his lips, a distinctly bad taste filled his mouth; *because technically...right now I'm a liar to these two girls.*

He tried to get comfortable in his squeaky seat as he flexed his shoulders, attempting to mentally shrug off an odd sensation of doom. Rick suddenly felt overwhelmingly saturated with the strange weight of responsibility towards this delicate family.

Without another thought Rick hastily jammed the key into the ignition, cranked the radio to The Rolling Stone's 'Brown Sugar' and drove out onto the highway. He crept around the block until he found the ancient gate that lead into the lower portion of the property, hopping out to unlock the padlock and secure the gate open wide enough for the truck to pass through.

"Huh...that's funny." Curiously he grabbed the dangling, rusty chain registering that the lock was gone. Running his hands through his hair he noticed that the gate had been recently used and fresh tire tracks were in the mud. He bent down, searching with his hands through the tall grass, trying to look at where the lock should have been abandoned, but it was missing. "Weird." Rick mumbled to himself as unease crept up his spine making him rub his face, standing up and ambled back to the truck. He drove through the gate by simply pushing it with the front bumper of his truck, until it was stuck open in the grass. Driving across the bumpy pasture he pulled the truck up along the longest portion of the fence that ran along the highway. The heat from the mid-day sun felt good on his face while he got out of his truck and stretched. *Ahhh, it feels great to be alone, away from the house and without any females to contend with.*

***

Rick's back throbbed from the ongoing hard work of unloading the truck, setting everything up and digging holes for the new lumber to fix the broken bays. A slight breeze cooled off his skin while he was squatting down contemplating how to jimmy rig a part of the fence together. His head snapped up when Anne's truck rapidly pulled off of the highway emitting a cloud of dust.

Rick fanned the dirt away from his face, coughing while it swirled around his head, causing him to straighten up and rub his lower back while watching Anne storm out of her vehicle. *If I'm reading her body language correctly, she's pissed about something again.* "Ah, shit." He let out his pent up breath as he stood his ground and watched her heated approach. *Now what the hell did I do?*

"Have you seen Beth?" Anne's surly words came out in a venomous accusation the second she stopped on the opposite side of the fence and fumingly crossed her arms over her heaving chest.

"Why Anne...what a pleasant surprise and a good afternoon to you, too." Rick condescendingly replied as he tipped his hat back to wipe the sweat off his brow with his forearm.

Anne indignantly stared blankly at him while she barely contained her wrath and waited for his answer.

"Yeah, sure...I saw her this morning, before I came down here to work. She said something about going over to Suzie's."

"Well that's funny because Suzie isn't home and her parents are out of town," she practically yelled at him as she struggled with the evolving overbearing predicament.

"Look Anne, you need to calm down." Rick cautiously approached her, but decided to keep a safe arms-length distance, while she started to maniacally pace along the road in front of the fence.

Anne incoherently muttered profanities about the male gender as she desperately tried to reign in her temper. "I come home to some stupid note, call all of the freaking unanswered numbers and more, only to find out she's nowhere to be found and you tell me to calm down!!" This time she did yell the last couple of words at him at the top of her lungs.

"Hey, hey, hey -- hold on a freakn' minute. I can't help it if you can't keep a leash on her. You're acting like it's my fault she took off," Rick replied defensively and immediately crossed his arms.

"You were the only adult here! She's just a teenager, didn't you take a second to think about how much trouble she could get into. How could you let her leave?" She indignantly rammed her hands on her hips and glared at him.

"Look…I'm just your employee, not a babysitter." He closed his eyes when he realized that what he just said was more defensive than helpful, took a deep breath and tried to reign in his rising temper. "We're wasting time standing out here trading insults. Give me a second, let me pack up some stuff and we can figure out where she could be."

Anne looked him over in a dour way and gave a very unfeminine snort at his offer. "What kind of help are you going to be? You don't know your way around the outlying areas, towns or any one she might hang out with." The moment her sentence ended, a pristine black Lexus skidded to a dramatic stop and then slowly pulled up along the fence as the tinted passenger window rolled down. Dave waved Anne into the car and leaned over the passenger seat to open the door as he called out to her. "I haven't seen her on the roads. Anne, hurry up and jump in. Let's head into town and start combing the streets before it gets dark."

Rick watched Anne's shoulders slumped in defeat, leaving her anger deflated for a moment as she walked briskly towards the car and Dave's Cheshire cat like smile. She looked like she had sold her soul the moment she opened the car door wider and began to sit down.

"What the…" Rick hesitantly moved down the fence line towards her. "Hey, hey Anne, what do you want me to do? Where do you want me to look?"

Anne looked up at him through shattered, tear brimmed eyes and whispered, "Don't bother yourself…she's not your responsibility." Without another word the window began to move up and she quickly closed the door. Dave peeled his car out throwing dirt and rocks everywhere as they rapidly pulled out onto the highway.

While the dust began to diminish, Rick silently watched them leave and cursed himself at being so gullible. He glanced up at the sky and realized that the sun had become precariously low. "It's going to be dark soon." He knew he had to help; Anne's last look had seared itself onto his soul. *Shit, if anything happens to that idiot sister of hers, I won't be able to forgive myself. And if I find her before anyone else…I think I'll ring her juvenile neck.*

Resolve in hand Rick, sprinted back to the truck to toss the expensive tools into the bed, drove out of the pasture and raced down the highway in the general direction of town. With every mile he racked his brain trying to formulate a plan on out how to get information. *Shit. Where would I hang out if I was a teenager in this town, where would I go? Who should I talk to?*

An idea crept into his thoughts the second his truck passed the Red Apple, which if his memory was correct, happened to be the only grocery store in town. He violently jerked the steering wheel, making the truck tires screech as he turned aggressively into the parking lot and glanced around. There were only a few cars haphazardly parked across the area as the parking lot lights were just beginning to flicker on. He quickly maneuvered the truck into a spot at the back of the lot facing the store and waited, suspiciously monitoring the lot's activity. *Please, please, let somebody show up.* After a long couple of aggravating minutes of drumming his fingers against the steering wheel and searching every car, a tricked out, low riding car pull into the lot. The ground shook with the bumping music blaring from inside of the car, Rick clenched the wheel as he listened from across the parking lot. A bunch of teens rolled out of it, stumbling, pushing, and laughing at each other as they headed into the store.

"Bingo." Rick's mood lightened with the single word, leapt out of his truck and tried to inconspicuously follow the teenagers inside. "Alright, here we go."

As the group arrogantly ambled around the store, loudly boasting to one another about all the girls they had left back at the party and punking each other throughout the aisles, Rick hurried around the last aisle and made himself available near the alcohol. He registered that there was a limited amount of people shopping in the section while Rick waited, acting like he was interested in the miniscule wine selection and waited for the teenaged bunch. Rounding the corner one of them disengaged himself from the pack, went over to grab out a few cases of beer, threw them into a cart and headed to the front of the store. The boisterous group made their way back to the registers, still loudly engaged in their adolescent bantering and completely disrupting the entire store, each of them oblivious of the resentful stares coming from any of the other shoppers.

Rick abruptly made his way around the unaware teens, out of the store and quickly jogged back to his truck. *If my guess is correct and I know anything...there's definitely trouble where they're going.*

Anxiously drumming his fingers against the wheel, Rick watched as the group left the store and piled back into the car. He hastily threw the truck in gear and carefully followed as they made their way out onto the highway and towards the next town down Highway 101 Grayland, Washington.

Rick racked his brain, trying to recall anything he'd heard about the area; only that it was a more remote area along the Pacific Ocean while he slowly followed the bunch of cars. It wasn't until he drove past a highway sign indicating they were approaching Willippa Bay, and the name suddenly jogged an occurrence from his memory.

During one of his endless errands to the feed store, he recalled overhearing Lois discussing Willapa Bay with a small crowd. Curiously it seemed that it was a legendary area, was locally called Wash Away Beach because the sea was slowly engulfing the desolate area that graced the coastline. Over decades, bit by bit the merciless ocean had swallowed up miles of the shoreline, including tress, livestock, land, highway, barns, cars and even homes.

Engulfed in his roaming thoughts, he suddenly startled and almost missed that the tricked out car had slowed down. Swiftly he took his foot off of the gas pedal, allowing his truck to slow down, calculating where the car was attempting to turn off the road and park next to several others. It slowly crept down a driveway that looked like an abandoned stretch of highway, blocked at the end by a huge mound of dirt with a large stump lodged on top and curing around a deserted path that led down to the beach glistening in the distance.

Rick continued to drive by the abandoned road, then carefully turned around and hastily drove back to the general area to park his truck across the street. Lunging out of the cab he rushed along the highway and attempted to become invisible as he followed the boisterous teens down along the unseen path.

He stumbled over the uneven terrain, down the dirt hill, through the tangled undergrowth until the scene opened up to an eerily beautiful spot where the ocean had dismantled huge chunks of the earth and simply swallowed them. Some of the houses still clung bravely to the mangled cliffs, balancing precariously as the water invitingly churned and waited to pull the rest of them into its depths. Strewn across the coastline were hundreds of fallen trees that littered the beach, creating an unimaginably twisted, wooden graveyard. Over to one side of the beach under a huge fallen tree's gnarled roots, was a large bonfire with hordes of kids huddled together as Imagine Dragon's 'Radioactive' floated up from someone's portable radio.

Rick scrambled the rest of the way down the sand dune, attempting to follow the group until they separated across the beach in the dying light as the sun began to set. He kept up his pace, frantically scanned the beach and desperately willing any sign of Beth. *Come on, come on, come on...please be here.*

From the disheveled look of some of the kids he passed by, the party must have been going on pretty much the entire day. The secluded beach had the appearance of an adolescent war zone, with teens scattered all over the area lingering in different designs of debauchery. Some were sitting or dancing around the fire enjoying each other's company, while others were frolicking in the surf, ambling along in pairs, passionately intertwined or simply passed out.

Dumbfounded, Rick rubbed his face, rolled his eyes as some of the teens spotted him and began to humorously nudge each other while drunkenly pointing to indicate his presence. *Ahhh...great, the teenage years, how does anyone ever live through them?* Rick took a second to mentally find his Zen, inhaled a deep calming breath as he approached the first partially intoxicated but fully clothed teen and carefully enunciated his word creating a sentence, emulating as if he were speaking to an errant toddler.

"Hey kid...do you know where Beth is...Beth Jones?"

"No, man. Never heard of her." A quirk snaked across his face when an idea crossed his liquor infested mind. "Hey, aren't you a little old to be around here? Or are you one of those kinky guys?? Are you looking for some fresh, young, new meat, Old Man?" The greasy boy slurred as he elbowed a buddy to punctuate his joke.

Apparently from the stifled laughter emitted from the group, the kid who answered apparently had to be one of the clowns of the crowd. *Obviously since he doesn't have a girl huddled in a secluded corner.*

Rick ignored the kid and his continued jesting about Viagra and old age performance issues, without another thought continued to wander through the tangle of youths while he reminisced about his own partying teen adventures. *Shit, if I remember correctly, if she's here it's going to be unlikely that I'm going to find her anytime soon, especially without any help...drastically less once the sun's gone down.*

"Hey, hey...Mister." A slight whisper floated on the breeze, making Rick jump at the interruption from his dismal thoughts until the quiet voice mumbled. "Excuse me." A cute young girl had detached herself from the unruly group around the fire and was hesitantly walking in his general direction while Crazy Town's 'Butterfly' was cranked in the background.

"Yeah?" Rick paused for a second, waiting for the shy girl to say something. *Anything.* The entire time his anxiety spiraled out of control in the back of his mind, concluding that with the ebbing, golden blaze, every second the sun was sinking, his chances of finding her were going with it.

"I knew we shouldn't be here. Look...I, I told her so. But you know Beth."

Rick peered closer at the girl and euphorically recognized Suzie, Beth's BFF, who occasionally stopped by the ranch. He mercifully closed his eyes and thanked his lucky stars that he'd made some kind of leeway.

"Suzie...right? Rick hesitantly asked the innocent question as if he was approaching a frightened animal, instantly praying that he had the girl's correct name.

"Yeah," The young girl perked up at the idea that Rick had recognized her, causing a surge of a blush that tinged her face and assertively nodded her head.

"Suzie, you know what... don't worry about anything right now. At this moment, I don't really care about anything you two have been up to, except making sure that I get you both home safely. So can you help me out?" Rick crossed his fingers as he watched Suzie glance back and forth between him, and the clan of drunken teens around the fire. *Please, throw me a freaking bone...and make a smart decision.*

"I told her not to...but she went down the beach, with Bobbie in that direction," Suzie's voice ended in a whine as she angled her chin in the opposite area of the beach from the bonfire. Rick's disbelieving eyes followed her invisible direction straight to a sea encroached dilapidated house, that magically had somehow managed to hang onto the edge of a hill, barely suspended in air, above the wet sand and raging water.

"Shit." Rick realized the emanate danger that Beth was in, instantly wanted to grab Suzie or one of the other stupid, drunken kids and shake them until their teeth fell out of their skull. *Are you shitting me? She went up into some condemned house that is perched to fall into the ocean at any second with some loser... and she's more than likely drunk! Thank the Lord Anne's not around, because if she didn't kill her right now...I'm sure as hell going to!*

"Look Suzie, I want you to take my truck keys and get out of here before the sun sets. My green truck is parked right across the street. Please wait in it while I go get Beth. Promise me that you'll just stay put until we get there and we'll get out of here without any mishaps."

"OK...I'll be there." Suzie's voice squeaked with doubt about his instructions.

Rick wanted to grab and kiss her, but instead he settled on a conspiring wink before turning to quickly trudge down the beach, calling back over his shoulder, "Good girl. Now get going."

He continued to move down the beach towards the house, loudly mumbling about the atrocity of youth, their surprising but idiotic decisions and how society should improve their knowledge with mandatory classes about how to raise children. *Shit, you have to have months of classes, take a test and receive a license just to drive a car, but not even simple common sense to raise children. Damn, Beth...this whole thing is freakin' stupid and outrageous!*

As he cautiously approached the base of the sandy hill until his steps faltered and became motionless, listening for some sort of sound to give any indication of her location. Rick jumped and began to heedlessly move the second he heard slight coughing carried by the wind from somewhere around the house.

He clamored up the dune, uncaring that he was underneath the foundation of the suspended house, only pausing in astonishment when he reached the opening. It wasn't merely a doorway that he faced, but a large section of the wall that had been ripped off by the sea. Heedless of danger, he pulled himself up, pausing when the realization sunk in, *Shit…I'm alone, precariously perched in a gigantic hole, where the living room should have extended out over the beach.* Trying to shake off a surge of apprehensiveness, he tentatively clambered up the rest of the way and found himself standing in the middle of the devastated room. Everything looked normal with the hardwood floors gleaming, red brick fireplace adorned with a substantial mantle and even the curtains still semi-covering over the windows; except they were billowing with the constant breeze blowing off the surf through the ripped open side of the house. The moment took on an eerie quality, holding his breath it became suspended and seemed surreal as he pivoted around to gaze through the gaping hole, out onto the endless merciless sea. *Man, I thought my place had a vista,* talk about a room with a view. *This tops everything I've ever seen.*

Rick redirected his wandering thoughts while cautiously snaking through a hallway down through the living quarters to check every room and back into the kitchen. Gazing incredulously at the appliances still in tack, Rick realized there was a back door and silently reached for the door knob. He forced his mind to keep his attention focused on any incriminating sounds, and not of the persistent roaring sea, except the undaunted eerie feeling crawled back into his head, *I'm standing in the middle of a house that's freakin' half perched on a bluff, along with the obvious fact that the sea has already claimed a large chunk. Shit, the only thing left to happen is having the house gratefully releasing its foundation, lifting up and sliding down into the murky abyss… with me in it.*

He deftly opened the ravaged back door and stepped into a typical back yard that opened up into a small covered patio with a clothesline strung from the side of the house and tied to a tree. Everything seemed normal, except that the half of a swing set had unnaturally been submerged into a sandy hill, a gigantic fallen tree laid with its top engulfed in the ocean and roots claimed most of the yard, where his gaze riveted on the young couple huddled together next to it.

"Ahem." Rick stumbled forward out of the house intent on breaking up their youthful embrace, until he heard the some more choking sounds coming from one of the figures.

The young man swiftly glanced up alerted by some foreign sound and took a guarded stance next to the other person, ready to courageously protect them.

"Hey man look...we're kind of busy here. Get Lost!"

Rick imploringly raised both of his hands, gave him a grateful smile and then nodded towards the crouched figure as he said. "Look kid, I think I can help you out."

Beth's head whipped around causing her to careen forward and almost stumbled over an exposed root. "Rick, is that you?"

"Yeah Beth, it's me." Rick's heart broke as he watched the poor girl turn back around and continue to get sick next to the tree.

"Dude, it wasn't me. She she's been sick like this all afternoon. I didn't know what to do!"

Rick shook his head disgustedly at the two teens and then gestured towards the bonfire glowing in the fading light.

"No worries, just go and join your friends...I'll take her home."

Rick could almost see the young man's mind physically churn as he measured his options; he could hang out tending a sick girl, argue with the older man or party the rest of the night down at the campfire. The decision was simple, he gratefully nodded in Rick's direction, scurried down the dune like an escaping prisoner and lightheartedly headed across the beach back to the fire.

Rick slowly made his way forward to Beth and gently set his hand on her back. "You okay?"

"No! Um, I -- I think I want to die!"

Elated when the realization that he'd found her firmly set in, Rick chuckled to himself and ruffled the top of her hair. He instantly stopped when suddenly she began to despairingly moan and then gag again.

"Let's get you back home." Rick comfortably rubbed her back, helped her stand up, took her clammy hand and led her down the abandoned driveway. By the time they carefully continued to wander down through the deserted woods and arrived back on the street, darkness had descended. It took them a little while to blindly trudge through the overgrown driveway, but calculating their position, Rick knew that they'd end up a short distance behind the truck.

"Whew," he let out an exasperated sigh of relief when he spotted a slight silhouette through the fogged up windows sitting in the passenger seat. He closed his eyes and said a silent prayer, knowing that Suzie had made it safely to the truck and stayed. Rick gently guided a moaning, sick Beth over to the passenger side of the truck and lightly tapped on the window.

"Oh my…Beth, are you okay?" Suzie guiltily jumped out to help assist her friend into the cab as Rick euphorically made his way to the driver's side. He turned the key while Suzie silently scooted in first to give Beth the spot next to the open window, switched on the headlights and headed back towards Westport.

As they drove back to the ranch the cab's interior was thick with tension. Rick tried to lighten the mood by switching up the volume as Katy Perry's 'TGIF' started to play and sarcastically whistled in time with the song.

After all of the drama at the beach the drive seemed pretty uneventful, until they began to round the bend to the house. Beth started to agonizingly moan louder while Suzie started babbling uncontrollably, searching for any feeble excuse for their decision to leave, any solutions to the issues that they'd gotten themselves into and mentally preparing for Anne's wrath.

Rick randomly grinned at their incoherent ramblings while he loudly announced that they were taking the last turn into the drive. As the truck sputtered and ascended the hill, the house loomed ominously, a glowing contrast that startled him, the dark gloomy night became an eerie backdrop to the illuminated interior lights, set ablaze from every window; as if the house stood like a homing beacon for a wayward ship.

Rick took a deep breath after pulling up to the front of the house, throwing the truck in park, turning off the key and readying himself for the impending doom at hand. He cautiously opened the door then paused to turn and sympathetically regard the two frightened teens. They were frightfully huddled together against the door, the light reflecting in their huge eyes as they surveyed his every move.

He couldn't help himself as he chuckled at their youthful innocence. "Hmmm. If I was the two of you --um…I'd stay in here. I'll go and try to smooth things out with the Dragon Lady before you have to deal with her."

The truck door closed with an ominous click, thankfully blocking their combination of small whimpering and agonized moans while the teens cowered below the window. He allowed himself a small pat on the back and a second for another chuckle as he rounded the truck.

Rick jumped when his attention was disrupted by the front door immediately slammed open with a resounding bang and Anne came barging down the front steps, with a smirking Dave in tow.

"Where on earth did you go? It's not bad enough that I can't find my sister…but then I have you to worry about too!" She nearly screamed the last few words as she approached the gate, while Dave lingered a few paces behind her heels, smiling serenely. When she skidded to an abrupt halt in front of Rick, Dave clamored forward to clasp a supportive arm around her shoulders and suavely tried to assist her.

"Anne, why don't you let me take care of this…issue" Dave started draw her physically away and comfortably pat her shoulder while eyeing his adversary.

"Are you shitting me?" Anne angrily brushed off Dave's advances, ramming both hands on her hips and threw a menacing glare at Rick, while her ire boiled over making her belligerently continue, "Well, Rick…what slick excuse do you have for yourself?"

Undeterred by Anne's dismissive brush off, Dave moved a step forward, placing himself next to Anne and lamely added, "Yeah -- RICH…what DO you have to say for yourself?"

Out of the corner of his eye Rick watched both a guilt ridden Suzie and ailing Beth scrunch further down into the seats of his truck. He silently stood his ground for a second regarding the pair with open distain, until moment became awkwardly suspended between the three. Curious at what their next verdict would be, Rick leisurely shoved his hands deeper into his dirty jean pockets and rocked back onto his heels. He maintained his silence, which outweighed any explanation he could give either of them and simply waiting to spring his check mate.

"Yeah--" He elongated the single word while critically narrowing his gaze at both of them, then pointedly fixed it on Anne. Before another word could be uttered, he turned and walked defiantly to the passenger side of the truck as he called out. "Shit, I should have figured, that's the way you'd view me."

Anne's attention became mesmerized watching him maneuver around the truck, raise his hand and lightly tap his knuckles on the window. Unexpectedly the passenger door appeared to magically open and revealed the two missing girls, who guiltily slid out of the cab.

"Ohh…shit." Anne sucked her breath in through her teeth as her sister stumbled around the truck with the aid of her friend.

 The deafening silence was broken by the crunch of rocks as the girls tried to sneak around the obvious adult stand-off. The teens hope soared stealing a quick glance at Anne's strained profile, quickly averted their gaze from either of the men, maneuvered widely around the group and bolted towards the house.

"Ah-hum--." Anne uncomfortably cleared her throat, trying to redirect her scattered, questioning thoughts and address Dave. Without breaking eye contact with a fuming Rick, she attempted to find the appropriate unobtrusive perspective and dismiss the unwanted help. "Dave, um…I don't know how to thank you enough for your support tonight, but right now...I believe that I need to put an end to this horrible situation, and go in to look after my sister."

Dave searched her face for any indication that she was being coy or too proud to ask for more of his help. Her stoic gaze softened for a second as she gave him an off handed shrug, then continued to glare at Rick. The realization that she wanted to handle reprimanding the other man registered, then limply gave her a lingering supportive squeeze on her arm, "I know...it's hard. Remember Anne, if you need me for anything, I'm just a couple blocks away. I can be here at a moment's notice."

Rick dramatically rolled his eyes at all of the melodramatics, casually leaned his head into the passenger side of his truck and started assessing the interior of the cab. *I just want to make sure Beth didn't leave any physical evidence from her drunken excursion.* As he completed the thorough inspection of the floor, he watched the stealthy headlights from Dave's car slowly drove around the drive and leisurely turn out onto the highway.

Resigned that the idiotic event was over he blew out a tired breath, stood up and attempted to shut the door. A slight movement caught his eye causing him to swivel around in defense, only to find Anne irately standing next to him, hands on hips, openly regarding him with disgust and physically blocking any move. *Shit, this isn't the appreciation I should be receiving!*

"Yeah...Dragon Lady, you want something?" Rick disrespectfully nudged her out of the way with his elbow and slammed the door shut, waiting for her to release her fury and take him on.

"Where'd you find her, Grunt?"

"I decided to try an old trick I remembered from my own adolescence."

"That is?"

"Common sense...where there's smoke, there's fire."

"What do you mean?"

Rick inhaled attempting to reign in his reply, without success and pivoted to face his opponent, to finally really take her on. With the delivery of each overtly enunciated word, he stepped firmly forward and intimidated her to slightly back away.

"You seem to be a smart girl Anne...so use your brain. It's a small town, seems like if she's been missing for that long...there was probably a party somewhere. And if there were a party, they'd need refreshments. So -- I looked at the only place I could think they'd be able to get it, followed the trail of drunken teens hoping that I was right and find her before it got dark." By the end of his tirade, Rick suddenly became overwhelmed and exhausted by the day's drama and threw a hand on the back of the truck. Anne's back slammed into the bed of the truck while Rick loomed over her, his body pinning her in an awkward position and causing a startled squeak. He narrowed his eyes bringing his face closer to hers, scrutinizing her silent response, shrugged and maneuvered around her angry stance to abruptly dismiss her. "Whatever Anne, you're going to believe…whatever you WANT about me, no matter what I do or say…even if I did find your sister." Rick gave up hope that she'd come to terms with the evening and indignantly waved an un-apologetic hand, tiredly moved away from her and made his way back towards the barn. "So fire me."

Listening to the crunch of his retreating footstep, feeling to cold mental seep through her shirt Anne found herself at a cross-roads. "Hey," Anne unconsciously made a rash decision, quickly shoved off the truck and tried to quickly close the distance between them by picking up her pace into a light jog. "Hey…hey, wait a minute,"

"What?" Anger overrode his common sense, her inane plea only fueled his defensive fire. Rick had enough of their verbal fencing abruptly stopped, swiveled around and began to menacingly advance towards her. "What…what do you want Anne? Do you want to condemn me again? Find a reason to finally let me go? What, what is going to be the 'issue' this time…and show you that I'm not good enough to work here?" Enunciating each specific question he resumed an aggressive pace defined with giant steps, immediately intimidating her to shuffle back towards the house.

"What do you want?" Rick's shoulders slumped as he felt his threadbare tolerance crack, resulting from constant accusations, strain from rescuing Beth, chaos of the day, but with the thought of her distrust, disappointment made everything evaporate into thin air.

After a few shaky steps, her back hit the fence with a thud, making her grapple for something tangible to hang onto as he loomed over her. Her hands weakly clung onto a broken board, her balance wobbling with the gate as she stared up into his daunting face.

"No," Anne squeaked.

"No…What?" Rick's voice lowered dangerously as he pinned her body tightly against the fence.

"No…I just --" Her eyes searched his for an answer.

"You know Anne…I really didn't sign up for any of this shit. If you need some help with Beth and your life…then you need to figure that all out, yourself. That's not why I came here. Right now I could use a shower, food and some sleep…after a really crappy day that has *YOU* written all over it."

Anne's shimmering eyes sparkled bright in the moonlight, partially because she was slightly frightened, but more intrigued by the man leaning into her. A second passed, then she carefully laid a delicate hand upon his cheek and hesitantly inched her face up to his.

Confused by her actions his menacing glare softened into a question, until she quickly touched her lips to his in the briefest kiss imaginable. Rick felt frozen as he felt her lip linger; like a whisper from a fleeting dream and then it was gone.

Embarrassed at her spontaneous decision she attempted to move away, without thinking he dipped his head down and captured her mouth in a passionate kiss to see if it was real. He seductively braced the small of her back with his hands as he leaned in and savored each second of their embrace. A slight current coursed through his veins as he closed his eyes and savored the moment while he thought of...nothing.

Anne brought her hand to the back of his head and began to lingeringly fondle the nape of his neck. As she opened her mouth to his, she moaned slightly and willingly clung to his body. Rick's hands dove under her sweatshirt, touching the heat of her body and began slowly inching their way up to cup her breast. Feeling his hands roam over her body, she lightly traced his chest, began to train her fingers down his stomach to the edge of his pants and slid them barely below to feel his skin. Anne moaned when Rick suddenly pushed her harder against the fence with his thighs, indulged in feeling the length of her body and deepened their kiss.

Rick's subconscious began to emerge while he realized where he was headed. He took a steadying breath as he gently lifted his mouth, searched her face and raised a hand to gently disentangle their arms. He contemplated their intimate position, looking away in an attempt to search the vacant arena, giving time to ease out of the situation, and register his thoughts on anything else than the accusations in her eyes.

Finding courage to face her after the brief respite, he looked down and realized she was openly staring at him, her mischievous lopsided smile in place, he grinned back at her.

"Um...I just wanted to thank you, for finding my sister." Anne adverted her gaze to uncomfortably examine the ground while the aftermath of their intimate situation hovered in the air.

"Well...I'll tell you what. If it's going to be like that from now on out..." Rick chuckled huskily attempting to keep the atmosphere light hearted and lightly flexed an arm to keep her in a semi-intimate embrace. "Well, then you can thank me anytime...and for anything."

Anne's lashes fluttered coyly at his jest, while she unconsciously mimicked his husky laughter. Rick felt a jolt of shock by the combination of her flirting and the heat from her body, making his body instantly respond in ways he couldn't believe.

She punched him slightly on the shoulder "No...really, I want to say thank you. I was wrong to say those things and I don't know how you found her...but you did and I'll always be grateful." Anne tipped her face up to search his, her expression mirroring her gratitude.

The honesty in her face hit him like a rock, Rick unpredictably let go of his hold, took a giant step backwards, bowed semi-submissively and responded with his best attempt at a British accent, "Well...I'm at your service, Mum."

When he glanced back at her, she was glowing with the most beautiful smile he'd ever seen. Uncomfortable Anne racked her brain trying to stumble through something witty to retort. "Um...I...uh...thanks, I really don't know what to say."

"Anne...I think you'd better go inside. From what I remember, seems like Beth is going to need serious some help tonight. Besides, I'll bet you all my chores that you and Beth are in for a long night and a date with either a bucket or the toilet."

Anne uncomfortably chuckled, silently nodded in agreement, but found herself continuing to stare dumbfounded at his face. Then with a shake of her head she abruptly realized that she was acting like a teenaged idiot, the thought caused her face to guiltily flush. Without a second thought she quickly turned to make a hasty retreat, accidentally ramming her legs into the gate, sending it flying backwards with a crash.

"Shit, I...um...shit. You're right, I better get inside, I've gotta go and help the girls." Anne attempted to restore her state as an influential adult as she busily fussed with the edge of her jacket. With each step she berated herself, desperately wanting to steal a couple backward glances, instead she swept around, and resumed down the path climbing up onto the porch. Opening the door she attempted to suavely sneak another peek over her shoulder, instantly registering that he was standing in the silvery moonlight at the end of the path watching her. Her heart momentarily lodged in her throat as she traced the outline of his body with her eyes. With a slight smile she lifted a hand, quickly closed the door and clumsily made her way up the stairs to check on the girls.

Rick waited in the drive until the lights were slowly turned out one by one on the second floor and finally in her room. He shoved his hands into his pockets and began to whistle Neil Diamond's 'Sweet Caroline' turning to slowly make his way back to the barn. The only other sounds disrupting the evening was the soft crunch from the gravel, the rushing of the wind and an owl in the distance. He thoughtlessly wandered through the barn, turning out the light, then distractedly meandered into his room and lay down across the bed. The combination of his thoughts and the overwhelming silence began harassing him, so he stretched across to switch on the radio. He flung his arm over his eyes as visions of Anne's face raced through his mind and Lady Antebellum's 'Need You Now' lyrics found a hidden place in his soul. A war ripped through him as he urgently tried to any kind of make sense between his actions and his feelings. A strange sense of loneliness engulfed the room after he stood up, switched off the lights, stripped off his clothes, and returned to bed trying to diminish the confusion by staring lethargically into the darkness. *What am I doing?*

He found himself holding his breath when suddenly seasons of his childhood flashed through his thoughts and seemed to play across the darkness of the room. The excited feeling of the Last Day of school, bicycling for hours with buddy's with the soul intention of finding a hidden treasure or a secret club house, swimming for endless days in a deserted lake that seemed to have no end, the fear of getting into trouble, the gentle of touch from his Mother when there was an accident, the exhilaration of trying to determine the second life would change, listening to his Father's car rumbling up the drive after work, Christmas morning, enjoying simple fireworks on the 4th of July, costumes on Halloween, when the entire world was just a couple of blocks long, remembering and knowing every neighbor, while time overlapped the constant security of home, family, friends.

Shit...What've I been doing? When was the last time I actually talked to my family, do my siblings have more kids...and what the hell did I get them all for a present last Christmas. I hope Mike didn't send the fruit basket...again. I miss the outdoors, clean air...real people.

After lying in bed for hours reliving his past and trying to conger names of his child hood friends, Rick fell to sleep. The next morning Rick opened the door to magically find two brown paper bags filled with either breakfast or lunch placed neatly outside his door and a heaping plate full of dinner in the evening.

14

Nervous about Anne's demeanor after their little tryst, Rick attempted to retain the amicable truce with her, by determinedly improving with his jobs each day and steering clear of any situation that had the outcome of being alone with her.

But by the end of each day he found himself inevitably drawn to the barn, to stand silently in the shadows and watched Anne carefully train Star. Rick became addicted to the simple pleasure of her graceful movements with the youngling, seeming flawless in a composition of beauty in raw motion. He mutely admitted that he honestly marveled every time he inadvertently stumbled upon any moment when she was training the other horses. *She really has a natural gift, no wonder Mike wanted me to come and work with her for the movie.*

One pleasantly warm evening Rick was standing, safely tucked in the shadows outside the barn, caught in the darkness that engulfed the landscape at twilight and watched her work with a mammoth black stallion. She was training the horse by lunging him in a tight circle, changing directions every so often, as they un-seemingly danced in time with Elton John's 'Tiny Dancer'. Her fluid movements were naturally graceful, resembling a ballerina, but there was no doubt that she held the authority with the imposing horse the entire time.

Rick found himself silently captivated, *I can't believe that huge beast doesn't get fed up with her constant demands, turn and completely trample her into pieces.* As his mind envisioned the aftermath of his daydreams, he guiltily jumped in surprise when she abruptly stopped the horse and determinedly turned towards where he'd thought he was invisible in the dark.

"Hey Grunt, come here for a second," Anne mockingly called out.

"Ahhh...yeah." Rick felt slightly embarrassed having been caught watching her like a predator, uncomfortably cleared his throat, and stepped into the glaring light of the barn's arena.

 "I think it's about time you start handling some of the horses and learn how to ride."

"What? Uhhhh -- you mean now?" Rick's knees wobbled, threatening to collapse at the idea as her approached the menacing duo.

"Yeah, I mean now." Anne laughingly mocked, then involuntary smiled at the slight waver in his voice and nonchalantly waved her hand to guide him over.

"Okay--." Rick nervously shuffled his feet across the arena, juvenilely kicking up little puffs of dust as he approached the large black animal. Just the initial immense size and coloring made the horse seem incredibly intimidating. It pawed anxiously at the ground while patiently standing next to Anne with its massive head towering over hers and dark eyes never wavering as it questioningly assessed his timid approach. *Can't that thing look somewhere else; it's scaring the shit out of me.*

"Alright, you've got me over here Dragon Lady...now what do I need to do?" His voice erupted in a high-pitched, overwrought sound and immediately made the animal skittish.

 Instinctively Anne tightened her hold on its reigns, gently whispering to sooth his reaction to Rick. "Well, first thing, you need to calm down. Horses can sense your nervousness and it'll make them a little on edge. Remember when you helped with Bella? Just try to think the same way with good old Demon here."

"Demon...really? His name is Demon? Why couldn't he have been named Buttercup, Blackie, or Velvet or...or something a little more approachable than Demon."

"Oh well, a name's a name. Don't worry about that part, just give him your hand, pet his flanks and make sure you have a firm stance with him just in case he bolts or tries to flex his muscles. In that case it's better to be knocked down because you're close, than kicked because you're too far from their body. It's a good insurance plan when you're working alongside horses." Anne's eyes danced at the sight of Rick being absolutely uncomfortable.

Holding his breath he stepped closer to its warm body, began to gently pet the massive horse and monitor for any aggressive movements. Rick let out his breath with a whoosh as his confidence started to grow with each passing stroke.

 "Now listen...I want you to take the lead and continuously walk him around the arena while I go and get a few things done." Anne simultaneously finished her sentence, thrust the lead into his hand, walked quickly away from the arena and switched off the radio on her way out.

Rick's brain froze while nervousness began to seep through his body and disbelievingly listened to her softly mumbling off an imaginary checklist as she left the barn.

"Wow, thanks Rick; maybe I can get the dishes done, fix that leaky faucet, watch some TV and give my hair a good deep conditioning. You know...important stuff."

"What the...Anne, but...I...aw--." His complaints fell on deaf ears while Anne's voice faded into the night. Shit."

Rick despairingly glanced up at the horse's nose, gave him one last pat and began to obediently lead it around the arena. Rick sucked in his breath as his conjured up his confidence with each step, coincidentally as long as Demon submissively walked calmly behind. After a couple speculative glances back, he realized that Demon was pretty tame and decided to enjoy the leisurely walk with the horse.

The interior of the barn became pleasantly tranquil while Rick began to comfortably bond with the horse. With every other pass he decided to switch back and change directions to see if Demon would comply. "Well Demon, you're not so scary after all." He paused to give its mammoth head a gentle stroke, his hand in mid-air Rick suddenly noticed that Demon's ears had perked up, moving in different directions and his head instantly became tense while his eyes began to fretfully scan the area.

"Ahem." He uncomfortably cleared his throat when the hair stood up on the back on his neck as he registered the distinct impression that someone was watching them. He tried to sooth the horse's agitation by softly whispering, turned to walk along the back of the arena and tried to remember every word of Anne's insurance policy. *Be ready to jump if this guy decides to bolt. I don't need to get banged up cuz I don't even know if there's a hospital around here.* For a few seconds the only thing that Rick could hear was the distinct sound of his heartbeat thudding in his ears, combined with the hum of his nerves and his hands began to sweat with the reigns in his hands. He tried to listen for anything odd, but only heard the steady clomp of Demon's hooves.

"What the --" Rick's head snapped around at the definite sound of softly crunching gravel coming from somewhere around the outdoor arena. *Shit. It's probably just Beth and Suzie… trying to spy on me again.* Rick pivoted the horse around, walked boldly in front of the door leading out to outdoor arena and paused. Covering his eyes from the glare of the interior light, he squinted into the darkness to try and determine where the two annoying teens were.

"Hey, what are you trying to do out there?" Rick angrily called out into the darkness. Immediately he spied a stooped over shadowy form scurrying darting out of a dark corner of the outdoor arena and dove into the outlining bushes, immediately disappearing into the darkness. His attention instantly was redirected from the mysterious figure, to a nervous Demon who had begun to physically shy away from the forceful tone of his voice and the unknown darkness.

 "Whoa --Demon. You're okay boy…just calm down." All of Rick's senses switched into survival mode while he worked on relaxing the agitated horse. Time slipped by while he exerted all of his mental strength on maintaining his command, soothing the situation and resuming to walking the animal at a steady pace.

"Nice...nice job Rick." Anne's enthusiastic voice startling him, causing Rick to quickly swivel around with a gasp, slightly stumble and attempt to pinpoint where she magically appeared at the edge of the arena's fence without him noticing.

"What the --, what are you two trying to do...kill me?" Rick said while he desperately struggled with his fright, besides pride at being foolishly scared.

"What are you talking about?" Anne shot him a semi-curious glance, while stepping through the gate into the arena.

"Shit...just a few minutes ago, Beth and her buddy were hiding outside in the corral and now you're creeping in here spying on me." Insulted at what seemed like obvious mistrust, Rick continued to sooth Demon while he warily watched Anne approach.

"Look, I don't know what you're talking about. I just walked in the barn two seconds before I said anything and Beth is spending the night at Suzie's tonight...so she's not even here." Anne made her way to quickly close the distance, stopped in front of him and defensively crossed her arms.

"Anne, I swear I heard some kind of shuffling noise outside and then I saw something dart off in to the darkness. I thought maybe...it might have been your snooping teens again." Rick lamely finished while he watched Anne's shoulders relax and quirk a smirk at his explanation.

"No problem. It can get a little weird out here in the barn, especially when you're alone" She lifted her hand to give his shoulder a supportive squeeze, conspiringly whispered out of the side of her mouth. "I don't know. Sometimes I have a feeling that someone is watching me." Rick found himself mesmerized at her slight touch, then shook his head and began to walk away from her.

"Me too!" Rick exclaimed loudly, startling the horse and making Demon immediately shy away.

"Well, at least we have something in common." Anne chuckled while she took over the reins and soothed Demon with a few gentle strokes. "Where do you think you're going?" She asked turning around to watch his retreating form.

"Oh -- I thought we were done for the evening, I was just going to hit the hay." Rick paused at the edge of the arena.

"Oh no, you're not going anywhere. You're getting up on Demon here and taking a few turns around the arena before we quit for the evening." Anne led the horse over to where he stood contemplating her suggestion, firmly handed him the reigns and pointed at the saddle. "This is going to be your saddle; better get used to it because you're going to be sitting up there for a while."

Rick exaggeratedly rolled his eyes at her rudimentary explanation of its purpose. "Yeah, yeah, yeah. Ha-ha -- very funny. Now, get on with the rest of it."

"Now these are the stirrups, you put your foot in here and try to gracefully pull yourself up." Anne exaggeratedly bent her knee, followed her own directions and gracefully landed on top of the horse. Once demonstrated, Anne swiftly reversed her actions and when her feet were planted on the soil, motioned with a fluid motion for Rick to utilize the stirrups and offered a shoulder to help hoist him up.

"Really—." Rick purposefully elongated the single word while his eyes became curiously round and gave her precarious stance an unwelcomed glance, ignoring her offered shoulder. *Shit...I've seen the stunt guys do this on set a thousand times. I don't need any damn help from some girl to get up on a freakin' horse.* Rick cocked an arrogant brow and jokingly pushed her slightly out of the way. "No problem, I don't think I'm going to need your help."

He quickly lifted a foot and inserted it firmly into the stirrup; his awkward position caught him off guard, causing him to hop slightly and precariously grab the side of the saddle.

"Hey...now, quickly grab onto the horn up on top, then try to hoist yourself up and over." Anne hurried out of the way while she amusingly watched Rick hobble, lunge and flounder at the horse's side.

"Whoa...whoa...whoa --" Rick continued to dangerously hop while Demon began to hesitantly move away from the pull of the saddle.

"Hey Rick, let me help you." Anne swiftly jogged up, steadied the horse, and then moved to tuck her knee under Rick's dangling foot to give some extra support. Rick instinctively pushed down on her knee, throwing his foot helplessly over the mammoth animal and launched himself across the back of Demon, ending with an exerted huff.

Anne cheerily stood to the side while enjoying the amusing image of Rick semi-lying on his stomach, wiggling to keep his balance and ultimately struggle to sit up in the saddle. After a few disgruntled moments, in addition to openly voicing a few choice profanities, he finally managed to completely throw a leg over the opposite side of Demon and helplessly clutched onto the horn.

"Well, ok...now what?" Rick's voice came out in a gulp of air, while clumsily waiting for her instructions.

"Ok, now...hang on while I just lead you through a few rudimentary exercises." Anne had to rudely redirect her head and openly began to chuckle at his obvious discomfort before she attempted to physically lead the pair around the arena, simultaneously coaching him on how to maneuver the horse and off handedly humming along with Snow Patrol's 'Chasing Cars'.

During a few frightfully token minutes, Rick unconsciously obeyed every one of her distinct instructions and undeniably found himself slowly enjoying being perched in the saddle.

Anne leisurely took a step back, surveying his extraordinary progress while he unknowingly rode solitarily around the arena. Inadvertently she gasped finding her naughty thoughts fleeting down the taunt stretch of his t-shirt to the seat of his jeans, until she embraced that her gaze had finally gravitated to openly examining the display of his body.

"Hmmmm....Nice seat," She lightly murmured out of the side of her mouth.

"What?!?" Rick called out while he tried to remember the exact way she'd instructed to stop the horse. "I hope I didn't just hear what I think I heard."

"What...I was just commenting on your form, that's all." Anne innocently batted her lashes while he rounded around the arena and slowly pausing the horse in front of her. "I think you've had enough for one night...I'm going to need you to be able to walk tomorrow."

Rick glanced over his shoulder to give her a curious but dumfounded look, dismissed her compassionate offer to help, as he disengaged a leg and decided to attempt to slide off the horse, unattended.

He shut his eyes in humiliation, realizing that not only was his butt was provocatively bent over the side of the horse, but he didn't have the strength to slither with dignity down with the support of the saddle. *I'm sure she's enjoying this.* The second his shaking feet touched the ground, he tried to quickly turn around to catch her eyeing his discomposure, but instead she was naively staring up at the rafters like an angle, but held the guilty tell-tale sign a tinge of pink flushing her face.

"Right...Nice, Anne. Catch a guy in a helpless situation. I hope you got an eyeful," He crossed his arms in mocking defiance and stated to belittle her open display of indifference.

"Oh, wow! Rick you're already down. Ohhh...I was thinking about how I'm going to clean out all of the cobwebs out of the rafters. Anyway...wow, good job and we'll try for some more training in the morning." Anne flippantly said as she guiltily averted her gaze, took the horse's reigns and began to guide him back towards the stalls. "I'll just take old Demon off your hands and cool him down for you."

"Yeah – I think I can tell you who needs a little 'cooling down '." Rick muttered at her obvious unease and hastily retreating back, amusingly shook his head to attempt to walk over to his room. That was until an aching kink surged up his upper thigh, striking his head like a brain-freeze, and instantly commanding him to pause with a complaining moan. Bending over, he trace the muscles of his legs, began to massage and vigorously rub out the painful knot from his lower back down to his calf.

"Oh my…" The suggestive timbre in Anne's soft voice floated across the arena.

"What?" Rick swiftly jerked his head in her general direction and glared.

"Ummm…night." Anne said offhandedly as she slammed the stalls door and threw some feed inside.

The only evidence that she had made an inappropriate comment was the bouncing movement of her bouncing ponytail as she left Demon to hurriedly skip across the planks, turn up the radio causing a slight giggle and suddenly humming along, but enthusiastically off-key with Def Leppards "Pour Some Sugar On Me."

"R-i-g-h-t…I know you got an eye full." Rick hollered then chuckled at her obvious enjoyment, while he humorously shook his head watching her impish retreat and continued his agonizing limp into his room.

15

A few weeks later Rick sneaked into the barn, conspiratorially looked around and stealthily approached Anne, giving her backside one of his most devastating smiles while mesmerizing it.

He caught her bent over as she busily concentrated on her routine of pampering Bella and Star with a luxurious massage, brushing and a quiet walk. Anne gently whispered while handling Star in the center of the barn illuminated by the sun beaming in through the open arena doors, while the proud new mother hovered close by. She had become so engrossed with the beautiful new addition that she hadn't even noticed Rick sneaking along the outskirts of the arena while Sheryl Crow's 'Soak up the Sun' was on the radio and her body seductively swayed in time with the music.

"So...I heard from a little bird that it's your birthday today," Rick leaned over and hovered above her shoulder while whispering close to her ear and then darted back for safety.

"Holy shit!" Anne yelled and jumped at the nearness of his voice. She narrowed her eyes, instantly contemplating how she'd accomplish doing him bodily harm, mentally calculating which body part she could attack with a shovel, without showing bruises and callously threw over her shoulder. "Don't *ever* sneak up on me when I'm working with any of the horses." Anne swiveled around attempting to shake off the lingering feeling of embarrassment at having been startled out of her mind, the closeness of his voice and the conscious feeling of being alone with him. She determinedly gave him the cold shoulder while silently resumed to soothe the newborn.

"Ah, come on now...don't get your panties in a bunch. I think your birthday makes a great excuse to cut out early and enjoy some of this perfect weather we've been having." Rick guiltily kicked the dirt know her indifference was because he had startled her, wandered over to the edge of the arena and propped his back up against the fence. He watched Anne desperately trying to ignore his presence as she continued working with the young horse. "Come on -- I won't tell the boss that we're going to play a little hookie, that is...I won't, if you don't," Rick said through his smile as he continued to openly watch her stiff back slightly turn to address him.

"Well...your boss already knows what you should be doing, Grunt...cuz right now it looks like you're not doing a damn thing!" Anne's voice softened for a second as she looked over her shoulder to add, "Anyway, I don't believe in celebrating my birthday...so don't sweat it." Her defenses rankled up her back while she tried to ignore the sight of him standing in the sunshine and remain focused on the foal.

Anne's muscles tensed waiting for one of his wisecrack remarks but instead all she heard was silence. Her brow angrily furrowed and she seriously started to question his mental abilities, rotated around the horse so she could pin him with one of her arrogant stares.

"Well, are you going to get off your lazy ass and…" Anne's mind instantly went blank, immediately forgetting what she'd intended to say. It was as if her words ended up hovering in the air, caught in an imaginary balloon when she spotted Rick lounging on the arena fence, with the sun gracing his body and smiling as if he didn't have a care in the world. His handsome looks had gone from being a rough bad boy when he first arrived at the ranch, to a really naughty man. His dark hair had grown out so it fell shaggily across his eyes, his skin remained beautifully tanned enhanced from working out in the yard, complimenting the tight white T-shirt and Levi's that hugged his form.

Suddenly Anne felt her stomach fall to her feet, palms start to sweat and her mouth went instantly dry at the mere sight of him. *Oh no, what am I going to do with this guy? I can't start feeling like this every time I'm around him and I can't avoid him. Just pull it together Anne… he's just your employee and you are not a child.*

Rick kept a serene smile plastered on his face as he watched the blatant irritation rise across her face while abruptly maneuvered around the foal and approached him.

She was striking in the midmorning light that came streaming in from the opened barn doors. His body uncomfortably tightened echoing each step as she strode across the arena with an angry determination. Her hair was haphazardly tucked up under her usual dirty baseball cap with a ponytail trailing down her back. He realized with a jolt that instead of her oversized work jeans and sweatshirt that he'd become accustomed to seeing her in, she was dressed in a fitted black T-shirt and snug cut-off jean shorts. She had a couple of smudges of dirt rubbed across her chin and nose, but as the sun made her eyes brilliant, everything suddenly complemented her youthful appearance.

With the seamless end of a beautiful spring the weather continued to be unusually hot for June and everyone was embracing it with high spirits because of the endless opportunities to be outside. Even Lois and Chuck hadn't given him such a hard time earlier that morning when he'd picked up their supplies. The unusual jovial mood from the disgruntled two must have rubbed off on him and continued by the time he'd arrived back at the ranch. Whistling while unloading everything from town he found himself having a fast discussion with Beth.

"OMG Rick…its Anne's birthday today and I can't think of anything I could get her." Rick stood in awe as Beth absentmindedly lifted a box of supplies, consumed with her plight. "We've always done something, but with the weather and everything…I just forgot."

"We'll see what we can come up with, no worries. "With a little inspiration he lightheartedly tousled her hair, ignored any of her teenaged complaints about her style and off handedly thanked her for the bit of information. A brilliant idea began to brew while he finished unloading the truck, ran into the kitchen to make a couple quick calls, asked Beth for her help and whistling off-key made his way down the barn. Turning his face towards the sun he felt positive that he'd come up with secure a plan that he'd make something happen that evening to celebrate Anne's birthday.

Except once his naughty thoughts about her began to stream though his mind, Rick had doubts about not only standing in the isolated barn with her, but started to question his sanity. Chewing on his bottom lip he tried to redirect his lingering thoughts off her tight t-shirt and his strong physical attraction towards her. *I don't know, maybe it's because I haven't been with a woman for a few months, but she's starting to look better every time I see her. I should stay away from her. Nothing can happen between us anyway...I'm leaving.*

"Well, Dragon Lady. I think we've worked pretty damn hard around here lately and could use any excuse to go out of here...even your birthday. Hey, and don't worry you're silly head about what to wear. I figure, you should clean up PRETTY good...at least good enough for around this town." Rick made it a point that during his speech, to allow his gaze to travel from her toes of her boots, slowly up her body while obviously lingering on the most appropriate areas. Rick finished his speech by staring into her eyes and gave her a charming, innocent smile he could muster. "I heard there's a great band playing in town at some bar, where they serve an amazing catch of the day and really strong drinks. Look, it's finally going to be an absolutely pristine night out and we shouldn't waste it." Rick leaned too close for Anne's taste, raised an eyebrow and stared down tracing her lips with his eyes, making her nervously lick them in response. "I double dog dare you." He casually slapped the bill of her baseball hat ending his verbal challenge, causing it to cover her eyes and jokingly nudged her shoulder as he made his way around her. "Double dog dare."

"What the f--?" Anne struggled for a second with the brim of the hat and finally pulled it off her head, causing her hair to cascade onto her shoulders in a tangled mess.

"Oh --. Um...and Anne by the way. I don't take no for an answer, so I'll see you at six sharp." With that he turned to slowly make his way out of the barn, whistling in time with Roy Orbison's 'Pretty Woman' playing in the background, to casually maneuver through the outdoor arena.

Anne struggled to lift her hair out of her irate eyes as she swiveled left and right in a futile attempt to search for Rick. She opened her mouth to find the choice words that she wanted to hurl at his retreating back, but instantly became speechless, mesmerized by his nicely shaped ass sauntering out into the sunlight and disappeared from sight.

"Well—,"she muttered while heatedly kicked the dirt, her actions making the foal startle, cautiously move over to his mother's side. "I'll be damned."

Anne scurried to pick the lead rope up off the ground, walking over to gently tuck it over Bella's head. The idea of Rick taking her out for the evening began to run errantly through her mind, a small shiver of apprehension ran down her spine while she attempted not to envision a few naughty scenarios that the evening could promise. Anne pulled her thoughts out of the gutter and paused in front of the foal, leaned down to gaze into his eyes and whispered conspiringly, "I'll just let him think he's going to take me out for the evening, pompous ass, but instead I just might have some kind of errand to run…or 'female' issues in the meantime." Rubbing Bella in between her ears, she secured the lead over the horse's head then started back towards the row of stalls. The idiotic idea that she'd probably be backing out of a dare kept creeping into her mind. *Shit, I can't believe that he's doing this, like I can't cleanup enough for this town. Double dog dare…my ass! I'll show him.*

Anne hurried to lead the horses precariously to their stall, tactlessly threw in some hay and feed inside, then quietly shut the stall door. She instinctively paused on the walkway, closed her eyes, imagined the outcome of her options for the end of the evening and pondered on which option she was going to take.

A slightly wicked smile spread across her face, then with a loud whoop she turned, skipped down the planks and giddily made her way over to close up the barn for the day.

"Shit, if he wants a night out…I'll show him a night out. Hang on Westport, here we come." Her rapid steps sped up into a slight jog as she neared the front of the house, abruptly skidding to a semi-halt, barged in with a slam of the door and raced up the stairs like a maniac.

"What's wrong…Shit, is there a fire?" Beth called out perched on the couch painting her toenails in an outlandish pink, watching thoughtless TV. "Hey…Anne, what's the rush? What are you up to?" Beth yelled out towards the front stairway, listening to the indistinct ruckus, without an answer. "Argh!" She grimaced trying to scramble off the couch without injuring her pedicure, cautiously hobbling across the room with tissue paper sticking out from in between her toes, to aimlessly follow Anne upstairs. By the time she caught up with her sister, Anne was tearing off her clothes, throwing them into a haphazard heap onto the bathroom floor, behind a closed the door while the shower was running.

"Ok…out with it." Beth flopped down on Anne's bed, her feet sticking out precariously rod like and patiently waited for her sister to answer.

The second after Anne jumped into the shower and began soaping up, she stuck her head out and called out from in between the shower curtains, "Funny thing happened today...someone told Rick that it's my birthday."

Unseen Beth guiltily bit her lip and began to trace the intricate patterns sewn into the quilt that covered Anne's bed. She took a deep breath, clearing her guilty, dry throat before answering. "Oh, I guess that I might have said something, to someone...sometime today."

Listening to her inadvertent answer, Anne quickly popped out her head, full of bubbles from washing her hair and called out to Beth, "Yeah, well he wants to take me out tonight! He stood right in the middle of the arena, told me to clean up as best as I could...and meet him downstairs at six."

Beth let out a whoop, clapped her hands ecstatic by the news, then sat ramrod straight and panicked, looking over at the bedside clock. "Well...that's in half an hour!"

"I know! I wanted to tell him to shove it up his, well...you know where I wanted to tell him to go and what to do."

Beth smiled at the sound of her irate sister's muffled voice yelling from behind the partially closed bathroom door. She jumped off of the bed, wiggling off the tissue ignoring her toes and began to vigilantly rummage through Anne's closet.

"Ok...you're going to need MY expertise with this one. I'm going to lay out some of your outfits, and HEY...don't forget to shave...everything, while you're in there!"

Bemused at Beth's request, Anne quizzically stuck her out from behind the curtain and yelled out, "Now...why would I do a thing like that?"

Beth took a deep breath, raised her eyes up to the ceiling and mentally asked for patience for her naive sister. "OMG!! When was the last time you shaved *anything* on your body...like maybe two Christmas ago?"

Irritated silence radiated from behind the shower curtain, becoming a blatant answer to her knowing question. Beth smiled as she heard slight shuffling, then muttering and banging around as Anne looked for her razor.

"Now...where did you hide all of your sexy party clothes from when you lived in Seattle?" Beth whispered to herself as she stepped into the vast space and combed through the closet. She found herself digging deep into the back recesses, until she found the small cluster of clothes that definitely did not belong in Westport. As her fingers instantly touched the beautiful material of the clothes,

Beth found herself reminiscing about how she'd duck into the lonely closet, loving to secretly try on every outfit when Anne had first arrived back home. *Shit...that was until the afternoon Anne caught me in that dazzling, sequined dress...tucked over my dirty work jeans, bad call and made them all off limits.* "Ok, where is that one little dress...the one that would be perfect for tonight...aha!"

Anne disgruntled threw the offensive razor into the trash, shut off the water and grabbed a towel hanging next to the shower door. The hairs on the back of her neck started to raise as she quickly dried off stepping out of the shower, instinctively pondering on what kind of unnatural phenomena had appeared to keep Beth so quiet. Tying a towel under her arms and hurriedly tucking her hair up in another one, Anne stepped into her room expecting the worst.

"What..." She asked stopping dead in her tracks. "Do you think you're doing?"

"Sit." Her sister commanded, motioning towards an abandoned seat tucked neatly in front of her and flicked on the radio while patiently waiting. Beth defiantly crossed her arms, clutched hard on the hairbrush held in her hand, and insistently tapped her toe in-time with the smooth melody of Norah Jones' 'Come Away with Me' that lingered in the background.

"Well--." Beth peevishly arched a brow, impatiently waved her hand in a come-hither motion, then pointed dramatically towards the stool.

"Yeah...what?" Anne curiosity piqued, returned a raised eyebrow at Beth's silent command, but obviously refused to move an inch while she visually measured what her sister was up to.

"Argh..." Beth exaggeratedly threw her arms up in exasperation, taking a moment to reason with Anne. "Look, you have less than twenty minutes to get ready and I hate to say it, but...you need all the help you can get." She decided to throw all caution to the wind and went in for the kill, while Anne stubbornly regarded her with an indifferent opposition. "Let me guess...I bet you were just going to throw on your one pair of clean jeans, a T-shirt and hoodie...then race out with your wet hair tied up in a ponytail and no makeup. Shit...Anne, when was the last time you did anything other than shovel shit and actually get all dressed up to go out on a freaking date?"

Anne stood in a reluctant, but semi-interested response rolled her eyes and huffed in defeat as she obediently plopped down on the stool.

Behind her Beth silently did a little victory dance and embraced her moment of triumph.

"Don't celebrate too much...I still need to leave." Anne ended her sentence with undistinguishable, but annoyed noises and maintained a rigid disposition while primly trying to cover her bare knees with the worn towel that was precariously wrapped around her.

"Shit, Beth. You act like I'm some old maid. I know it's been awhile, but I'd like you to know that I've been on plenty of dates," Anne tried to grudgingly defended herself through clenched teeth, becoming silent, and closed her eyes at the pain as Beth roughly dragged a brush through her tangled hair.

"Well…,"Beth tried to untangle a large knot, administering a little more pain than necessary while mischievously grinning down at her sister's head. "I know Anne…but you only have smidgen amount of time to get ready, and you know how much I love to dress up, so sit back, relax and let me have some fun."

Anne closed her eyes against the pain and smiled while she remembered when she silently observed an exuberant Beth, youthfully imagining herself as a queen holding court in the barn, toes dug into the wet sand, treading across tide pools as if elegantly walking across a stage and running hell bent through the fields all decked out in either her ballet tutu or her mother's old formal gowns.

Beth was quick with pulling her hair off of her face and allowing it to dry naturally while she started to apply her makeup.

"Ahhhh --"Anne started to nervously fidget, recalling the rather horrifying images of a particularly 'tween phase Beth had gone through, ominous memories of when her makeup application resembled between some sort of animation character, Twisted Sister or someone who'd just rolled off the circus' freak sideshow wagon.

"Shhh…Be still. We'll be done in a second." She finished with Anne's makeup with a couple of deft strokes of eye shadow, liner and mascara. "Okay, now hold your head upside down while I dry your hair. Hmmm, let's see if this old thing works."

Anne instantly obeyed, too frightened to look at what she looked like, while Beth attempted to turn on the ancient hairdryer…sputtering because it hadn't been used in years. She blankly stared at the wood on the floor, listening to Beth hum while spraying a couple of different products in her hair, slowly working them through.

Anne's eyes started to grow heavy with fatigue, closing with the constant hum of the dryer until a loud honking broke through from outside, the shrill resounded over the high-pitched noise of the dryer.

"Ouch!" Anne's head shot up, accidentally knocking it against the dryer and glared at the red numbers illuminating the clock.

"OMG, he's just a few minutes early. He can just cool his horses and wait a few more...I'm saying, that's what he gets for being obnoxious and honking," Beth muttered, angrily switching off the dryer, stomped over to the window and stuck her head out having every intention to yell down at Rick. Beth paused for a second, watching as he casually leaned against the trucks door with his legs crossed at the ankle, eyes closed and face raised to the sunshine. "Hey, Hot Shot! Hold onto your horses. She'll be down...but it'll be when she's ready!"

Rick genuinely smiled up at Beth's mockingly irate attitude and hollered back, "I'd appreciate it if you made sure the she's at least changed out of her dirty work clothes, we don't want to scare anybody tonight!"

Beth smiled and replied in a mocking tone, "Oh, don't you worry...she'll look just fine for a night out...but I don't know about being seen with the likes of you."

She popped back into the room with a silly grin pasted to her mouth, triumphantly ending their friendly banter in her favor. Beth found herself plummeting from being carefree, to being stuck in an uncomfortable moment locking gazes with a terrified Anne, who was staring back at her through a massive curtain of hair.

"Well, now...what's next?" Anne nervously asked her muffled voice barely heard through her hair. "Should I hide?"

"Knock it off, you're going to have a great time...Ta-Da!" Beth decided to do an outrageous, but improvised dance, shimming over to Anne's closet and whipped open the door, demonstrating her Vanna White impression by pointing to the back of it. Anne gasped as if on cue, hanging up against the door was the sexiest, little black dress, making her rapidly blink in denial at any memory of ever wearing it, because she never had.

"Oh...Beth, I don't know if I can wear that! I didn't have the balls to wear it even when I lived in Seattle, how am I going to pull it off in Westport?" Anne visually paled at the idea of putting on the slinky black dress for the evening; but she recognized the feeling bubbling inside was torn between being nervous and excited. *It's been forever since I've felt this kind of apprehension about getting ready for a night out.*

"Sorry...you don't have time to think about it or make another choice." Beth sauntered over to the closet, gracefully lifted the hanger and balanced the dress on her little finger. Silence hung in between them as Beth held the dress up in front of Anne's face and gave it a happy little shake. "Besides the lack of time, with all of his smart assed remarks, don't you want to make him eat a little crow tonight?" Beth asked with an exaggerated shake of her eyebrows.

"Shit." Anne abruptly stood up and made a quick grab for the dress. Beth was prepared for her sister's reaction and held tightly onto the dress; deftly dodging Anne's clutch and leaned back to grab something else that had she'd tucked under the pillows at the top of the bed.

"Now, now…just wait a minute. First things first," Beth said in her best matronly voice. While displaying a matching set of sexy black panties and bra.

"What …exactly… do you expect will happen this evening?" Anne asked then instinctively paused mid-swipe, rammed her hand back down on her hip and give Beth an annoyed look.

"OMG! I was counting on *something*, but nothing that you wouldn't want to happen…at least if you'd let it. Anyway, you are only as sexy on the outside as you are on the inside. What were you going to wear this evening, cotton panties and your sports bra?" Beth replied, giving the delicate items one last thrust in Anne's face.

Anne gave her sister a look that was a mixture of immense pleading and accusing glare, then grabbed all of the clothes out of her hands and stormed into the bathroom.

Beth did another jig, quickly walked around the room to turn up Lady Gaga's 'You and I' and then rummaged through the closet for a pair of shoes. "Perfect!" she murmured. With a Cheshire cat grin, she did another triumphant little dance while grabbing a sexy pair of strappy heels. Backing out of the closet Beth heard Anne opening the bathroom door, turning around to find her sibling forlornly standing in the doorway.

The dress fit her body perfectly, with wide straps that tapered down to a V at her cleavage, ended at the knee, plunged into a deep V in the back and material that hugged every curve. Beth let out a low whistle as Anne unconsciously chewed on her lip, trying desperately to find an excuse to back out of the evening.

"Look, don't start trying to get out of this…I've worked too hard and you don't have time. Sit down so we can finish, you're already late." Beth responded as if she was reading her mind.

"You're so exasperating!" Anne laughed at her sister's enthusiasm.

Beth kept up her busy pace, working her hair with the blow dryer and some spray, tossing her mane in different directions. The room seemed uncannily quiet with the music lightly floating on the air after Beth shut off the dryer and started to brush her hair off of her face. "Okay, now lean forward so I can get this all secured with the pins."

Anne hesitantly leaned down and watched her bare toes as Beth grabbed the top of her hair twisting it loosely back on both sides of her face, leaving the rest to fall in waves around her shoulders.

A few seconds Anne hovered between hyperventilating and refusing to go, until she finally had the gumption enough to glance at her reflection. To her surprise her makeup was tastefully simple, light liner angled her eyes as mascara accentuated her lashes giving her eyes an exotic look. The shimmer of a warm glow graced her cheeks that brought out the hint of sun from the past few days. After Anne's hair was secured in place it had a carefree feel to it that softened the appearance of the sexy dress. She sat there, mesmerized by her transformation in the mirror and tentatively touched her face as she astonishingly regarded the youthful image starting back at her. Beth busily rummaged across the dresser to grab a pair of chandelier earrings, her favorite perfume, black shoes and a warm pink lip gloss. *What am I doing all of this for...some two-bit cowboy? I must be going crazy! Damn, I have to hand it to Beth...she's getting pretty good at all of the beauty stuff. I look pretty good for this evening.*

"Hurry up! Throw your shoes on and I'll grab a purse for your stuff."

"Oh man, I forgot how much I loved these!" Anne exclaimed at the sight of the shoes. She bent down to put on the sexy black patent leather shoes that hadn't seen the sunlight in years. As she cinched up the strap around her ankle Anne turned her foot this way and that, feeling better by the minute. Standing up she gave Beth a loving hug and accepted the small black clutch while they simultaneously stuffed everything she was going to need for the evening.

"Now, go and have a great time tonight! I've already called to have Suzie come over and spend the night. So...take your time, there's absolutely no hurry to get home..." Beth added with an exaggerated wink.

Anne linked her arm with Beth's while they left the room to walk down the front stairs, both of them giddy over the excitement about the evening. Anne took a deep breath as they approached the front door and pulled her sister to a stop before they opened it.

"I don't know why we're making this such a big thing out of this." Anne turned to give Beth a hug and laughingly whispered into her ear, "You make me feel like I'm Cinderella...I can reassure you that nothing is going to happen and everything is going to turn into a pumpkin at midnight. We won't be that long; we're only going into Westport, not even Olympia...and from what I remember there isn't that much to do around town."

Beth laughed lightly and returned the hug, grinning as she replied, "Oh, I place a bet that you guys will be able to think of something to do to pass the time...in Westport or wherever."

She caught a glimpse of Rick through a crack in the blind covering the doors window over Anne's shoulder. He was irritated, kicking a bunch of pebbles next to the truck pacing back and forth, impatiently waiting to leave. Bubbles of anticipation grew in the pit of her stomach while she anticipating Rick's reaction. *OMG -- is he in for a big surprise. I'm sooo glad we made him wait a little longer than necessary...the look on his face... this is going to be great!*

Noticing the shadows poised in the doorway, Rick decided to casually lean against the side of the truck seemingly bored and squint to watch the sun making its slow descent towards the horizon. A speedy shower had left his hair slightly disarrayed, with the appearance of stubble created a striking combination. He decided to accompany his disheveled appearance with a casual white short sleeved button-up shirt, his worn Levi's and new cowboy boots.

"Okay Cinderella, time for you to go get into your carriage and off to the ball," Beth giddily said as she dramatically threw open the front door and walked across the porch. Beth began to teasingly offer a few options of the limited activities that would be existing local flavor for the evening. "Let's see, you could go whale watching, hang out at the Crab Pot for some outrageous seafood, head on over to the Knotty Pine for a little ping pong and shuffle board, Cowboy Billy's for music...or The Local for pool and darts. What do you have in mind?"

"First off, how do you know about Westport's nightlife?" Anne nervously tried to distract her wavering thoughts and mono-tone answered, robotically following her sister. "Well, I thought casting a line at the jetty for crab would be a starter."

"Ha...I might be young...but I do notice things." Beth kept her eyes trained, waiting for Rick's instant reaction instead of paying any attention to Anne's attempt at flippant answers. The two giddy girls continued their inane banter as they descended the stairs and enjoying their creative choices of local entertainment for the evening.

He'd apparently recognized Anne's laugh, the sound of it made him casually turn in their general direction from watching the sunset. He had to blink a few times before his vision cleared, because was still marred by black spots and slightly out of focus. Once he could see clearly, Rick awkwardly pushed himself off of the truck in astonishment while the two casually walked arm and arm down the path. As his gaze skimmed down the length of Anne's body, he felt his jaw almost drop. *Shit, I knew she had a hot little body, but I wouldn't have guessed how hot.* He mentally appraised her appearance from head to toe, her hair was loose, moving with the slight warm breeze blowing off of the sea, a little black dress that clung to her body like a glove and as she walked the edge had a habit of creeping up her thighs, with every other step her hand instinctively reached down to pull it back down.

As she turned to give Beth one last hug, he caught a glimpse of how low the dress plunged down her back. His eyes lingering, traveled down, resting on her nicely shaped ass then lower to a pair of shiny black shoes that wrapped her ankles and had a bit of a heel. Agitated Rick shifted his feet, unconsciously wrestling with the way his body immediately responded to her appearance. Rick rubbed his face and suddenly realized that he was going to have absolutely no control over the evening. *Damn, I hope I made the right decision to do this tonight.*

Uh-hu…YES…Uh huh, yes, that's what I thought. The look that was plastered across Rick's face said everything, reaffirming her success in her sister's transformation. Beth sweetly smiled as she gave Anne one last squeeze, sincerely whispering, "Remember, you two have a great time tonight."

Anne clung tightly to Beth, basically because she felt like bolting back across the porch, into the house, throwing on her sweats and cowering under her blankets. The mere thought of walking alone, towards Rick made her feel extremely uncomfortable. Hesitating for a second, she took a few timid steps forward, then glanced longingly back at her sister, standing forlornly alone on the path. Beth gave her a lopsided grin, shooed her away with her fingers and silently mouthed, "OMG, chicken shit…have fun."

"Wow Wee! Look at you all dressed up for the evening, you look like a million dollars!" Suzie's squeaky voice shattered the awkward moment as she hooted a lengthy catcall as she lumbered up drive carrying her backpack.

"Thanks…thanks a lot!" Embarrassed at all of the attention, Anne turned to look in Suzie's general direction, nonchalantly waved and laughingly called back. "Great!" Anne muttered under her breath as she desperately searched for her absent pride, "That's just what I need, an optimistic teen making suggestive remarks about my looks." Nervous at being targeted as the center of fascination, Anne tugged tartly on the hem of her skirt and turned mid-stride to make her way towards the truck…ramming smack dab, directly into Rick.

"Um, sorry…. I didn't see you," Anne said instinctively placing her hands on his chest for support while tilting unsteadily on her heels.

"No problem… I thought I'd help you over to the truck." Rick readily grabbed her arm, allowing her to take a moment to breathe and collect herself before she fell down. *Or tried to run off is more like it.* In a lame attempt to redirect the awkwardness, Rick gallantly bowed then held his elbow out for her to take.

"Why...thank you." Anne laughed and allowed him to tuck her hand possessively under his arm as they sauntered towards the truck. He held open the passenger door and adverting his gaze while he assisted her to climb into the cab.

Anne listened to the squeaking springs as she scooted across and with each annoying noise, she desperately wanted to sink deeper into the ancient vinyl seat. Suddenly feeling cold against her skin, she attempted to retain some dignity by securing the hem of her dress with one hand as it naturally migrated north up her thighs and quickly squirmed across the seat. Her face instantly went beet red as her terrified eyes darted up to see if Rick had noticed her plight, but when the door shut with a firm click, she began to mentally calculate the different ways she was going to string up and beat Beth when they arrived back home. *I'm going to throttle her; she's the one who got me into this damn outfit and absurd situation.*

After getting an eyeful, Rick shut the truck door, then casually strolled around the bed to give Anne a necessary second while she wrestled with her dress and arrogantly called over his shoulder to the two girls on the porch, "Girls don't wait up...I don't know what time we'll be back tonight." Listening to their giggling, he instantly pause to give them a stately salute, then hastened the rest of the way around the truck, jumped in and started the engine. Rick didn't waste a precious second, instantly throwing it in gear, deftly maneuvering around the drive and pointing it west towards Westport, *I'd better keep the speedometer at an dangerous speed, cuz if I know Anne, she's about to throw herself out the window and run back home at any second.*

As the truck sputtered out of the drive Anne craned her neck to imploringly watch the house disappear from view and waved at the laughing girls standing on the porch. A nervous sob choked her throat, making her readjust her position on the seat as they sped down the highway. Stevie Nick's deep sexy voice unexpectedly lulled over the radio as Fleetwood Mac's 'Sara' began playing. Humming to herself, Anne turned her head towards the window enjoying a slight, warm breeze that drifted through causing her hair to move as her fingers kept time with the rhythm. Her mood gradually lightened as she lifted her face up towards the blue sky and enjoyed feeling the warmth from the sun. A slow, sensuously lazy smile touched her lips as she suddenly felt...*free.*

"So –,"Anne cleared her throat when her voice came out a little husky, twisting slightly in her seat so she could face Rick. She wanted to create some sort of conversation to break the silence that hung over the cab of the truck. "What have you planned for the evening?"

Rick struggled to keep both eyes on the road, pretending not to notice that her skirt had, once again, risen to mid-thigh as he cleared his throat. "Well, I asked around town a little bit...and it seems like the only 'happening' is Cowboy Bob's. They don't accept reservations, so I'm hoping we can arrive a little early, before it becomes too crowded to get a table and have some dinner. Then there's supposed to be a great band later." Instantly he couldn't help his hot gaze slide across the seat, barely pausing as he skimmed her exposed leg, up her body and finally rested on her face.

"Humm…" Anne felt a sudden sinking sensation in her stomach and her face flushed as their eyes locked for a few seconds. "Dinner and dancing sounds great…" *Are you shitting me, who the hell talked me into this? Oh that's right, freakn' double dog dare my ass. I could just kick myself for agreeing to this.*

 Companionable silence settled over the cab for the rest of the drive and Rick determinedly kept his eyes on the road as they slowly meandered through town. There seemed to be quite a few tourists still out enjoying the boardwalk and harbor, browsing some of the small gift shops that remained open.

 Nick slowed the truck down to a snail's pace as they drove past the front of Cowboy Bob's. "Sorry, it doesn't look like there is any parking available in front. I'll have to drive around the block again to see if there's anything close…or would you rather I drop you off at the door?"

Instantly disturbed, Anne sucked in some air through her teeth, while embarrassing images crept into her mind. *Oh, I can just picture it now: me waiting alone next to the restaurant's entrance dressed like this, while hoards of locals snidely snicker and make indecent proposals as they lumber past. No thank you.* "Nope, I'll be fine where ever you find a parking spot. It's still nice out; a little walk and fresh air would do me some good," Anne responded in an uncanny, singsong voice.

Without a word, Rick knowingly smirked at Anne's futile attempt to cover up her uneasiness. A few seconds later he found a parking spot about a block away, deftly angled in the truck and quickly jumped out to stride around to open the passenger door.

Anne leaned over to quickly assess her make-up in the rearview mirror and involuntarily began watching him walk around the truck. She instinctively licked her lips, forgetting all about touching up her make-up and became consumed with checking him out. *Hmmm…he is one good looking man. Too bad he's probably really an ax murderer, besides being my employee… something might just have happened tonight.*

Rick reached for the handle and opened the door as Anne grabbed her purse off of the truck floor. He diligently coughed while he let out a pent up breath as his gaze moved to her exposed upper thigh while she retrieved her purse. Rick immediately averted his wandering eyes, trying to give her some dignity and pretended not to notice how high her dress had traveled.

"Yikes! How did that happen?" Anne floundered with her purse when she noticed the position of her non-existent skirt and his obvious discomfort. She cautiously stepped down from the truck using his hand for leverage, dutifully pulled her dress down to a near decent length and gave him a saucy wink as she looked up at him through her lashes simultaneously accepting his arm while they started down the street. "You're going to have to help me watch out for my little, um, problem. It's my first night out in a long time and I don't want to cause a scene tonight if my skirt rides up a little too high."

"Oh…well now Anne, you won't have to worry about that. You can count on me to be watching out for any kind of slip ups in that general area all night…and if you need some assistance with your skirt, you just let me know. Hell, I'll give you a couple of hands to help you out with any kind of help you might need in that area. You might say that some even call me an expert in that department."

"I'm sure they have…" Instead of being offended at his jest, Anne good heartily smiled, smacked his shoulder and shook her head.

Companionably they continued to stroll down the street, indiscriminately pausing every so often to laughingly search the shop windows. They took turns making outrageous comments about the typical local flavor for sale that spanned from glass balls in nets, crazy kites, dried starfish, sea-shells and fishing gear.

Every once and a while, out of the corner of her eye, Anne found herself dreading the two-storied weathered building that loomed ahead. Her jovial mood escaped and seemed to deflate her personality as they approached Cowboy Bob's Restaurant; even with Jimmy Buffet's lively 'Margaritaville' playing over the loud speakers, mixed with the voices from a crowd sitting out on an open deck. Anne nervously stole a timid glanced up towards the deck and slowed her pace to almost a crawl as they neared the entrance door. *I sure hope I don't run into anyone I know tonight. I wonder if there is any way I could get Rick to call off the evening and head back home. A stomachache… or headache maybe, I'd even go as far as twisting my ankle in these damn shoes.*

Rick felt a curious slight tug on his hand that caused him to break their friendly ambiance, glance down and register Anne's panicked expression. *Oh no you don't…You're not backing out on me now.* He gave her hand a quick, but reassuring squeeze and then stepped quickly ahead immediately yanking her towards the doorway. Rick decided to heedlessly pick up their momentum as they precariously neared the stairs. *Determining the height of those heels and any kind of speed…she won't be able to stop without making a huge scene.*

Hitting the first step, they propelled through the dark street-level entrance and unwaveringly continued awkwardly up the stairway to the busy restaurant upstairs. The entire time Rick made sure that he kept a firm grip on her hand.

Anne tried to forcefully yank her hand out of his grip and venomously glared when they reached the top of the stairs. Realizing what he'd just accomplished, she irately opened her mouth, prepared to give him the dressing-down of his life; instead clamped her mouth aggravated shut, with an uncomfortable click when a sultry feminine voice spoke softly from seemingly out of no- where.

"Mmmm. Hi, there. Are you here for dinner this evening?" A young, curvy blonde stood seductively poised behind the reception desk, deliciously inspecting Rick with an open invitation written across her overtly made-up face.

Rick gallantly slid his hand onto the small of Anne's back, applying brute pressure and practically steered her unbending body over towards the desk.

"Why yes, we're looking at having a bite to eat this evening. Is there any chance there might be an available table out on the deck?" He paused their unwavering plight next to the reception desk, precisely the second Rick ended his question. Realizing that the restaurant was a full capacity, he knowingly leaned closer to the blond and bestowed her one of his trademarked sultry looks. "You know...I'd really appreciate it, if you could make anything happen tonight."

"Well..." The girl barely tore her open interest from Rick, then became immediately flustered by his transparent innuendo for a response, redirected her gaze down at the seating chart as her face flushed pink. "Oh, I think I can fit YOU in somewhere..."

Shocked, Anne's jaw almost dropped and rolled her eyes listening to the hostess' overactive, hormone stammering as she made a tremendous effort to find them a table. *What a schmooze. I bet he rolls out his charms every time he's around a female, just to get what he wants. I swear...men make me sick!*

"Why...don't you follow me, I think we have a quaint table available right outside." She clumsily grabbed their menus while unconsciously wiping the perspiration off her palms onto her black skirt and turned to guide them through the dining room with an inviting smile aimed at Rick.

"You know, you need to move so we can sit down this evening. I don't know about you...but I'm hungry!" Rick gave Anne a slight shove prompting her to start moving before they lost sight of the hostess. "Get going."

Anne felt her knees turned to liquid while Sugarland's 'Want To' floated through the room, wobbling slightly in her heels, she made her way around the front desk with Rick arrogantly sauntering in tow. Her frayed nerves began to explode as they weaved through a sea of circular tables overflowing with carefree customers. Out of the corner of her eye she recognized an elderly couple, noticeably pause and gawked when they spotted her waltzing through the room. Anne lifted her head a little higher, then quickened her pace as she began to identify quite a few of the other patrons.

Rick witnessed with humored curiosity, as some of the customers abruptly did a double take at Anne's uncommon sexy form and openly appraising her. It seemed like the restaurant came to a standstill while most of the patrons unashamedly froze mid-stride with what their intentions, to regard the newcomers. *Freakin' small town...she looks hot.*

Anne rushed as quickly as her cumbersome heels would allow her to follow the blonde outside onto the deck, directly to a tiny table that was set up in a secluded corner. Gratefully spying the table and without ceremony she surged forward to quickly scoot into an empty chair. Without thought she snatched an abandoned refreshment list, flipping it around and struggling to frantically conceal her overly flushed face.

"Oh!" Anne jerked the list down in surprise when she felt the chair next to hers move closer as Rick casually sat next to her thigh.

"Don't mind me." Rick winked at her, then turned his undivided attention to the hostess.

"Just to let you know that the catch of the day is alder-smoked salmon, served with fresh veggies of the day and rice..." The hostess sing song voice faded into the combined chaos of the restaurant.

Anne's interest became piqued, halfheartedly listening to the sexy blonde reciting the meal, until it started to sound like it was an adulterous invitation. As her monolog began to sound like Marilyn Monroe singing 'Happy Birthday' to the president, Anne gradually lowered the menu barely below her astounded eyes to watch what the other woman was doing. "Oh, my --"

The blonde had audaciously stretched over the table, slowly pouring water into Rick's empty glass. She pouted her overly glossed lips while intentionally spilling some water, innocently batted her lashes and attempted to make eye contact with Rick. "I hope I didn't get you...wet." Her eyes flashed him an open sexual invitation and finished with, "Now if you need anything else or have questions, just let me know. My name is Michelle...I'll be here for the rest of the evening."

Anne's eyebrows shot up while observing the indecent lingering gaze that Michelle lingered on Rick and then lazily sashaying away from the table, but before she was out of sight casting one last sexy gaze over her shoulder to make sure he was still watching.

Rick simply leaned back in his chair, arms crossed over his chest and smiling at her production as he watched her disappear.

"Huh." Anne snapped her menu open appallingly in front of her face, muttered silent profanities out of the side of her mouth and finished with, "Shit…I believe she's decided to be *your* special for the evening."

Rick was involuntarily pulled out of his interested stare by the irritated tone in her voice and her quiet, off-handed comment. "Ah…I'm sorry, I didn't hear that. What did you say?"

Anne reverently leaned her chin into her hand and placed her menu aside, giving him a momentary look of mocking ignorance from across the table. "I was just making the assumption…that she considers herself to be the catch of the day. But…now that I think about it, and see your reaction, I realize that I'm mistaken."

Realizing he was stepping into a trap, Rick squint and became heavily guarded as he hesitantly ventured to ask, "Okay, I'll take the bait. Why do you think that you're mistaken?"

She saucily peered at him as she primly pinched her lips into a fine line and snapped her menu back in front of her face. Pretending to become immensely engrossed in the dining selections, she replied in a dry haughty tone, "Why, I actually believe…that she wants to be your *dessert* this evening."

Rick good humor rose to the occasion, chuckling to himself at Anne's displeasure and carelessly leaning back in his chair to look out at the view. *Ha…Looks like someone has already started to get her panties in a bunch, this should end up being a very interesting evening.*

As his gaze scanned the harbor he became instantly engrossed in the beautiful evening. The entire day the skies had been a clear blue; with the encroaching sun beginning to set, it was now streaked with orange, red and gold. The harbor was enclosed by an enormous rock jetty in the distance, the shadows making the water look like black molten tar as the colors from the sky reflected the movement of the waves; rippling and churning the warm tones. Single dark silhouettes identified plenty of fishermen still posed on the rocks with their bait on one side and pole sturdily gripped in their hands, with the white breakers sweeping onto the glistening rock with the encroaching tide, for a moment there seemed to be a natural truce between both man and nature. Far off in the distance a fleet of charter fishing boats slowly made their way back into the harbor and against the sun's glorious descent, all of the boats began to fade into shadow against the glowing warmth of the sky. All around the docks families searched anxiously for the ships' return to see what their loved ones would be bringing in. The scene was tranquil and mesmerizing while Johnny Mathis's 'Chances Are' hovered in the air. *Damn, this sure is a beautiful place…well -- when the sun finally decides to come out. Maybe I was a little too quick to judge a book by its cover.*

"Ahem--." A dignified male cough transported his pondering thoughts back to the present situation of sitting alongside of an irritated Anne and an inquiring waiter next to his elbow. Anne's clear eyes were innocently round as the annoyed young waiter decided to repeat his inane question in a somewhat stale tone. "Sir, would you like anything to drink?"

"Ah...yes, yes I would. Um, I called ahead and had something special ordered for the evening, you'll find it under Rick Short." He reached over and arrogantly stuffed a twenty dollar bill in the waiter's palm, "and I'd appreciate it if you could ensure that there will be a sufficient amount served for the rest of the evening." He looked over at Anne, cocked his eyebrow at her then winked, "It's a very special evening."

"Wow, absolutely. Sir, if there is need of anything else...just give me a wave, my name's Justin." By the end of his bumbling sentence the young man made a slight awkward bow, took two steps backwards and then scrambled towards the bar to disappear into the kitchen.

Rick stole a dubious glance over at Anne while she sat sipping her water entranced by the spectacular view. *She's so beautiful sitting there unguarded, admiring the ongoing scene as the evening's transforming.* He unconsciously reached for his glass, as his fingers grazed the slick surface, unconsciously noticing beads of water that had collected on the outside of it. Rick traced a slight pattern across the moisture right before raising the glass up to his mouth, while his gaze lazily slid back over to her.

He watched as Anne decided to take a sip. His eyes instantly became riveted on her, poised lifting his glass in mid-air, because at the exact moment a large drop of water that was precariously dangling on the bottom of her glass, slipped off the end and fell onto her bared chest. Unintentionally he became mesmerized between her hair gently moved in the breeze off of the ocean and the drop, as it made an agonizingly slow, lingering wet path down between her breasts. The physical sensation caused by the combination of her warm skin and cool water caused her to involuntarily shiver and hug her arms.

"Ahem...Anne, are you cold? Would you rather we go and sit inside this evening?" Rick had to embarrassingly clear his throat as the words came out in a suspicious gravelly voice. He achingly watched her mouth as she leisurely licked her lips after taking another sip and placed the glass back on top of the table.

 "No...I'm alright, but thanks for asking." Anne raised her shining eyes up to his and gave him a lopsided smile.

Rick uncomfortably cleared his throat and shifted in his seat trying to redirect his roaming thoughts and resolving instead to taking a long drink. *I need to forget where that damn drop of water disappeared to.*

"So--, Rick. One thing I'd like to know is where on earth did you learn how to manipulate everyone to do your bidding? Seems like you're used to having people do what you ask them to, especially the way you've managed to set this entire birthday charade up tonight." Anne rhythmically slid her finger slowly up and down the sides of her glass, then smiled sweetly to soften the abrupt delivery of her question, and take a little of the bite out of it. The cool wetness felt good under her finger as she traced patterns on the heavy condensation layering the glass.

"Huh? What do you mean?" Startled out of his reprieve by her direct question, Rick found his mind drawing a blank, not quite sure how to answer. He opened his mouth as he urgently searched for a decent explanation, but was heroically saved by the approaching waiter.

"As you ordered sir...Schramsberg, Blanc De Blanc 2001. I hope I said that right." The waiter had some difficulty setting up an awkward stand next to the table, and set the heavily laden tray down with an ungracious thud. Anne shot a questioning glance towards Rick while Justin started to scrimmage the iced bucket, bottle and glasses among the table.

"Ummm, I knew you wouldn't approve...and I only get the best for the best." He boyishly shrugged his shoulders in response to her silent deploring question. Anne jumped as the waiter audaciously popped the cork and made quite a ceremony while he filled each of their glasses completely with foam.

Rick quickly grabbed his and took a small sip of fizz. "Perfect, Justin. Thank you."

He obediently lingered while they placed their orders, allowing enough time for Anne to take a few quick sips of her de-fuzzed champagne. The taste was perfectly light and airy as the tiny bubbles tickled the inside of her mouth. By the end of placing their orders she felt a little more relaxed and narrowly gazed at Rick lifting his glass in a toast.

"To...a perfect day. You only live once and to be honest...I wanted you to have a great birthday. Here's to your special day, Dragon Lady...besides, it seemed like a great excuse to get out of work early." He gave her another lopsided grin.

"You have certainly outdone yourself this evening, Grunt." Anne genuinely smiled at him after their glasses clinked, both savoring their drinks and his spontaneous speech. "Just the name of the champagne sounds pretty fancy."

"Before we continue on, I...um...I purchased you a gift." Anne sat speechless while Rick rummaged clumsily through his pockets.

"Ahhh--," She desperately racked her brain to summon an appropriate response, until he produced a small lumpy square wrapped package. *I hate to admit that it kind of looks like a six year old wrapped it.* "Really Rick, you didn't have to. I don't know what to say." She smiled politely at him and tentatively took the box delicately from his out-stretched hand. She slowly opened the taped paper, opened the box and found a pair of beautiful thinly mallet golden loop earrings lying in the center.

"I...I...I really wanted you to have something to open today; Happy Birthday, Anne."

"Thank you." Tears of gratitude stung the backs of her eyes while she picked up each earring and speedily replaced the ones she was wearing with the new pair. Anne rapidly blinked back tears, gave him a girlish lopsided grin, took his hand and gave it grateful a squeeze.

They were both saved from the uncomfortable moment of having to say anything, as a few of the ogling patrons began approaching the table in the pretense of appearing to see how Anne was enjoying the evening, but actually being obviously nosey. The intensity of the evening seemed to wane while Anne stumbled awkwardly through the introductions between each person and Rick. After the first couple departed, another curious group immediately resumed their vacancy, causing Anne to quickly conger up a weak, generic explanation about her mysterious date; "So and so...I'd like you to meet my new employee, Rick Small, who happens to be the culprit who talked me into celebrating my non-existent birthday this evening."

Rick offhandedly leaned silently back in his chair, surveying how diplomatically Anne handled each unique posed question and fumbled about their situation. *Shit, she's making it worse...we seem so deceitful, as if she's trying to absolve our uncomfortable moment by explaining who I am and reiterating our innocent intentions, I'd just tell the fuckers off.* With each second listening to her explanations, he found himself completely entranced with her casual confidence and his admiration grew. Evidently since she had been raised is such a small town; everyone knew something about everyone and everything. Anne sat poised in her chair like a queen, taking the time to follow along with each of their conversations, occasionally making a comment or suggestion. It seemed like everyone held a high esteem for her which made Rick even more conscious of their genuine concern for her and her sister, besides the malicious glares he was receiving.

As the continuous stream of well-wishers filed by and filtered out, the evening had started to fade and Rick dutifully kept their glasses full. By the time they'd finished the first bottle of champagne and started on another one their dinner was served.

After the waiter clumsily set their dishes on the table with a thud, Rick raised his glass and made another toast. "Here is to the Dragon Lady…to one hell of a hard working woman, who will always end up on her feet because of her knowledge, ingenuity and pure talent with horses; Happy Birthday." Anne freely smiled up at Rick after they'd cheerfully clinked glasses and took a sip from her glass. Rick's pulse managed a slight flip when her smile suddenly curved into a devilish leer and she raised her glass to summon another toast.

"And here is, ummm…to the hardest working man in all of Westport. Grunt, you're the only guy within one hundred miles that would have the guts to double dog dare me to get me out for such a wonderful evening, besides all of your help on the ranch. I don't know if I could have gotten this far without your help. Thank you." Anne set her empty glass down with an indelicate clink and picked up a fork. "Well, it looks delicious. Let's eat before it starts to get cold."

Frank Sinatra's 'Summer Wind' lingered in the background while they enjoyed their meal in a companionable silence, pausing to direct a few token comments about the breathtaking view from the deck. The sun set in a glowing fiery red ball, slowly slipping into the never-ending depths of the dark ocean. A comfortable sense grew, until each of them stopped to simultaneously comment about the brilliance of the food and pure beauty of the moment, causing a burst of hysterical laughter.

Justin came around to remove their dinner plates and refill their empty glasses, as Anne wiped her eyes, nervously glancing around the deserted deck realizing all of the tables were cleared and night had descended, creating a slight chill in the air.

 Anne felt her body shiver and began to rub her arms. "I should have brought a coat or sweater, I didn't realize it would be so chilly out tonight."

Magically the staff was on queue as they started to pull large portable heaters onto the deck. The petite blonde arrogantly strutted through the deck, lit candles on each of the vacant tables and completely ignoring theirs. Justin rolled one of the heaters over to their table, carefully ignited it, and as the warmth illuminated.

"Justin, thank you so much." Anne sighed in deep appreciation.

 "No problem." He smiled, snatched a candle for their table from the grumpy blonde and continued into the restaurant to help in repositioning all of the tables.

"So Rick, now what do you have in mind for the rest of the evening?" Anne took another sip from her glass and realized she was beginning to feel a little lightheaded. *Wow…I better stick with water for a while.*

"Well, I thought we might order a little dessert and then there's going to be a band here this evening, The Locals. I heard that they're pretty good. I thought it would be kind of fun to watch, let your hair down and maybe do a little dancing."

"Yeah, well...it does sound like a lot of fun, but you have one small problem...I don't dance," Anne laughed as she openly admitted one of her many flaws.

"What? Are you shitting me...everyone dances!" Astonished Rick leaned a little over the table to peer quizzically at her, trying to read her stoic look and recognized the truth in her unbending silence, causing him to lowered his voice suggestively, "Well...I bet by the end of the night, we'll find a way to cure your 'no dancing' issue."

Anne felt herself become mesmerized by the depth of his rich brown eyes, straining to come up with a witty rebuttal, but found herself sinking further into his intensity.

Their charged second was instantly broken by an abrupt male cough that suddenly erupted loudly from next to their table cutting through the heated silence.

"Yikes!" Anne guiltily jumped backwards as if she'd been burned caught entwined in their intimate situation to hastily glance up. Embarrassment rushed to flush her face with a red haze when she awkwardly realized that Dave was standing silently next to her seat. "Oh! Um, Dave... how long have you been here? I...I didn't see you." Anne bounded out of her seat; almost turning the chair backwards in her exuberance to quickly stand up and give him a light hug.

"Not very long, I just walked in and saw you out here. So...I thought I'd say a quick hello." Dave stepped back, took her hands in his large ones and spread her arms wider apart so he could admire her thoroughly. "My lord Anne, you sure do look beautiful tonight. I don't think I've ever seen a prettier woman in my whole life."

"Ummm...thanks." Anne tried to smile at Dave, but felt a little too uncomfortable at the way he clicked his tongue with a smack while mentally undressing her.

Rick felt suddenly disturbed at Dave's intrusive display over Anne. He attempted to unclench his jaw, instantly deciding to embrace the awkward moment and put a halt on continuously being ignored by the newcomer.

"Yeah, Wow...she certainly is a vision, just like that sunset...Anne you are a beautiful sight tonight. How are you doing Dave?" Rick roughly scooted his chair out to allow enough room to stand up and congenially extend a hand.

As the two opposing men squared off, Anne seized the opportunity to abruptly release Dave's hands to plop back down in her chair with an unladylike thud and grab her drink.

Dave arrogantly smirked at Rick, then obviously ignoring his extended hand by shoving both of his into his pockets and irreverently gazed out at the harbor.

The result of Dave's insult was Rick left clumsily standing with his hand stretched out in midair, extending it to Dave's back. Rick looked down quizzically at Anne then dropped his neglected hand to his side and gave a disregarding shrug while returning to his seat. *Oh, I see how this is going to roll. This freakin' asshole thinks he's all that…big fish in a little pond. Well, he's going to have to take a back seat to me tonight.*

"Oh, hey there…Rich. I almost didn't see you. Yeah…yeah…I'm doing well. Thanks for asking." Dave barely turned his head, intentionally mispronounced his name and nodded while warily regarding Rick through narrowed eyes.

Rick ignored the evident insult of the mistake, loudly scooted his chair closer to Anne and haughtily saluted him with his glass of champagne taking a healthy drink.

"Wow, so…what brought you out this evening, Dave?" Anne hastily rambled off her bland question attempting to diffuse the male infested, nerve racking silence hovering over their table.

The impertinent tone in her voice and direct question snapped Dave out of his spiteful trance. He craned his neck as if he was trying to adjust it, then took a lengthily moment to regroup and focus back on Anne. "Well, I heard about The Locals, they're supposed to be pretty good. I ended up getting done early this evening, so I wanted to get here before too many people started to show up."

On queue Anne checked around noticing that the interior of the restaurant was beginning to fill up with people and the band was busy setting up on a small stage in a corner. The tables had been cleared away from the center of the room to create a small but efficient dance floor in front of a makeshift stage. Anne began to feel a tingle of excitement at the prospect of listening to the sound check and being in such a festive atmosphere for the evening.

"What are *you* doing here tonight, Anne? I thought you were always too busy to go out…and hated to dance," Dave attempted to mockingly accuse her but his last few words sounded sully and juvenile. He leaned near her cheek appearing to patiently wait for an answer, then surprisingly he intently dipped his face closer, searching her eyes and seem to lean in for a kiss.

"I, ah--." Anne began to nonchalantly lean her head away from his, but was suddenly filled with guilt. *For years I've dodged Dave's overbearing attempts to persuade me into taking some time off of work to go out with him, instead I get caught red handed with a transient worker over him.* Agonized at being trapped, she gave him a half-hearted smile while urgently tapping into her mental reserves and find courage to squirm out of the uncomfortable situation. Startled out of her thoughts, her head snapped around at the sound of Rick clearing his throat.

"Wow...I'm surprised you didn't realize this Dave, but its Anne's birthday today. I thought it would be a nice surprise to take her out for the evening. You know, I just didn't feel right about her sitting alone in that big house on her special day!" Rick gave the other man an ignorant expression punctuating the end of his sentence and allowed time for him to take a hint. He innocently smiled while intentionally draping an arm around her shoulders, bestowing a longing look and topping it off with a gentle squeeze. He turned up his brilliant smile a notch while casually reaching for his glass, arrogantly tipping it in Dave's direction and took another long swallow. Sighing, he contentedly gazed back at Anne's fury and gave her a conspiring wink, all the while he deftly attempted to deflect her manic efforts of thoroughly kicking his shins underneath the table.

"Oh Anne, I'm so sorry. I didn't realize it was your birthday. Gosh, I feel like such an ass." Dave put his hands firmly on the table next to Anne's and leaned slightly forward. His actions making her look up as he locked his gaze with hers and continued to move intimately closer, having every intention to obviously go in for the kill.

"I guess...I'll have to figure out a different way to try and make it up to you." He slowly bent his head towards Anne's as he determinedly aimed to kiss her.

Rick clenched his hands tightly while he helplessly watched Dave's head descend and Anne's eyes widened with surprise.

"Oh look! Here comes our dessert!" At the sight of their waiter, Anne took the opportunity to giddily pipe up with relief and abruptly leaned her body to the side to deftly avert her face away from Dave's.

"Justin...my man, great timing. We are famished." Rick's smile widened at the perfect reprieve as he approached the table with the tray loaded with quite a few choices of decadent desserts.

Disgruntled by the unwanted disruption, Dave blew out an exaggerated huff and slightly stamped his foot. As he pushed away from the table he turned to calculatedly search over his shoulder, as if he needed absolute confirmation that the waiter was approaching.

Anne quickly reached out, grabbed her glass of champagne, closed her eyes and downed its entire contents. The liquor burned her throat, causing her eyes to water as she tried to hold back from coughing out the fumes out.

"Anne, I don't want to intrude on your evening any longer." Dave took Anne's hand and bent over to give it a lingering kiss. Slowly standing up, he gazed into Anne's watery eyes and meaningfully said, "I'll just have to figure out my own special surprise for you another day. Have a great evening and if you need me, remember...I'll be right here."

Watching Dave slowly saunter away Rick happily became consumed by his small victory, leaning forward and poured the remaining champagne into their glasses. Rick listened to Anne clearing her throat, the first few strums from a guitar as the band loudly tuned up and Anne fleetingly picked out her dessert. Turning in his chair, Rick took a second to enjoy scanning all the action that was going on inside the bar. *What a car wreck this is going to be...I can't wait.* His gaze lazily slid from one partying patron to another, enjoying their joie de vivre, until he noticed a disgruntled Dave had decided to belly up to the bar. Their gaze locked for a second while Dave continued to indifferently stir his drink, ignoring the partiers and openly watch their table.

"Creepy..." Rick mumbled, restraining himself from either giving Dave an exaggerated wink, throwing him two thumbs up or the bird, *but I can't decide on which one...Fucker*. At the last second he decided to simply smile, then turned around to say something to Anne and instantly froze when he registered the look on her face.

"What?" Rick asked innocently.

"Really--." Anne rolled her eyes, "Oh, I don't know...just that was so much fun! You know, I've heard about 'origami of the penis', but I never really thought that I'd be able to get to see it up close and personal." She angrily grabbed her glass, taking a sip as the waiter approached with their desserts.

Rick silently waited for the waiter to move to the opposite side of the table and decided to slowly inch his chair even closer to hers. The loud scraping sound that emitted from his chair unnerved her as he continued to tactlessly scoot.

"You know Anne, I could have left you two love birds alone if you wanted me to, but I didn't get the impression that's what you wanted to happen." Their knees intimately brushed against each other, his close proximity continued to silently disturb her creating a slight warm shiver. Justin began to meticulously place each of the scrumptious dishes on the table, watching how sluggish he was being, Rick took a calming breath, waved him off and assisted in re-maneuvering the generous desserts to sit delectably in front of them.

"OK...OK, I agree. The testosterone inflated ego did get a little intense there for a couple of seconds. But you have to admit most of all that bluster was from your friend, not me." He put his fork into the rich chocolate cake, removed a bite and lifted it to her mouth. When he didn't receive a response, he wiggled the fork and decided to try a different approach.

"Question...what is it between the two of you anyway?" Rick gave her an imploring look.

"W-h-a-t?" Anne gave him a droll gaze, shut her mouth in a prim line, refusing to take the bait as he moved the scrumptious bite playfully back and forth in front of her mouth.

"Look, it's your birthday...so you have to take the first bite. Plus, for the explanations on the new seating arrangements, it's easier to sit on this side next to you so we can share. Besides that I have a better view on what's going on inside." He assertively wiggled the fork under her nose trying to entice her out of her bad mood with the morsel and get her to say something.

"I really don't feel like discussing any of my past history with you this evening...or any evening, for that matter!" Anne leaned over and whispered. "You better be grateful, because the only reason I haven't gotten up and left your ass is because these desserts look too delicious...it'd be a sin to waste them." In conclusion she quickly opened her mouth and snatched the bite off of his fork.

Rick hadn't realized that he'd been holding his breath until he began cutting a bite of the raspberry cheesecake. His lungs gratefully stretched when he started to breathe and stealing another sideways gaze at her as she gave him a dreamy smile. He felt slight physical agony as he watched her savor the taste of the chocolate cake and tempted her again lifting the fork back in front of her mouth. *Hmmm, she looks exactly like a tiny bird, willingly opening her mouth to accept my new offering.*

Anne closed her eyes in ecstasy the second her mouth captured the morsel, simultaneously The Locals came on to play. Rick shoveled a piece of chocolate cake in his mouth attempting to pull his naughty thoughts back from where they had strayed. The taste of the cake went unnoticed as he shifted uncomfortably in his chair, the entire time thinking about her mouth. *Damn. I've never wanted to be a piece of dessert, until now.*

The band opened their set by played a romping rendition of Neil Diamond's 'Kentucky Woman'. Their lead singer had a rich gravelly voice that reached out and captured not only the originals style, but the song's essence.

By the end of the song Rick happened to glance down, noticing that they had polished off both desserts and another bottle of champagne while another waiter was clearing it all away. The band flawlessly rolled into the next song Van Morrison's 'Brown Eyed Girl', while he semi-turned in his seat so he could watch Anne from the corner of his eye. She had begun to move slightly with the melody, unconsciously drumming her fingers in perfect time to the beat, while her face was softly illuminated by the light from inside the restaurant. *She looks so young and without a care in the world.*

They sat through the entire first set enjoying the music and each other's company in silence. After the group finished the Rolling Stone's 'Honky Tonk Woman' and left the stage for a short break Anne eagerly turned towards him. "That was great! You were right, this group is wonderful."

Rick watched as she tapped her feet to imaginary music and happily sipped her drink. *I might as well try this while she's in such a good mood.* He rubbed the back of his neck and ventured to say, "Well then…with the next set you'll have to dance with me."

Anne quickly frowned and opened her mouth in an attempt to protest, until Rick held up his hands in surrender.

"Look, I know you say you don't know how to dance, but it's been a great evening and it's your birthday. You have to at least try. Come on…I double dog dare you." He winked and whispered the dare.

"We'll see." Anne returned to watching the crowd, attempting to enjoy the evening and completely forget about all of her responsibilities.

After a few token cat calls the band reappeared and promptly started the next set off with The Clashes' 'Rock the Casbah." With a small smirk, Anne clamped her mouth shut, narrowed her eyes over the rim of her glass and tartly responded to his questioning stare, "Nu-uh…Nope not this one."

Rick watched while a bunch of overtly drunk people who'd been sitting around the dance floor rushed out and started to dance. Taking a sip of his drink he allowed his mind to wander, as it instantly started to wonder about all of the people out on the dance floor. Abruptly he realized it was the first day he hadn't cursed his decision to come to Westport. *Hm. Funny.*

He had become so absorbed in his thoughts that when the next song started, he startled when a girlish squeak of pleasure split the air and turned in surprise at the noise. Anne was standing next to the table, almost wiggling out of her skin trying to contain her enthusiasm while she held her hand out to him.

"I love this song! Come on…let's dance." She chirped.

Rick jumped at the chance, grabbing her hand and tugged her through the maze of people until she excitedly hopped out onto the dance floor. By the time they reached the mass of dancing people who had joined in singing he recognized the entertaining rendition of The Police's 'Everything She Does Is Magic'. Feeling someone nudge him in the ribs, Rick caught himself gawking when he glanced down at Anne, who was dancing extremely close to him because the floor was packed. She had both of her hands over her head, swaying suggestively to the music and singing with the rest of the crowd. Rick laughed and started to sensuously move in time against her body following her lead.

All too soon the song was over and the crowd began to disperse; Anne and Rick made their way back to the table and fell back into their chairs laughing.

"I don't know what you were talking about. You dance...very nicely." Rick made the saucy comment while he watched Anne's flushed face.

"Well, it's pretty easy when you're a human sardine squished between bunches of people and can barely sway to the song." Anne took a quick sip of her drink as she hummed in time with the next tune and watched the dancers inside.

"As long as you are having fun, that's the only thing that matters. But now that I know you can move...so, don't be surprised when I ask you out onto the dance floor when there's a song that I want to dance to starts playing."

Smiling naughtily over her glass at Rick, Anne cocked an eyebrow and said, "Well Grunt, we'll see about that." Right then the first few chords to John Mellencamp's 'Hurt so Good' started.

Anne quickly set her drink down with a thud, batted her lashes, puckered her lips and silently begged Rick to dance.

Rick set his drink down with an exaggerated sigh then quietly stood up, reached out his hand and jokingly yanked Anne out of her chair so they could join the mass. Once they hit the dance floor Anne twirled, lifted her arms above her head and laughed. *I am having the time of my life. I need to get out more!* She giddily thought as her vision was blocked by Rick's tall form. Looking up into his grinning face she threw all caution to the wind, stepped forward and began to intimately dance against Rick's rock hard body.

By the end of another set of songs the room was beginning to get a little too hot, people were singing loud and drunkenly off key. Everyone started to exuberantly whistle and clap as the lead singer announced the next song would be their last for the evening. When the band started to play the first few notes of a slow melody, Anne fanned herself with her hand, nonchalantly shrugged and started to make her way back towards their table.

Seconds before she had the chance to step off the dance floor, she felt the heaviness of a solid hand on her shoulder, the pressure startled out of her reprieve and made her instantly picture Dave standing behind her, looming in for the last dance. Anne closed her eyes, held her breath and reluctantly turn to accept Dave's invitation to dance. When she opened her eyes confusion set in when she realized that it was Rick intently studying her. His face broke into a smile at the confused look plastered across her face as he silently motioned with his head to join him back on the dance floor. He gently took her hand in his and gave it a supportive squeeze before he whispered, "Remember, it's my turn." The singer walked up to the microphone and started a heartfelt performance of Elvis' 'I Can't Help Falling in Love with You'.

Anne allowed Rick to guide her slowly out onto the dance floor. Her heart was beating in her ears so loud that she could barely recognize the beginning of the song. Anne closed her eyes, stepped into his embrace and licked her dry lips as she prayed, *Please, God....don't let me trip, or step on his toes, and hopefully I don't smell or have sweaty palms.*

He kept her hand lightly in his while steadily inching their bodies closer together, until she felt the heat through his shirt and started to sway. Anne jolted the second she felt his other hand settle on the exposed skin at the small of her back. His hands felt warmer than his body while he guided them in time with the song, until he dipped his head into the crook of her neck and pulled her body snug against his. Her eyes widened in surprise, but only for a second then she simply inhaled, closed her eyes and welcomed the feeling of his warm body pressed intimately into hers. Slowly she leaned her head onto his shoulder, clung to him a little tighter and dreamily smiled, listening to him hum softly along with the song. Anne's breathing stopped when his fingers started making lazy circles across her lower back sending shivers racing up her spine and felt him breathing on her neck. A fleeting image of the two of them intimately moving in time with the song, tracing each other's bodies with their fingers, suspended without a care in the world, flashed through her mind. Suddenly Anne had the uncanny feeling that they were the only ones on the dance floor. *I don't want to open my eyes...I want this moment to last.*

Anne dreamily moaned, opened one blurry eye and cautiously peeked around the room. Her eyes slowly re-focused on the back of the restaurant where a swarm of people were noisily filing out to walk down the stairs, towards the exit.

"Oh...oh, my." Her eyes shot open wider when she realized that the band was packing up and they were still slightly swaying in the middle of the dance floor. *Alone.*

"I couldn't tell if you were awake, I thought you just might've fallen asleep. So...I didn't want to disturb you...at least not yet." Anne felt a tingling sensation surge up the base of her neck when felt his breath as he gently whispered the innuendo in her ear.

"No, Grunt." Anne pulled back, a little unsteady on her heels and unable to focus on his face, peeking up through her lashes to respond with a mockingly indignant. "I was just, um...playing possum."

Rick smiled down into her drowsy eyes, his grin widening when he noticed the slight slur in her words. He placed his hand lightly on her jaw and then lightly moved it along her cheek to tenderly place his finger on the tip of her nose, "Let's get you home."

Anne became embarrassingly alarmed when walking off the dance floor took a little more effort than she expected. Even though Rick steadily helped to make their way towards the exit, Anne found herself inadvertently veering in the wrong direction. After a couple attempts Rick reached over, tucked her arm safely under his and bodily guided her towards the stairs.

"Gosh --" Anne murmured out of the side of her mouth, too dizzy to peek back. "I hope we didn't leave anything at the table."

Alarmed at the thought, Rick stole a quick glance at the deck to see if anything was abandoned at their table. Instantly his gaze froze, as it ended riveted on Dave sitting at the end of the bar with the voluptuous blonde who had been working the reception desk. She was sitting prettily on the bar stool next to him animatedly chatting away, slowly moving her hand up and down his inner thigh. Rick suddenly had an odd feeling, exactly like the moment had become suspended in time, because he realized that Dave hadn't moved an inch the entire evening. *He's had a perfect view, watching our every move from his perch.*

"C-r-e-e-p-y..." Rick elongated the word while muttering it through the side of this mouth. "Hold on Anne, watch your step." Rick happily disregarded the other man while he assisted Anne clumsily down the stairs, out onto the sidewalk and slowly maneuvered her towards his truck.

Once Anne was outside she started to inhale deep breaths the fresh cool evening air, seemingly enjoying the tell-tale sign of salt from the ocean. With a whoosh her mind began to reel, causing her to pause midstride as she started to feel the complete impact from all of the champagne they'd drank that evening.

Giggling at nothing Anne tried to stay silent, mainly because her intuition screamed that she'd say something stupid. After weaving happily down the sidewalk, with Rick's arm cinched around her waist and a couple of near mishaps they finally approached the green truck.

"Um, 'scuse me...how much did I drink tonight?" Anne inquired in a sing song voice as she stumbled off the sidewalk the second Rick got his keys out to attempt to open her side of the truck. He turned just in time to catch her before she caused any major damage and planted her pretty face on the curb. He stood there gripping her shoulders, shaking his head at their situation and enjoyed looking into her drunkenly amused face.

Rick smiled reassuringly and brushed the hair out of her squinting eyes. "I think we did enough damage for one evening. Lucky for us I've been keeping pace with you and only had water after dinner."

"Did I tell you I L-O-V-E my new earrings?" Anne looked suggestively up at Rick, gave him an outrageous pout and batted her eyes while fondling her new earrings.

 "Oh, good!" He shook his head in obvious affirmation trying to keep her still, attempting to hold her leaning stance up straight, smiling at her up-tilted face while he fumbled for the truck keys. Rick redirected their bodies so she was neatly tucked, pinned between his thigh and against the truck, then safely leaned his other leg against her. Holding onto her waist gently with one hand, he unlocked the door with the other. After an aggravating second with the ancient lock he opened the door, bowed slightly and directed her promptly with his hand. "Your chariot awaits, my lady --"

Anne covered her mouth to stifle a giggle and attempted to independently launch herself into the cab of the truck. All of a sudden the step seemed a lot higher than it was earlier and she completely missed stepping into the truck. Luckily Rick had some sense to cautiously hold onto the back of her dress, so she wouldn't plant her face onto the concrete.

"I, I don't think I can make it up. You'll...you'll have to leave me." Anne dramatically sighed and forlornly leaned against his warm body for support. "Just get me a freakin' blue plastic tarp, a pillow, some water and I'll sleep in the reeds. Ha...it's no problem, not like I haven't done something like this before."

Rick watched her sleepy face illuminated in the street light, while she looked like an old comedy act, attempted to visually search out a convenient spot to lie down and smiled enraptured at her drunken idea. "Look...Anne, I don't think we're going to have to go to such an extreme. Let's see...why don't you put your foot onto the floor of the truck, grab hold of the seat and I'll push from behind."

Anne's face hilariously lit up at his simple suggestion, "Great idea!" She covered her mouth, realizing that she'd just yelled and hysterically giggled to gushingly add, "HA, HA! More like you'll be pushing my behind."

She turned towards the truck, lifted her leg just as he suggested and planted a foot on the floor, making her dress move indecently up her thigh and with a mischievous giggle she suddenly spun around to face Rick crashing into his solid chest. She angled her mouth in a disapproving way, squint one eye, lifted a single finger and accusingly pointed it at him adding, "Don't get any fresh ideas, Grunt. I know all about you kind of boys and itchy fingers...so watch it."

Rick gave her a militant salute, patiently smiled, watching her amusingly struggle to put her foot back up, grab onto the side of the truck and desperately tried not to allow her skirt to rise up past mid-thigh.

"Ok…I'm ready!" Anne loudly counted to three, pulled on the seat as Rick put both hands on her firm bottom and pushed. Suddenly she found herself face down, ungracefully landing cock-eyed across the squeaking seat. Rick chuckled immediately averting his eyes from her lumped on the seat, firmly closed the door on the view of her exposed backside and sauntered over to the opposite side of the truck. Taking his time with the lock to give her some time to pull herself together and jumped into the cab, Anne was sitting, poised like a queen with her hands demurely in her lap, looking haughtily out the passenger window.

Rick shook his head at her embarrassment. "I can almost guarantee that you won't remember most of this in the morning." He revved the engine, turned up the radio as The Eagles 'Desperado' began to play and made their way out of the silent town. As they stopped at the only blinking light, Rick glanced in his rear view mirror and noticed Dave's sleek black car parked in front of the restaurant. In the dim light he could barely make out a single dark shadow standing next to it, but couldn't quite distinguish who it was.

16

Rick couldn't shake the myriad of questions that kept nagging in the back of his mind during the drive home. Each random question seemed to take its own sweet time, suspended on the tip of his tongue, but before he had the nerve to ask, it would silently drift away like a flock of vultures waiting to rip into their meal.

He glanced over at Anne, chuckling just as they turned onto the main highway on the outskirts of town. Her head was beginning to slightly bob like a buoy from left to right and then she'd pop upright, valiantly trying to stay awake.

Casually drumming his fingers to Roy Orbison's 'Crying' on the steering wheel, Rick abruptly cleared his throat and decided to dive in to ask, "Soooo...what's up between you and your uptight, but very persistent neighbor?"

"E-x-c-u-s-e...me?" Anne had to squint across the vast blurry wasteland of the seat, after turning her head too fast towards Rick. She cocked an arrogant eyebrow, trying to peek at his non-descript shadow, taking an essential few seconds for her eyes to focus in the darkness of the cab.

"Well--. Look I'm not trying to stir anything up, I was just wondering what's going on between the two of you." Rick became uncomfortable with the abrupt question and patiently kept his eyes carefully trained on the road, wondering if she'd answer.

"What would make *you* think there is...or ever has been anything going on between Dave and me?" Anne asked in an absurd tone.

"What?" Rick ignored the road for a brief second, ignorantly stared over at her as if she'd lost her mind. "Are you shitting me? Ever since I've started working at your place, he's been over more than is typically necessary for a 'hospitable neighbor'. Besides that, he seems overly concerned about you and most importantly, the simple fact is that...he seems to show up nearly every time you're around the house, in town or even leave the yard."

"Well...you can't blame him for showing up somewhere, it is a very small town," she resentfully quipped towards his side of the truck and folded her arms defensively across her chest.

Rick mutely waited for her to answer his question, deviously smiled into the dark while out of the corner of his eye he watched her squirming in her seat. *Obviously I've hit a sore subject. I feel kind of bad forcing her to decide if she's going to talk about this or not.*

"OK, ok, ok. There's a small amount of history between us. When I was a freshman at Ocosta High School, Dave was a senior." Anne turned her head, staring out the window at the passing darkness as if she was watching her past flow across the glass while they sped along the highway. "I was the bright, naive, nerdy girl with a head full of dreams, about getting away from here, going to Seattle to college and someday travelling the world. I wanted to have a different life than what a small coastal town offered a young woman; fishing, working in a factory, crabbing, marriage to a local or child rearing."

"Ok." Rick muttered trying to prompt Anne when the silence stretched uncomfortably between them across the cab. "I totally agree with your decision to leave and find your way in life, you shouldn't feel guilty."

"What?" Anne snapped out of her thoughts, whimsically smiling at his statement. "Oh no, I never felt any guilt with my decision to leave. It's just this odd situation began to occur just before I left; Dave started to take a huge interest in me. You see, he wasn't just the average cute guy next door; he also was the gorgeous captain-of-the-football-team kind of guy. It seemed that every girl within a hundred miles had either heard of him, wanted to date him or had dated him. When he started to come around and ask me out, well...people started to talk." She took a deep calming breath before continuing with her story. "Like I said, it's a small town. When my parents heard about him pursuing me, they began to worry. I can recall many nights I sat out on the front porch with my parents having long conversations about life, dreams and reality throughout that year. They knew me and didn't want to watch me settle on just another pretty face, especially when I had endless possibilities waiting just around the corner."

"Hmm?" Rick raised his brow after a lengthy pause, curious when a girlish chuckle bubbled from across the darkness.

"I hate to admit...it was quite hard to say no to a pretty face." Anne shook her head at her amusing weakness.

He gave a quick smirk at her honesty as they drove around the final corner before the grand old house came into view.

"Towards the end of my senior year I found myself and Dave in some pretty ardent situations and we also had some very heated arguments. The last occasion I remember...and I'm not proud of, is lying to my parents, sneaking out and going to a party with him. It was the middle of summer, I can still remember being nervous about leaving the house and running through the tall grass in the lower pasture to meet him. He was so handsome in the moonlight standing by the gate, bringing me flowers to sweetly attempt to win my heart and convince me to stay. But, after the first hour we ended up leaving the party because we had another infuriating disagreement about my decision to leave for Seattle the next week." Unconsciously Anne began to nervously finger the edge of her skirt, uncomfortably reminiscing through her memory about that evening.

Rick patiently waited realizing how painful it must be for Anne to struggle with her past, his silent support began to make his hands start to sweat while he gripped the steering wheel.

"After we left the party, that's where of my memory about the rest of the evening gets pretty sketchy. I can recall being in Dave's car while he was trying to simultaneously talk me out of going to Seattle, and more importantly out of my clothes, I knew that he'd been sexually frustrated because we were never intimate. Thank God for my dad...I don't know how he knew where we were parked, but all of a sudden he was there, banging on the car window. The next thing I remember is sitting in the front seat of my dad's car sobbing in a torn dress as we drove silently home. That was the last time I was alone with Dave, I left soon after that for my new life in Seattle." Anne ended her story in a whisper.

Shit...sounds like he Ruffied her drink to me. Bastard. Rick irately thought as they pulled onto the dirt driveway. He slowly parked the truck along the front gate, got out and assertively walked around to help her out. The back of Anne's eyes ached with unshed tears watching him casually move around the truck.

"Thanks for telling me about what had happened, helps to make some sense out of him." He said when he slowly opened the door and leaned across the opening. Rick gave her hand a gentle squeeze as he took it and carefully helped her step down onto the ground. As he turned to shut the truck's door, Rick noticed that she was oddly staring down at his hand while she clung onto it tightly. Something surged through Rick as he watched her sad beautiful face stare at their joined hands. *What am I doing?*

"Hummm..."When she finally glanced back up at his face and sighed, "Who would have thought?"

Rick instantly tried to lighten the mood by giving her a quizzical look as he waited for her to continue with her sentence. When only her silence answered his patience he simply shrugged his shoulders realizing that she wasn't going to say anything, turned and began to direct her physically towards the house. He could feel the heat of her body as she followed his lead but scooted closer next to him to keep warm. Abruptly Anne stopped at the gate and tugged on his hand to make him stop. Confused by her actions Rick obediently stood still, causing his body to sway back slightly and stay with her.

"I don't think I can handle going into the house right now. I don't know…all of the champagne, talking about the past and too many memories. I just don't think I can handle going in there alone," Anne whispered as if her confession was a conspiracy, causing her to nervously fidget and uncertainly peeked at him from under her eyelashes waiting for his reaction.

Rick detected that she was wound up tight like a spring and guiltily admitted, *this is all because of my insensitive questions.* With a nonchalant shrug, gallant sweep of his hand making a grand gesture while he formally bowed and ended in a silly British accent. "Well then my lady, the night is young and beautiful…what would you care to do?"

Anne impishly smiled, then thoughtfully tapped her lip with her finger as she contemplated their lack of options and enthusiastically clapped her hands to announce, "Why don't we have a bonfire? We used to do that all the time when I was young. We'd throw down some blankets, stay up talking all night, lie around and watch the stars."

"Sure…alright." Rick uncomfortably hedged at the thought of being alone with her, laying under the stars. "I think I have some scrap wood that needs to be burned. I'll get the fire going if you'll run in and find some blankets. Meet you back at the fire pit in a few."

"OK." Anne happily called over her shoulder, weaving slightly as she raced around to the back of the house in search of some old blankets.

"Shit." Rick disbelievingly shook his head while he headed for the side of the barn murmuring into the night, "What am I doing?" Rummaging around to find some decent wood, Rick took his time in dragging all the old lumber back to the fire pit, *Damn…I hope that Anne's going to forget or pass out somewhere in the house during her quest for blankets.*

Fate showed its humor when he lumbered up to the pit on his final wood searching trip Rick found Anne demurely sitting next to the non-existent fire with a mismatched assortment of blankets spread across the ground, newspaper and matches. She looked deliciously young dressed in a new change of clothes; a simple black sweat suit, flip flops and her hair pulled up in a ponytail. Anne had moved a portable CD player out onto the porch and put in U2's ' Joshua Tree'. The poignant melodies opened into the air creating a fitting background for the unexpected evening.

Silently Rick heaved a tired sigh while he began to stack the kindling, creating an obnoxious display of ripping paper, piling into a pile and started the fire. He remained squatting on his haunches until the blaze took off on its own, then hesitantly walked over towards the blanket and begrudgingly sat down on the only available spot…next to her.

192

"So, Anne." Rick tried to lighten the uncomfortable mood by changing the subject, "You were talking about seeing the world...is there a specific place that you'd prefer to visit?"

"Ah...yeah." Anne looked at him as if he was completely out of his mind. "Have you ever heard of the Palio di Sienna?"

"Nope. I've heard about a lot of things, but that doesn't sound familiar. What is it?" Rick shifted so he could watch her face while she animatedly describe her dream.

"Well, it's the most famous horse race in Italy. I'm surprised you haven't heard about it, I thought everyone knew about it!"

Rick gave her a droll stare for his answer, then silently waved his hands to keep up her momentum with her descriptions and attempting to keep her sidetracked.

"Ok, it's held in Siena, Italy twice a year, one on July 2nd and another on August 16th. The tournament consists of only 10 riders who ride bareback around the Piazza del Campo 3 times, which only takes about 90 seconds but thousands of people go every year to watch." Anne ended with an exuberant whoosh and excitedly turned towards Rick, "Can you imagine being shoulder to shoulder watching the pageant, Corteo Storico before the horse race, then the thrill of watching the riders racing around the ancient square, waiting to see if any fall? Besides the festival, atmosphere and just standing in Italy, I can't even imagine how it would feel. I even tried to learn a little Italian, but there never seems to be enough time"

"Humm, maybe someday you'll be able to go there and see firsthand." Rick stared up at the stars, wondering how it would feel to take her to Siena and give the dream to her.

"Yea, right." Anne smiled at the side of his pensive face as he quirked a brow at her comment. "Not while I'm stuck here trying to figure out how to maintain this place and try to keep Beth in line, besides I can't even imagine how long it'd take me to save up that much money."

"Well, I'm just saying, you never know...something might come up and help you get there." Rick grinned while she rolled her eyes obnoxiously in response.

"Sooo...now it's your turn." Anne uncomfortably cleared her throat and leaned slightly back to scrutinize his face glowing in the firelight.

"What are you talking about?" Rick inquired furrowing his brow, attempting not to look back down at her lovely face, instead he redirected his line of vision to stare at the fire.

"It's your turn to tell me a little about yourself…a story for a story." Anne gave him a quizzical look and finished with "It's only fair that you tell me a little bit about your past."

Rick felt the comfortable heat emanating from where her thigh was pressed delicately against his. *Ah, are you shitting me? All I want to do is inch my hand slowly up your calf, grab a thigh and drag you closer.* Instead Rick rubbed his aching hand over his face, abruptly stood up and silently, but thoroughly cursed the sexually charged situation.

"Alright…go ahead and ask your questions," He miserably stated while surrendering his control on the situation, stomped over to grab some wood and continued to pile it on the fire.

Anne happily bounced up at his consent to conjure up her options, trying to pick one that wouldn't offend him. "Well, the only thing I know is that you've continually moved around throughout your life and have had a rough time in the past." Anne reached out, picked up a stick and began to push around some of the glowing embers forming underneath the logs. "Have you ever gotten into a sketchy predicament…like the one I was in?"

Rick tentatively sighed, contemplating his amazingly opulent life that waited back in California, contrasting his experience living on the coast; *At least I won't have to lie about this story. Well, at least not all of it.*

"Well…before I arrived here, I was recently in a situation with a woman that I think would be pretty comparable to yours." He timidly answered, while weighing the complete story to find a way to give it honesty, without fumbling around too much with the truth. Rick pushed some of the glowing embers for a second, then tossed the unwanted stick next to the fire while he stood up to wander over to the woodpile selecting another piece to toss it onto the blaze. He stood there for a second, transfixed by the fire as it began to ravage the wood and emitting bursts of heat that quickly warmed his face. Rick shook his head realizing that he'd become ominously mute, immersed in his thoughts and turned to silently searched Anne face. Picking up a stick he resumed aggressively stabbing the embers as he began to voluntarily describe his life, recalling the plastic warmth of L.A. and how distant it had become.

"The first time I saw this particular woman I was completely awestruck by her beauty. This was during a time…well, to be honest back then it seemed like I was always doing something rash and upsetting my friends. I wanted to live life to its fullest and completely by my rules, without a care about the effects on anyone, residual impact, consequences or anything. When I started to ask around town, trying to get any information about her it seemed like everyone's response about her life was either negative or evasive and I found that's what made her so mysterious. It drove me crazy not knowing anything about her and physically unable to have her. One evening there was a small party and through a few of my resources, I knew she'd be there. So, I decided to attend…even though I wasn't invited." Rick closed his eyes while the glamorous images of his past flooded back to him in unrealistic waves. Memories of all the amazing glitz, social networking, audacious parties and overwhelming expectations swirled around, sucking him in. The odd balance of beautiful people and continuous deception was still evident to even though he was thousands of miles away.

"I couldn't wait to be introduced. To be honest, I really didn't want to know anything about her…I just wanted to have her. It was as if she had some kind of magnetic pull and I couldn't resist." Rick gazed over at Anne and gave her a quick lopsided grin. "From the second I touched her hand, we were together all of the time. I created this amazing magical world where only she and I lived. I placed her high upon a crystal pedestal where no one else could reach her."

"That doesn't sound so bad…actually it sounds quite lovely." Tilting her head Anne absentmindedly smiled back at him and then turned to stare into the fire. She dishearteningly began to poke at the edges of the burning wood, creating tiny black patterns in the glowing wood while she mentally berated herself. *I bet she's beautiful too…why did I ask?*

"Ha." Rick barked a caustic laugh then strode around the fire, casually took the stick away from her and started to annoyingly poke deeper holes into the glowing embers. "Yeah it was, until a few days went by and I really got to know her. She was everything I never wanted to get involved with. She's vain, manipulating, lazy, a liar and ignorant. She's the epitome of someone who was shallow enough to take the world for more than what it's worth, just because she's beautiful. Shit…I'd be surprised if she's ever read anything more important than an article about the trendiest shoes in a fashion magazine."

Disgruntled over the obvious facts about his past history, Rick threw the stick on the fire, dropped onto the blanket, placed his hands behind his head and leaned back, watching the stars shimmer in the midnight sky. Marveling at the endless sparkling jewels forever cast in the heavens, but became momentarily intertwine with the tiny glowing orbs of sparks while they soared high into the air. *It seems like the embers are desperately trying to reach the stars before their light burns out.*

"After we'd been with each other for a while I was approached by overly concerned friends and started to listen to the rumors. I tried to blow them all off entirely, not because I trusted her, but because I was so infatuated with her looks." The image of Ava's beautiful face floated in the sky when he continued on. "Then, one evening in the middle of the night…there was a knock at my door. When I opened it…another man stood in the doorway, I was completely shocked to be confronted by her irate husband. There was a huge fight between the three of us, leaving me to do the only honorable thing…to stand behind my decision and continue to date such a soulless person, while I watched her husband's entire world crumble. When I shut the door on his vacant eyes, the crystal pedestal I had her on turned into glass and shattered at that exact moment. To be honest, I think a lot of my heart shattered along with it that night."

"I don't get it." Anne asked, puzzled at the ending of his story. "Then...why did you want to stay with her?"

"I do have to admit, one of my greatest faults...I hate being wrong. Besides that, I was embarrassed that I didn't trust my friends who warned me and it would look rather pitiful if I suddenly dropped my relationship with a married woman, whom I stole away from her supposedly happily married life. No one would see the truth, that the situation that had gone so sideways, that she had overtly lied and actually I was the one who became caught in her trap. So now...I'm the one who's majorly screwed. I guess I'll just have to ride it out until I can figure out another solution."

"You mean...she's still waiting for you, even after you've been here for this long?"

"Trust me, this girl wouldn't let go of any kind of meal ticket, especially since she's lost her husband, publically ensured that we're a loving couple and bottom line is that if we breakup, she'd have to thrive on her own. Right now I don't think I'll ever have enough strength to deal with a crazily vindictive, scorned harpy."

"Gee, Rick, I really can't imagine a more depressing way to live." Anne said off handedly while she resumed to blankly staring at the fire instead of watching all of the confused emotions play across his face. The first few anguished cords to 'Running to Stand Still' began to play as Rick got up and walked over to toss more wood on the fire.

"What do you mean?" Rick muffled question hung in the air while his back faced her.

Anne took a soothing, deep breath as she felt the lyrics dig into her soul and started to nervously wring her hands. "Well...it just seems like such a sad, shallow existence for the two of you. Being with someone...but never really knowing whom you're with, where you're going to be or what you're going to have. Your story makes me thankful for everything I've had in my life."

"I...I still don't understand what you're getting at." Rick squatted down next to the fire and gave her an open but quizzical look.

"Well...when I found out that I had lost my parents, the pain was beyond crippling and I wanted to give up, allow it to suck me in. But, somewhere in the back of my mind I knew I couldn't be consumed by it, simply because I knew I inherited the responsibility of raising my sister and running the ranch, those two things alone kept me from leaping over the brink of a dark oblivion."

The fire greedily transfixed Anne's gaze while she unconsciously pushed the logs around with her stick, causing an eruption of embers to shoot up into the sky. The riot of flames leapt hungrily into the air, creating a warm glow across her face. The immense pain submerged from the past, became evident mirrored in her vacant eyes as she gazed into the blaze. The years of sadness that should have engulfed her soul, rapidly surged to the surface while she unabashedly relived it.

Rick realized as he carefully watched her, *she's never faced her emotions about what she's had to endure. All of the years she's had to sacrifice herself and her being to be strong for everyone else…anything else…except for herself.* Unexpectedly a wave of compassionate understanding hit Rick and for the first time in his life all he wanted to do was give her his heart, to try to comfort her…help her heal. He felt frozen entrenched with the foreign need to go to her, an instinct that was completely overwhelming, but all he could do was distantly observe while she re-experienced her pain.

"I couldn't let my parents down by turning my back on their dream and I would never lose my sister to her grief. There were so many times when I caught her trying something stupid, I can't imagine being so young and having to cope with such a staggering loss, my grief seemed so insignificant in comparison to hers."

The second Anne raised her head and hollowly stared at Rick over the fire, he was shocked by how devastated and beautiful she was. Her bright eyes brimmed with unshed tears, longingly searching for any kind of comfort while vulnerability seemed to seep through her skin. Suddenly the night became a perfect moment of pure honesty given from someone who had never complained to anyone in the world to a stranger and she'd simultaneously would have given anything up for the opportunity to trust him.

"Rick…have you ever lost something you knew that you could never replace? Have you ever woken up in the middle of the night ready to scream…except you can't see through the horror filled fog of your dreams to remember what exactly it was that you were so terrified of? Instead you lie there in a cold sweat while the swirl of intense emotion begins to dissipate and you trust the night enough to finally settle back into bed. When everything seems to become normal and you calmly lay down, close your eyes…only to become instantly petrified with the realization that it was actually your life that just woke you up." Rocking back and forth Anne put her head in her hands, grabbed handfuls of her hair and began to rub her scalp. "Then as your throat begins to close the only thing you want to do is scream…only you can never make a sound."

Rick silently reached out to gently touch her shoulder with one hand and stroke her hair with the other. Anne startled away because in her grief she'd become completely unaware that he'd moved closer and was shocked by his gentle gesture. Her eyes stared intently into his as if she was trying to reach his soul.

"Everything was so sudden, I never had the chance to say I'm sorry, goodbye or I love you…nothing." Tears began to slip from her eyes as Rick drew her closer towards his shoulder and wrapped his arms comfortingly around her. "Life is so precious; there are millions of moments in our lives…but only one of each of them. I always took it for granted that they'd be here until they were old, I never considered that they'd die too soon." Anne buried her head into his shoulder and began to cry in earnest.

Rick closed his eyes and tried to steel himself from making the wrong decision, but the desperate need to be with her overrode any of his common sense. The next second he unconsciously started to whisper heartfelt sympathies into her ear and gently brushed her hair away from her face. When Anne's face emerged from under his shoulder, tears readily flowing down her cheeks creating inky rivers of makeup while a slight hiccup accompanied her breathing. Her eyes, lips and the skin around her cheeks had become red, swollen and blotchy from crying. Giving her a soft smile, Rick found himself memorizing everything, because every second became a moment that was seared on his heart. *I know I'm never going to forget her.*

"I…I'm so sorry. I don't know what…" Anne started to sloppily sniffle and apologize, until she felt the warmth when Rick held his finger against her lips to silence her unnecessary rambling.

Before Rick could stop himself from leaning down and captured her lips in a soft tender kiss. Gently he moved his hands through her hair trying to sooth her ragged emotions as the kiss lingered. He trace her lips, gingerly while he attempted to slowly pull back and prepare for some kind of instantaneous rebuttal or outrageous rib to deflect the uncomfortable situation.

But what he found lurking in the depths of her eyes was something quite different.

Anne sat dazed after Rick stopped kissing her. Blinking confused into his questioning face she realized that she wasn't so much shaken up by the fact that he had kissed her, *but by my own reaction.* Years of yearning settled while she recognized that it had been years since someone had touched or shown her any kind of affection, especially sexually. With the death of her parents she had closed that door tightly and readily determined never to re-open it; trying to survive, only having enough strength for what was needed to do; any kind of outside complication would be too much once she'd committed to making the ranch her life. She set her sights to solely conquering her inner, but tormented goals and never giving anything else but a passing glance.

Her started eyes snapped open, comprehending the fact that she was lying half drunkenly next to a fire, with a man she barely understood, revealing her darkest secrets and disappointments of life; the mere idea of exposing her soul and trusting someone else, was an idea that had become a strange figment of her imagination. *It's been so incredibly long since I've touched another person…I've forgotten what it's like.*

Unsteadily she hesitantly reached up her hand to Rick's cheek, feeling the roughness of stubble, taking a moment to gaze into his rich brown eyes and assess the man that she'd been struggling to place on the backseat, simply so she wouldn't have to deal with anything. *I've never considered there was someone with a past, future and dreams. I never paused in my hectic life to take the time to search beyond what was situated in front of me.*

Throwing any unresolved ideas to the wind, she firmly took his face in both of her hands, arching her back off the ground and brought his mouth back down to hers. The second she felt the heat when their lips met Anne moaned deeply, the sound sent an electric jolt through Rick. He leaned into the kiss and began to deepen it on his own accord, slowly memorizing her mouth while sensuously lingering with his tongue, totally consuming with each other. Anne slowly leaned back, touching her back, firmly pressed upon the ground as Rick rolled on top of her body, making their kiss deepen while they pressed their bodies intimately against one another.

Rick's hand began leisurely roaming up the side of her body until he detected the curve of her breast. The thought of touching her skin made him achingly moan while his fingers began to fumble, searching for the zipper on her sweatshirt. Rick instinctively deepened the kiss as he listened to the zipper being slowly guided down just below her belly button. He opened the fabric barely enough to brush his hands across her bare skin, shock immediately made him realize, *oh my god…she isn't wearing anything underneath.*

Anne felt like her body was on fire feeling the light grazes of Rick's warm fingers as he unzipped her coat and began to trace them across her naked body. As he captured her mouth with his, she slowly inched her tongue along his lips and moaned as he responded by slowly tracing her mouth with his tongue. The feel of his hands on her bare skin made her shiver in anticipation, wanting to feel his fingers tracing a trail all over her body. She reached down to quickly tug the hem of his shirt out from his pants, completely ignoring the buttons, bunching it in handfuls up his torso and yanked the unwanted material over his head. Anne held her breath until his hot skin touched hers, replacing his searching mouth and continued his assault by lowering her sweat pants a friction of an inch down to lift the edge of her panties. Anne began to trace the hair across his chest and slowly followed it with her fingers down his treasure trail, just past his belly button and began to manipulate the button of his jeans. She smiled when it opened and listened to the zipper begin to move down.

Rick was the first to realize what was about to happen, slow down the direction of their intentions and break their embrace. While breathing was still a little ragged he lifted his head, tentatively dropped a soft kiss on the end of her nose, fell to the side of the blanket and cradled her head onto his bare chest.

Anne's head started to spin listening to the combination of her heart beating wildly and Rick's attempt to take long calming breaths, while hers hysterically caught in her throat. *What's going on? I can't believe this is happening to me...Oh my God, he doesn't want to be with me!*

"Hey. Don't even start thinking that way." Rick muttered immediately noticing the change in her ridged body language. He lifted up his hands to gently turn her head to face him and looked her directly in the eyes. The intensity of the fire had died back and her searching gaze oddly emulated the glowing embers, the growing emptiness pierced his soul. "It's not that I don't want you, I believe that's pretty evident." Rick raised an arrogant eyebrow, moving his hips to firmly press against her so she could feel the evidence of his excitement rub against her thigh. He genuinely smiled at her innocent but startled look and began to stroke his thumb along her jaw line while continuing. "It's just that I don't want to put us in an awkward situation in the morning, so...I think we should just give this a rest and let time show us what's going to happen. I don't ever want you to think that I took advantage of you."

Anne tried to give him a tangible smile as she nodded, not wanting to chance saying anything while her thoughts were reeling with too much emotion. She instinctively curled her hand into his, returned her head on top of his chest, as he lay motionless beside her.

Rick silently brushed her hair soothingly away from her face and fixed his gaze up towards the stars, almost instantly he felt her body soften and her breathing slow down into tiny puffs. He fumbled around the ground, blindly searching for the extra blankets next to his head and awkwardly draped them over their bodies. Brushing her hair back and stared at her face while she slept. *With all of her daily stress stripped away by the abyss of sleep, she's so peacefully beautiful.* Unknowing how she was complicating his life, she achingly had begun to reveal herself more each day, while Rick unconsciously felt his air tight resolve slip away.

I've never met anyone like her and I probably never will again. He felt a surge of sadness while gently kissing her forehead and then laid his head back, willing sleep to come. For a stolen moment he enjoyed her warmth while he memorized the stars and simplicity of her body while he yearned for some guidance to prepare himself for whatever fate had in store, a mystery that was yet to come.

17

Hu... funny how time just creeps along without a trace, Rick contemplated while pausing for an idol second to contently lean against the rake, glance around the yard and survey the reward of his hard labor. He reminisced about when he first laid eyes on the exterior of the grand old house, it had been dismal with years of neglect, littered with trash, and numerous abandoned mundane jobs that took the back burner because Anne never seemed to have enough time. *It had been a disgrace the way the yard had been completely neglected.*

He felt a surge of pride standing next to the tidy back porch and surveyed the surrounding area that was litter free, all the trash and discarded items had either found a home or went in one large load to the dump. Rick had made it his daily mission to try and restore the yard to its original beauty. Everything was pruned, weeded, edged and mowed in his attempt to accomplish something of purpose with his own bare hands.

A cool breeze picked up slightly tugging him out of his thoughts making him close his eyes and inhale deeply in for a moment. Rick willed his mind to remember the comfortable feeling of being there and in a somewhat insignificant way, knowing he'd made a difference. *No matter how minute, at least there'll be a small reminder that I was here and cared.* He opened his eyes and return to finishing lopping down a huge rhododendron that after countless years had encroached across one of the backyard windows. He wiped the sweat off his brow after struggling with the last couple cuts, Rick stepped back to survey the damage. *Nice, I didn't do very badly, this time. At least I didn't kill it like the first one, hopefully that one will come back next year or I'll just grab another one.*

Rick placed both hands on his lower back, enjoying a lengthy stretch of his over-worked muscles. He briskly rubbed his arms as he realized that the final rays of sunshine were diminishing, announcing that once again time had gotten away and he needed to finish cleaning up before dark. Bending over Rick grunted, grabbing a large section of limbs and started to drag them over to the fire pit. While the light started to become ominously softer, Rick carefully heaved the large pile of rubbish to the designated to an area where he'd been storing all of the yard waste. After throwing his burden down, he turned to meander back towards the rest of the debris, but paused halfway where he unconsciously found himself near the open kitchen window. He smiled then chuckled listening to the typical evening noises as Anne finished cleaning up the dinner clutter. After a few days of yard work Rick realized that her nightly ritual was singing a plethora of Neil Diamond songs accompanying her preparations and clean up.

Rick found himself from chuckling to having to cover his mouth to suppress from laughing harder. *Ha, well… seems like "Sweet Caroline" is the favorite of the day*, after his thought the song began to immediately replay for the countless time. His stomach loudly growled at the smell of the delicious meal cooking, causing him press a hand firmly across his midsection, trying not to disturb the moment. He started to pivot and was about to leave, when out of the blue he recognized that Anne had decided to make the song, into a duet. Rick squinted in agony listening to her painful attempt at singing, she was not only off key but also out of sync with the song. The melody was timelessly fun and enjoyably beautiful, but Anne added some spice while completely butchering it in such an innocent way. A forlorn smile touched Rick's lips as he tried to picture her dancing in the dimly lit kitchen, impressed with her karaoke abilities and immersed in the peaceful moment alone. Then he questioned he sanity and hearing when she decided to engage in an encore, attempting to tackle the lyrics, but this time with even more enthusiasm.

He dismissed the entertainment with an amused shake of his head and wandered over to the pile of littered limbs dragging another load over to the fire pit where Rick's thoughts ventured into a darker web of unknown. *It's amazing how life changes and time relentless continues. Seconds fly by, minutes turn to days and days have melted into months. Funny my mail for Mike is lying untouched next to the bed and I'd rather be out here.*

Attempting to shake off his meandering thoughts, he turned his attention back to raking up some of the smaller debris as his mind floated back to a particularly strange moment that had transpired earlier that day. *I'd counted on painful experience when Anne sent me on another humiliating errand to The Local Feed Store.*

Rick grudgingly pushed the catawampus over-loaded cart towards the front of the store after an agonizing hour to accomplished shopping in the cave-like store and bravely reigned in his patience when he spied the ever calculating Lois. The veering cart hit the checkout stand with a thud making Rick nervously gulp while gingerly placing the first item on the counter, expecting some kind of reprimand for the dent, but paused in astonished silence. *Holy shit, Lois is actually smiling at me.*

"So, Rick how's everything going up there at the big house? Are they treating you alright?" Lois snapped her gum, desperately tried not to check out his body, efficiently scanned each item and ungraciously continued on before he could answer. "Well, I drove by there the other day and Lordy be! I couldn't believe my eyes! You sure have made quite a difference up there. The yard is coming along great!"

"Um, thanks Lois." Rick steeled himself for some kind of off handed attempt to dismantle his manly pride or make a discreet sexual reference.

"I haven't seen much of that Dave nowadays. It used to be that he would saunter in anytime Anne showed her pretty face in town. Now, if he notices either of you two pulling up, he usually makes a bee line for his car parked out back and high tails it out of here like a bolt of lightning." Lois punctuated her monolog with a creative snap of her fingers coinciding with her gum while grabbing the black credit book and easing it across the counter to him.

"There you go…you know what to do, Sweetie." She silently kept her hand on her hip and waited for him to scribble his initials. "Chuck's waiting out back with your call in. You have a great day now, Hon."

Rick hesitantly shoved the cart towards the entrance, uncertainly mumbling, "Um, thanks?"

His head was still spinning with astonished questions about Lois's uncommon treatment as he pulled around to the back. Training his thoughts back to backing the truck to the loading dock he warily watched Chuck sitting in his favorite white plastic chair, reading the paper and lounging in the sun. With a slight nod of his head he mutely directed Rick towards the stacked bales of hay, then continued on with his paper. *Ahh, at least something around here is normal. If Chuck actually spoke I'd know I was in an episode of the Twilight Zone.*

After he secured the bales he heard the scratch of the speaker while Lois's irritated voice hollered over the microphone, "Hey Chuck, tell that young whippersnapper that they'll need to call in earlier for their feed next time…it's on back order." Chuck's answer was to merely lower the paper below his eyes, cock a graying brow after making eye contact with Rick and then resumed reading silently continuing with his busy day. Bewildered at the sudden change of atmosphere, Rick froze in confusion trying to determine what to do next, then casually shut the tailgate and uncertainly turned towards Chuck giving him a tentative wave.

"Hey, thanks again, Chuck." Rick whipped around the truck to yank open the door, intending a rapid departure. He glanced over to ensure Chuck's typical, completely uninterested response, until he nonchalantly returned the action and gave Rick the equivalent of a half-assed wave. Astonished Rick's mouth hung open as he stared incredulously while the corner of Chuck's stoic mouth ticked slightly, and then knowingly lifted into a pleasant grin. A sudden quiver of unease reverberated through Rick. *Are you shitting me? I feel like I've been on the set of the Twilight Zone with the way these two are acting.*

Unbelievingly smiling, shaking his head at the audacious memory he mindlessly maneuvered around the bush, laughing out loud while he continued to rake the errant leaves. *Funny, you'd think that those two had been hitting the juice or taking a hit off a pipe during the day.* Without a pause his thoughts migrated to uneventful days of amiably chatting with an overtly animated Beth about teenage drama, school, rival girls and irritating unaware boys. By the end of their heated debates that resounded with her youthful enthusiasm about life, he continuously left the house light-hearted, punctuating the evening by annoyingly tousling her hair until she jokingly complained about his high-handed treatment. *But at the end of every evening, I find my ritual at be leaning against the corral fence silently waiting for Anne's bedroom light to fade out and only then I can make my way back into that damn tiny room.*

Scraping the blades of the rake farter under the bush he absentmindedly noticed a large, stray limb that had fallen, pinned against the wall under the window. Squatting down to army crawl his way under the bush, Rick grumbled to himself about his situation until he got closer to the window. Unconsciously he froze, as the hairs on the back of his neck stood up accounting for the strange feeling of dead the second he recognized the outline of a large pair of footprints indented in the dark, moist soil. He tried to shake off the odd sensation, deciding not to give it an extra thought until he realized, *what the hell...shit, I've never worked on this side of the bush.* A surge of unreality enhanced an oppressive feeling, every muscle instantly tensed screaming to immediately crawl out from under the bush, he instinctively obeyed by scooting backwards, standing up and cautiously made his way over to the opposite side. Carefully stretching against the house and lifting the last branch, Rick placed his foot next to the footprint to ensure that it wasn't his. *It seems slightly larger and a completely different type of shoe, kind of like a boot.* Scratching his head Rick surveyed the area until a shiver of fear went up his spine when he found himself looking directly eyelevel into the living room of the house. The bushes decoratively covered some of the window, but from this hidden angle he had a perfect view through the living room and into the kitchen. He instantly ducked just as Anne stepped into the living room and unknowingly raised her arms over her head in an elegant, but sexy stretch. Rick fearfully slid onto his hands and knees to carefully snake out of his hiding place, praying that she wouldn't catch a glimpse of his shadow. *Damn, what the hell is this all about?*

Later Anne was finishing up humming the last few bars of the song, enjoying the end of the evening while she dried off the final dinner plate and placed it gingerly in the cupboard. With a contented sigh she walked over to lay the dishcloth on the sink to dry, until the manicured yard's multitude of colors shimmered in the evening glow, the beauty immediately catching her eye. *I really need to thank Rick in the morning for putting so much hard work into cleaning the place up on his days off.*

Anne tiredly yawned and turned off the lights making her way out of the kitchen. She shook her head amused by the memory of Beth informally announcing that she was going to spend the night at Suzie's house the moment they sat down for dinner...with Suzie. She didn't have any complaints until that second, when the absolute silence engulfed the house still and waiting to hear someone bothered her whenever she was alone. *I hate it when the house is so dark and the silence concretes that no one else is here*

Anne felt a lump of sadness well up in the back of her throat causing her to become motionless in the shadowy living room dimly lit from the front hall, unconsciously reflecting on the distant images that began to carelessly run through her mind. *All of the moments I never appreciated that are lost forever...everyone squished on the couch fighting over the remote laughingly commanding what program to watch, Christmas mornings when Mom would bake homemade cinnamon rolls as Dad would sneak Bailey's in their coffee until neither of them cared who was complaining for the rest of the day. We'd become drones playing with our gifts, listening to endless Elvis' 'Blue Christmas' and our parents would quietly drift off to sleep, napping with one limb overlapping another their bodies tucked into the end of the couch.*

A tear achingly slipped from the corner of her eyes while she desperately became torn between trying to stop the memories and cherishing each precious moment. With a loud sniff Anne abruptly brushed the moisture out of her eyes and turned to mechanically make her way towards the stairs.

 "Oh man, I've got to get some sleep," she whispered into the dark, solemnly leaning against the wall to switch off the light. Instinctively Anne clasped her hands firmly over her mouth, violently sucked in a frightened breath and attempted to suppress an unexpected shriek. Seeking safety she took a few clumsy steps backwards, blindly stumbling until her back was firmly pressed against the cold kitchen wall. She gasped for a calming breath while her mind silently screamed, *Holy shit...someone is standing outside the living room window!*

For a few seconds the only thing Anne could hear was the intense drumming of her heartbeat while restraining from becoming physically ill rammed against the wall until she'd regained enough control to mentally force her body to relax. In the inky darkness a horrifying thought crossed her mind sending her to silently creep through the mudroom to double check that the back door was securely locked. She blew out her pint up breath and summoned her common sense to find some kind of resolve to walk into the other room and look out the window. *OK Anne, think...if there is someone outside, then as long as the lights are shut off...they can't see a thing inside. Come on, you can do it!* Hugging the wall with her back, she tentatively took the first few steps, an odd tingling sensation like she was treading across broken glass with bare feet. Her lungs felt like they were going to explode from holding her breath, while she terrifyingly waited for the ghostly white face to show itself in the window again. Keeping to the shadows Anne hedged around the middle of the room until realizing that she was standing in the darkest corner next to the door and exhaled the rest of her pent up breath. *Whew, I don't think anyone is out there...or am I crazy.*

While Anne watched the blackened window, she realized that the view was clear through the evening darkness of the yard all the way down to the barn. The hair on the back of her neck stood up immediately when she noticed Rick's shadowy form was just closing the arena door while a grating suspicion reared its ugly head. The thought firmly drove itself home making her shake her head in silent denial. *No, it couldn't be. Maybe I'm just tired and my minds playing tricks on me.* Without another thought Anne hastily swept into the entryway, switched off the remaining outside lights, double checked the front door locks and then sprinted upstairs. Once she skidded safely in her room with the door tightly shut, she giddily laughed at herself for acting so foolishly. *No more daydreaming for tonight, you won't be able to go to sleep!* Anne quickly changed her clothes, switched off the bedroom lights and crawled into bed begging for sleep. Instead she lay imprisoned in the darkness, awake for hours, listening to either the rhythmic pattern of her breathing or every creak that creepily moan that shattered the silence throughout the old house.

18

Tourists began to steadily pour into Westport in unheard of hordes when the forecaster's prediction of uninterrupted sun-filled weather was intended for the northwest. The quick couple hours' drive to the coast had made the destination an essential weekend family vacation for generations.

Typically, the ordinary coast scenery surrounding the Westport area would never be as magnificent as its immediate neighbors. Up towards the north, near Neah Bay or the Hoh Rainforest, the majestic landscape moved with an ancient combination of sea and rainforest creating breathtaking visual waves of primitive grace and beauty. In addition, the raw beauty of the scenery across the southern coast of Oregon carved a name of its own in Newport and Cannon Beach. The unprecedented coast embraces its unearthly grace with craggy weathered islands of rock suspended against the churning sea's elements that's captivated anyone's attention around the world. Normally on any beach across the Northwest when the weather cooperated, anywhere on the coast was a tantalizing morsel of a holiday. Once the sun began to shine reservations started pouring in daily and the brief weekends of summer began to fill up from May until way through Labor Day weekend. The result created an essential gift for the local businesses who found themselves outrageously thriving during these magical moments, even at Anne's ranch, any negative outlook seemed to miraculously lift with the intention of Westport's success until the end of the season.

Anne thoughtfully scratched her head and hung up the phone from booking another family for a weekend reservation. *Well, I'll be damned. This whole horse business is starting to pan out.* Consumed with the enlightened feeling of a new optimistic thought, she waltzed across the kitchen to happily gaze outside at the thriving property. She became entranced admiring how the dismal countryside had flourished with the changes summer had brought with the weather heating the earth. Everything seemed to glow with a multitude of budding color, blue skies and the promise of a new day. Anne's gaze aimlessly scanned towards the lower pasture, creating a slight devious smile creep across her face as she realized, *Holy shit...I'm sitting here staring at Rick.*

He'd taken the day off work with every intention to finish some final touches to secure the lower fence gate that had been missing a lock and a few other safety features. It was one of the last imperative job he needed to finish to protect the lower pastures before the onslaught of visitors. At that second Rick was bent over intently tending to something low on a fence post, while beautiful, huge Demon paused slightly towering over his kneeling form. The horse playfully nudged Rick's back, demanding his immediate attention by almost shoving him over. Rick playfully pushed him off a few times, then with a disgruntled laugh he gave in and stroked the horse's nose.

The endearing sight of the two brought a warm smile to her lips. *I have to admit that a lot of the success that's been made around here couldn't have been accomplished without Rick's help.* Anne acknowledged that she'd had her doubts at first, but after Rick's first few riding lessons with Demon his skill dramatically developed and absolutely impressing her with his commitment to learn. *I have to admit his confidence and working with the horses has grown tremendously over the last few months.*

The combination of the ranch's daily schedule along with the overload of taking weekend beach excursions with clients had taken its toll on Anne and Rick had become an invaluable daily asset. At first he'd nonchalantly began to prepare the gear and horses for each day's excursion. Realizing that some of the weight had been lifted, until he realized it was nothing compared to the burden of Anne's daily responsibility of conducting her business. Without Anne's knowledge, Rick had silently made the decision to help with preparing the group, assigning horses, directing any wayward person towards the beach excursions and ending the day by tending the horses alongside her.

After the first few stressful weekends of 'family' excursions, every evening Anne fell into bed exhausted from the overwhelming stress of redirecting family members' horse inhibitions, recurring domestic disputes, leering males with suggestive opportunities and aggressive sibling rivalry. She habitually lay quietly across her bed with her eyes thankfully closed after another event, breathing deeply trying to accomplish some healthy meditation and tried to prepare herself for the next day's unknown chaotic events. *Ah...the illusion of domestic bliss, white picket fences and the beauty of child rearing...more like prison and angry daycare. Thank the lord, I haven't condemned myself to that type of prison.*

"Anne!!" someone shouted, causing her to lift out of her tranquil dreams. Unknowing where she was, Anne cracked opened an aching bloodshot eye to another beautiful morning with the birds singing and a slight crisp breeze flowing in through the window.

"Mmm," she deliciously moaned low in her throat while she rolled over and pulled the blankets tightly over her head. Trying not to be too selfish, she floated backwards allowing herself a precious moment to lay motionless imprisoned deep in her warm blankets without a care in the world, until the door slammed open

"OMG," A few seconds later when an irritated adolescent voice rang as Beth tapped her toe emphatically, only to find herself faced with a lengthy moment of silence for a response. She stormed over to Anne's bed and attempted to yack the top layer of blankets off. Beth made an aggravated sound when her futile attempts couldn't compete with the secure, multicolored quilted cocoon that Anne had encased herself inside. "You are not still in bed! Do you know what time it is?"

Silence resonated from the depths of the bed.

"Argh…fine!" Beth let out an exasperated sigh and stormed over to the door. "Just to let you know, you've slept in to the point that the family for the afternoon excursion should be arriving at any minute! And trust me…I'd be more than happy to see you on top of a horse in your PJ's, but I don't know about you, I'd like to eat this week. So, hurry up!"

It took a second after the door's slam resounded through her cocoon that Anne's unbelieving eyes popped open with alarm. She desperately struggled to disengage herself from the sheet and find her way into the bathroom barely throwing herself into jeans and a T-shirt.

Beth whistled surveying the room, knowingly positioned herself leaning against the kitchen countertop and listened to the familiar sounds of her sister frantically rummage through her room, then stumbling down the stairs.

"Ah…shit," Anne unconsciously muttered racing through the kitchen, while Beth mutely held out a mug filled with coffee making Anne skid across the room in her sock feet.

"Shit…damn it all to hell." A string of quiet ranting began accepting her mug, she took a burning gulp and began to run around in erratic circles desperately searching for her shoes.

"Yikes!" Anne yelped as Beth loudly slammed her weather worn cowboy boots down on the countertop next to her elbow.

"Here you go."

"Aw, shit." Anne half glared and half rolled her eyes in response to her sister's dramatic help as she grabbed the boots. Anne muttered another string of profanities while she struggled to forcefully tug them on, hopping unsteadily from one foot to the other.

"Ok, I packed a great lunch for the both of you and I'll have dinner ready for the barbeque when you get back home." Beth calmly walked over, refilled Anne's semi-depleted mug with coffee and waited for her sister to finish the daily fight with her boots. "Have a great one!"

"Yeah, ok… right, great." Without hesitation Anne grabbed the brown bags and coffee mug as she sped out the back door. She continued to speed walk down the drive trying to make up time, only allowing a half second to pause and take another necessary sip while she approached the barn door. She mentally accounted, *Alrighty…not only do I need to get what I have to get done for the day, but also incorporate Rick's daily assignment... while I'm completely discombobulated. Lord help me, I don't have time for this shit.*

Maneuvering around the catawampus barn door with her arms full, Anne was greeted with the familiar combination of musty smell from the barn dirt, horse and fresh hay. She had to blink rapidly a few times to get the sleep out of her eyes and adjust to the dim interior light of the barn.

"Rick?" She called attempting to close the broken door with her foot, but with a negative shrug she decided to leave to it open and mentally prepared to throw herself into high gear. Anne prayed desperately, *please let it look like I'm competent and ready for this family that's due to arrive at any moment.*

"Hey Rick." Anne bellowed while mentally berating herself for sleeping in again, nervously glancing at the clock and sulkily realized, *I am going to have to beg him to give me some assistance with this next group if I'm even going to attempt to be on time.*

She walked over to the small table holding the radio and switched it on as Crowded House's 'Fall at Your Feet' sprang to life then slammed down the lunches and coffee. Anne pinched the bridge of her nose, wondering where Rick was hiding and mentally listening to the ticking of precious time that was being lost while searching for him.

"R-i-c--" Anne opened her mouth with every intention to bellow his name and release every ounce of irritation.

"Ahem." Rick made a slight noise that came from the general direction of a darkened arena next to the outer doors.

"Yikes!" Anne squeaked as she simultaneously jumped and turned towards the sound of his voice.

"Um, shit." She let out an embarrassed sigh of relief to find Rick standing in the middle of the interior arena nervously kicking the dirt with the toe of his boot. Anne's jaw dropped in astonishment, all the horses were standing next to him at attention like a small battalion, meticulously saddled and prepared for the day, including Demon. Expecting her wrath, Rick brought up both hands and began to hesitantly make his way towards her, imitating actions like he was approaching a wounded animal.

"So...before you say no, I've been thinking." He shoved his hands deep into his pockets creating a mild distraction as Anne's eyes suddenly became riveted onto the taut fabric stretched across his groin. "Look, you need some help out there on the beach with the excursions and tending the tourists. I can help you now that I can keep my seat on Demon. Especially when you're going to have such a large group like you do next week."

Anne's mute reply was to arch a skeptical brow, then opened her mouth to comment.

Rick quickened his pace towards her and held up a hand for her to stop as he continued on. "Please Anne, just listen for a second. I've noticed you have an extremely hard time letting things go and can be a little bit of a...um, control freak, in your own special kind of way, I mean. All of this continuous hard work is taking its toll on you and I'm tired of watching you kill yourself with everything day in and day out. "

Anne's eyebrow instantly shot up higher, uncomfortably cleared her throat at his honest observation and defensively crossed her arms in front of her while he finished.

"I've finished all of the large projects around the grounds and organized the daily routine. I figure that if I can get everything out of the way during the week, then I'd be able to help you out with the weekend rides. Look, it's mainly to indulge me by giving me a breather from being in the barn all day and give you another pair of hands while you're dealing with the crowds. You have to admit, you could use my help." Rick found the last few words lamely running together and stood poised in front of her waiting for some kind of witty, but scathing rejection.

Anne stubbornly put her hands on her hips, objectively regarded him for a quick second and then shrugged her shoulders. "Great, let's get started and see how you do," Anne said before she turned around.

"Uh, hey...thanks! Anne, you won't regret it," Rick called out while a sheer look of surprise shot across his face, giving her a light punch on her shoulder and gave her a lopsided grin that made her heart miss a beat. For a quick second a rush of attraction raced through the air like static electricity making them pause and stared wordlessly at each other.

Without another thought Rick broke the tension by giving her an exaggerated wink, turned to leave and began to whistle Neil Diamond's "Sweet Caroline" as he sauntered outside to finish up his daily morning routine.

Anne stood perplexed in the middle of the empty arena, raised her eyes towards the rafters and let out a little laugh as she shook her head. "Now what have I gotten myself into?"

After running around to accomplish the last few chores, Anne was amazed that by the time the first carload of tourists pulled up to the house they looked organized, professionally geared up and ready for the afternoon. Anne watched as Rick walked around the corral to thoroughly inspect that everything on the horses was in order for the day. His lean body captivated her attention as his shirt became taunt stretching down to check one of the horse's holsters. She guiltily jumped when her daydreaming was shattered by the unexpected startling screech of children piling out of a vehicle.

Each of the errant children ran to the fence intent on picking out their favorite horse for the day. Anne laughed at the chaos, turning towards the two haggard parents making their way out of the 'well-loved' minivan and seeming to tiredly limp behind their hoard.

"Hello, Mr. and Mrs. Jones, you have perfect timing and it's great that your reservations for today. The weather is cooperating and it should be an amazing day for a ride." Anne called out with a friendly wave.

The couple nervously approached the corral fence while dismay spread across their faces and silent fear filled their eyes while they assessed the horses. A drivel of complying commands formed in their frozen mouths, while they attempt instruct some kind of verbally parental restraint to their children that were dangerously climbing all over the corral fence.

"Hi," Mrs. Jones replied absently as she hovered next to the fence, nervously wringing her hands while mutely watching her children's antics accelerate in their obnoxious misbehavior.

Anne cautiously observed the nervous woman's frightened eyes dart from the horses lined up for the ride, to her children and immediately return to the van. She was about to give Mrs. Jones a bubbly pep talk about the joys of riding and the benefits that her perfect children were going to receive from their experience, that was until she witnessed an odd but immediate change in her posture and disposition the second she adverted her gaze.

The mother's beaten-down sagging shoulders suddenly straightened, jutting her buxom chest out, lack-luster eyes instantly sparkled and widened with feminine curiosity as she noticed Rick discussing horses with Mr. Jones.

"Hmm," Anne's lips became pursed, while angrily narrowing her eyes at the other woman. Anne's female intuition leapt up a few notches, assessing the weary mother's transformation as she eagerly straightened the collar of her wrinkled shirt, readjusted her ill-fitting pants, fluffed her hair, openly adjusted her bra, and completely ignored Anne.

Really? Quizzically Anne shook off her irritation at the outrageous feminine antics the other woman was displaying, elected to exaggeratedly lift her shoulders and clap her hands to get everyone's attention. She deftly ducked under the slats of the fence, began her opening speech and attempted to educate them all for their upcoming experience.

The excursion finally commenced after a grueling hour of assigning mounts, patiently redirecting each of the children and answering a mass of insignificant questions posed by Mrs. Jones intentionally directed towards an unsuspecting Rick. With the sun heating her face as they made their way over the dunes and out onto the open beach, Anne became well aware of Rick's presence.

Throughout the day she enjoyed watching him confidently ride behind the group, galloping through the surf when he noticed one of the younger children having some difficulty with their mount. Anne unknowingly smiled taking pleasure in the sight of him working in the spray of the ocean with the sun shining on the water as he maneuvered the beautiful horse over to help out another lagging child. Shaking her head in denial, noticing how Mrs. Jones was holding on to the horse for dear life but, craned her head with any movement that Rick made, Anne giddily spurred her mount forward to check the rest of the horde and galloping through the water a small laugh escaped her lips. *With Rick's help, things might possibly be looking up for the summer.*

* * *

With the extensive late summer clientele intense demands began to bear down on the ranch, everyone's nerves had become a bit frayed. It wasn't anyone's fault, but the tension at the barn was at an all-time high, even with the weather staying brilliant. Visitors flocked to Westport while the end of summer was riding high on the wind and there wasn't a care in the world down on the coast.

Rick found himself alone in the barn trying to tie up assembling the gear on the horses for a demanding excursion with their largest group of the summer. His brow furrowed as he manically tried to wrap up numerous tasks on his mental checklist bending under the last horse to check on its saddle, only to become too engrossed with the tack to recognize the crunch of gravel as a truck maneuvered up the drive.

Listening to the slamming truck doors, Anne quickly tied her hair in a high ponytail and walked out of the house ready for the day. She immediately skidded to a halt, dejectedly groaned as she spied a large gaggle of late teen girls ambling out of a beautiful new Cadillac Escalade SUV. The half-naked limbs from the scantily clothed girls continued to pour out of the vehicle and instantaneously shifting into pairs, maliciously whispering to each other while casting heated glares everyone. A dark-haired, long-legged beauty who was obviously the leader, disengaged herself from a pack and approached the fence to present each one of the teens with an "I told you so" bored expression, creating a ripple of rolled eyes in silent but unified agreement to ignore the adults.

Sizing up the obvious difficult bunch, Anne stood frozen on the porch, closed her eyes to mentally send a small prayer out into the universe for strength and reinforcements to get through the day. *Please give me some kind of distraction when we get down on the beach, like an unscheduled all male volleyball tournament right on the main beach directly past the dunes. That way they'll demand to*

213

pause and watch, while we run out of time for the excursion. Hell, right now I'd even enjoy some time off to watch that. Ambling down the steps she softly whistled Garth Brooks' 'Friends in Low Places' while her hopeful thought clouded her mind and rounded the side of the truck.

Like a flock of birds, all of the girls unexpectedly swiveled around and started to twitter candidly amongst each other. Before Anne could wonder what was transpiring, the girls started to nonchalantly migrate towards the corral fence connected to the barn. Right at that moment their overtly weary chaperone poked her disheveled head out of the vehicle, spotted Anne with a wave and clumsily approached her.

"Hi. Um…I'm with them. We're here for the beach ride today. I hope we aren't too early. I can't seem to keep these girls entertained for the life of me." The chaperone rambled searching Anne's face for some kind of silent understanding.

"No, no, you're fine." Anne said as she paused next to the truck and attempted to smooth the flustered woman's nerves. "I have a sixteen year old sister. I know exactly what you're going through, just leave everything to us."

"Oh…bless you. Any kind of distraction for a little while will be wonderful." The woman looked as if she should rest with a nap inside the vehicle instead of ride, while she eagerly followed Anne towards the barn.

Anne's piqued curiosity got the better of her while she ignored the other woman's babbling about the horrid mischief the gaggle had been up to, instead attempted to listen to what all the high-pitched whispering was about. She continued to mindlessly discuss the day's itinerary with the exhausted woman until they strolled around the back of the vehicle and openly wondered what had the girls in such a heightened state of awareness.

Shock rocketed through her limbs making Anne stop dead in her tracks the second she witnessed the atrocity unfolding. Most of the girls were leaning alluringly over the fence, seeming to innocently talk amiably to each other, while a couple of them had boldly crossed over the fence and bravely stood inside the corral audaciously bantering with the rest of them. But underneath all of their display of coy poses, bantering complaints and flirtatious demeanor, their feline attention was obviously directed towards the same object. *Oh shit, they are all in heat…and it's because of Rick.*

"Oh my…it must be our lucky day, why I haven't seen the girls get along this well since we left Seattle," the chaperone energetically interjected, unaware that her enthusiastic words were like rubbing salt on a wound to Anne.

Rick was completely preoccupied, still struggling to saddle up all of the horses for the day in the barn, his back illuminated by the sun shining through the door. Anne's mouth gaped while she stood there amazed at their audacious behavior as few of the bolder ones began to approach Rick with an openly coquettish curiosity. *Dear lord…they are slowly circling around him like a pack of hungry freakin' hyenas!*

The pack of inherently overzealous hormones focused their female powers on redirecting his attention away from the horses as the leader took a turn at boldly asking a question, a second casually flipped her hair and another loudly giggled making a witty comment. Anne watched in horror as all of the adoring girls ended up either hanging along the fence or angling their young, voluptuous bodies to display their best assets in all of their youthful exuberance, every one of them desperately vying for Rick's undivided attention.

"Oh my God!" Anne rolled her eyes and blew out a frustrated breath imagining the desperately long ride that she was in store for the entire day. She clapped her hands loudly to get all of their hormone-aroused attention trying to begin their lesson and explain the itinerary for the day. Her prediction about the day's outcome became painfully obvious while Anne talked and observed each girl urgently attempted to get some sort of individual attention while they assembled alongside their assigned horses. Honing in on his unaware with their juvenile manipulation that spanned from painful ankles, dust in their eyes, to how to determine if they were saddle sore, how that kind of sore would feel like and pleading to have him demonstrate the art of massage, was a dalliance of persistent questions aimed at Rick.

Throughout the girls lusting teenaged tirade, their frazzled chaperone sat petrified on top of her horse, ramrod straight barely keeping a seat in her fright.

Anne wanted to scream in frustration, throw her hands up in the air and cancel the entire outing, *but the thought of losing so much cash is outweighing my better judgment.* She jumped onto her horse, spurring it around to plow through the sea of estrogen and approach Rick's mount. Seething fingertips of jealously riddled up Anne's spine as she wielded her horse through, tactfully disengaging and creating a path through the disgruntled female pack.

Unknowingly her lips drew into a persnickety, thin line as she saddled up alongside of Rick deploringly warning, "Hey there Grunt…you better watch your back today and anything else you've might be thinking about exposing. You never know, you might get a little more than you bargained for."

Without another word she eyed him sitting in his saddle, heatedly spurred her horse out onto the trail that led off of the property, over the dunes and down onto the beach. An excursion of ten for the entire day would usually be a piece of cake, *except for the continuous fiascos that seemed to take place whenever Rick idiotically rode his horse haphazardly through the crowd of overtly, hormonal young females.* Anne hopefully crossed her fingers the instant she disengaged her mount from the pack as they crested the dunes. She disdainfully heaved a sigh of defeat while the party made their way down the beach and the sound of twittering voices resumed their aggressive pace towards Rick. Anne miserably searched the horizon in either direction, *Damn it...where are all of those half-naked professional male volleyball players, oiled up in a heated competition on the beach when you need them?*

* * *

By the end of the day Anne was ready to relish in any sort of solitude, even preparing the horses to be washed alone seemed like a novelty after babysitting obnoxious girls. Once she had everything in place she sauntered over to the radio, flipped in her favorite Chris Isaak compilation CD and played it on random. His crooning, but despondent voice hovered through the warm summer air embracing the darkness of the barn.

Heaving the over sudsy bucket of water with one hand and a garden hose with the other, she made her way outside into the late afternoon sun intent on washing a couple of the horses. Humming low in her throat keeping in time with the first couple of songs, she made a quick job with the first few horses and released them to run into the lower pasture. Anne took a brief moment consumed in her solitude to stop and raise her face towards the sun, purely indulging in the feel of its fingers tracing her bronzed skin across her face. The heat felt good as she inhaled deeply and pleasantly felt all of the day's tension begin to dissipate, until the first notes of 'Wicked Game' floated through the speakers.

"Ohhhh no...I don't think so, I'm not listening to any sappy songs today." Anne ungraciously snorted, immediately dropped what she was doing, stormed through the barn to the radio and grumpily switch songs. Her mood immediately lifted as his voice began singing the first few bars of 'Cheater's Town', inhaling another deep breath to restore some of her angry determination and focus on finishing the remaining horses. She hummed along with the tune while marching back outside to resume where she'd abandoned the dirty pail of water sitting along the side of the barn. Anne absentmindedly swirled the murky water around, tossed it out in the pasture and pivoted around to refill with clean sudsy water.

"Awww....nuts." Turning off the spigot Anne sighed when she gazed down at her dirty work boot only to realize that she was standing in a huge mud puddle in just her tank top and a pair of cut-off shorts.

With a quirky lopsided grin Anne absentmindedly shrugged her shoulders, maneuvering around the last couple of horses and walked one to the gate.

"Not like any of you guys would give a hoot about how I look; besides I know I can clean up real good. So, don't go getting your panties in a bunch, I'm just trying to have a little fun."

She took a second to watch him run through the pasture with the rest, Anne went to grab the last horse. Her gloomy mood began to lift while enjoying the heat of the sun as it began to burn her face, shoulders and arms. She impishly smiled while the horse followed her lead over to the washing area and "American Boy" kicked her mood up a notch. Anne instinctively began tapping her feet, humming and loudly semi-singing in time with the song while mimicking the beat with the spray on the animal.

The second the suds were dissipated Anne untied the horse, carelessly sauntered across the corral and releasing it into the pasture simultaneously the beginning bars of 'Baby Did a Bad Bad Thing' insistently seeped its way across the barn.

Despite any inner restraint or pride, Anne let out a girlish squeal when she recognized the tune, then sensually rolled a shoulder, pivoting and returned to the wash area with a sexy catch in her step, attempting to imitate a Victoria's Secret model strutting across the catwalk. A small bubbly giggle escaped her lips, making a giddy feeling overcame her senses as she exaggeratedly bent over and picked up the hose, intending to clean up the mess. Instead she began to twirl the water, creating sloppy, muddy patterns across the ground.

Then a silly idea struck her and without another thought she slowly started to rotate her hips with the beat of the music, mentally deciding to throw caution to the wind and embrace the moment by breaking into a sexy dance, enjoying a token second alone. By the time the song reached a handful of heated verses, Anne had attempted every sensual move that she could conger up and what her agile, feminine frame would allow. Her lack of expertise at imitating anything remotely sexy revealed itself when she slightly tripped, making her desperately envision herself between a pole dancer and a backup dancer for either Madonna or Lady Gaga. By the end of the song and a little out of breath, she erotically sauntered over towards the corral humming along with the lingering chorus to regally bow towards her captive audience of horses. *Well, at least it's only you guys who could appreciate my attempts.*

Humming she switched on the faucet, set the hose down next to some of the refreshed bubble-filled buckets and began to walk over to open the gate leading out to one of the exterior pastures. Anne gave her hips a couple of twists while enjoying an mental extended version of the song, whistling the tune and keeping up with her sexy strut as she rounded the corner of the barn, but only to come to a screeching halt.

Casually swinging a leg, Rick sat perched on top of the fence just a few feet from where she'd been absorbed in her evening duties. He uncomfortably cleared his throat, gave her an awkward expression and started to applaud her techniques as his eyes devoured her body.

"Ahem. Wow…Anne, I really don't know what to say. Ummm…that was great." Rick asked. "But I have a quick question,"

"What?" Anne could only spit out the single word through her clenched teeth, while she felt the food of embarrassment rush across her face.

Now that I've seen all of that…do you hire out for private functions, bachelor parties…?" He could barely keep a straight face as he delivered his question, then burst out laughing as he barked out the last couple of words. "Maybe, retirement parties?"

"W-h-a-t?" Anne couldn't think for a second while her mind swam with complete humiliation at the combination of her anger at having been caught and the unconcealed, but through sexual assessment he was giving her.

"Nice. Aren't you finished ogling…or should I say drooling over the overexposure of feminine attributes for the day? You know, I probably could have done a public service this afternoon and passed out free condoms to all of those lusting girls today. I would've had parents across Washington sighing with relief at my consideration for their child's safety, or possibly erecting a monument in my honor." Anne rammed her hands onto her wet hips, tapping her foot as jealously reared its ugly head and disintegrated any of the common sense she'd ever held in high regard while she impatiently waited for his reply.

"I guess you could say, that I decided to save my best ogling for the last." Rick's lips quirked sexily while he took a second to close his eyes and acted like he was savoring the last few moments. "This experience was like trying a foreign dessert; kind of odd, not really knowing what to expect…but in the end, delicious and absolutely worth the wait."

"Wow!! I really don't believe…I've ever been compared to a bizarre food! I don't know if I should thank you or, or try to create a catchy slogan for my 'delectable' assets after watching how interested you were in to younger ones today."

Rick cocked an eyebrow at her snide statement, decided to ignore her as he slid off of the fence and walked over to the spigot. Bending over he grabbed the discarded hose and began to adjust the pressure of the water from a light spray to a steady stream. Slowly he began to clean up the flat poured concrete area where the makeshift horse shower was established.

"Look, I never gave any of those girls an invitation," Rick said defensively.

"Are you joking? You were practically a performing monkey from the moment those girls paraded out of the truck, until they left. Let alone the fact that you probably had to wipe off tons of drool after you suggested they try to gallop trough the spray in their freaking tank tops!"

"I can't help it if a carful of over-heated teenage girls were scheduled for a ride today. Maybe you should have thought about that before you penciled anyone in."

"Oh...that's rich. You're going to blame me? I guess with you around I'll have to develop a new registration form so we don't have any angry fathers lurking around the property with a shotgun after hours."

At the end of her tirade, Rick abruptly shut off the hose, angrily turned and advanced upon her. Anne's senses were nervously heightened while she involuntarily listened to the slight trickling of the remaining water that suddenly captivated her senses after the complete silence once the spray was shut off.

"Is, is that really what you think of me? That I'd be attracted to a bunch of adolescent girls?" He searched her face for some kind of response. "Thanks Anne...thanks a lot."

"I, um, I..." Anne opened and closed her mouth while she struggled to find some ingenious retort to validate how she felt. Her mouth went dry when Rick moved so close that he towered over her for a second, his brown eyes slowly raking down her body and she could almost feel the heat radiating off his body. Anne visibly shivered as his intense gaze wreaked sexual havoc throughout her body. Her mind screamed 'stop!' as it lamely attempted to instruct her take a giant step back and make some kind of sense of the situation.

Instead she allowed her stubbornness to win as she jutted her chin out, angrily squint her eyes in silent determination and remained ramrod straight in defiance.

"Really?" Rick gave her one last seething glare as her murmured under his breath. "Just so you know...I don't mess around with young girls."

"Well, it didn't look like that out there to me."

"Well Anne, maybe you should try looking a little harder."

"Why should I? I think I can see perfectly what was going on right in front of my nose."

"Are you joking? Teenagers? Are you serious? Is that what you think about me?"

"Yeah."

"Well, if you'd open your stubborn, obstinate....argh...."

By the end of Rick's attempted sentence, the two of them had squared off and their voices had risen to a fevered pitch. Anne's condemning silence hung in the air as she watched him turn in aggravation and Rick angrily kicked at the dirt, then turned on her.

"Come on Anne, I think you better seriously reconsider what you're saying right now before either of us say anything else detrimental adding fuel to this stupid situation."

"Maybe...you should learn to keep it in your pants, especially before the next time a group of women are scheduled for an excursion."

Rick silently ignored her while he kneeled over to turn the water back on and attempted to finish up with cleaning platform. He kept his placid face turned away from her while he desperately tried to regain his composure and diffuse his anger. *Freakin' obstinate, self-centered, sexually repressed female...probably couldn't handle a man around here. No wonder you can't find one around for miles, men are probably too scared to deal with her.*

"Why don't go on up to the house and cool down. I'll finish up out here." Rick commanded snidely over his shoulder giving her a rude backwards glance and dismissing her without another thought.

Rage ripped through Anne's veins at the thought of being so completely dismissed, clouded by the image of Rick animatedly chatting with the alluring young beauty while lingering in the surf. She heedlessly grabbed one of the buckets of cold sudsy water and straightened up, causing it to slop some of its cold contents down the front of her tank top. Without hesitation or thought about what she was about to do, Anne carelessly turned towards Rick and angrily yelled at his bent over frame, "Well Rick...why don't you just cool off."

It wasn't that she had even considered the outcome that the reckless decision of tossing the cold water would create in reality, but the actual feeling of her mechanical movements that brought her sensibilities down to earth. The last thing her mind registered at that moment was the sensation of bringing both of her arms back, then forcefully forward and throwing the entire contents of the bucket of cold water directly over Rick's head.

Regret instantaneously whipped through her veins while she stood transfixed, watching Rick instinctively react to the chilled water running down his face, causing him spring to life with startled amazement. Anne felt like she was in a movie as everything continued to play out in slow motion and her stunned eyes calculated the repercussion for her rash decision. *What the fuck did I just do?*

Soapy water slowly dripped off the tip of Rick's nose as he standing in shock, soaking wet with his white t-shirt shirt plastered against his torso.

Anne momentarily lost complete sanity while appreciating his masculine form, her wide inquisitive eyes leisurely lingered up the entire wet length of his body. Relishing a surge of sexual temptation, Anne's tongue instinctively licked her bottom lip and she completely forgot about her compromising predicament. A slight flick of water from his hand landed on her face and shattered her roaming thoughts as the wetness made her redirect her astonished gaze abruptly locking onto his maliciously narrowed eyes. Anne shook her head in denial while a slight suggestive look played across his face, Rick took a firm step through the soapy mud towards her, causing her to hesitantly mimic one backwards.

Terror began to close her throat as she desperately surveyed the situation and a way out. With each calculated step, the splash of mud signaled his approach, while Anne urgently tried to formulate some kind of lame excuse for her decision. *What the hell am I going to do now?*

"I, ummm…well, you know you pissed me off and I don't like being told what to do" Her lame excuse rang hopelessly short of any type of an apology, making her sound completely daft. *Well, that was a stupid thing to say, even if I do say so myself.*

"Oh…I think you'll agree that on the contrary. With what you just did, I think you're the one who needs to cool off." Rick maliciously grinned as he whipped the nozzle of the hose and directed it at her face.

Anne's eyes widened in shock, denial clouding her brain as she tried to assess what was about to happen, making her breathlessly scoot backwards until her back rammed against the side of the barn making her stumble as she frantically tried to get away.

Without any hesitation Rick smiled ecstatically and opened the mouth of the nozzle on high, a rushed stream shot out and proceeded to drench her entire body.

Anne incoherently began to screech as the ice-cold water hit her body, wiping any constructive words right out of her mouth. She flimsily raised a hand out in front of her for some kind of protection and braced the other against the wall trying to maneuver out of the way of the steady stream. *What the shitting hell! I'm trapped between a wall and the corral fence. WTF!*

Listening to the rumble of laughter emitting from her attacker, Anne attempted to turn her back on the intense spray and scramble under the fence. The effort caused her awkwardly slip and land in a new mud puddle that accumulated during Rick's persistent attack. Stranded with her knees stuck in the mud, she began to wave her hands in front of her face and decided to surrender.

"Ok, ok. I surrender, I surrender!"

With her affirmation the hose was abruptly shut off and Anne found herself humbly hunched over, huddled in a somewhat protective ball. She spread open her ice-cold fingers off her eyes and took a peek attempting to determine what Rick was up to. Anger shot through her when she noticed that he was casually leaning against the barn silently laughing at her with a smug smile spread across his face. *I'll freakin' wipe that arrogant look off your damn face you SOB.*

"Ha, ha, ha, very funny. Now give me the damn hose." Slipping slightly while she attempted to straighten her stance with some kind of grace, fuming inside she determinedly turned to face him her chest heaving and sparks flying from her eyes. Treading lightly through the mud she marched assertively to where he calmly stood with the hose dangling and his mirth intact.

"Shit. Not on your life! I think you owe me an apology...until then you're not getting anything."

"You've got to be joking! I believe after that escapade everything is e-v-e-n." Anne jammed her hands onto her hips and glared at him harder.

"Nope, you need to apologize." Rick smiled and raised his eyebrows a notch interpreting the string of muttered unfeminine curses that cascaded from her mouth. Without uttering another word she stubbornly raised her nose, pivoted on her heel and stormed into the barn. Rick's smile faded as he watched her drenched backside and transparent tank saunter furiously away, disappearing into the darkness of the barn. He strained listening for any clue, attempting to determine some sort of idea to what she was up to.

"Damn pig-headed stupid woman, probably sitting in there cold and bawling her eyes out because I wouldn't back down. Ah, shit." Rick kicked the dirt and ran a hand across his wet face, trying to wipe some of the wet residual out of his eyes. With a sigh he walked over to the spigot, with a hard twist completely turned off the water and set down the hose. Mumbling under his breath outlining a list about how stupid women were, Rick quickly stood up hearing a slight crunch of gravel and spun around to see what was going on.

In a flash his brain registered the sight of Anne holding a large red bucket filled to the brim with water. The moment became surreal while he absentmindedly watched the bucketful of water slowly inch through the air and land promptly in his face. Peels of Anne's hysterical laughter could be heard over the splash of water smacking his head, making him frozen as the icy cold water penetrated his brain.

Shivering for a quick second, Rick peered through the water running off the top of his head and spotted Anne a few feet away standing protectively in the corral with arms wrapped around a fence pole that seemed to hold her up laughing hysterically.

Anne wiped the tears out of her eyes with the back of her hand while enjoying the sight of a drenched Rick standing frozen in the late afternoon sun, for a second the sight of him made her pause.

"Too bad you don't know where all of the spigots are in the barn, Grunt. Maybe next time you'll think a little differently when you try to…yikes!" Anne unconsciously yelped when she realized that Rick wasn't going to sit there and listen to her ranting.

Unexpectedly he moved like lightening towards her, refusing to allow her a moment of victory.

"Shit!" She barely had seconds to turn and attempt to dash back into the barn for protection, listening to Rick grunt as he climbed through the fence and rushed in hot pursuit. Anne made it through the indoor arena and nearly past one of the stalls, until a strong arm grabbed around her waist and lifted her off her feet. She gasped for air as the wind was knocked from her and suddenly found herself unappealingly deposited face down in a giant bale of hay that had been freshly strewn inside one of the back stalls.

Anne felt her teeth click loudly when she ungraciously landed with a loud, "Oomph." Stars swam across her sight as she tried to focus when she felt a thump next to her in the darkened stall. She turned to find Rick lying next to her, his wet shirt covered with hay, impishly smiling back, the image made her start to laugh. Grateful at the change of her mood Rick found himself randomly laughing and watching as her face became illuminated with happiness, then hesitantly lifted himself onto an elbow and cupped her jaw with his hand. His thumb slowly traced her jaw line, while his warm brown eyes suddenly became dark and intense. Anne raised her hand up to his cheek and gently brought his head down to hers, the second their lips met Rick moaned and deepened their kiss. Anne found herself completely accepting his lead, opened her mouth and pulled him firmly on top of her as she felt heat course throughout her body.

Fueled on by Anne's eager response Rick mindlessly pressed his body harder against her and maneuvered her deeper into the hay. Shock coursed through their senses as the pressure from their bodies pressed intimately, the icy wet clothes molded against their skin. Unconsciously they inhaled at the abrupt shiver that sent tingling needles rage throughout their bodies.

Embracing the momentary lapse of contact, Rick registered the split second of coherent rationalization that willed itself into the situation and diminished the heat of the moment. The clarity of what was about to happen completely sobered him up enough to look down into Anne's face and realize how close they were to making a mistake. *I can't do this. It isn't right... I'm leaving.*

He gently raised his body off of hers, rubbed his face and crouched down on his knees to regretfully stare at her, fighting with every instinct to take her and make love to her all night.

Anne propped herself up leaning on an elbow, completely confused by his abrupt actions. Her eyes were half closed and smoldering with unabashed need, wet hair hung in clumps around her face with undetected pieces of hay stuck randomly as evidence of what they were about to do.

"I can't do this," Rick mostly whispered to himself as he stood up, turned away from her and braced his hands against the stall. He close his eyes, wrestling with his guilt and the desire to turn and look at her, completely consumed with their dilemma. Silence engulfed the stall, Rick startled when he felt the warmth from her hand as she firmly grabbed his shoulder and turned him around to face her. Rick found himself entranced by her sensual eyes, swollen lips and her black bra showing through her white tank top. Mesmerized he watched as her mouth whispered a single word.

"Please."

Rick didn't know if he'd heard her or imagined her delicious lips move, giving him permission to swiftly resume his intent, ending with a deep heated moan.

Instantaneously he backed her against the stall wall as he ravished her lips and his hand trailed up the side of her wet tank to find her breast. Pulling the cup of her bra to the side he began to play with her taut icy nipple until she began to unconsciously moan into his mouth. Without hesitation Anne followed his lead by quickly unzipping his pants, tugging them down his hips with an urgency that was caused by his forgotten hesitancy. The movement allowed just enough room for her hand to slowly wander inside the material, slipping down to cup him. Fueled by the feeling of her fingers touching him, Rick yanked her shorts down enough so he could put his foot in the crotch and shove them to the ground. Simultaneously he lifted her higher against the low wall, situated himself between her spread naked legs and with a single thrust he drove himself deep into her. He instantly paused from the shock of her slick warmth, leaning his forehead against hers as he struggled for control and listened to their ragged breathing. Rick's eyes snapped shut when he anguishing realized that as she shifted the weight of her position, the movement caused him to enter her fully. Without another thought he sucked in a deep breath through his teeth and his mind went completely blank, as he continued to heedlessly drive himself into her to finish what they had started.

Guilt riddled through his thoughts by the time his head cleared, feeling her slightly wiggle suspended off the ground and felt her breath on the side of his neck. Silently he anguished realizing what he'd done and gently tried to slip her onto her feet.

"I'm so sorry, I couldn't help…I've been imagining this for so long," He whispered into her hair as she silently stroked the back of his neck.

"Um…" Anne allowed herself a moment of pleasure simply by relaxing against his frame and enjoying the feeling of his warmth. "No problem. To be honest, I've been having the same ideas for a while. Because…"

Rick curiously lifted his head in tuned to the way she saucily annunciated each word, the questioned ending and evident pregnant pause. He gazed down into her mischievous eyes, only to have his attention distracted again by her swollen lips, exposed low cleavage from her askew bra and his instant sexual reaction to her, trying to patiently wait for her explanation.

"Because Mister, if you think you're getting off that easily, you've got another think coming." Anne lifted her mouth, capturing his lips in a long suggestive promise. "No pun intended." She laughingly whispered while she pulled away and gently nipping at his lips.

"Mmmmm…" Anne licked her lips as she gradually slipped from his embrace, kneeling to gracefully retrieve her shorts off of the ground. With a nod of her head she wordlessly pivoted around and began to sensually walk across the uneven planks towards Rick's darkened room. She turned her head, glancing over her shoulder and gave him her best smoldering 'come hither' look.

Rick's already slackened mouth dropped to the floor as he watched her sauntering away clad only in her black bra, layered by the transparent tank that rode the top of her exposed naked ass. With each step as Anne approached the door she unhurriedly stripped off her tank, followed unhurriedly by her bra and called over her naked shoulder, "Hey Grunt, are you coming?"

"Uh, yeah." Rick took a moment to shake the adulterous thoughts out of his head after witnessing her enterprising departure, but when he went to move forward the action caused him to stumble precariously making him grunt and grab onto the stall fence. *What the…ah fuck.*

Listening to the twinkling laughter coming from the general direction of his room, Rick instantly knew Anne had probably surmised what had happened.

"Shit!" The tug around his ankles made him glance down. Rick unbelievingly realized that in his haste, he'd forgotten his unbuttoned pants dangling around his calves. Thoughtlessly he gave a quick jerk and haphazardly pulled them up while rushing out of the stall.

"Oh...don't you worry, I'm coming," he lethally muttered under his breath and humiliated hobbled his way into the darkened room.

19

The feel of Anne's lips while she slowly traced the outline of his mouth with her tongue was torture. Rick groaned as he pulled her tightly against his body and leaned deeper into the mattress, causing it to emit a loud groan of protest. Rick wholeheartedly chuckled while he lifted his head and gazed down at Anne's beguiling smile.

A thousand questions swirled through his mind while their eyes continuously searched each other's for some kind of silent answer. He traced the side of her face with a gentle finger as he dipped his head down to lightly trace her mouth with his.

Suddenly the tender moment was broken by a flashing light and persistent alien noise. Rick snapped his head up and peered across the room to see what was causing the rude interruption. A small green light was blinking in time with the irritating noise as he incredulously realized that it was his forgotten cell phone. *You've got to be shitting me.*

"Wow, you mean that thing really works?" Anne chuckled while she traced a finger down the side of his arm, lingering gently on his chest.

Rick slowly lay back on the bed throwing his arm over his face and groaned in response to her question. He could feel Anne's body straining against his and realized just how close they had come to making love again. The reality of what he was going to have to do washed over him like the bucket of ice water, engulfed with the fact that time was truly cruel. *I'm leaving...now.*

Rick took a long deep breath as he felt Anne's fingers tracing imaginary circles on his bare skin. The immense pain that was sinking its talons into his chest was numbing as he gently reached for her hand. Slowly he took it, held each finger to his lips and intimately savored kissing each one. Closing his eyes he turned to embrace her, trying to ignore his hollowed solitary moment.

Suddenly he felt her chin lay gently on his chest as she tried to peer through the darkness, into his face and decipher the sudden change in his mood.

In the distance of the barn soft music was still playing on the radio, the first solemn strains of Peter Gabriel's "In Your Eyes" floated across the distance and haunted his breaking heart. The words seemed all too familiar as he strained to listen and memorize them. *This wasn't supposed to happen. I'm not supposed to leave her like this.*

"Hey," Anne whispered softly, as if she sensed his turmoil. "You ok?"

"Yeah, I'm ok." Rick stroked her hair back from her face, cupping it gently to lower his mouth and languidly memorize her lips. He wanted to show her what he was going through, wanted to give her everything with that one kiss. Gradually he pulled away and traced her swollen lips with the end of his finger.

"I don't want to pressure you into anything. Everything went so fast out there. I just feel like we need to slow down for a second."

"No problem, I never had much luck in the sex department anyway. I'll tell you one thing; I have never felt so good with anyone in my whole life, corny, huh?" A sad, lopsided smile came to Rick's mouth as he imagined how much it took for her to admit her feelings and how red her cheeks would be if he could see her face clearly.

"No, actually I totally understand. That's why I'd rather we slowed this down a notch and consider everything before we go on from here." He felt her oddly hesitate at the end of his sentence and gradually pull her hand painfully from his grasp.

The dead weight of her arm while she uncomfortably slid it across his chest emulated her uncertainty about the reality of their situation. Anne rolled onto her side as an unnerving emotion descended upon both of them, layering their bodies like a smothering sheet. Before she could make another rejecting move, Rick instinctively rolled over and pinned her body under his. He bent his head swiftly and captured her mouth. He proceeded to kiss her until he felt the uncomfortable strain cease, rekindling the heat that burned underneath each of their skin. Rick lifted his head when they were both panting and couldn't take their eyes off of each other. He gently lifted his head as he attempted to gaze down into her face as he lightly traced the delicate areas along her jaw, desperate to say the appropriate thing but cynical enough not to open his mouth to say just anything. Rick closed his eyes, listening to David Gray's 'Sail Away' and prayed that what was going to come out of his mouth would be enough, eno*ugh for forever*.

"It's not that I don't want to be with you…but if I could do one foolish thing in my life, it would be to make love to you right now. I have to be honest because if I start, I'm going to want to keep on going. I just can't promise you forever, at least not right now." Watching her reaction in the faint light coming in through the slit of the door, he tried to read her thoughts. Her face was serenely beautiful, framed with her hair fanned all around and in her eyes he could see… *forever*.

His heart tightened heavily when he decided to give her hand a reassuring squeeze, then carefully got up and tugged his shirt over his head. Immediately following his lead Anne awkwardly rolled off the opposite side of the bed and hurried to put herself back together while his back was gallantly turned.

She made an uncomfortable slight coughing noise once she was done and added a quiet, "Alright, I'm ready."

Rick simply turned to take her hand in his while he led her softly out through the barn and into the night. He tried to memorize the feel of her hand. *Don't think about anything else but this moment.*

The night was enchanting with the moon shining in the semi-clear evening throwing shadows across their path from the small clouds that passed over it. A delicate breeze moved Anne's hair as they listened to the crunch of their feet on the gravel as they walked in silence. Rick wanted to grip her hand and yank her back towards the barn. *I want time to stop so I can stand with her outside the house and never have to leave.*

As they neared the porch Rick slowed their steps to a crawl and tentatively walked up the stairs. He stopped once he reached the middle step and grabbed both of her warm hands securing them around his shoulders. He turned slowly and brought her in closer to face him, carefully placing both hands on either sides of her face like he was cradling a jewel. His eyes searched each angle of her face as if trying to find an answer to a never-ending question. He silently lowered his mouth to hers and gave her a kiss to stop all time, attempting to force his heart into hers, *because I know it isn't ever going to be mine anymore, not after tonight...not after I leave her.*

Anne placed her hands over his as if she accepted everything about him, anything she didn't and knew his secrets, but wanted him to stay. She willingly opened her mouth and her heart to show him exactly how she felt. Life seemed to spin around them in the twilight of the evening.

Rick deepened the kiss once more so he would never forget their perfect moment, as Anne desperately clung to him in her own personal battle with letting go. When they parted Rick lowered his head and pressed it against her forehead, listening to their combined breathing as it calmed down while the sounds of the night penetrated their minds. His fingers lightly traced her face while she innocently toyed with the back of his neck. Closing his eyes he slowly bent and kissed the tip of her nose, then opening them he gave her a halfhearted lopsided grin.

"You'd better get in. It's a little cold this evening."

"Mmm hmm." Anne watched his face as he stood back, reached around her body and turned the knob to open the back door.

Rick's features seemed shuttered and withdrawn, but his eyes were violently alive, searching. She smiled reassuringly at him as she gave his hand a squeeze, allowing her fingers to trail off his as she moved to stand silhouetted in the doorway. The light from the inside created a shadow across his face so she couldn't determine what he was thinking. "Thanks for everything Rick."

"It was my pleasure." He graciously bowed with the last word to take the awkwardness out of the situation.

"Soo, I'll see you in the morning," Anne nervously laughed at his gallantry.

"Yeah," Rick's voice awkwardly wavered in the darkness. "I'll see you."

Anne turned to walk into the house when suddenly a slight sinking feeling made her stop and look back. She couldn't put her finger on whether it was his tone or his disposition, but something wasn't sitting well. As she watched Rick walk away her eyes swam with unshed tears. His broad shoulders slumped and his hands shoved in his pockets, *he's the image of a defeated man*. She waited for a minute while her intuition surged to the surface, gripping the doorknob as the overwhelming feeling that she should forget her pride and run after him haunted her soul. The heartbreaking words from Jewel's 'Foolish Games' circled through her head as they floated downstairs from Beth's room. Leaning in the doorway Anne waited to see if Rick would turn back and catch her watching him. *If he'd just pause for a second, turn to see me, smile, anything. Just return to me.*

Instead he kept his head low and walked at a steady pace across the drive until he completely disappeared into the darkness after her vision was blocked by the old barn door. Anne's heart sank while she silently closed, locking the door and turned to switch off the lights, but the persistent feeling of the heavy fragmented moment remained.

"Oh… Anne you're being silly." Laughing away any negative thoughts, Anne began to recount with a devious smile every sexual moment that transpired in his room and giddily continued upstairs to her room.

Rick was still wrapped in his pensive thoughts after waiting for hours as he watched the lights switch off in her room. Noiselessly he made his way out to the truck, carefully opening the door, jumped in and tossed his packed bag onto the empty passenger seat. Leaning across the steering wheel he stuck the key into the ignition and gave it a quick turn. He let out his pent up breath when the truck smoothly came to life. The radio crackled to life as Damien Rice's tormented voice singing 'The Blower's Daughter' overwhelmed and haunted the interior of the cab. Rick despairingly closed his eyes and laid his head against the cold steering wheel thinking about her reaction in the morning. Taking a tortured second, Rick moved outside to stand in front of the idling truck and mutely watch Anne's blackened window. Sorrow poured from his heart as he desperately wished that she'd open her curtains and foil his carefully laid out plans for his exit. The wind caught the curtain and momentarily startled him out of his daydream. *I need to remember there's nothing to keep me here and everything waiting for my arrival back in California.* It happened in a blink, his life had changed. He would give anything to stay with her, if only there was a way.

Rick closed his eyes as agony ripped through his soul and anguish engulfed his thoughts. He stood captivated by the beautiful lyrics and Anne's darkened window. He rubbed his face and took a steadying breath, determined to empty everything in his very being while he prepared himself to commit to the choice he was about to make. *All I have to do is turn the truck off.*

The pale light from the moon illuminated the soft movement of the curtains blowing in the breeze and outlined Anne's sleeping form. Her arm was flung over the top of her forehead with part of the blankets intertwined around her legs and pulled catawampus across her chest. A slight moan and a residual smile lingered as she curled deeper into the warmth of her bed and pulled the blankets higher over her shoulder while sleep stole all of her thoughts.

In the colorless early morning light Anne never heard Rick's truck pull out of the drive, out onto the highway and out of her life.

20

The ocean was magnificent, the pristine mirrored surface reflected the color of the cloudless blue sky, sparkling white with the cascading waves that lazily crept against the shore. Marine blue seemed to swirl into azure and crested within the gentle endless expanse of the sea. The atmosphere seemed tranquil, even though the shore was haphazardly chaotic complicated by hordes of sun tanning people lazing up and down the sandy beach.

Watching the commotion, Nick's brain registered that technically it was the same Pacific Ocean; it just wasn't the image that had captivated his heart.

That was the image of the ominous, threatening churning grey waters that seemed angry even in the brightest light of day. Wind whipping through your veins as the sea beckoned, tempting anyone to stray too near, waiting for an opportunity to display its sheer power and whisk anything in its path away. During his time north, the only exception he'd found was during his long walks in the night. *That's when the water becomes tranquil, its movements glowing with the enchantment of phosphorous illuminating the waves. It was during the endlessness of night, under the moon that I found a peace and beauty that rivaled here.*

Nick couldn't stop torturing his soul, continuing to simply listen to the guilt his heart was screaming, trying to blindly accept his decision to leave. He closed his eyes and leaned his head against the back of the couch, allowing the small pleasure of remembering what he'd had for a perfect moment. *This is all wrong…I'm not supposed to be here, I can't be here.*

It had taken a moment to leave his dented truck and hesitantly set foot in the beautiful Malibu house. After braving his ghosts Rick found himself emptily lounging engulfed in the couch facing the huge bay window for the better part of the morning. The Kings of Leon were playing 'Use Somebody' over the high definition stereo that ran throughout the house. *I feel so trapped and alone.* The corners of his mouth turned up at the ironic thought, *Yeah right. I'm sitting in a beautiful house located on the busiest beach in Malibu, totally surrounded by idle strangers.*

It had been a difficult three day drive back to California, the second he'd found enough resolve to turn the old truck out onto the highway, he couldn't seem to shake an anxious feeling in the pit of his stomach, *like I've left something behind.* Nick remembered shaking his head trying to tear his thoughts from the guilt, knowing the anguish that had washed across Anne's face when she realized he was gone, tried not to think about what he'd done. As he watched the street lights flash by he couldn't allow his mind to travel down that road, knowing that he was completely distressed with the realization if given a choice, he would have turned the truck around, dismissed his commitment and driven back to the ranch.

It wasn't until a few hours past Portland that he became absolutely sleep deprived and felt far enough away to pull into a hotel for the rest of the night. Mechanically he'd checked into some random run of the mill hotel off of I-5 and found himself standing zombie-like in the middle of another dismal transient room did he allow the enormity of his decision set in.

Nick lethargically threw his bags onto the bed, turned on the bedside radio and walked into the nondescript bathroom. Tiredly he switched on the light, turning to look at his defeated reflection in the mirror, The Airborne Toxic Event began playing 'Sometime Around Midnight' through the broken speakers. Nick found himself momentarily caught up in the music as he adjusted the shower, grabbed the trash bag and set it on top of the sink. Leisurely he began to remove all of his prosthetics, followed by his clothes dropping each item solemnly into the trash and walked into the hot shower. By the time the water began to make his skin feel pruned, Nick started to feel human again. Shutting off the tap he stepped out of the warmth, tied a towel around his hips and wiped the condensation off of the mirror to stare at his reflection. He startled when his million dollar blue eyes stared vacantly back, while an emptiness engulfed his soul. He switched off the light with an exasperated sigh, walked to the bed and flopped down on the stiff generic mattress.

What seemed like hours passed in the sterile room and he still couldn't quite grasp what had just happened. *What have I done?* The odd feeling of deja vue flooded over him, lying in another strange nondescript hotel bed and only then he allowed his mind to wander through the inconsolable pain seeping through his veins. *I can't believe this. I left. Anne will never be able to forgive me. I couldn't stand to see the look on her face when she realized that I'd deserted her, just like everyone else. I can't ever go back.*

Nick hardly slept at all, waging a war on himself, tormented throughout the night by his conscience. Blurred eyed he left the hotel in the drizzly morning, thoughtlessly launching into the truck and maintained the resolve to continue driving south, because hope was tucked in the back of his mind, knowing that if he gave himself the opportunity, *I'd immediately turn the truck around and go back in a second.*

A loud sound penetrated through his dismal thoughts, startling Nick until he realized that the front door had briefly opened and closed. He couldn't find the strength to move, listening to the comforting sound of Mike's slow familiar whistling while he moved about the house. Nick closed his eyes again attempting to mentally pull himself together before meeting his friend, when unexpectedly the sound of the music diminished to a slight hum in the background. A genuine smile creased Nick's face while he recognized the memorable sound of Mike's clumping walk as the other man ungracefully approached the couch.

"Hey there buddy, how you doing? I heard you just got back in town."

Nick wearily opened his eyes, but remained motionless in front of the window and continued to stare at the beautiful surf until he felt Mike ease next to him on the couch.

"Wow," Mike gave a low and long whistle coinciding his intense stare while he checked out Nick's disheveled appearance. "What the hell did they do to you up there? You look all Sasquatch...or Yeti-ish. Man Nick, did you even take the time to change since you got home? Damn, maybe I shouldn't have sent you up there."

Nick decided to completely ignore his friends concerned comments, arrogantly glanced at his friend from the corner of his eye, gave him a half-hearted smile and placidly lifted the remote to turn up the volume as the music changed to The Verve's 'Bittersweet Symphony'.

"Hey Mike, I knew you'd be here soon enough. I'm surprised you didn't show up in the middle of the night when I arrived last night." Nick nonchalantly reverted his attention back to numbly gazing out at the endless scenery. "I was just enjoying the view."

"Hm...yeah, we'll see. Shit, man. You better go and change because I think Ava was hot on my heels." As if on cue, the front door quickly opened and slammed shut, followed by the indelicate clicking indicating a stampede of very high heels. Nick started to itch his nose when her sticky sweet perfume premeditated the air in the living room before Ava even reached the couch.

"Nick, you fucking asshole! You've got some serious explaining to do! I can't believe that you just up and left me without a word...ME!" The irritating clicking sound loudly manifested as she crossed the room and stopped directly behind Nick's head resting on the back of the couch. "What the Fuck!" Ava practically yelled into his trancelike face, realizing that her presence was obviously being silently ignored and her frayed nerves surfaced. Unchecked rage built making her eyes widened in astonishment at his lack of interest and resumed her childish fit with a constant irate tapping of her stiletto heel.

Nick kept his eyes blissfully closed and envisioned Ava standing there beautifully attired, perfectly made up, painfully coiffured and absolutely seething.

"Well, Nick...What do you have to say for yourself and explanation for your tirade?" Ava practically spat the last word while she narrowed her gaze at his head, waiting for an appropriate response.

"Well, come on over here girlie and give your Daddy some sugar. I can tell...you missed me sooo much. You probably cried every day with the thought of missing me, didn't ya?" Nick answered, imitating a thick southern drawl as he stood up, spread his arms out wiggling every finger towards her and smiled in a naughty half-uncle kind of way. He knew he looked like shit, still dressed in his AC/DC T-shirt, worn Levi's, dark-circled eyes, hair askew and week's growth of stubble. "I should have brought some candy for my sweet lil' Miss Superstar."

"Ha..." Mike quickly swiveled his head in the opposite direction to cough and politely cover his laughter listening to Nick's unexpected response.

"Ha, ha, very funny." Ava calculatingly narrowed her eyes, waiting for a different response. "What have you done to yourself? Did you have a mental breakdown or go into rehab...or something that's tangible?" She sniffed as one of the Kris's handed her a tissue and she indelicately blew her nose. "Can you even imagine what I've been through these past few months...dealing with the press, excuses about you're absence and...everything?"

"Hmmm..." Rick eyed her with curious disapproval watching her irritatingly lean a hand on her hip waiting for some kind of sympathy or apology, but received nothing but unflattering silence. Ava's pursed lips creating an unbecoming huff and then threw her hands distraughtly into the air.

"Argh! What the hell...I need a drink." Ava yelled without any consideration to anyone in the room. A loud huff punctuated her command then swiveling immersed in a fog of perfume, the sound of her irate clicking heels faded towards the kitchen followed by Ava's high-pitched voice yelling for one of the Kris's, making the unsuspecting duo clumsily stumble attempting to catch up with their mentor. "Kris...Kris, get me a drink...Pronto!"

"Well buddy, welcome back. I'm sure she missed you somewhere in her black heart." Mike solemnly leaned closer beside Nick and sympathetically patted him on the back. "Why don't you go take a break...a nice hot shower, clean clothes and shave...I'll get Ava situated and her goons taken care of. But...come back here when you're through, because we need to get some things rolling on this project. We can't afford to miss a minute on this opportunity."

"Hmmm..." Exhausted, Nick refused to answer but gave Mike a distracted shrug, stood up racking his memory and ambled towards the distant recollection of his suite. He absentmindedly rubbed his face attempting to remove any of Ava's venomous residual and disappeared into the shadows mumbling incoherently, but sarcastically to himself, "Oh...it's so good to be back."

Nick confidently strode down the hall well over an hour later feeling like a new man. After a long hot shower, shave and a change of semi-familiar extremely expensive clothes, Nick finally felt like he could take the two of them on. Rounding the last of the halls corner he instinctively stopped, shrouded in the darkness of the shadows, allowing a token few seconds to study the two strangers posed for war, but showing every indication of semi-patiently waiting for him.

The odd nemesis's were haughtily stationed on opposite sides of the couch, positioned like opposing enemies waiting for a valiant savior, and thankfully the Kris's had mysteriously vanished. Nick found himself watching them as they cautiously cultivated their movements to a honed precision, one seemed to leisurely enjoy the view and the other inspecting pleasantly restrained from acknowledging the other's presence.

Mike was warily avoiding Ava, simply by watching the gregarious scene of tromping sun worshipers outside on the beach. He sat idly sipping on his whiskey on the rocks, occasionally clinking the ice unconsciously against the glass.

Ava sat ramrod straight focusing her venomous glare towards Mike whenever she had the chance, her eyes flashing as if mentally conjuring a spell to have him combust into flames at any second. Her long slim legs were crossed at the knee and with every futile huff, she began frustratingly swinging them while sipping on her 'healthy' cosmopolitan; her only validation of 'healthy' was that it was being made with organic cranberry juice.

Nick's eyes roamed back to Mike's docile face and smiled. *Thank the lord for him...I always feel self-assured when I'm around Mike, knowing he's always had my best interest at heart.*

A few seconds later his vision swiveled back to Ava immediately he felt the physical feeling of his earnest smile sag away and altogether disappeared. Nick took a second to evaluate her perfectly, but surgically maintained profile and realized that because of the healthy dose of reality from his reprieve from tinsel-town, time gave him the chance to dissect his past and regurgitated the shallow reasons that surfaced that compiled his addiction to her. *She's an exquisitely beautiful woman, almost in a surreal, plastic sort of way from head to toe,* the thought made the corners of his mouth sardonically turned up as he chuckled. *Shit, I'm sure there is enough Botox, filler, nip, tucked and whatever 'plastic' shoved in every area of her body to maintain complete perfection, with a hefty price tag that she can afford...which is a lot.*

A dark feeling overwhelmed him making him feel like something was missing, but couldn't or wouldn't put his finger on it. The foreign emotion was too huge to even reflect on at the moment, so instinctively he tucked it away. He braced his shoulders back prepared for battle and loudly cleared his throat to give the pair a considerate indication that he was coming into the room.

"Don't you think it's a little early to partake in happy hour?" Nick asked while he glanced at his watch, realizing it was still midmorning as he approached them. "Wow, it's not even eleven yet."

"Oh, Nick...there you are." Ava elegantly swiveled her head, longingly watching him walk across the room until he uncomfortable perched on the opposite arm of the couch.

"Well darling, we're celebrating the fact that you're back. Why don't you just sit down next to me and make yourself a little more comfortable," She purred, leaning forward to help enable him to take a nice lingering glimpse down her shirt, smiled like a predator and then invitingly patted the empty spot on the couch next to her extensively bared thighs.

"I, I'm just fine right here...but thanks." Nick cocked a questioning brow at her brazen actions then dutifully turned his attention over to Mike and realized he was holding his breath waiting for whatever impending doom waited to fall.

"Ok, well enough of this trivial talk. We have serious business to attend to." Mike scooted closer to the edge of the couch while Nick decided to accept the invitation and walk over to sit next to him. Listening to the mewing sounds coming from the other end of the couch, he patiently waited while openly ignoring Ava's spoiled-little-girl pout as she threw a brief but silent tantrum about his declining her invitation. Even though he couldn't actually see the daggers he knew she was imagining hurling at his head, I *can sure feel them from here.*

"So, now that we have you back, we can jump into this with both feet. We've been filming on a blue screen since you left and have a large chunk of it completed. We need to catch you up to speed on the script, cast and crew. Also I have ordered your wardrobe and it should be finished by this evening for the final fitting," Mike hurriedly continued as Nick waved his hands as he tried to keep up.

"Whoa, hold on a second Mike, back up. I have no idea what you're talking about."

"The movie. We've been hard at work on it for the last few months while you've been gone. I want everything done by the end of September. We have a tiny window to get this through production to be in the running for the Oscars. I want us at the head of the awards this year."

"Ok, I totally understand all of that...but what are all of the particulars concerning me?"

"You received most of the script while you were away, now we just need to start shooting on location." Mike uninterestedly nodded towards Ava as he continued on. "We've cast Ava as your leading lady. With the press's influence on your relationship, we're going to over publicize the two of you starring together for the first time. The public's demand for the finished product will shoot the picture over the top. We have to capitalize on your situation; you've been missing for a while, the public has been fed some rumors and your relationship is still the hottest 'it' couple."

"Nick...now that I have all the information, I absolutely understand why you were gone and I...I forgive you." Ava graciously tipped her head in the direction of the two astonished men, giving her regal acceptance of being written into the script.

Sidetracked for a second Nick appallingly rubbed his face of how idiotic Ava sounded and tried to stay on track with everything Mike was referring to.

"So...you're telling me that Ava and I will be starring in this new movie and we need to start shooting on location right away, that way we'll make it in time for the next Oscars?"

"Yep," Mike simply finished by lounging back on the couch, sipping on his drink and started to nervously bounce his knee. Noting Mike's guilt disposition, Nick's calculating gaze moved over towards Ava and noticed she'd simultaneously become engrossed at looking into her compact, trying to find a flaw in her exquisite makeup.

"Hmmm, I don't see any catch. What is it? Ummm… what am I not seeing here?" Nick said mostly to himself reassessing the fidgety calmness the two were equally displaying. "There has to something that I'm missing."

Mike uncomfortably cleared his throat and apprehensively glanced at Ava for some kind of support. Her response was to look astoundingly annoyed, merely closed her compact with a snap, shrugged to deploringly gaze out the window and silently resumed sipping her drink.

"Um, we have to start shooting hopefully within the next few weeks. Everything that has been possible to accomplish in your absence is finished. That means you're already extremely behind schedule and we need to get your part going, ASAP."

"Ok...what do I have to do?" Nick asked deflated of any objection, he sat down preparing himself for a list of unachievable tasks.

"We need to get you into costume/wardrobe, fix your hair, makeup, hire doubles, negotiate a contract and memorize the script...all by the end of next week."

"What? That only gives me a handful of days!" Nick irritatingly stood up almost spilling Mikes drink and began to pace the living room.

"Nick…B-a-b-y, it's not like you haven't done this before. You're a pro, you'll be fine…Kris!" Ava reminded him in an exasperated tone while she leaned over the sofa and unfeminine bellowed out for someone to bring her another drink.

"Hey look…I feel like this is too much, it's different. You can't understand how this is, I can't explain it…it's, just different this time." Nick finished his statement by towering over Ava and frustratingly regarded her, while she arrogantly lifted her shoulders then dumped her empty glass onto the coffee table.

"Oh, you think too much. Don't be so negative…it'll all be fine!" Ava annoyingly waved him off as one of the Kris's walked around the corner balancing a tray laden with not only her drink, but one for each of them.

"There's another catch, isn't there?" Rick eyed the offered libation as if it was poison, until Mike grabbed it and shoved the glass into his empty hand.

"No, nothing…well the only problem is the location. We need to hurry and capitalize on their situation." Mike paused to semi-excuse the Kris by silently nodding in the direction of the kitchen, waved his hand for another drink and continued to answer Nick's question. "The family has had a tragedy, is in a horrible financial situation, and they're a little hesitant about filming on their property. All of the papers have been signed and monies exchanged. We just need to swoop in and get this going before anyone on their side has second thoughts."

"Hmmm…" Nick suddenly felt sick while an intuitive sinking feeling formed in his gut. Without another thought he shot to his feet and began pacing. "So, where exactly are we going to shoot on location?"

"Why…didn't Mike tell you? Ha, isn't it just so hysterical how Mike always gets his way." Ava snidely muttered as she neatly swirled her drink in the crystal glass and then flicked the side with a fingernail making it ominous clink.

"The place is perfect…and the price was exceedingly right. Even though the owner is a bit of a shrew and made us agree to a shitload of improvements to the old place before she'd sign anything. In the end it took a lot more money than I'd like to talk about to suffice the harpy, get this movie going and finished to keep on schedule. Stupid old coastal house…seemed like no one had maintained the place for freakin' years."

"What!" Nick visibly paled, instantly stopped pacing and turned to face the conniving pair. "Mike…where exactly are we going to be shooting this movie?"

"Nick, you silly...well, why do you think he sent you to that God forsaken place? Mike wanted you absolutely familiar with your surroundings, comfortable with the animals so you could concentrate on perfecting your part more and physically know the ropes of the location."

Nick groaned as he rubbed his hands over his face and waited for a moment. "Where...exactly...will we be going...to shoot on location?"

"Well..." Mike looked at him like he had completely lost his senses. "What would be a better place to shoot than the very spot where you've been trained and lived, you should know everything like the back of your hand, it'll be the perfect set up!"

"Hhmm...What's wrong Nick? Didn't you like it up there?" Ava smiled wickedly as she punctuated her question with another sip while watching his reaction for any incriminating evidence, eyeing Nick like a hawk over the rim of her glass.

"I... I...think I'll have that drink now." Nick mechanically finished the one in his hand, called out for another and sank down on the couch next to Mike. Apparently the Kris's were prepared for his reaction because without notice they magically appeared with a round of fresh drinks, quickly sitting one in front of each of them and then loyally flanking Ava's side.

Without another thought or objection, Nick grabbed his glass, lifted it in a mocking salute to the deceptive couple and asked in a raspy voice.

"So...when exactly do we leave for Westport?"

For Centuries our lives have evolved to the music that artists created, the perfect backdrop to a multitude of melodies.

What's on your playlist?

David Guetta & Sia – Titanium   Virgin/EMI
Fugee's – Killing Me Softly   Ruffhouse/Columbia
Calvin Harris & Florence Welsh - Sweet Nothings   Columbia/Decoustruction/Fye Eye
Justin Timberlake – Sexyback   Jive/Mosley
Maroon 5 – Moves Like Jagger   A&M Octone
Rod Stewart – Maggie May   Mercury
Joe Walsh – Life's been Good   Asylum
Eagles – Life in the Fast Lane   Asylum
Beyonce – Single Ladies   Columbia
Martina McBride – Suds in the Bucket   RCA
Wings – Maybe I'm Amazed   Apple
Muse – Madness   Warner Bros.
REM – It's the End of the World   I.R.S
Bruce Springsteen – Glory Days   Columbia
Bob Seger – Hollywood Nights   Capitol
Garth Brooks – Papa Loved Mama   Liberty 57734
Bruce Springsteen – I'm on Fire   Columbia
Bruno Mars – Locked out of Heaven
P!nk & Nate Ruess – Just Give me a Reason   RCA
Mona – Lean into the Fall   Zion Recordings/Mercury
Justin Timberlake – Sexyback   Jive/Mosely
Pearl Jam – Elderly Woman behind the Counter   Epic
Lenny Kravitz – Are You Going My Way   Virgin
Evanescence – Bring me to Life   Wind-Up
Eagles – Tequila Sunrise   Asylum

AC/DC – Back in Black   Atlantic
Katy Perry – The One that got Away   Capitol
Brandi Carlile – The Story   Columbia
Elvis – Suspicious Minds   Sceptor
Red Riders – Lunatic Fringe   Capitol
Neil Diamond – Sweet Caroline   UNI/MCA
Rolling Stones – Brown Sugar   Rolling Stones Records/Interscope/Universal
Crazy Town – Butterfly   Columbia
Imagine Dragons – Radioactive   KIDinaKORNER/
Katy Perry – TGIF   Capitol
Lady Antebellum – Need You Now   Capitol Nashville
Elton John – Tiny Dancer   Uni
Snow Patrol – Chasing Cars   Interscope
Def Leppard – Pour some Sugar on Me   Mercury
Sheryl Crow – Soak up the Sun   A&M
Roy Orbison – Pretty Woman   Monment
Norah Jones – Come Away with Me   Blue Note
Lady Gaga – You & I   Streamline/Interscope
Fleetwood Mac – Sara   Reprise
Jimmy Buffett – Margaritaville   ABC
Sugarland – Want to   Mercury Nashville
Johnny Mathis – Chances Are   Columbia/Mercury
Frank Sinatra – Summer Wind   Reprise
Neil Diamond – Kentucky Woman   Bang Records
Van Morrison – Brown Eyed Girl   Bang Records
Rolling Stones – Honky Tonk Woman   London
The Clash – Rock the Casbah   CBS/Epic
The Police – Everything Little Thing She does is Magic   A&M
John Cougar Mellencamp – Hurts so Good   Riva
Elvis – Can't Help Falling in Love   RCA/Victor
Roy Orbison's – Crying   Monument 447
Eagles – Desperado   Asylum
U2 – Joshua Tree/Running to Stand Still   Island
Elvis – Blue Christmas   RCA/Victor
Katy Perry – California Gurls   Capitol
Crowded House – Fall at Your Feet   Capitol
Garth Brooks – Friends in Low Places   Capitol Nashville 44647
Chris Isaak – Cheaters Town/Wicked Game/American Boy/ Baby did a Bad Bad Thing   Warner Bros

Peter Gabriel – In Your Eyes   Geffen/Virgin
David Gray – Sail Away   Atlantic
Damien Rice – The Blowers Daughter   Vector
Jewel – Foolish Games   Atlantic
Kings of Leon – Use Somebody   RCA/Sony
Airborne Toxic Event – Sometime Around Midnight   Majordomo/ Shout! Factory / Island & Mercury
The Verve – Bittersweet Symphony   Hut